SEEING JULIA

by

KATHERINE OWEN

ALSO BY
KATHERINE OWEN

NOT TO US

WHEN I SEE YOU

SEEING JULIA

by

KATHERINE OWEN

The Writing Works Group

Seattle

COPYRIGHT INFORMATION

SEEING JULIA
Published by *The Writing Works Group*
FIRST EDITION
Copyright © 2011 Katherine Clare Owen
All rights reserved.
ISBN: 978-0-9835707-3-8
Print Edition

This book is available in print at most online retailers. Ebook editions are also available; check Amazon.com.

Cover art Design and Interior by: *The Writing Works Group*.
Visit our website: http://www.thewritingworksgroup.com
Cover art Photo images:
Copyright © Konstik|Dreamstime.com;
Silhouette of girl, jumping in waves of ocean
Stockfresh |Stock photo: Woman in white dress at seaside
Copyright © Julija Sapic (simply)

Discover other titles by Katherine Owen at the website:
http://www.katherineowen.net

DEDICATION

To Dad, I miss you.

SEEING JULIA

PROLOGUE

Before after

There was *before*. And, there was *after*.

Before was magical, embraced promise,

and bequeathed good things.

Before was for the innocent.

After was haunted,

and relinquished all promise.

I HAD LED A MAGICAL LITERARY LIFE in New Haven—a college town admired for its Ivy League status and an innocent sentiment held by its residents that nothing bad ever happened there. I had two famous novelists for parents. Yes. A magical literary life.

In one of the last days of *before*, my father's best friend from Yale came to visit with his family. At seventeen, the man's son, almost two years older than me, would inspire one of the last carefree days of my life, and exemplify a touch point for me for all the ones that followed.

All of him would captivate me—his crooked smile, lean tall build, and clear blue eyes. He wore denim blue jeans with a black Nirvana t-shirt that professed his nostalgia for the band, while his golden hair swung around his face, impersonating the revered Kurt Cobain. I remember sweeping it out of his eyes without thinking, overcoming my normal shyness, and being spellbound.

I'd never known enchantment before, but, somehow, he stood in front of me that day. While our two families talked inside my imposing house, the golden boy and I hung out in the backyard under the sweeping branches of our cherry tree on a swing. Hidden, we were. Secret, we were. His lips tasted of the cherries we'd eaten earlier, when they first met mine. My first real kiss. He stirred feelings inside of me I'd never felt before, and I remember wanting to kiss him forever, to savor the surprising desire that overtook my body and mind.

No one, my own age, had ever taken that much of an interest in me. He'd asked me all kinds of question about my life. Where did I want to go in the world? I told him all about my travels with my parents to Madrid, Paris, and London, and the upcoming trip to Athens. I blushed, thinking he would find me boastful, but he'd only expressed admiration for my worldliness. When he asked me what I wanted to do when I grew up, I'd shared my secrets to be a doctor and save people, a ballerina if I managed to get up on toe shoes by the end of summer, a veterinarian, if only, to fulfill my love for animals, and, of course, the ultimate, I hoped to be a famous novelist, just like my parents. He asked about my favorite music, but, by then, I was too captivated by this strange rush of feelings for him, so I said, "I loved Nirvana," even though I never really played their music. One of his last questions had been what was my favorite movie? I had stammered out *Jerry Maguire*, before I could rein in the truth about my secret fascination with romance. His engaging laugh was not at me, but with me. He stole the second best line from the movie, when he said, 'You complete me.' I stole the first, when I said, "You had me at hello."

I remember being so awestruck by him. He gave me the courage to share more of myself and my secrets. Why he took an interest in me, I would never know. I had always been the bookish girl with famous writers for parents. As a freshman, everyone, in the exclusive Hopkins School I attended, had known who I was, who my parents were, but they hadn't really known me.

I blushed under his gaze, when he held on to my hand. Already, his familiarity and possession of me was complete, even as he'd tucked a strand of my hair behind my ear and kissed me, again. I laughed more that day than I ever had before, and drank him in, like fresh cold water on a hot day. I remember the feeling of being forever altered by him. And, when he said goodbye, and reluctantly left with the rest of his family with a promise to write and call, I believed him.

How could I have known he would be the last of the magic that had been my world? It would be a sliver of time I would never get back. A modicum of happiness, in the *before*, I would never fully let myself experience, again. How could I have known that it would be the last of before? And, in the *after*, everything I had ever loved would vanish. In the *after*, I forgot his face, even his name. There would be no letters. No phone calls. I'd never reach out to him, again. I would only be able to recall his words, 'you complete me, you're all I see', and that acknowledgment, alone, would save me, in the aftermath, and serve as an everlasting promise of how things could have been. My new reality would take away the magic, turn my dreams to nightmares, make my memories imagined, when before ended, and the after came.

He saw me that day.

And then, the *after* came, and I disappeared.

CHAPTER

ONE

In the after again

I'VE BEEN HERE BEFORE. I'VE DONE this before. At sixteen, I buried my parents, at twenty-three, my fiancé, Bobby. And now, almost four years later, my husband, Evan. I'm here, again, in the *after*. Here's what I know: death abducts the dying, but grief steals from those left behind. There is less of myself with every loss.

I stare at the red glow of the cigarette for a long time, and then, inhale deep. A rush of nicotine courses through me.

I don't smoke. Except, today, I do.

The lit cigarette provides the only light in the church stairwell. I take comfort in the cloak of darkness and estimate having another five minutes of anonymity, before Kimberley comes looking for me. Five minutes to get it together, to let the Oxycodone and nicotine do their thing. One to get me to an anesthetized state, the other, because breaking the rules seems like the one thing I should do for him, this day. I lie back and willingly suffer the sharp metal edge of the stair that digs into my back. The pain is real enough, but it's nothing compared to the steady ache that already pulses inside of me. I close my eyes and allow this stairwell sanctuary to envelop all of me.

A few stair flights above, Christian Chantal's distinct French accent and the southern drawl of another man's voice pull me from oblivion.

"I'm glad you came. He'd be glad you were here," Christian says.

"I had to come. I still can't believe he's gone. I just saw him."

The stranger's voice catches with emotion. "I'm taking the red-eye flight back to London, tonight. There are things that need to be taken care of over there. Here, too. What does she want to do about Hamilton Equities?"

"I don't know. She's pretty broken up, right now. I haven't had a chance to talk to her."

"What will she do?"

"I don't know. She's been through a lot, even before this happened. She's amazing that way. We just have to help her get through it," Christian says.

"I don't know … Evan getting married again, so soon, after Elizabeth's death, and no pre-nup with this one." The way he says, *this one*, causes me to wince.

"He wanted to give her the world. He really loved her. Julia's the real deal."

"And, she loved him?"

"You're so cynical," Christian admonishes. "Of course, she loved him." The men's voices get farther away. The echoing sound of a metal door opening, and then, banging shut drowns out the stranger's response.

Weary, I lean my face against the cool cement wall. *How many others at this funeral were going to be suspicious of me? How many would question my motivation in marrying Evan so soon after we first met? Do I really care? Does it even matter?* I just want to rewind back time, to ten days ago, when it was just Evan and me playing with our baby and watching the storm rage outside.

The light bursts on overhead, and I sit up, startled, even though I knew she would find me. My respite ends, as Kimberley runs up the stairs toward me.

"There you are." She appropriates the lit cigarette from my hand and takes a few tokes of her own. Then, flicks it to the ground and steps on it with her black Stiletto. "It's almost time."

I nod. She flashes me one of her I-know-this-day-sucks looks. I allow myself a wan smile, as she helps me up.

"Did you find her?" Stephanie leans through the doorway below and wrinkles her nose at the smell of smoke that still drifts in the air. "Julia, you don't smoke."

She fishes out fresh mints from her handbag and adroitly hands them out to us.

"I can do whatever I want." I manage to say, though raw emotion constricts my throat.

I think our kindergarten teacher is at a loss for words, as my assertion reminds her of why we are all here. The empathy for me emanates from both of them.

No one wants to be me on this day.

"I need a drink," I whisper to Kimberley.

"Julia, we all need a drink. In another hour, we'll do just that."

If anyone can make something better out of this day, it will be Kimberley Powers. I almost smile at this thought.

We enter the foyer at the back of the church. I glimpse all the people inside. A mixture of panic and sorrow rushes at me. *I will not cry, not today.* My two best friends link their arms with mine, and bestow me with their strength. The Oxycodone begins to kick in and man-made serenity slides over me. We enter the hushed church of four hundred restless strangers. All eyes are upon me, as the three of us, dressed in variations of designer black, make our way down the middle aisle to the front pew.

I keep my head bowed, not wanting to be here, not wanting to be any part of this day. Yet, I am here, and Evan is not.

Kimberley has outdone herself, even against the high measuring bar as one of the best public relations specialists on the eastern seaboard. I expected a nicely planned gathering after the funeral, but I look around, amazed at the opulence of this get-together on the Upper East Side, and muse Evan would have loved it. There are more than a hundred people here to honor him. I have already thanked and been hugged by most of them—family, friends, and employees.

Now, I'm flanked by my entourage. Kimberley, to my left, dispenses a continual stream of a chocolate martini mixture in my glass, fulfilling the role as my personal bartender. Christian's older brother, Gregoire, sits on the other side of her, intent on keeping Kimberley entertained. Stephanie and Christian are to my right, attempting to ply me with food. Mr. and Mrs. Chantal take turns, encouraging me with, "Try this, Julia." I do not openly refuse their offerings. I eat a little, but drink more.

I cannot feel my toes any longer. I vaguely try to contemplate if this is due to the vodka or the Oxycodone. I give the group a reassuring smile, as my head swims with a mixture of pain killers and alcohol.

This is a non-smoking lounge. I lament that fact, when I dangle an unlit cigarette between my fingers. The bartender continues to eye me in this vigilant way, surely wondering of my intention with the forbidden cigarette. I've already shared my theory about breaking the rules with him. I think he would like to agree with me that rules are meant to be broken, when your loved one dies, but the hotel general manager hovers, just twenty feet away from all of us, and eyes me, in particular, with worry and uncertainty.

Kimberley orders another chocolate martini and slides it over in front of me. I look up at her reflection in the mirror behind the bar, lift my glass in gratitude, and take a sip. I try not to grimace at the amount of alcohol that assails my tongue with this semi-sweet concoction.

I'm a light-weight. Kimberley knows this, but we keep going. I have not informed my co-conspirator about the vial of Oxycodone—an inheritance—an unexpected gift from the god, himself, from a knee injury that Evan suffered skiing the winter before. I've already pilfered two more pills from the vial in the last hour.

I catch the edge of the bar, as grief plunders me with this fresh memory of Evan, whose life we celebrate.

He is gone. I am still here.

I cannot reconcile these two incongruent thoughts.

I hazily continue with my performance for my two best friends and their significant others, showing them all, that I will survive this, although I am not at all sure how I will.

Despite all of these people around me, I feel alone. The thought cuts across me in a peculiar, ominous way. I am alone in the *after*. Again.

The crowd has moved on to dancing—the signs of a good wake, so I'm told, by one of Evan's nostalgic uncles. I perform a waltz in a semi-daze in the older gentleman's arms. Even when his hands stray to my right buttock and give it a firm squeeze and I feel his hard-on accost my right hip, I keep up the pretense of dancing with him, for a few more minutes, with a fake smile pasted on my face. Evan's Uncle Joe gives me a lustful look, and then, he mutters under his breath that I am a sweet young thing and he can show me a good time.

I step back away from him, more unsteady now, but too weak to actually slap his face because my imbibitions are beginning to catch up to me. I sway and take another precarious step. Someone comes up behind me and squires me away from the lecherous old man.

"I'm so sorry for your loss," drawls the voice from the stairwell in my ear. He puts his arm around my waist and we move together across the dance floor. "The old guy is a real dick and to do that to you here, on this day, unforgivable. He's perfectly harmless, I think, though I would have thought Evan would have warned you about him, long ago."

His invoking Evan's name upsets me. I pull away from my intended rescuer, intent on making it back to my appointed place at the bar.

"Don't talk about *Evan*," I say in alarm.

Tears threaten, again, but I've already resolved not to cry, not here. I haven't cried at all.

Not yet.

"Careful, Mrs. Hamilton, someone will get the wrong impression."

I'm startled by the disdain I detect in his voice and turn back and give him a beseeching look. His blue eyes are mesmerizing and I stare at him, this golden god, and try to place his face. *Do I know you?*

"Jake Winston," he says with diffidence, extending his hand toward me. "Evan's best friend from Yale."

I gaze at him through a haze of inebriation and a self-induced drugged state and attempt to focus. Then, I lift my head in defiance and shake his hand, half holding on to him. *Steady.*

"Hello, Evan's best friend from Yale. Julia Hamilton, *the real deal.*"

With sudden ingenuity, I sweep my arm outward, with an exaggerated Vanna White move, and almost fall down. He catches me around the waist and steps back from me, as if he's been burned.

"I apologize," he says with an embarrassed flush. "I guess dark stairwells are not the place for private conversation. You never know who might be there lurking in the dark."

"You never know who's lurking in the dark. And, don't worry about Uncle Joe, I'm sure he's just trying to show the grieving widow a good time."

He gives me a deliberate look, and then asks, "Are you … having a good time?"

His implication is not lost on me and my temper flares. "Fuck you." I take a deep breath. "You're deplorable, you know that? I realize the idea of a deep relationship doesn't extend beyond fucking someone more than twice, but my marriage to Evan was very real and I love … him."

I've run out of words and lost control all at the same time. I'm mortified at my behavior, and retreat from Mr. Jacob Winston and, unsteadily make my way back to the safety of the now empty bar. Frantic now, I search around for Stephanie and Kimberley and finally spot them both out on the dance floor.

I am alone. The realization overwhelms me.

I ask the bartender for my evening bag, and he reluctantly hands it to me, while asking if I'm okay. I nod and give him a contrived smile. The sight of myself, smiling, in the mirror behind him, almost makes me cry, but I turn away and make a hasty retreat. The bartender calls after me. I do a backhand wave and keep moving.

In the lounge restroom, I pop two more Oxycodone. The funeral was too painful, and now, all of this is too much. Desolation overtakes me, as I try to envision a life without Evan. The grief is too much. I don't want to feel it anymore. I can't feel this pain anymore. Not again. For good measure, I take two more pain killers.

CHAPTER

TWO

Not starting over

MOVING ACROSS THE LOBBY OF THE hotel toward the bank of elevators takes all my concentration. I experience increasing listlessness, and vaguely acknowledge I've taken too many pain killers, and drank all of the martinis put in front of me. The grief over Evan still rages. I cannot escape it, no matter what I do. I'm exhausted by the time I reach the elevators and lean back against the hotel wall for support, while pressing the up button with an incessant backhand motion. Finally, the doors to one open. Someone calls my name from behind me, but I'm too intent on my escape, and practically fall into the waiting elevator. As the doors begin to close, I glance over, just as Jacob Winston jumps his way on.

"I'm sorry," he says. "I've upset you."

"S'okay." I turn away from him and sway with the speeding rush of the elevator as it soars to the nineteenth floor. "It doesn't matter," I say with an absent wave of my hand. "I shouldn't have said what I said. Sorry." I open my handbag and search for the card key to my hotel room. Somehow, everything in my handbag ends up on the floor. I collapse down on all fours, trying in vain, to pick up everything. "God… damn it."

"I've got it." Jake Winston kneels down next to me. He hands me my hotel key card and begins to pick up my things: cell phone, lipstick, compact, wallet, hotel receipts. He holds up the Virginia Slims Menthol cigarettes. "You shouldn't smoke," he lectures.

"I don't smoke," I say airily. "Except, today, I do. Breaking the rules. Evan would want me to." I have trouble hiding my devastation, in sharing this secret with him, and almost succumb to the grief. I let my hair fall forward, to hide my face, and try to recover from this fresh onslaught of pain.

"Are you taking these?"

He holds out the vial of Oxycodone in front of me. I don't answer. I just continue to kneel, managing to steal a covert glance in his general direction and watch him slip the vial into the inside pocket of his suit jacket.

He stands up again, and I look up at him, lost in this wondrous state—part alcohol-induced, and part something else I cannot name. He reaches down, and pulls me up. I feel this instant rush from the sudden motion and try to steady myself with the help of the elevator wall and him.

"The pills? Are you taking these?" he asks, again. When I still don't answer, he reaches back into his jacket and holds them out in front of me again. I flinch at the anger I detect is his voice and he looks at me in surprise. "Are you taking these, Julia?" he asks in a more gentle tone.

"Maybe," I finally say.

He stares at me and I return his gaze as best I can, although the elevator's constant motion is making it difficult to remain still, and I sway into him, a few times.

We're startled by the ding of the elevator and its sudden stop. The doors open and we step into the hallway, moving in tandem towards the penthouse suite. After my two unsuccessful attempts with the door lock, he takes the card key from me, and swipes it through. The lock clicks and he turns the handle and opens the door. I walk past him, gripping the furniture as I go. I'm assailed by the smell of too many dying funeral flower arrangements, which brings the threat of tears again. *I will not cry.* I close my eyes for a moment and feel the direness of my life settle all around me. The darkness I can't outrun.

"Nice digs." I open my eyes and watch him as he performs a self-guided tour of my opulent hotel suite. He moves further into the room and turns on the gas fireplace.

"Kimberley's idea. She thought it would cheer me up," I offer in a faraway voice.

"And, did it? Cheer you up?" He gives me a speculative look seeming to assess my every reaction. *For what?*

"No."

I open the bar's refrigerator. After a moment's contemplation, I grab the Dom Perignon, tear the foil from the cork and manage to open it without losing too much and pour the champagne into two crystal flutes. He comes over to the bar, takes one of the filled glasses, and clinks it with mine.

I return his gaze, though a little disconcerted by his obvious appraisal of me and vaguely concede he is far too good-looking, from this distant place, in my mind, that used to care about stuff like that. Evan was always handsome. My husband, the cliché, the golden god, bigger than life—the man everyone loved. This guy is more of a walking advertisement for a Calvin Klein underwear model. Another golden god, but, the one, who stands in shadow, exuding sex appeal with the white flash of a smile and far too attractive to be real. He flashes me his white smile, in the semi-darkness of the room, now. I've been staring too long, and blush at being caught. I busy myself with draining my glass, and then, pour another.

"You should probably go slower."

I shake my head slowly side-to-side, and try to smile. "Why? The whole idea is to forget, Mr. Winston, to get to the point of numbness. So, when I close my eyes and see his face, I don't feel … anything. Or, better yet, I don't see his face, when I close my eyes."

I drain the second glass of champagne with a flourish, and pour myself another, and unsteadily refill his, spilling some of it on the counter, as I go.

From my vantage point behind the bar, I study him. His light golden-brown hair sweeps back from his face, with a bit of a wave, I'm guessing he has trouble taming it each morning. He runs his right hand through it, now, demonstrating this truth for me. He is tall, even taller than Evan had been. I struggle thinking of the past tense and have to rest my head against my forearms, for a moment. The dark granite countertop is cool against my face, and I close my eyes.

"Are you okay?" Jake asks.

"No." I slowly lift my head and find him studying me, again.

He was Evan's best friend, and yet, I've barely seen the man, and I wonder why that is. "Why? Why, Mr. Winston? Before London. You declined every dinner invitation I ever extended? Why have we never talked before? Had a drink? Gone bowling?" I giggle, a little, at the idea of any of us going bowling, and find I cannot stop. I put my hand over my mouth to stem the uncontrollable mirth. Jacob Winston is looking at me in bewilderment. I go on. "When you're here, you have a house in Amagansett just down the road from ours and yet, we ... I ... never saw you. You went sailing, skiing, rock climbing, had drinks with him. *With him.* Never with *me* and him. Why?"

I wipe at my face in irritation, and stare at the wetness on my hand. *I'm crying?* I haven't cried. Not yet. I'm beginning to lose it, talking about Evan like this. Without answering, he turns away from me, walks over to the fireplace, and stares at the flames.

"Why?"

"I live in London, now."

"Why?"

"Evan wanted to expand Hamilton Equities. I was contracted, for the legal services, to help him out. It seemed like a good place to start."

"A good place to start," I murmur in confusion. "To start what?"

"To start over."

"Why? Why would you need to start over? That's what I do."

He grimaces, as he looks over at me. "So, you'll start over. Good for you." His southern drawl is more pronounced, as he says this.

I realize I know next to nothing about the man who was Evan's best friend from Yale.

"No," I say in agitation. "I'm *not* starting over. Not this time." I'm emboldened, suddenly anxious to share my secret. "It's too much. Too hard. And, for what? So, I can lose it all again? *I believed him.* I believed him, when he said we could have a wonderful life together. I believed him. Look what happens, when you *believe* them. He's gone. They're both gone. My life is over. I can't do it, again."

I cross over to the sofa and drop down onto it and close my eyes. I'm pulled to the present, again, when he grips my forearms and kneels in front of me. I try to focus on him.

"What are you talking about?"

"I'm not doing it again," I say slowly. A plan, a decision of sorts, comes together.

"Starting over?"

"Right. No starting over." My words come slower. The pain from grief diminishes as he holds on to me. He doesn't let go. He seems to need an answer of some kind from me.

"What will you do? What will you do? It'll be up to you. What you decide to do." He's looking at me with this desperate expression. He seems to be searching for the right words. "With the London office, now, that he's … gone."

"London?" I ask in confusion.

Why are we talking about London? I move my hand to my forehead, as if to physically stop the thought. "God, I miss him. Why did he leave me in charge of his company? We talked about it, when we redid the will, when Reid was born. I told him, no. I told him—"

"I don't know, but, at some point, you'll have to deal with it, Mrs. Hamilton." There's an edge to his voice and I try to focus on him more closely.

"At some point, I would have to think and do something about a lot of things. Or not," I say in a conspiring tone.

I reward him with my best smile and lean forward and look into his eyes. He has this strange, almost haunted look on his face. I reach out and trace the outline of his face. He has these amazing blue eyes that seem to draw me in. I put my arms around his neck and pull him to me. My lips trail along his chin and find his and I kiss him.

This pent-up release, for all the emotional turmoil I've been carrying, takes over. I just buried my husband and the overwhelming sense of loss that's been with me seems to fade away as I give in to the sensation of being held. This fiery passion comes out of nowhere for this stranger. He sighs, encircles me within his arms, and I kiss him more deeply. At first, he doesn't really respond. I sense his hesitation, but then, he groans, and starts kissing me back.

The room seems to catch fire as we come together. The difference between what is right and what is wrong evaporates, within seconds, under the heat of our coming together. His lips are on mine, then trail along my neck, causing these pleasurable sensations to ignite. I respond to him in kind.

Time just seems to stretch out into infinity as this unexpected attraction, that neither one of us seems prepared for, takes over. It dominates all of our senses. We shift in our movements and occupy the length of the sofa. His body is draped over mine and his kisses travel to my breasts, my neck, and back again to my lips. I luxuriate in being able to feel *anything*, even this sexual desire for him. I feel his physical response to me. The barrier of my black silk dress and his suit seem surmountable. He makes me feel alive, again. On some level, I acknowledge I shouldn't feel this way, but my body betrays me, in wanting him, to feel more of him. He seems almost shy, and I smile with encouragement, and give in to this brazen desire for all of him. I pull him even closer and kiss him again. I want him. I need him to fill this pervasive emptiness that's invaded me for the past ten days. *Fill me up; take away this pain.*

His fingers trail along my body, setting it aflame, wherever he touches me. We acquiesce to our mutual need in desiring to possess the other. On some unknown level of consciousness, I accept this. His kisses take me to this sanctuary, where time seems suspended and gravity is nonexistent. I feel this release, at a soul level. I open my eyes and try to focus on him, again. This mysterious golden god, dreamlike, just above me. I unbutton his shirt and run my fingers along his chest, and then, trail kisses along his neck and face. In a desperate frenzy, I work at the button on his pants and finally make it work and unzip him. At his liberation, he stops moving, and I cry out in protest at his stilled movements.

"Julia? We can't do this," he says against my neck. He sounds help-less, unsure, and even fearful.

I feel hopeful and certain. I lift my head and try to focus on his face. "Yes. Take away this pain, Jake … please."

"No," he says again. He pulls back away from me and searches my face for a moment. Then, he pushes off the sofa in a single motion, and strides across the room, and begins to pace, back and forth, running his hand through his hair in agitation.

"Please. Take this pain away." I don't attempt to hide the despera-tion in my voice. I can feel myself spinning out of control.

"I can't. I can't do this." In a daze, I watch him as he tucks in his shirt and zips up his pants. He has this tortured expression as he moves toward me. He seems wary of me, now.

"Please," I say back to him as he comes to stand in front of me.

I stand up, unsteady now, and reach out, and pull him closer. My lips find his again and he kisses me back. I lift my head and attempt to smile up at him. He holds me close and I register his heartbeat, pulsing at my cheek.

"We can't do this," he says in a resigned final kind of way.

I'm desperate to stay in this heady state of feeling nothing, in this unfamiliar place, where grief hasn't yet found me. I hold on to him even tighter and close my eyes and savor the feeling of falling backward into the dark abyss, as I feel his arms around me. Unafraid now. The pain of grief is far enough away and there's this sense of peace I haven't felt in days.

"Oh, God. Please. Jake."

He answers me with the most gentle of kisses. This peaceful feeling comes over me. I can't even be sure he's actually kissed me again, as I fight to stay conscious now. My arms and legs begin to feel strange, as if, somehow, separate from me. I let go of him and seem to fall away.

"Are you okay?" I hear him ask me from this faraway place. "Julia! Are you okay?" He sounds worried and I struggle to open my eyes to see why that is, even as he shakes me.

"I'm fine. Not … starting over," I whisper. The sweet darkness engulfing me is interrupted by this roiling sensation in the pit of my stomach. "Oh, God."

I push myself away from him and stagger toward the master bath. I'm dizzy from the sudden movement and clutch at the furniture as I go. On some level, with swift clarity, I know I'm going to be sick. Just in time, I lean over the toilet basin and vomit up all the food and drink I've ingested in the past two hours. I sink to the floor.

Water is running. I turn my head, and spy him at the sink, holding a hand towel under the faucet with shaking hands. He looks scared and I wonder why.

"Just go," I say from my resting place at the toilet. Moving my head side-to-side causes me to feel nauseous again.

Then, Jake's there, pulling me up. He towels off my face with the wet cloth, grabs my chin, and looks into my eyes.

"How much did you take?" He shakes the vial of Oxycodone at me.

"Enough."

I pull away from his grasp, violently vomit again, and slink further down to the floor. My world of cognizance continues to shrink. I hear the shower water running. I'm suddenly pulled up again and shoved into it, still clothed in my black silk dress. I shriek at the cold and feel as though I'm drowning as water runs over me.

"You've got stay awake!" Jake yells over the din of the shower. He adjusts the water temperature, until it runs cold. "How many pills did you take?"

"I don't remember." I shiver from the ice-cold water, while the narcotic chases through me at an ever increasing velocity.

"Try," he commands.

"Eight or ten. I don't remember. Maybe, twelve. Enough," I say with hostility. "I'm *not* starting over."

"Jesus!" He props me up against the tiled wall and steps away from the shower. Dully, I watch him go. From the open doorway, I gaze at him as he gets on his cell phone. Snippets of his conversation resonate with me. "Emergency. Peninsula Hotel. Possible drug overdose. Oxycodone. Ambulance. 19th floor."

Uncontrollable shivering takes over, and I lean against the wall for support, and give myself over to the cold. It numbs me further. I close my eyes, unable to keep them open.

"Does your friend Kimberley *know* that you took the Oxycodone? Open your eyes."

When I don't answer, he grasps my chin through the open shower door.

"No."

Like a child in trouble, I squeeze my eyes tighter and tremble even more. I blindly reach for the nozzle, but he slaps my hand away.

"You have to stay awake, Mrs. Hamilton."

The frigid water temperature causes me to shake violently now, but he keeps a firm grip on me and forcefully holds my head under the spray.

"I hate you."

"I didn't get that impression."

I open my eyes to look at him.

"I … hate … you," I enunciate slowly, as if teaching him English. This inexplicable wounded look crosses his face, and then, it's gone.

"You're sure you're the real deal?" His implication cuts across my soul.

"I'm not ... what you think I am. I ... loved Evan. He loved me."

I finally start to cry. Jake eventually lets go of me. I stare at him through my tears and glimpse the same haunted look, from earlier. Two incongruent thoughts assault me at the same time: *Evan is dead. I've just kissed and almost had sex with someone else, another man.* The grief returns, full force, at this silent admission.

I slide down the marble wall of the shower and let the water all but drown me. My cries of sorrow and this endless pain come from deep inside. The bathroom door opens, and then, closes. I'm thankful for the privacy, in which, to bear this horrible resounding heartbreak, alone. The pain is worse than ever.

Indeterminable time goes by. I struggle to come to a stand, and finally, reach the faucet and turn the temperature from cold to hot. I wash the residue of vomit from my hair and face with a mixture of water, soap, and shampoo. Eventually, I regain enough sense of self to turn the water off.

The black silk dress clings to me now, in ruins. Like me.

I emerge from the shower, dripping water everywhere, just as he returns to the bathroom suite. He holds on to me and strips off my dress. Naked, I stand before him and tremble, uncontrollably, as the tears stream down my face. Now, I can't stop crying.

Dispassionate, he wraps me up in a bath-size spa towel and pulls me along into the bedroom. I sit on the edge of the bed, dazed, watching him search through my suitcase and the dresser for clothing.

Tears still stream down my face. He returns to me, a few minutes later, takes the towel away and pulls a black Van Halen t-shirt of Evan's over my head and helps me shimmy into underwear and black jeans and coaxes shoes on my feet. Then, he towel-dries my hair, and then, combs it through with his fingers. This ritual is done in complete silence.

I close my eyes to avoid looking at him. I feel his hands on my face, wiping away my tears.

With reluctance and this rising shame, I open my eyes, but avoid looking directly at him. Instead, I try to concentrate on the Monet replica on the wall behind him, while the room still shimmers.

"I called an ambulance," he says. "The vomiting probably helped, but you need to get checked out at a hospital." With a resigned sigh, he sits down next to me on the bed. From the faraway recesses of my mind, I experience surprise at his conciliatory tone.

"No." My body sways against him. "I'm not going anywhere."

"Yes ... you are. How do you feel?" His attempt at a clinical bed-side manner saves my dignity.

"Tired. I haven't cried. Afraid I wouldn't be able to stop. I was right about that."

He just nods.

There's an out of control resurgence in the sharp edges of grief that's plagued me for the past week and a half that an endless supply of pain killers or kissing a stranger can't take away for long. He puts his arm around me and I lean into him and just sob. He strokes my hair, over and over, and I take solace in this simple gesture.

"I used your cell phone to call Kimberley," he says after a time. "She's on her way.

"Okay."

I look over his shoulder and vaguely note he's hung up my ruined silk dress over the shower door and draped my bra and panties over the desk chair. His unexpected optimism and act of kindness almost make me smile.

"Julia," he drawls. "I'm sorry. I wasn't thinking clearly before. I'm so sorry. I loved Evan, like a brother. I ... there's no excuse for my behavior. I'm so sorry."

"I wasn't thinking clearly, either." I close my eyes, but experience this spinning sensation, so I open them again. "I just wanted him back." I swallow. "Holding you, felt like him, and I just want him back."

"I know."

"Too much sadness. Too much grief. Just like Bobby," I whisper.

The blackness begins to surface again. I lean against his chest, confused by the rhythm of his heart beat and what he's saying me.

"Who's Bobby?" Jake asks in this guarded voice.

"My fiancé, Bobby Turner. Killed in Afghanistan. Almost four years ago."

"Bobby was killed? Oh God." Remorse and this profound sorrow emanate from him now. "Who are you? Tell me."

"I'm Julia Hamilton." Blackness drifts closer. "Mrs. Evan Hamilton."

"Before that," Jake says. "Who were you, *before* Bobby? Do I *know* you?"

"I don't talk about *before*."

I can feel myself slipping away. He seems distant now. I can't hear him anymore. I attempt to smile, but the narcotic takes all control and I can't feel or do anything.

"Hold on, Julia. Stay with us," a voice interrupts the dark tranquility invading all of me.

I try to open my eyes, but I'm too tired. I'm lifted up. My arms sting from the urgent movements. I cannot feel my hands and my feet feel unbelievably heavy. I'm beyond cold.

"Julia, can you hear me? Oh, God, Julia, don't do this to me."

I feel the fall and rise of the elevator. I hear slamming doors and feel the rush of speed. "It's going to be okay."

I don't believe you. I try to say out loud, but no words come out. *I don't believe you. It's not going to be okay, ever again.*

I try to open my eyes, but there are too many lights, too bright, too much.

All these voices calling my name, over and over. "Julia! Wake up! Stay with us!"

I wish they would stop saying my name. I don't want to wake up. I don't want to stay here, wherever here is.

Something is shoved down my throat and I feel myself gagging from this faraway place.

"Mrs. Hamilton, can you hear me?" A voice whispers voice near my face.

I am Mrs. Hamilton.

I was Mrs. Hamilton.

Now, Evan is dead.

I am no one, now. I am no more.

The pain is too much, the loss too great.

There is no more *before,* and the *after* is too devastating.
There isn't enough of me left to go on.
Grief has stolen too much of me, now.

Chapter

Three

Confessions

I'M NOT DEAD. I ONLY KNOW this because I see the redness behind my eyelids, as if I'm looking directly into the sun and can only watch the hidden world of blood veins and cell movement, experiencing a complete understanding of mitochondria. Extreme warmth invades all of me. There's this fiery heat at my hands and feet. The tingling pain affects all of my outer limbs, but I cannot move. My throat burns and I long to speak, but something heavy weighs me down, as if I'm being held under water, even moving my lips proves to be too much work.

Kimberley's voice assails me as she argues with someone and uses her best don't-fuck-with-me tone. "She's my *sister*. I have to be here. She'll want to see me when she wakes up."

"Visiting hours begin later this morning, not the middle of the night. We need to get her stable."

"She *is* stable. You already told us that. I'm her *sister*. Her only family, now."

"Fine. Just please try not to upset her. We'll engage psyche to further evaluate her."

"Psyche! Julia would never intentionally try to kill herself. She's been through a lot, but she has all of us, Reid—"

"I think what *Kimberley* is trying to say is that Julia has a lot of support around her and this was just an accident. Too much alcohol mixed with some narcotic intended to help her get through the funeral." My mind jolts at the unmistakable southern drawl of Jake Winston, but I don't actually move. "That's all, doctor. I was with her most of the evening and she was extremely grief-stricken, but getting more lethargic. That's when we put it together that she had over-indulged in the pain killer. We were all unaware of how much she had taken or been drinking. Just a mistake in judgment. Nothing more."

"Well, thank you ... Mr. Winston, is it? For all of that," says the voice I don't recognize. "We'll see what Psyche has to say. We take these kinds of situations very seriously."

"I'm sure you do. I'm the executor of the estate and her lawyer in charge of all her domestic affairs. The family would like to keep this quiet. Evan Hamilton was quite well known. His death has been publicized all over Manhattan and throughout the states of New York and Connecticut. We just want to ensure Mrs. Hamilton's privacy, allowing her to grieve in peace."

"Of course."

"I'm staying," Kimberley announces as her final answer. The sweet scent of her expensive French perfume drifts over me as she grips my hand. Desperate to see my best friend, I struggle to open my eyes, but they won't move. The door clicks shut.

I feel the weird high from drugs surf through my system and try to fight the inevitability of unconsciousness.

"You just making it up as you go, Winston?" Kimberley hisses. "What the fuck happened?"

"She took an overdose of pain killers. Did you even *know* that?" Jake asks. "You want her to lose custody of her baby?"

"Jesus, you think they'll try to take away Reid?"

"If they don't think she is capable of taking care of him. Yes. And, they will, if we're not three steps ahead of them. As her *family*, we can show them how much support she has around her, while we try and get this situation under control. Get the checkbook out. Get a press release ready, because we're going to bury this whole thing so far under, it will be a faint reference in the footnotes of all that's happened to Mr. and Mrs. Evan Hamilton."

"Where did she get the pills?" I hear Kimberley take a jagged breath. "Oh God. Julia, what have you done, baby?" Her hand brushes at my face. "How did you find her?"

"I followed her up to her hotel suite. I upset her with some things

I said, and wanted to apologize. We let things get … she started to pass out and it was pretty clear she was in trouble."

"You need to just stay away from her, Jake."

I try to smile through the edges of my drugged state, as Kimberley takes her familiar protective stance over me. I attempt to follow her heated lecture about not getting involved with me.

"She's been put through enough," Kimberley warns.

The man has no idea what he's in for because being on Kimberley's bad side is never a good thing. I want to hear more, but I lose the fight for consciousness with the remnants of the narcotic still running through me.

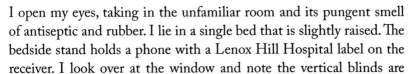

I open my eyes, taking in the unfamiliar room and its pungent smell of antiseptic and rubber. I lie in a single bed that is slightly raised. The bedside stand holds a phone with a Lenox Hill Hospital label on the receiver. I look over at the window and note the vertical blinds are half-open, which provides a glimpse at a daylight world on the other side, just as Stephanie comes in.

Our blonde version of a living Barbie sails into the room, as if she's on ice skates. One minute she's across the room and the next she's right at my bedside. She pulls up a chair next to my bed, takes my hand, and gives me a forced smile. Worry lines mar her beautiful face.

Kimberley and I share Stephanie as our best friend. For five years, the three of us lived together, during our UCLA days with Bobby, and again, in Manhattan after Bobby's death, until I married Evan early last January. Then, Stephanie married Christian last summer.

Evan. I'm brought back to my reality in an instant. I am here and my husband is dead. I glance at Stephanie as the tears stream down my face.

"Julia," she says now. The soothing way she says my name serves as some kind of benediction that things are going to be okay without the perfunctory announcement. It causes me to cry harder. I try to smile through the tears, but fail. Things are so far from being okay.

"Where am I? How did I get here?"

"You're at Lenox Hill. Do you remember what happened?"

The distant memory of being picked up and put on a stretcher rushes forward. The memories of the potent aroma of rubbing alcohol mixed with the sterile scent of medications, the sensation of high speed, the inquisition of bright lights, and all these frantic voices calling my name flood my mind. Bits and pieces of the puzzle come back to me. I remember taking the pills. I remember being in the hotel room. I remember the cold shower. I remember Jacob Winston. *Oh. I remember.* The guilt of kissing Evan's best friend, Jacob Winston, and the grief of being Evan's widow take turns with me, penetrating my soul.

"Do you remember what happened?" she asks again.

An intense need for Stephanie's continual approval and self-dignity has me answering, "No."

Stephanie looks at me in earnest. I think she wants to believe the lie I've just told, but she cannot quite reconcile my answer with what she actually knows to be true.

"No, I don't remember," I say.

She nods, as if she's made the decision for herself and plunges forward. "You're suffering from … an overdose, Julia. Jake Winston found you and brought you here. You almost died. You would have died, if he hadn't been there."

Fury erupts from her. Her anger is unusual. Stephanie is the serene one, the peacemaker, among us, but today, on this day, she is livid, so irate that she doesn't seem to know what to do. I watch her, as she slides from my bedside, and then, begins to pace the room.

I cringe, inwardly preparing for the onslaught of judgment, before saying, "I was sad. I didn't know how many pills I took." I don't quite believe what I'm saying, and note it's having little impact on Stephanie's belief systems, either. She continues her back and forth ritual across my hospital room floor.

"You took *six* times the dosage. Any more pills and you would have…" Her voice falters. "If he hadn't been there…"

I've never seen her get this upset before, especially with me. "Oh. I just wanted—" I cannot come up with a lie to explain the pills.

"What, Julia? Were you trying to kill yourself? We've been so scared." Stephanie sits down, again, and takes my hands in hers. The anger has worn her out. The diplomat is not used to the draining edge of such strong emotion. "We know it's hard, almost unbearable, but

Julia…" She stops for a moment, and then, says, "We love you so much and if something had happened." She starts to cry. "What about Reid? He needs you, Julia."

I have not really considered my seven-month-old son, not since the day Evan died. The grief just took me. I have not been able to really look at Reid, I've been too afraid that I would see too much of Evan's face in his features and literally break down. My son serves as a constant reminder of all that I've lost. Grief has had its way with me, breaking me apart. "I'm not … good for him."

"Don't say that. It's not true. You're the best mother, the best. We love you."

Her voice holds such conviction. I want to believe her.

For a single moment, I'm thankful that I'm still here, among the living, and Reid's mother. Then, the moment is gone. *How will I live without Evan? And, I'm not good for Reid, not now.* The grief travels through all of me. I think of Jacob Winston and feel the edges of shame. *I keep making mistakes.* I can't reconcile all these competing thoughts.

"I'm not good."

Stephanie holds my face between her hands. "Yes, *you are.*"

Her arms come around me and I attempt to hug her back. The IV line gets in the way. I struggle with hugging her. Stephanie and Kimberley have never experienced the grief of this world as I have. I love and resent them, at the same time, for this reason, alone. But I am bound. I am bound to these people who love me, and now, to a life without Evan. I am bound. I am here, saved by Jacob Winston. I am here and Evan is gone. I cry these endless tears of profound sorrow. I am here and Evan is gone. *Gone.*

<hr/>

Hours later, Stephanie disappears in search of better coffee and some decent food for all of us. Kimberley sits at the end of my hospital bed in a jogging suit I've never seen. She does not jog, so the sportiness of the navy blue outfit bewilders me. She's barely wearing make-up and her long mane of dark mahogany hair is in disarray. All anomalies.

"You didn't have to stay the night," I say in a mollified tone.

This lone comment seems to ignite her aggravation. She slides off the bed, comes to stand right in front of me with her arms crossed, and leans directly above me. I physically shrink away from her scrutiny.

"I've been here for two nights, Snow White. You've been out of it, for two days, with the stuff you took."

Her eyes fill with tears and she moves away from me, suddenly intent on looking out the window at the dreary landscape of Manhattan in December. After a few minutes, she sighs and comes back to me.

"Spill it," she commands. "I'm not leaving, until you tell me what's going on. You can start with the continual delivery of flowers from one Mr. Jacob Winston all the way from London. Why is he doing that? If I didn't know better, I'd say…" Kimberley stops and takes an uneven breath. Then, she leans over me, tucks a stray strand of my hair behind one ear, and says, "I've let you down. I'm sorry. I know you've dealt with grief before, with Bobby, with your parents, but I should have seen it. What it was doing to you."

"I messed up," I say dully. "I took too many pain killers. I drank too much. I just wanted the pain to go away. Lecherous Uncle Joe propositioned me and Jake…" My voice falters in just saying his name. "I said and did … some things I shouldn't have." I struggle with my confession. Now, Kimberley watches me intently. Her radar is up and engaged.

"Like what?"

"Like, I know, his idea of a serious relationship involved two consecutive fucks with the same girl," I say this with such profound distress that Kimberley starts to laugh.

I feel this release deep inside of me. She understands me. I return a wry smile.

"I left the bar, upset, and took some more pills. Truly, I just wanted the pain inside to go away. He caught up with me on the elevator. Then, everything fell out of my purse. He found the vial of pills and put them in his jacket. I don't know why, but I remember asking him about why he never did anything with Evan and me. It was always just the two of them. Skiing, hiking whatever. Never, all of three of us."

"Did he tell you why that was?"

"He started talking about London being a place he could start over."

"Start over? Why?"

"I don't know. Then, I started talking about starting over. How I had done it, too many times, before. I told him not again. I remember him getting this strange look on his face. Almost haunted. He looked sad. Then, he was holding me, and he felt like Evan. And, we were kissing, and it almost led to more." I give Kimberley this mortified look.

She looks momentarily stunned at my confession. Then, she gets this huge grin on her amazingly gorgeous face, even sans make-up.

"It was so *wrong*. I can't believe I almost did that. Oh, God. I'm a terrible person." I catch my lower lip between my teeth to keep it from trembling and avoid her intense appraisal. "I can't believe I almost did such a thing."

"Almost did what? Making out with a guy is not wrong," she says in her thou-shall-not-be-judged-by-me voice.

This absolution comes from the most promiscuous girl I know. I bestow her with a withering look. "Okay. You marry Gregoire, you have a child with him." I watch an unfamiliar blush steal over her face. "Almost a year later, he dies, and ten days after that, you're making out with Gregoire's best friend. How do you feel about yourself, now?"

"You lost me at the marrying Gregoire part," Kimberley says with this silly grin.

"Fuck you," I say with a modicum of affection and frustration.

"Funny," Kimberley retorts and rolls her eyes. She grips my hands in hers. "Julia, you cannot get hung up on the Jacob Winston thing. I want you to forget about it. *Really*. You were in a weak moment. So, you *kissed* the guy. You did something reckless *for you*. And, let's face it, completely out of character, but, you don't have to berate yourself over it. You loved Evan, we all know that, but I refuse to participate in a discussion where sexual foreplay is considered an immoral act. I'm not a priest. So, stop this guilt tripping, right now."

"You're not a priest," I say in a mocking tone.

"I've *done* a priest, but I'm not one." She gives me the all-famous-Kimberley sly secret smile—the one she saves for getting out of tickets with policemen, or with bartenders, when she fails to bring her ID. I actually start to laugh at the triumphant look on her face she's giving me. Then, she comes over and hugs me. "Don't take it the wrong way when I tell you I'm proud of you."

"God, Kimberley, *why* would you say that?"

She pulls away and looks at me intently. "You're *living*, Julia. You want to. Maybe, this is a new beginning."

"What? I get to take over the famous Kimberley promiscuity record setting? You're retiring?"

"I just might," she says with airy wave of her hand in my general direction.

I choose to ignore her get-out-of-jail-free speech. "So anyway, to finish my story, before the whole sexual exploration of the Catholic Church was revealed, I started feeling really weird and got sick. The white knight threw me into a cold shower, and, apparently, called an ambulance. The end."

"If he hadn't been there," she says with reverence. "God, Julia, he saved your life,"

I give her an exasperated look. "You just *told* me, five minutes ago, to forget about him."

"I told you to forget about the guilt of almost doing him." She just laughs, when I blush. "Not the parade of flowers from him over the past three days."

I don't miss her speculative look. I can almost see the wheels turning in Kimberley's head.

"I don't intend to ever see him again." I give her a little shrug for emphasis.

"Sure."

"I don't know why he's sending the flowers. I guess he feels bad about what almost transpired, and the things we said to each other."

"Like what?"

"I think he thought I might have married Evan for his money." I grimace. "But, I'm pretty sure, my literal breakdown changed his mind. I cried a lot. *Too much.* We talked about some weird stuff. Bobby. But, I don't remember why."

I turn away from her concentrated gaze. Kimberley has a way of knowing my innermost secrets, sometimes, even before I do.

"You talked about Bobby?" Kimberley asks in surprise.

I never talk about Bobby. It's an unwritten rule, among all of us, never speak of Julia's dead loved ones, especially Bobby, and now, Evan.

"A little," I say, defensive now.

Kimberley stares at me. I become more uneasy.

"Enough about Jacob Winston," I say in a firm this-subject-is-now-closed voice.

"Thank God, he was there, Julia. What were you thinking?"

"I wasn't. The grief over Evan was consuming me."

Kimberley stops pacing, comes back over the bed, and grips my hand.

"Promise me you'll never do anything like this ever again."

"Almost sleep with Jake Winston? I can't believe I almost did that." I give her an anguished look while the guilt of that chases through me.

"It didn't get that far," Kimberley says in a consoling tone. Then, she frowns, shakes her head side-to-side, and gets this serious look. "But no, that's not what I'm talking about." Her blue Topaz eyes seemingly penetrate my green ones. "Promise me, you'll never do anything like this ever again."

"I promise."

I'm not convinced of my promise and from the dubious look on her face, I know she doesn't quite believe me, either.

Why I hate Advil

THE PSYCHE QUESTIONNAIRE ASKS ME TO list the things I dislike. Why don't they just use the word, *hate*? Why is everyone so afraid to admit they hate something? I write Advil, and then, add Athens, Afghanistan, and the U.S. Army. In conclusion, I hate a lot of things that begin with the letter A, I write in the space provided.

Dr. Bradley Stevenson's office is one of understated opulence done up in these chartreuse and gold tones. He has these over-bloomed white roses in various vases around the room. I find myself actually smiling.

"These are my favorite, just like this." I bend down and sniff at one of the arrangements, savoring the pungent smell of over bloomed roses. I walk around the room surveying it, taking everything in.

This is day three of *my tour* at Lenox Hill. My first day out of the ward. My first day where I get to meet privately with the venerable Dr. Bradley Stevenson, in his office, instead of my hospital room.

He lives up to his billing and his name. He is another golden boy. I have flashes of Jacob Winston and my own Mr. Evan Hamilton, but I damp down these two errant images, intent on concentrating on this less painful replica in front of me.

"Tell me about your husband. Tell me about what happened to Evan," he encourages me in this cajoling tone.

I look over at him with a deliberate stare. He's not going to let me off the hook this time, I can tell. We're not going to experience a session of absolute silence, like yesterday afternoon.

I sigh, take a deep breath and say, "There was a storm. One of those early December storms that obliterate daylight. We'd been hanging out all day, but … I had a headache. And, we are out of Advil." I pause for a moment, taking in air.

"That's how it started. I had a headache and Evan volunteered to go to the little market, a mile away, to get more Advil." I shake my head side-to-side.

"It's a fifteen minute trip, there and back, maximum. Only he's not back in fifteen minutes like he promised. I remember the rain whipping against the windows of our beach house and staring out at the churning waves of the Atlantic just counting off the time by one-minute increments. Forty-five minutes went by. Now, I was anxious, headache forgotten. I bundled up Reid and carried him in his baby carrier out to the garage and loaded him in the car. I kept thinking, this is silly. This is silly, going to see what's keeping Evan, but I did it anyway. I kept thinking, I'll see him coming from the opposite direction. He'd pass me and give me that legendary smile of his and shake his head at my angst. He wouldn't be mad. Evan understood my fears better than anyone else. He'd just tease me. He'd tell me he got a present for the baby or fresh strawberries for me, or he stopped at the post office, or he saw an old friend, all possibilities in that small town."

I take a deep breath. "But something stopped traffic in both directions. All the innocuous errands he could have been doing get obliterated by the punctuating sound of sirens, the flash of blue and red lights. A semi-trailer truck sits jack-knifed in the middle of the two lane road. Police cruisers, fire trucks, and ambulances surround it." I shake my head and look over at my psychiatrist. "I remember thinking, it's like a prized collection of vehicles—a boy's playground strewn with Mattel hot wheels left out in the rain, only life-size."

I close my eyes and the frantic scene comes to life in my mind again. It conjures up the horrible scene of Evan's last moments and takes my breath away. I gasp for air and open my eyes, disoriented, for a few moments. Then, I'm brought back Dr. Bradley Stevenson's opulent office at Lenox Hill hospital.

I look over and discover him watching me from one of the char-treuse-colored Thai silk chairs in the west corner. His dark blonde hair haloed by the muted sunlight that's trying to make its way in through the slats of the fashionable gold-tinted blinds at his office windows. I stare at the angelic effect the sun is having on my psychiatrist, and try to take some solace in the fact that I'm alive and in this room across from him, though it still feels like my life is over. I struggle to hide the true devastation from him.

"Go on," he says in this neutral Greek god-like tone.

Adonis has come to life, here in Manhattan, in the human form of the exceptionally good-looking Dr. Bradley Stevenson. I mean, if you have to be *committed*, if you have to go down the abyss, this is the man to take you there, or be accompanied by.

I take a deep breath and start again. "So I parked the car in the middle of the road and grabbed my baby, my purse, and keys. I kept thinking, I might need these: Gum. Keys. Mints. Money. Identification."

I catch my lower lip, remembering my weird obsession with having *everything*. *Where was I going to go?*

"There was a little boy, he just stood, there, in the pouring rain. He was, maybe, eight-years-old, crying on the side of the road, next to his bike. I remember him pointing at the accident and just sobbing. His bike askew. The front tire flat. The spokes bent at a weird angle. It was, as if he'd recently met up with a ditch. I kept looking from the boy, to his bike, to the accident."

I swallow hard. My breath becomes shallow and I glance over at the good doctor again, trying to find the will to go on with the story. The minutes tick by, one by one, while he patiently waits for me. I swipe at tear.

"And then, I found Evan." I shrug, involuntarily, to ward off this bad feeling with this gesture, alone. "Well, I found the *proof* of what was Evan's charcoal-grey Porsche, just an hour before. Now, it was mangled steel caught under the massiveness of a semi–trailer truck that was wrapped around his sports car, like used tin foil."

My voice holds traces of bitterness and I can practically feel the bile coming up my throat in evoking this last memory of Evan.

He's gone.

Gone forever.

I clasp my hands together, and attempt to control the shaking, and automatically turn away from the intense gaze of Dr. Stevenson.

"Go on," he says into the growing silence.

I nod in slow motion and try to chase away the nightmarish feelings of terror that recalling the memorable scene of the accident still invokes. It still holds such sway with me.

"The firemen worked fast, calling out orders I couldn't comprehend." I close my eyes re-envisioning the horror of that afternoon. "I watched them work, at a frenzied pace, at the twisted metal, attempting to pry open the crushed driver's door with the Jaws of Life. Evan. His Porsche looked too small, half the size of what it should have been," I whisper. "I remember the smell of gasoline infusing with the salty air and the smell of the chilling winter rain, unwelcome. So incongruent."

I push up from the chair opposite from the good doctor and walk back over to the window and stare out through the slats at the bare tree branches just beyond. "Deciduous." I touch the window, as if I can reach them from here.

"I remember glancing down at Reid and seeing his one-tooth gaping grin, *pure joy* just emanating from him that day. And, I remember thinking, where does it come from? I reached out and touched his face and said it's going to be okay. I told this lie more for myself than Reid. I said what everybody says to you in a time of crisis. His baby-like sounds seemed to reach at me from so far away, *already.*" I turn back from the window and lean up against the sill and inspect the room, trying to discern its magnificence.

"There were these seagulls, just calling, cooing, whatever the hell it is they do. These seagulls flew overhead in frenzied formation, diving, seemingly spying at the unexpected activity. They flew away, all at once, disturbed by the building crescendo of unfamiliar sounds, I guess. I kept wondering, why do they do that? Are they frightened? God-damn birds." I take another unsteady breath.

"So, I stood there in the pouring rain, held my hand over Reid's face, so he'd get less wet." I look at the good doctor in this conspiring way, acknowledging the futility in that action. "Then, this state patrolman came over to me and said. 'Lady, you're going to have to step back.' He's tall. Tall like Evan. Broad shouldered, steady, and safe, just like Evan. I remember his face. It was so grim, already undone by the reality of being up close and witnessing … *the unthinkable*. I remember trying not to look at him, but I did. I couldn't help it. The look on his face. It still haunts me."

I push off the ledge of the window sill and step to the center of the room.

"So, I say, 'That's my husband and pointed toward the Porsche. He's late. He went to the store about an hour ago.' I remember holding out my wrist to the officer. My Seiko watch glistened in the pouring rain. The gold watch—the first gift Evan ever gave me."

I take another unsteady breath and look over at the doctor. He just nods, encouraging me. "Evan told me he could hold time in his hands." I smile at the memory. "And, when he opened them, there was this beautiful Seiko watch for me. He promised to love me forever. Forever. Time," I say slowly. "Fuck." I shake my head and grimace at the good doctor in silent consolation for my swearing. He just inclines his head again. "Sorry."

"Go on."

"I remember the officer glancing at my watch, and then, back at my face. 'You should sit down,' he said. His voice held such *consolation*. It was the same kind of voice my mother used, when my cat, Seraphim, died. I was ten. The end of a ten-year-old's world, when the cat dies."

I try to smile at my weak effort for contrived humor. Dr. Stevenson tries to smile, but it doesn't quite work. He looks as devastated as I feel.

"I remember thinking, *and this? This* really is the end of my world. Lot more than a damn cat."

I lick my lips and traipse back to the window again and stare out at the gloomy semblance of daylight in the middle of December.

"I remember the sound of a saw distracting me, then. It made this whirring sound, like a bee does, when it's pollinating flowers. Not an *it*. A *he*? I'd asked the state patrolman about that. 'There's the queen bee, and then, all the other bees are *he's*, aren't they?'"

I nod my head, remembering.

"He'd answered, 'Mostly he's, I believe.' I remember his arm sliding through the handle of Reid's baby carrier and how he held on to me with his free one."

"I'd said to him, 'You rhyme.' I remember trying to laugh. 'Mostly he's, I believe. That's good.'"

I glance over at Dr. Stevenson. His pen is poised in the air, he seems frozen in the moment, dismayed by my awful story. It appears that I have broken through his impenetrable shield where he constantly emulates that everything is going to be okay.

"I remember just nodding my head, up and down, like it wasn't attached to my body any longer. My head was just pounding, pulsing out of control, just like my heart and lungs, with all this extra energy I no longer knew how to expend. I took in the scene like a gaping teenager, as if witnessing my first horror film, wanting to scream, but willing myself to keep silent. I slept with the lights on for weeks after that movie. And, I remember thinking I may have to employ that technique again."

I turn back from the window.

"The thing was, *I knew*, even then, I was saying goodbye to happiness. I felt it seeping away from me. Gone forever. Just this feeling of suspended disbelief. *Suspended disbelief.* You know, the feeling you get, after you've cut yourself, a silly accident where the carving knife goes astray. You're cutting tomatoes, and then, you've cut yourself. It's stupid, really. And, you stare down at your finger, and before, the pain starts, you watch the hint of blood ooze from sliced skin, then, in the next instant, it's everywhere. The horror of spurting blood that can't be stopped. The horror takes hold, and then, the pain comes."

I pause, take another deep breath, and glance over at the good doctor. He just regards me with those grey eyes of his, too much like Evan's, takes notes, and watches me.

"I said to the officer. 'It won't be stopped. Will it? The happiness is really gone forever. This pain is never going to go away. Is it?'"

"You should sit down," he'd said back to me and asked me my name."

"I'm Julia Hamilton," I answered. I remember the sparks flying as one of the fireman wielded another saw and cut through the metal from the other direction. All the firemen exhibited this desperation, their faces contorted with stress and recognizable fear. And, I kept wondering; *does mine?*"

I inhale air and hold it for a moment. I count to fifteen.

My breath's uneven now. I practically gulp for air.

"Then, I said, 'And, that's Evan,' and pointed toward the Porsche again. 'My husband, Evan Hamilton. He's twenty-eight, more than a year older than me. This is Reid, our son, he's six and half months old.' I remember reaching for my baby's hand. His fingers felt so small in mine. 'What's your name?' I'd asked the officer."

"He answered, 'I'm Lieutenant Grant.' His voice was so soothing, a priest giving benediction, gravelly. He looked from me, to Reid, to Evan's car, and, back again, at me."

"I remember saying to the officer, 'I think I'll sit down.' And, then, all I saw was ice cream, and the post office, and the little market a mile up the road from our beach house, and Evan's face. Then, just his smile. It's the last thing I remember seeing."

I look over at Dr. Brad Stevenson, now, and convey an are-we-done-here? look.

"And," I say with inevitability, "That's why I hate Advil."

The psychiatrist regards me with his steady professional gaze, but his hand trembles, betraying his own turmoil over my story. He glances down at his watch.

"Time's up," I say.

All he can do is nod.

CHAPTER

FIVE

Things that begin with the letter A

DAY FOUR AT LENOX HOSPITAL. IT's my third session with the good doctor. We spend the first fifteen minutes in total silence, but he manages to throw me off with his next question.

"And, Athens? Why do you hate Athens?"

I glance up at him and give him a dubious look. I thought he was going to ask me about Bobby, so I'm unprepared to talk about my parents. I sigh.

"Nobody should die on their vacation. My parents worked hard their whole lives. They spent months planning that trip to Greece. It was wonderful and magical. Then, one day, the magic just ended with a fated helicopter crash, when they were returning from Crete to Athens. I stayed behind at the hotel, bored with the idea of Crete, enthralled with the idea of the hotel swimming pool, of being on my own. I just didn't know it would be forever, after that day. I was an only child. Alone. In Greece. A ward of the U.S. Embassy. Instant problem child. A real-life Greek tragedy."

"Your parents died in Athens, while you were on vacation? You were all alone?"

"Yes," I say with weariness. The memory of my parents' untimely deaths still overwhelms me, with lightning speed, even all these years later.

"How old were you, then?"

"Sixteen."

"How did that make you feel?"

I move my head side-to-side, in a daze, as I remember. "How did it make me *feel? Alone.* No more magic."

I struggle to find my nonchalant footing and stare back at him. I watch him get uncomfortable with my open appraisal of him. He busies himself with taking notes in his leather-bound book.

"Do you go back and read those? I mean, some people take notes, and then, never read them. What do you do?"

"I read them."

"Good for you. I never read them. I'll take notes and commit them up here." I point to my temple. He watches me from this introspective place, trying to figure me out, I suppose.

I bequeath him with my most devastating smile, the smile Kimberley taught me long ago, the smile that gets a girl everything she wants. She's right, of course. It does. Only, I don't know what I want, so I falter with it, now. The good doctor shifts in his chair and gets this uncertain look.

Note to self: Got to watch who you smile at like that.

"Ms. Hamilton," he begins again. His fingers form a steeple in front of him, now, he seems in contemplative thought. *The thinking man.* My smile gets wider at my racing thoughts. "Tell me about Afghanistan."

My smile disappears.

"I've never been there."

"You hate a place you've never seen?" His feigned surprise amuses me, on some level, but I reward him with a withering glance.

"Sometimes, you don't have to see it, to hate it, Dr. Stevenson. Surely, you understand the power of hate."

"Who did you lose in Afghanistan?"

"I don't … talk about that."

"Whatever you say to me doesn't leave this room. It's between us. No one else. You wrote it down." He gives me a nonchalant shrug. "That's the first indication that, maybe, you want to talk about it. Tell me about these things that start with the letter *A* that you hate."

Stunned into silence, I contemplate my next move. The more I talk to him, the more I feel the emotional shield, I normally hide behind, begin to disintegrate. I take a deep breath and let it out slowly, as if I'm in a Hatha yoga class.

"If we're going to talk about Bobby, we have to start at the beginning," I say with deprecation. He nods, encouraging me with this sympathetic look and his rapt attention. "So, Kimmy," I incline my head, questioning him with a glance, to determine if he remembers Kimberley from the more than ten times he's seen her in my hospital room the past four days. He inclines his head again.

"So Kimmy sees me at Chicago O'Hare. I'd just turned eighteen. I'm incognito. I'd dyed my hair, changed my name. I was on my quest to get out of there. I had my suitcase with all my belongings in it, and I stood at the reader board, trying to decide where I wanted to go. But then, I saw Kimberley. Kimberley Powers. We'd gone to school together, at Hopkins, before the courts sent me away to live with my grandmother.

It'd been over two years, since I'd seen her. She looked even more awesome at eighteen. In my mind, I was unidentifiable, but I was still worried she'd seen me and struggled to remain nonchalant. But, she passed by me, like a model, swanking down the walkway with her long legs, wearing a black and white ensemble with black strappy sandals."

I shake my head and laugh at the memory of her. "I remember studying the reader board, even more intently, hoping she hadn't recognized me. Rio de Janeiro. Reno. Raleigh. South. West. East. Where to go? Her perfume assailed me, first, and then, her lyrical voice, when she said, 'Julia Hawthorne. Where have you been for past two years?'"

I smile over at Dr. Stevenson.

"She will not be *denied*. She convinced me to head to L.A. with her. As you can imagine, you don't say, 'no' to Kimberley Powers. She was the coolest girl at Hopkins. She was on her way to L.A., to meet up with a former classmate of ours, Bobby Turner. I *definitely* remembered him, from two years ago."

I walk back over to the window and look out at the bleak winter day. I stare at my own reflection. This stranger stares back. *Who am I now?*

"So, we boarded the plane for L.A., despite my normal distrust of people." I glance back at the doctor and see his slight amusement at my comment. "I spent the majority of the flight, filling her in on what had happened to me for the past few years. I even shared the finer details about my grandmother and her drinking and how I'd been little more than an indentured servant to her, while she waited to get her hands on my trust fund. That day. My eighteenth birthday. I'd been to the bank, cleaned out my account and shown up at Chicago O'Hare, and all Kimmy said was, 'Well, your double-down secret is safe with me.'"

I expel a gratifying sigh, now, and allow myself to experience a little happiness at the memory of Kimberley and her solemn vow. My secrets have always been safe with her.

"So we deplane. And, there's Bobby, just inside the terminal at LAX. He's leaning against the wall, with his arms folded across his chest, wearing these black jeans and a white Polo shirt with the UCLA Bruins logo, a true golden boy. I think I actually shivered, when he shook my hand, and said, 'Nice to *see* you, again, Julia.' I'd been away from New Haven for a few years, and the guy still remembered my name. I remember Kimberley looking at me funny, and glancing down, only to discover I was still holding Bobby Turner's hand."

I laugh at the memory and the feeling it evokes. I think it surprises the good doctor. He gets this incredulous look on his face.

"Somehow, with astounding ingenuity, Bobby manages to load all of our luggage in his white Porsche. The top was down and I sat in the middle, my bare legs straddling the stick shift. His hand was in constant motion, shifting the gears. I was trying to find air, while his hand was brushing against my inner thigh every few seconds."

I blush as I tell this part of the story and note Dr. Stevenson is still looking at me in veiled astonishment.

"We arrive at this fabulous beach house he's rented with Kimberley in Marina del Rey and I walk in with my suitcase and he takes it from me, and says, 'Your room is this way. Here, let me show you.' I smile over at the doctor. "My room was his room. Just like that, he loved me and I loved him."

I stop talking. It takes a few minutes to recover, to find enough detachment left inside of me, to go on. "The three of us attended UCLA. He's in the ROTC program and playing soldier on the weekends, every so often. I didn't pay any attention to that aspect of his life. He talked about law school and I talked about being a writer. Our life together was amazing and grand. Our future predetermined, like the stars in the galaxy. After graduation, we were going to get married right on the beach. We'd buy a house, have kids. He'd be a lawyer, I'd write."

My smile vanishes.

"Then 9/11 happened, and he talked about what he needed to do for his country, and I just didn't get it. I was busy planning our wedding on the beach at Marina del Rey, and he was talking about Afghanistan and duty. So, when he told me he'd made his decision, I thought, great he was ready to set a date. We'd been talking about keeping things simple, and I was saying, "June," at the same time, he was saying, "My orders are for Afghanistan." He was due to leave at the end of the January. He'd signed up to serve as second lieutenant in the U.S. Army. Not the Christmas present I hoped for." I walk back from the windows, stand in the middle of the room, and gaze at the good doctor. My breath comes less even, now.

"So, we're together, only I was in L.A. trying to breathe without him. And, he was in Afghanistan and had begun to wonder what he'd gotten himself into, going on three years. He sent me a letter every day. I had more than a thousand letters from him." I give the psychiatrist a pleading look, but he just inclines his head encouraging me to continue.

"Kimmy spent her free time trying to distract me. She was good that way, always up for distraction. She convinced me to go to a movie, and we had a few drinks at a bar, afterward, so it was late, when we got home. She'd kept reminding me all night that Bobby would be home in sixty-three days for good. Like I needed reminding, I remember telling her it was sixty-two days, twelve hours and twenty minutes and ten seconds, to be exact."

I smile at the memory, but then, it falters.

"I already had my wedding gown. I was going to marry that guy as soon as he got off the plane. No fanfare, no guests, just a minister; Kimberley; Stephanie, our other roommate; Bobby and me. So, we had just gotten back to the beach house and Kimmy pressed the blinking light on the answering machine. I remember Bobby's dad's voice filled the room in this inconsolable tenor, as he said, 'You need to come back to New Haven, Julia.'"

I stop and take a breath.

"My life had been over for twenty-one hours and thirty-three minutes. I just didn't know it," I whisper now.

I count to thirty, trying to take even breaths, in and out. All the while, Dr. Bradley Stevenson concentrates on me with this incredibly sad look on his face. With a sudden need to sit down, I steal into the chair opposite him, and put my head between my hands.

"Bobby was killed in *Afghanistan*," I say in a low voice. "He was twenty-four. They didn't keep him safe. The *Army* didn't keep him *safe*." There's open hostility in my tone. I raise my head and just look over at Dr. Bradley Stevenson clearly conveying, *solve that one, doctor*.

"I'm sorry."

"Everybody is. Everyone is always *sorry*."

"Sometimes, that's all we can be. No one can pretend to understand your pain."

"Right." I look over at him in distress. "But, everybody *tries*."

We share five minutes of pure silence. I watch the clock tick off the time. Five minutes, ten seconds. Five minutes, twenty seconds. Five minutes, thirty seconds.

I sigh. Apparently, I'm supposed to end this absolute stillness.

"Do you ever just want to say, fuck it? Fuck all of it? Because, I do. Sometimes, that's all I want to do."

I stand up and walk over to him and touch his hand, trailing my fingers along his forearm in the same suggestive way Kimberley always appropriates with men. Of course, I am way out of my depth, beyond my normal character fiber, but I press on.

"What do *you* want to do, doctor?"

"I'm here to help you."

He shifts again and eventually stands, towering above me, flustered. A red flush steals over his handsome features.

"Session's over," he says with a strangled cough.

I just nod.

And then, I say, "That's what I thought."

<hr />

Day five at Lenox Hill, session four with the good Doctor Stevenson. Back in my hospital room, we are back to neutral territory. My overt affections at the end of yesterday's session were apparently out of line. They were. He seems intent on getting back to the patient and doctor boundaries between us. I'm intent on getting out of here.

The good doctor is not completely buying my schtick about being fine and just needing time and solitude. Instead, he inundates me with questions. "How do you feel, Julia? Have you had bad thoughts?"

"Bad thoughts?"

I take a deep breath, preparing for the dramatic role of my life.

"A thought of suicide," offers the handsome Dr. Stevenson. He's not amused, his determined look confirms his frustration with me. I have not been a very good patient. Cooperative, yes, but not at the informant level, I believe he was hoping for. I am not willing to share my bad thoughts about suicide with the good doctor, with anybody, so it seems. So, it is.

"No, of course not," I say with the slightest edge of indignation. "Of course not. I made a mistake. I was too sad. I wasn't thinking clearly. I just wanted the pain to go away. I didn't want to kill myself."

I'm guilty now, too. I do not say this to the good doctor. With almost a week's worth of unspoken reflection, upon the almost sexual encounter with Evan's best friend, along with an attempted overdose of pills that led up to said incident, and the fact that my death would have left my seven-month-old son without a mother, I've added guilt to my continuous burden.

Guilt and grief consume me.

Jake's own remorse has shown its way through an endless succession of flowers and cards that apologize in a thousand different ways for what transpired. He has just made it worse. I stare at the flower bouquets, littering my hospital room that inundate me with constant shame. He does not stop sending them.

"Why would I have thoughts of suicide?" I've tried to master this manufactured attitude of nonchalance and hide my true pain from everyone the last few days. I even try to smile, after saying this.

Dr. Stevenson doesn't hold back, he counters with, "Why wouldn't you? You were married to a wonderful man, who's been tragically killed. Tell me, what you're feeling."

His questions make me cringe inward. I still can't imagine living without Evan, but I don't tell him this. I struggle to hide my true feelings, but take a detached stance. I think he is taken aback by my unnatural indifference even more than our coy banter about thoughts of suicide that disguise the true suspension of my destiny—my true mental state—a knife's edge for both of us. One wrong answer and I will find myself in a locked ward without a key, despite my generous donations to Lenox Hill in my dead husband's name.

I give him a measured look. "I am very capable of handling grief," I say to him in an even, patient tone. "As I've told you, I have a life's history with death: my parents, my fiancé, and now. Practice makes perfect, isn't that what they say?"

"All the more reason for me to be concerned."

He attempts this clinical attitude and continues to assess me with his penetrating stare.

Fuck. Just leave already. Just fucking leave. I want to shout this at him, but I don't. The good doctor is just waiting for that kind of reaction from me. I remain steadfast and silent and just stare at him in this practiced, I-don't-have-a-care-in-the-world kind of way and eventually say, "I'm fine. I've made it through all the others."

"Yes, but this was your husband. You had a child with Evan. Ties. Connections."

"He wasn't that great." My attempt at humor backfires. My flippant words come out as this strangled cry. Ties. Connections. The double meaning is not lost on me. I have trouble keeping the mask of serenity on my face in place. The warning signs of the grief and guilt I've kept at bay, during all these conversations, take hold of me.

"Julia, I shouldn't let you go home," he says without looking up from his notebook.

"I'll be good," I counter.

I'll be good. He shakes his head at me. I don't believe me, either. Good is a relative term any way. Good at what? I take turns with grief, guilt, shame, and heartbreak, and serve as some kind of punching bag for all of these emotions.

"I'll be good. I promise. And, you can't keep me here," I say kindly.

He can't keep me here without cause. And, I refuse to give him any. I have been here for five days and have done more than the standard three days of evaluation. The state of New York cannot keep me any longer without a court order.

I know this; and he knows this, too.

"No," he concedes with a heavy sigh.

We are at this impasse and we both recognize it.

I smile at him. He does not smile back.

His concerned look is touching. His resemblance to Evan, with his dark blonde hair and his grey eyes, is disquieting. The gold-rimmed glasses are not Evan's and my husband was taller, but it's there. I think all of this, as I smile at him in a practiced, captivating way that has always helped me get what I want, even with Evan. It's been working on Dr. Stevenson, too. I can see his hesitation. I can see his attraction to me. I still have that sex appeal, men find attractive, going for me. I certainly know this. A brief flash of Jake Winston's face comes to my mind. I struggle with the feelings his image brings with it, but I recover enough to give the good doctor a beguiling look.

"I'm going to be fine," I say.

Dr. Stevenson breaks away from my evocative gaze and picks up the small paper pill cup. He deftly opens my hand with his, and drops two white pills into it, and then, hands me a glass of water. My look of compliance disguises my disdain for these white pills. Dr. Stevenson steps back away from me, helpless, too involved, too captivated, in too deep. I believe he is indebted to the white pills as a last point of defense with me. I acknowledge the apprehension I see in his eyes with an inclination of my head.

"Don't worry so much. I'm *fine*," I say.

We look at each other, certain of only one thing, we silently concede the white pills won't solve anything, least of all, what is haunting me. Everyone I have ever loved is dead, and the handsome, beguiled Dr. Bradley Stevenson can't fix any of it.

CHAPTER

SIX

A never-ending roller coaster ride

AT THE RECOMMENDATION AND, SOMEWHAT, AGREEABLE terms reached with Dr. Bradley Stevenson, I return to the beach house at Amagansett, under the watchful eyes of Kimberley, while Gregoire Chantal stays at her place in Manhattan. Stephanie and Christian stay at Jake Winston's empty abode a mile down the road from mine, further delaying their return to Paris for Christmas with Christian's family, while Jake continues to oversee things for Hamilton Equities at the office in London. Jake. Thoughts of him and our strange encounter ignite new rounds of guilt over my reckless behavior. Silent self-castigation about kissing my dead husband's best friend from Yale assails me at unpredictable moments throughout each day now. What is wrong with me? Why oh why did I have to kiss him? Was I possessed? Yes. It's the only explanation that makes any sense. He reminded me of all those I've lost; and I was a little bit crazy. And now, I have to live with all of that.

The little white pills put me in an anesthetized state; I'm unable to feel anything too deeply. A living body wrung out and bereft of a soul, functioning in neutral on constant idle. The heartbreak is still real, just down deep; and I do my best to hide it, but based upon the anxious looks my inner circle exchange between them, I don't think I'm fooling anyone, least of all, myself.

Grief settles around me with the clear intention of staying for the long-term as my constant companion, a stalker I can't outrun. It's always there, lurking, and ready to pounce at any given moment. I can't get Evan's accident out of my mind half the time. At other junctures, I'm inundated with thoughts of Jake Winston, our strange connection and this guilt and shame of being Evan's widow and yet, kissing his best friend Jake. Incurable thoughts, all of them. If I could just stop thinking, everything would be fine.

Listless, I stare out at the grey canvas of the Atlantic. The harsh chill of the wind and the faint prickling sensation of salt spray barely register as these things race past me and obliterate all other sound with the exception of the agonized screaming inside.

A memory of Evan jogging along the shoreline, just weeks before, flashes at me. I look to the north and there he is, in his favorite grey sweats. I scrutinize the lone figure running toward me. This inexplicable exhilaration coupled with rising anxiety courses through me. *How can this be?* Before, I can stop myself, I've opened up my arms as the runner sprints my way. "Evan!"

Seconds later, I recognize the runner as Jim Hargrove from two doors down. In agonized disbelief, I watch him turn up from the path and take the stairs, two at a time, leading from the beach to his own palatial home. Despair follows me down into this momentary descent from reality but only the wind can hear my cries. For once, I'm grateful for the Atlantic and its ability to mask all sound. I need it, on this day, before anyone discovers how despondent I really am.

Tears run down my face, only part wind-driven. Grief fills up all of me. I look to the north again. My arms ache. *I will never hold him again.* This staggering thought brings me to my knees and I collapse into the wet wintry sand. The fierceness of the approaching waves lull me into this sense of acceptance. Evan's life is over. So is mine. Pain killers chased with a slew of chocolate martinis, and now, little white pills, or even thoughts of Jake Winston cannot stop grief's latest assault.

"Julia!" Kimberley's voice breaks through my numb state.

It's all been a bad nightmare. None of it's true.

I'm dragged to my feet, soaking wet and yanked back to reality. *It's all true.*

"God, what are you doing out here? I've been looking for you everywhere. You're ice cold. Julia, look at me!"

Glazed, I look at her, unseeing. "Kimmy?" I can't keep my teeth from chattering.

Kimberley grips my stiff hand and half-drags me back up the wooden stairs to the house. With reality revived, I stare at the home that used to be a haven that now serves as a constant reminder of Evan and all I've lost. "I can't … stay here."

"I know. It's just for a few days, until we figure things out."

Her sympathy propels me forward. A few days. *I can handle a few days. Can't I?*

Kimberley leads me inside, up the stairs, and down the long hallway. She pushes me under a hot shower, clothes and all, while I chase away the memories of Jake Winston doing this for me just days before. Tears mingle with the shower spray and I let them fall. Five minutes later, Kimberley strips off my clothes, wraps the towel around me, and pulls me back along the hallway.

I stop midway. "I can't. I can't sleep there, Kimmy." I point towards the double doors, leading to the master bedroom, where Evan and I slept only weeks before.

"I know. We're just getting you something to wear. We'll sleep in the guest room."

With trepidation and a shared sense of urgency, we enter the master bedroom and head straight to the walk-in closet. Kimberley searches the drawers for clothes, while I try to control my trembling. The farthest hallway light serves as the only source of illumination into this dim tomb. I peer over at Kimberley, who tries to smile, but the furrow at the bridge of her nose reveals her own distress as she wipes at a tear. She tosses me an old t-shirt and cotton pajama bottoms. I catch them one-handed. "Thanks."

Through the darkened hallway, we make our way to the guest suite. Then, I hear Reid's distinct cry from downstairs, and look over at Kimmy.

"Lianne's got him," she says.

How does she know? How does she know my pain?

She switches on the night stand lamp, turns down the bed, and pushes me into it.

"I'm going to change. Then, I'll be right back. Okay?" I crawl into the bed without answering. She brings the covers up to my neck and studies me. "I'll be right back," she says again.

I close my eyes at her words. 'I'll be right back,' Evan's last words reverberate through me. A tear escapes and makes a slow trail down my face. I open my eyes again and look at her.

"Don't turn the light out," I say.

"I won't."

Minutes later, she crawls into bed next to me, because that's what my best friend does for me. She was the same way, when Bobby died. In the semi-darkness, we face each other and hold hands.

"Kimmy. Thank you."

She nods. Her tears mingle with mine on the pillow we share.

Stirring awake, I glance at the red illumination of the numbers: two, one, five, and savor a few precious seconds, before I remember what's happened. Grief returns with fresh reinforcements. The battle seems to be waged for my sanity. While Kimmy sleeps beside me, I face the haunting imagery, grief has so eloquently prepared. First to arrive are those happy memories of Evan: his amazing laugh that captivated me the first time we spoke, the way he'd whisper in my ear when we were in public, the way he made me feel when we'd gaze at each other from across a room. Then, our last moments together, when he brushed his lips across our baby's forehead, and then, mine before he sailed out the door and called out: *I'll be right back.*

Then, other images of Evan re-emerge, painful ones that haunt: his crushed Porsche; his lifeless broken body when the firemen finally extricated it from the wreckage; his eyes closed forever; and, the first dawning moment when I began to comprehend he was really gone. The images play, over and over, an endless film reel I can't begin to turn off. "Evan," I say into the darkness, but only silence answers. *He's not coming back.* Kimberley sighs in her sleep, disturbing the early morning's daunting stillness, while I give into the grief swirling all around me.

Eighteen days. It's December 23rd. We spend the day in New Haven at the cemetery. There's this strange consolation in being there for me, while I watch Kimberley try to handle her high-powered public relations job with *Liaison* from a cell phone. She stalks with purpose in her black stilettos along the cemetery's stone path and gestures wildly with her hands. Since Evan's death, she's been running triage from Amagansett for *Liaison,* when she should really be in Manhattan, or at the new office in Paris. Even I can see, from this faraway place in which I inhabit, that it's time for everyone to return to a normal life, whatever that may be. All of us. Kimberley, Stephanie, Christian. Even Jake. Everyone has put their life and plans on hold for me.

Good girl. The whispered memory of Evan's voice encourages me now. I start to smile, but then, my heart lurches when I glance down at his grave. The permanent granite headstone isn't finished, so the freshly dug grave with its faint hint of new green sod laid over the top of it looks out of place in the middle of a snow-covered landscape. I gasp for breath in the chilly air and try to get warm by waving my arms around in the stillness.

"I miss you," I whisper at his grave, and then, rearrange the white roses I've put there. "I miss you so much."

I spend a few minutes more at Evan's grave, and then, retrace my steps along the familiar path to my parents' graves, and finally, Bobby's.

This haven holds all my dead loved ones. Tranquility drifts over me in just being here with them.

Kimberley drives my SUV back to Amagansett, since I remain incapable of really operating heavy machinery doped up on Dr. Stevenson's magic white pills and still plagued at unpredictable moments by this overwhelming grief that stays with me, like a chronic flu. If it were possible, I most certainly have it.

The three-hour plus drive, including the car ferry, provides this fleeting sense of serenity, a carry-over from the visit to New Haven. *Who gains solace in a cemetery? That would be me.*

Settling back in the passenger seat, I note the holiday lights seem to saturate the world. "What about Christmas?" I steal a glance at Kimberley.

"What do you want to do?"

"You should spend it with Gregoire. It's time for you to return to Paris. *Liaison* isn't going to run itself. I'm sure Gregoire's anxious to return home."

"Paris can wait. *Liaison* can wait, too. We should spend Christmas all together. Wherever you want to be," she says.

A scene from last Christmas comes out of nowhere. Evan and I were in the midst of wedding plans dealing with everything from the guest list to tasting wedding cake and dinner entrees and champagne to choosing theme colors and flowers. The fitting of my crème-colored wedding dress and Evan's black tuxedo led to an intimate evening with just the two of us. We dispensed with tradition that night, when he made love to me in my bridal gown, two weeks before January tenth's big event. The memories of being that happy overwhelm me. We were overjoyed at being pregnant and starting a new life together. Now, just a year later, Evan's gone from me forever.

"If I told you I envision a large pitcher of margaritas in my future, on Christmas Eve, drinking myself silly, and then, wanting to spend the entire day in bed on Christmas Day, but, I let you choose where, what would you say?"

"I'd say, sounds good. I'm there. But, you choose where."

"Amagansett," I say. "It's Reid's first Christmas."

Kimberley nods and casually wipes away a tear and stares straight ahead intent on the road ahead.

"Yes. Thought of that."

"But, no gifts."

She looks forlorn. "No gifts?" The only thing Kimmy likes better than sex is giving and getting gifts.

"One gift." I give her a determined look, wondering exactly what I'm going to get her, since my sphere of existence has not been to venture beyond the beach house at Amagansett, the cemetery in New Haven, my sessions with Dr. Stevenson at Lenox-Hill, or the one-time requisite appearance in Manhattan for Evan's funeral service and wake. This last occasion conjures up a clear image of Jake Winston's handsome face, just above mine, which practically jolts me out of my seat. *Don't think about him.*

Kimberley peers over at me, curiously, when she sees this, while

I shrink further down, as if this action, alone, will prevent further invasions of Jake Winston's persona.

"One gift." The way she says this already conveys she'll be breaking this rule. "We'll celebrate at the beach house. Serve margaritas for Christmas cheer. Just the inner circle."

"You, Gregoire, Steph, Christian, Reid, and me," I say.

"Right."

She has this bemused look on her face and I already wonder what I've gotten myself into.

Chapter

Seven

Not so perfect

Dr. Bradley Stevenson insists on keeping our weekly session, even the day before Christmas. I saunter in to his inner office sanctum and give him a rueful grin. "Happy Holidays." This salutation is as close as I can manage in acknowledging Christmas and my way of expressing my gratitude for him seeing me the day before, without actually saying so. I avoid his quizzical look and settle in one of the chairs across from him.

"How are you?" Dr. Stevenson asks.

"I'm fine," I say with a slight shrug.

He arches an eyebrow, looks in my general direction, and repeats his question.

"It's difficult. The holidays. Reid's first Christmas. We're spending Christmas in Amagansett. Santa's coming." I reward him with a wry half-smile.

"How does that make you feel?"

"Santa?"

He gives me a come-on-Julia stare.

I'm about to give him another one of my I'm-fine standard answers, when out of nowhere, I launch into a detailed description about my troubled morning. "I'm in the grocery store, earlier today, picking up things for tonight, and some woman comes up to me and squeezes my hand. 'I'm so sorry for your loss,' she says, and she starts crying. I don't know how to respond. She's wringing her hands and touching me and telling me how much she loved Evan. She was a neighbor of the Hamiltons, Evan's parents. She tells me she was at our wedding, and now, had just been at his funeral. She's going on and on, sobbing now; and I'm just standing there, trying to comfort her with my arms around her and trying to place her face. I don't know who she is. But, she knew Evan."

I stop and take a deep breath and look over at him.

"Then, she says, 'first Elizabeth, now Evan.'" I shake my head slowly. "After that, I couldn't take it anymore. I just left the basket full of stuff, went back out to the car, and sat there, and waited for Kimberley to find me."

I make the familiar trek over to his large office window and look out. "I just want to be lost somewhere, where no one knows me, or who I am, or who I've lost."

The good doctor sits silent, perhaps, in search of the right words for consolation in talking me away from this particular ledge. My propensity to fill silence takes over.

"Kimmy wants me to go with her to Paris, possibly take a position with her PR firm, *Liaison*. There's a project in Paris she'd like me to lead, for a while."

"I know the firm," he says. "Is that what you want to do?"

I turn back and lean against the window ledge. "It's all … a little overwhelming … what to do. Where to live. Right now, Paris sounds pretty good." I give him a wry glance. "The Hamiltons are … more than a little dismayed that I'd consider leaving."

"It's not their decision to make."

"Right. Doesn't mean they don't want to make it for me." I have trouble hiding my resentment. "I'm not their first choice for daughter-in-law. Not sure what I am now…" I turn and proceed to draw an imagined Christmas tree on the glass. "I had Evan buried next to Elizabeth, his first wife. You would think that would have made them happy, but it's never enough." I shrug, reaching for the semblance of nonchalance. "Elizabeth died, three years ago. Of cancer."

"How did Evan deal with Elizabeth's death?"

"He was devastated."

I make a conscious effort to hide my anguish over Evan's first wife by avoiding the doctor's insightful gaze.

"How did he make you feel about *her*?"

I shoot him a please-don't-make-me-talk-about-this look, and then, before I can stop myself, say, "I could never be Elizabeth. We both knew that."

"So, how did it make you feel that you could never be Elizabeth?"

I hesitate with my answer, knowing it could turn the tables on a lot of things we've discussed here. All the pretty, trussed-up stories I've put together for him, so far, could disappear.

"Our marriage wasn't perfect."

There. I said it. Just saying it out loud causes some sort of release inside. I breathe easier.

"I wasn't perfect and neither was he. We weren't perfect together." In defiance, I raise my head to look over at him, awaiting his judgment, I suppose.

"I didn't ask about the marriage. No one's is, by the way. I asked you how it made you feel that you could never be Elizabeth."

I shake my head at him and give him a pleading look. He just returns my gaze, imploring me to answer. With a heavy sigh I say, "Inadequate. I always wondered how much he loved me. I knew he loved me, but I was always left to wonder how much. He didn't always tell me everything, share everything. I wasn't Elizabeth. And, I sensed his disappointment in discovering that." I wince, and swipe at a tear that's escaped down my face.

Did I take truth serum or something? Stop saying these things.

Silence ensues. I struggle to keep from filling it.

As a distraction, I pace the room, while he just watches me for a moment, and then, starts writing in his notebook.

"What did she look like?"

His question stops me in my tracks. His perceptive ways are so eerie. I'm taken aback and unable to answer for a few minutes.

Finally, I say, "Long dark hair, blue-violet eyes, slender, tall, she had a Liz Taylor in Black Beauty thing going on."

Reluctance sets in. *Do I really want to put this together for him?*

"Like you," he says.

Pandora's Box opens. Chocolate anyone? An abundance of heartbreak. Rare happiness. Plenty of self-destruction. Take your pick. Julia's got everything in here.

I turn and face him and incline my head in his direction. "She looked a lot like me. Or rather, I looked a lot like her. We'd been married for a few months. I was almost eight months pregnant, when I made an unscheduled trip to the beach house in Amagansett—to the house that Evan had never taken me to—and discovered something I was never meant to see." I'm transported back to the bizarre scene. "There she was, in every room, this persona of a woman, who looked a lot like me, who had died, a few years before." I shake my head back and forth, and then, look over at him. *Are you getting this? Do you know what I'm saying?*

"Except my eyes are green. I'm not as tall, not as organized, not as accomplished as a gourmet chef, or a very good bottle washer." I smile at my own joke, and then, it fades. "I was a close second for the real thing, a fine-enough replica, but never as good as the original." I don't hold back my devastation from him as I say this. I don't have to.

Dr. Bradley Stevenson seems momentarily stunned, so stunned, he isn't even taking notes, but just stares at me. He's become the epitome of a man who is at a loss for words. Then he swallows, looks down at his notes, flexes his hands, and picks up his pen.

Is there an answer for me in there, somewhere, doctor?

"What happened when you discovered this house was a shrine to Elizabeth?"

My bravado fades a little, as this particular memory dredges up too much pain, all at once, but I recover enough to say, "I flipped out and told him he could basically fuck off."

I make a face. "Sorry for swearing."

He inclines his head and waves his pen, the wizard's magical wand, indicating I should continue.

"Where was I? Oh yes. The Elizabeth discovery. Telling him he could fuck off. Yes, Dr. Bradley Stephenson, I was a mess."

I sound like Stephanie must, when she's reading a story to her kindergartners, 'and then, this happened, and he said this, and I said that.' The pain begins to bubble up from deep inside.

"I thought we had this perfect life. We had this huge fight about it. He left."

Breathe.

I attempt to smile, but falter. "For a while."

The pain splashes everywhere inside of me, like paint violently thrown at a wall.

Tortured modern artwork, this is me. Someone interpret her, quick.

I voice my silent soliloquy, the one only I can hear. *He left for two weeks. No word. No phone calls. Nothing. I moved in with Kimberley again. I was eight months pregnant, despondent, broken, and disillusioned.*

The heartbreak for all of that traverses through me at lightning speed, calling up pain I haven't allowed myself to feel for some time. It performs a coupling with the all powerful grief. I practically implode, right there in front of him, with the pain that I must live with and carry. I stagger over to the window, look out, and see the nothingness.

The minutes pass. I take shallow breaths and try to assemble some sort of control over the emotions raging inside. I turn back and discover my handsome doctor has this hopeful look, like a child's, convinced there must be a happy ending to the story. *I almost feel sorry for him.*

"Then, he came back. We had Reid. I like to think we worked it out." I shrug my shoulders, perfecting nonchalance outward, while I quake inside. "Like I said, we weren't perfect. He wasn't Bobby and I wasn't Elizabeth," I say gently. "We were two broken people trying to make the best of a life as the two who were left behind."

At my words, he looks bleak, as if experiencing his first real heartbreak. I've pierced his life-is-good armor with my realism. This white knight struggles with the news that life is harsh, and that, I already know it.

My recovery from this latest revelation is faster than his. He fumbles with his note pad, his writing pen and hastily glances at the window, trying to recover himself. *Are there answers for both of us there, doctor?* I slide into the chair across from him and adopt the shield of indifference and wait him out.

Silence again. One minute. Two. Three. Four.

He holds out his notebook and peruses his handwriting. "What do Evan's parents want you to be?"

"They ... they would surely like me to hand over Reid and never return." I reward him with a cynical smile.

Dr. Bradley Stevenson just nods. "You're Reid's mother. In time, when you're ready, you can establish the ground rules with them. You don't have to do that, right now. They'll always be his grandparents.

There will be ties, connections because of Reid, but you're your own person, Julia. And, they're grieving the loss of Evan, too, and maybe, not considering your feelings as much as they should."

I clasp my hands together and attempt to control my irritation with the simple way he's seeing these things. "Evan always denied their preference for Elizabeth over me, but it was there. It was easy to see. How they spoke of her all the time, when I was *right there*. I thought, maybe, after Reid was born, things would change, like they did for Evan and me, but they didn't. Then, Evan ... dies." This conversation thread serves no purpose. "It doesn't matter."

"It all matters. But it takes time to work through it, for everyone, to work through it. Paris, for a couple of months, might be good for you. Kimberley will be there, right?"

"Paris might be good for me," I parrot back to him. "Kimberley's running the Paris office there, right now. And, Christian and Stephanie are close by. They split their time between New York and Paris. They've always been there for me. All of them."

"Friends are always good to lean on." He hesitates, before adding, "But, Julia, you're perfectly capable of handling things; know this about yourself. You've been through more than most experience over a lifetime. Take your time to discover what you want, more importantly, what you need."

"Wants. Needs. Like there's a difference."

He wanly smiles at my sarcasm. "There's a difference. What we need, often has nothing to do with what we want. What do you need in your life, Julia?"

I struggle to find the right response. I should just make something up that sounds good, but the truth meets up with me.

"I need someone ... to see me." A vague image of Bobby comes to mind and morphs into a clearer one of Jake Winston. I look over at him, study his face, and try to gauge his trustworthiness. "The real Julia, not the one everyone thinks they know, but the one I've always been inside, the one few people really see, besides Kimmy. Bobby."

I'm babbling like an overexcited teenager at a rock concert; I dig my nails into my palms to stop the soliloquy. *Why am I telling him all this?*

"Did Evan *see* you, Julia?"

My answer sums up the whole session. "He wanted to."

"You told me, once, you changed the color of your hair, your looks, even your name. Maybe, you need to start there. Show the world who you really are, by being, who you really are."

He rewards me with this all-knowing look, so similar to Kimberley's, it's uncanny.

The man is the personification of a Hallmark greeting card come to life, he believes in all he's saying. It just emanates from him—this belief system in needs and wants and gods and angels and all the good in the world. I'll be touched by his words and be saved. But my own reality rushes in, a cruel reminder of the truth of this world, of this life, I already know so well. This hoodoo voodoo greeting card script he adheres to gives me a headache and stirs up too much of the pain I keep buried deep inside. *Who I am? What I might need? Who gets those kinds of answers about life? Doesn't everyone struggle to be seen?*

"Show the world who you really are," he says, again, breaking through my reverie.

"I'll think about it."

We spend what little time we have left talking about Reid, my support system, Kimberley, in particular, and how I'm handling the dosage of my medication. At the end of our session, he hands me a business card with a referral to an American psychiatrist, who's an acquaintance of his in Paris.

I'm almost home-free, but guilt washes over me, and, like a rogue wave, it comes out of nowhere. I hesitate. He sees it.

"What is it?"

Oh God. Don't say it. Just go.

"I have something I need to say. Something I should have told you sooner. It's difficult." I take a deep breath. "I was … well, let's just say, I wasn't myself the night of Evan's funeral."

"Go on," he says in his now familiar, ever patient tone. He assumes his clinical stance with me, at the ready, to take more notes with his pen in mid-air.

I have his undivided attention. I smile in sympathy, when I see this. *Oh God. I'm going to disappoint him so much.*

"Okay." I take a deep breath and let it out slowly. "I let things get out of hand with ... someone. The night of Evan's funeral, at his wake, I was in the hotel suite with Evan's best friend from Yale. I kissed him. He was there. And, holding him, felt like Evan. And, I needed to be held. And, we had this connection. I can't explain it."

I seek refuge at the doctor's office window again, just out of his direct line of sight, and look out at the barren landscape.

"I can't believe I kissed him," I say in a low voice. "I'd just lost Evan, ten days before. Drank enough alcohol and took enough pain killers to escape the grief for a while. And, he was there, and he made me ... feel something. Alive, again, I guess. Kimmy knows. She said it shows I'm living, that I want to go on." I turn around to face him. "What do you think it shows?"

"You've lost more loved ones than most, Julia." His consolation reaches at me from the across the room. I'm undone by his kind words, but still ashamed and ready to do my penance. "You said it yourself. You needed to be held. He was there. No one controls the power of attraction."

I look over at him. He looks calm, collected, a priest used to hearing such things from his sinners.

"No one controls the power of love," he says.

"I didn't say I was *attracted* to him. And, I certainly didn't say I *love* him. I don't even *know* him."

"Love has nothing to do with knowing someone. And, everything to do with need."

There's that hoodoo voodoo Hallmark card schtick from him again. I avoid his direct gaze and make a point of looking at my watch. "Time's up," I say with a generous wave of my hand.

He finally nods in agreement.

Yes, indeed, time is certainly up.

We shake hands, and I thank him for everything, with one of my practiced winning smiles. I don't think I fool him with my jubilant state. I think, he sees right through me, but, for some reason, he's willing to play along.

Maybe, it's because Kimberley greets us in the next room. And no one, not even Dr. Bradley Stevenson, is immune to the charms of Kimberley Powers.

I can see the effect she's having on him in a matter of thirty seconds. Kimberley assures him she'll take good care of me in Paris and promises she'll make sure I continue my weekly sessions with his colleague. Dr. Stevenson gets this awestruck look on his face as he talks with her. The two exchange these evocative glances and business cards with a joint promise to keep in touch.

Is this, in case, Dr. Bradley Stevenson's services are needed in my future? Or, because Kimberley wants his number and he wants hers? I avoid rolling my eyes at both of them, just barely.

Intuitively, I know Kimberley could be swayed to take more than a passing interest in my psychiatrist, if she wasn't involved with Gregoire Chantal. I tease her about this, as we make our way to the car.

And, she finally admits it, by saying, "He's incredibly good-looking. How do you manage to concentrate?"

"With difficulty," I say, tossing my hair and mimicking the way she just did this to him.

We both laugh. It feels good to be normal, carefree, however temporary.

Chapter

Eight

For the love of white chocolate

BACK IN THE CAR AND NOW closing in to a long line of
traffic, we share in the unique luxury of being able to
spend uninterrupted time together after spending the
last year, more or less, apart from each other. Kimberley's been jet-
setting between New York and Paris for the past eight months, while
I've spent the last year getting married, having a baby, and establishing
a life with Evan. Now, only one of those life transformations is left for
me. Reid.

In revealing my feelings of inadequacy surrounding Elizabeth and
admitting out loud, to someone else, that my marriage wasn't perfect
and we weren't perfect together, the peaceful respite with Kimberley
begins to seep away from me. I'm weary, worn out, and definitely experiencing silent collateral damage for revealing so much of myself. Grief
takes the rest of me. I lean my head against the window and experience
the coldness as the weather reaches for me from outside.

Her cell phone rings.

She gives me a surreptitious glance and I look over. She holds up
the phone. I see Gregoire's name flashing.

"Answer it," I say.

With mysterious reluctance, she answers on the third ring. I'm left
to wonder, if there's trouble in paradise, and, again, reflect upon her
more than a passing interest in Dr. Bradley Stevenson. It's typical of
Kimberley to grow tired of her boy toys and begin lining up the next

one, although she's been dating Gregoire much longer than any of her past conquests.

I look over at her, realizing she's essentially put her life on hold for me, while my life has become utter chaos. I have no right to judge her. The sadness resurges with this realization.

Kimberley glances in my direction and I'm pulled from my anguished thoughts. "I don't know, we haven't worked it out, yet. Then, go. Yes. I'm absolutely fine with that. Gregoire, can we talk about this later? I'm taking Julia back to Amagansett. I told you I wouldn't be able to make it. I know. Look, let's just talk a little later. I'll call you."

"What's wrong?" I ask when she ends the call.

"Nothing," she says.

"You said I'm *absolutely* fine with that."

"I am."

"*Absolutely* fine with what?" I look at her closely.

"He wants to go to Paris for New Year's," she says. "I told him he should go."

"You should go with him. I'll be fine in Amagansett."

"No," she says. "Have we forgotten the little incident with the ocean, two days ago?"

"The medication's kicking in." I grimace. "I'm really okay. I can take care of myself. You should go with him. New Year's in Paris would be amazing. Go spend it with him."

She shrugs in contrived nonchalance. "It's all … getting so complicated anyway. At first, it was fun going back and forth between Paris and Manhattan. I think that's why it's lasted this long, the fated serious-for-the-last-six-months timetable."

She attempts to laugh, but I glimpse her torment. I sit up straighter, knowing this conversation has just turned into something more serious. We're not talking about New Year's, anymore.

"He lives in Paris. He can't spend all his time in Manhattan with me. There's no future in that." She leans forward looking straight ahead at the lineup of cars for the toll bridge. "I don't know. I thought opening the Paris office would be the ultimate. And, it's been great, don't get me wrong, but I miss New York. I miss you. This whole thing with Evan. It makes you think about what you really want. What's important."

"Isn't Gregoire a part of your life?" She looks over at me and gives me this pleading let's-talk-about-something-else look. "You can tell me anything, you know that."

"There's nothing to tell. It's been great, but it's time to end it."

She shrugs her shoulders and busies herself with getting the toll for the bridge from her purse. I hand her correct change and she looks surprised, for a moment, as if she doesn't know what to do with the money.

"Are you all right? Are we talking about New Year's or something else?"

"I'm fine."

Our conversation stalls, while she chats up the toll guy, an earnest twenty-something-year-old with amazing brown eyes and an instant attraction for my little PR queen. Lively banter, about the weather, the traffic, and the long lines, ensues between them.

I roll my eyes and look out the window and try to hide my irritation. It's so like Kimberley to avoid any deep conversation, if it has anything to do with her, while we can systematically dissect my life at every turn. Now, she lasers in on lining up another admirer for future reference. God knows we've been preoccupied with my life, but, sometimes, the way she treats the men, who might actually care for her, upsets me. She takes his card and gives him one of hers.

"What's going on?" I ask in irritation, when she pulls the car forward after one last-minute seductive look at her newfound friend and then, drives onto the bridge. "God, if Gregoire saw the way you looked at that guy or my psychiatrist, earlier today, you would be in a world of hurt."

"I'm not married," she says softly.

Her eyes narrow and she gives me the famous Kimberley-knows-best look. *But does she?* I can feel her spinning out of control, right here in the car.

"The Paris office is doing well. I'm putting Frederic Dupont in charge. I'm moving back to Manhattan." She sounds resolute as she outlines her future plans, but I'm not so convinced.

"Are you doing this because you think you should or because you want to?" I ask. "I thought you really liked Gregoire. It's been *more* than six months. You met him, two years ago."

"It wasn't so serious, then. We were just having fun." Kimberley sighs, and then, takes a deep breath and shakes her head back and forth. "He's *late* to everything. It drives me crazy. But, he just laughs when I call him out on it." Kimberley runs her life with a stop watch, so I'm somewhat amused, when she says this. "Then, he has this obsession for white chocolate. Just like you." She looks flustered now. "He's got me liking it, too." She moans at this admission.

"White chocolate isn't the end of the world, Kimmy."

She shakes her head and gets this bewildered look. "He knows everything there is to know about wine and food, in general. And, he *orders* for me and, you know, how I hate guys that do that." I nod, knowing this is true. "I let it go, at first, because I thought it was some kind of suave French seduction thing. And, it was working." She gets this secretive look of delight, and then, it fades. "But about a month ago, we're at Daniel and he orders everything, as usual." She rolls her eyes. "And, I realize I couldn't make up my mind about what to eat, even if I wanted to. What is that? And, he always chooses something different that I end up really liking. God, it's weird." She grips the steering wheel with one hand. "He's so ... linear." She moves her free hand across the horizon. "And, you know, how I'm up and down, up and down. "She makes a zigzag motion. "He's just so steady, like a burning candle, lighting the way. The complete opposite of me."

"Magical like you, but in a different way," I say. She gives me this withering glance.

"You're supposed to be helping me out here. Talk some sense into me. This *cannot* happen."

"You can't control who you fall in love with," I say, instantly reflecting that Dr. Stevenson would be so proud to know, I can, at least, recite his lessons.

"Love," Kimberley scoffs, and makes a dismissive motion with her hand.

I'm momentarily lost in the revelations with Dr. Stevenson from earlier about the powers of attraction and needs and wants and make this inevitable leap to thoughts of Jake Winston. I shake my head to chase them away.

Kimberley glances sideways at me, seeing this. "What?"

"Maybe, you're in love."

"I am, absolutely, not in love." She glares at me. "He just drives me crazy." I start to laugh. "What?"

"Absolutely." I make the quotation mark gesture in mid-air. "You're using our code word and everything."

"You drive me crazy, too, you know."

"I'm sure I do," I say with benevolence. "And, I know, you love me."

"It's just so…" She looks away from me and concentrates on the traffic. "Scary."

I reach out and touch her hand. "I wouldn't trade any of it, you know. Not one single moment, happy or sad." There's this sudden uplifting, from deep inside of me, the heavy burden of grief has left, however temporary, I still feel its absence. "Love's worth it, Kimmy." I surprise, even myself, at this assertion. My Hallmark Card psychiatrist would be so proud.

Kimberley looks bleak, undone. The woman is used to being in control. This much, I do know, she isn't going to accept my truth, until she finds it for herself.

"You think I love Gregoire?" she asks, after a few minutes of silence.

"He makes you crazy. You can't stop thinking about him. You're out of sorts, unbalanced. Eating white chocolate and letting him order for you. Seems like sure signs to me."

Kimberley groans. "This seems more like a cross between the flu and dementia. I can't think straight."

"I believe the term is *see straight*."

"I can't see straight, either. Oh God, this can't be happening."

"Kimmy, everything's going to be okay," I say in my best impersonation of her. We both burst out laughing and, for a few precious moments, grief retreats a little further away from me.

After our early afternoon return from Manhattan along with spending two hours in traffic, I sit out on the deck in an Adirondack chair with a thick wool blanket draped over me and stare out at the grey Atlantic and try not to think about the things and places starting with the letter *A* that continue to haunt me. Talking with Dr. Stevenson has brought all this pain, from the past decade, to the surface. And now, with my newest revelations about my imperfect marriage and my own inadequacy, pain, I thought I'd dealt with long ago, emerges now, synchronizing with my latest heartbreak.

Attempting to distract myself from the inner torment, I sip from a steaming cup of coffee Stephanie has doctored with heavy cream. She acquiesced to my request for freedom and allowed me come out on the deck by myself. "I just need to be alone for a while," I'd told her. She agreed to listen for Reid, who is taking his afternoon nap, while Lianne set off for the grocery store for more last-minute supplies and a list of presents to buy for me. My nanny promised to take care of everything and her assurance set me free from guilt, for a few hours, because I can't do it all today.

Our beach house overflows with people, yet, I'm alone. I wipe away a tear. It's Christmas Eve day. Late afternoon. My revelations with Dr. Stevenson have moved to the regret stage. Why did I have to share so much of myself with him today? It won't change anything. I am here. Alone, in the after, again. Evan is dead. Bobby's dead. My parents are dead. There's nobody left, hardly, even me.

I stare out at the Atlantic, willing it to give me some kind of answer. The white waves splash the shore with renewed fierceness.

"Evan, where are you?" I whisper.

The opening and closing of the French doors leading out to the deck stir me from my misery. Kimberley's lyrical voice reaches me above the roar of the crashing waves.

"Yeah, I sent them out. No. Not a problem. Look, once I had the list it was easy. Just a note card stating, due to the untimely death of Evan, you were postponing. Well, it would have been a little hard to do from London. Yeah. I got that impression. Look, I'm sorry. Frankly, I think it's for the best, right now. All right. The car service will pick you up at three. Yes." Kimberley gives me an appraising look and I lift my head in defiance. She has the infamous just-go-along-with-the-plans-Julia look. "Yes. We'll all be here with her. And, Reid. Right. Okay."

I take a sip of my coffee, which is fast cooling off in the bitter cold, and attempt to achieve some sort of nonchalance.

"I'm almost afraid to ask who that was," I say through chattering teeth, after a few minutes.

"Okay. I won't tell you."

I give her a dirty look. "Tell me."

"No." Kimberley shrugs, then grabs part of the blanket and burrows in to the chair next to mine. "You just continue to wallow in your little pity party by yourself."

She amazes me with her perceptiveness and I lash out. "It's Christmas, tomorrow, Kimberley. Give me a fucking break. *Please.*"

"We all *know* it's Christmas tomorrow. That's why I'm taking care of everything and making it a Christmas you'll never forget." She flashes me one of her do-not-fuck-with-my-plans looks.

"Now, I'm really afraid to even ask who you were talking to and what you're planning," I say with agitation. She just laughs, her wicked I'll-never-tell laugh, the laugh that has had the uncanny ability to set me on edge, since our college days. With Kimberley, *anything* is possible. "I don't want a big party."

"No big party. Just the inner circle."

"Fine. Like I have a choice."

"Being in bed. In the dark. With the covers pulled over your head all day is *not* an option."

"We … talked about this. The margarita plan. Hanging out. The inner circle. I thought I got to do what I wanted on Christmas Day." I almost laugh, my whining is so pronounced. Staying in bed all day on Christmas is the exact scenario I have planned. I've already arranged for Lianne to take care of Reid and plan to shut myself out from the world.

"No."

My plans evaporate, just like that, at the unwavering look on her face. I try another tactic. "Who was on the phone?"

"A new client." She leans back in the chair, sighs, and closes her eyes. "Jake Winston."

My body contracts deeper into my own chair. I don't want to have a conversation about Jake Winston. I don't want to know why he has become her PR client. I study the Atlantic and count the wave cycles. One. Two. Three. Four.

Kimberley sighs again, and leans over in my general direction. "He cancelled his wedding." She hands me the invitation and the subsequent note, announcing its cancellation, and awaits my reaction.

I manage to hold it together.

"Evan was supposed to be his best man." My deadpan tone gives absolutely nothing away about how I really feel about this announcement, but I'm reeling inside. How is it possible that I'd forgotten Jake was getting married? Evan had been talking about being in Jake's wedding for weeks. We were all getting ready to fly to Austin. How is it possible I forgot this? How much of me am I really missing?

"I forgot he was getting married Saturday," I finally say. Heat rises up my face. My anger surges from nowhere. "I know I was fucked up enough to kiss him, but what exactly was his excuse for kissing me back?"

I continue to rage in silence at how all the magnetism transpired between us, since he was engaged to be married to some Savannah Bennett and I am, most definitely, the recently widowed Mrs. Evan Hamilton. Kimberley touches my hand and breaks me out of my angst-ridden reverie.

"He cancelled the whole thing," she says softly. "His little fiancée is beside herself." She shakes her head. "I thought I was going to have to fly down to Austin and practically pry the guest list out of her southern-belle little hands to get the announcement out that the nuptials were cancelled. Little hard for him to do from London. His mom's been great. I'm not sure who was more relieved, his mother, or the groom-to-be, himself."

"She's from Austin?" I ask in surprise. Somehow, this fact about Jake's fiancée unsettles me. Kimberley nods. "I don't want to talk about Jake Winston," I say trying for indifference, but apparently not indifferent enough, because Kimberley laughs and points her finger at me.

"You may not want to *talk* about him, but you are, most definitely, *thinking* about him."

"Kimmy, please." I give her an exasperated look. "Look, I think, it's sad he's put off his wedding. I know he's upset about Evan, too."

"He is. But, I don't think that's the only reason he cancelled the whole thing."

I glance over at her.

"What are you getting at?"

"I think Mr. Jacob Winston is reevaluating his entire life and what he wants."

"And you know this, how? By spending a few hours on the phone with him, going over his guest list, and sending out cancellation notices on his behalf?" I stand up, irritated, and pull the blanket closer, taking it away from her at the same time. She stands up, too, studies me for a moment, and then, hugs me.

"Come on. It's almost Christmas Eve. I've made appointments for you, me, and Steph, in town, for the works."

I roll my eyes and just follow her back into the house. There is no point in arguing with her when she gets like this. I'll steal out for a run along the beach, before the day ends, despite Kimberley's protests, and her seemingly endless secret plans for my Christmas holiday. I know all of her efforts are part of the get-Julia-back-in-the-swing-of-life plan, and I only begrudge her, a little, for trying to lift my spirits, as she drags me back inside.

CHAPTER

NINE

Definitely, definitely the most alive among us

SOAKING IN STEAMING BATH WATER WITH aromatic lavender-scented sea salt revives me. My mind languishes as I feel at peace for the first time since the fifth of December, after a run on the beach, which practically undoes all the cosmetic efforts at the place in town Kimberley took Steph and me to. I'm determined to hang on to this elusive tranquility that I'm feeling now, but, minutes later, a knock on the bathroom door is followed by Kimberley's brazen stroll into my bathroom, modeling a risqué camisole and thong ensemble in a bright Christmas red.

"Gregoire's coming." I tease.

The whole mid-morning car conversation about Gregoire Chantal seems to have been forgotten, once Kimberley learned, he was on his way here.

"Yes. Everyone is. Christian, Stephanie. Mom and Dad, possibly Braden, and definitely Brian." Kimberley's seventeen-year-old twin brothers are like my own siblings. I experience this modicum of joy, knowing her family will all be here for Christmas Eve. "That's just about everybody."

She looks over at me. "Oh, and Jake Winston."

Momentarily stunned by what she's just said, I'm just watching her, while she casually inspects her freshly-painted red fingernails. Until, her announcement finally registers.

"Jake? Winston?" I rush out of the bathtub, sending water every-where. "You invited Jake Winston, *here*? Tonight? Christmas Eve?"

"Yes," she says. "He's feeling a bit low and just getting back in from London and his friends are *your friends*. He and Christian are like this." She twists together her index and middle finger, while I flip my middle finger at her for another purpose all together.

"You're killing me. I don't want to see him."

"He's just called off his wedding. Give the guy a break." Kimberley gets this weird speculative look as she throws me a towel. I begin drying off too upset to speak. "You're getting too thin."

"Don't change the subject. We're not through talking about this. Why would you invite him here?"

"Look, Julia." Kimberley adopts her most soothing tone. The one, she only invokes with her clients, when they're behaving badly. "He doesn't really have any place to go. He was supposed to be getting married this weekend in Austin. His best friend just died. He called off his wedding and pretty much everyone in that town is in an uproar about him canceling it. Apparently, the bride is related to most of them and these kinds of things just take on a life of their own. And, his ex-bride is in a raging snit over it. There are other names I would describe her as, if Jake wasn't a client." She uses her index fingers for quotation marks, when she says the word client. "So, give the guy a break. By the parade of flowers he's sent you, I think you can safely say, he's sorry for his momentary transgression with you. And, I think, we can agree, worse things have happened to both of you."

This is exactly why all her clients clamor to work with her, the woman is never fearful of calling things out, even though I'm stunned by what's she said. Kimberley rarely directs her wrath at me.

In a huff, she steps into a red silk dress and clips her hair back. She shoots me a dagger look. Remorse begins to filter through, but the guilt and grief I've been swimming with all day wins out.

"I'm sorry. You're right. Can I just tell you ... that it's been a very trying day?"

I pinch the bridge of my nose to stop the sudden threat of tears. Kimberley tosses lingerie my way, some all red and black lace ensemble to match the dress she's bought for me. I let my hair fall forward, to hide my face, so she won't guess I'm crying. I focus on producing more material from the skimpy bra, camisole, and panties, by pulling this way and that, but finally give up.

"What happened with Dr. Stevenson today?" she asks. "You were with him over an hour. What did you two talk about?"

There's that supernatural perception of hers. "Oh you know..." I attempt to smile, but fail. "I got to tell him about the whole Elizabeth shrine story today. How Evan left me before Reid was born and my feelings surrounding all of that."

I wave through the air with one hand and swipe at a tear with the other, but miss. A silent Kimberley holds out the dress and I step into it. She zips it up and hugs me from behind.

"Here I was complaining about Gregoire driving me crazy. Do you want to talk about it?"

"No. I've done enough talking about my feelings for one day. Thank you very much. I don't' know why I even said anything. He has this uncanny way of making me talk about things I've left unsaid for years. God. It's painful, like opening Julia's own personal Pandora's Box of everything bad that's ever happened. And I love Evan. I do. I love ... loved him." I struggle with even thinking past tense. "I still love him. And, I shouldn't have told the good doctor so much. It's in the past. None of it matters. I just wish ... I just wish, so much, that Evan was here."

"Me too. I loved him, too," she says with a sigh. "I just wish he hadn't hurt you before. God, Julia I just want your life to work out. I want that for you so much."

"It wasn't perfect," I whisper.

"No, but it was grand. He made you happy. This last summer. The two of you. I saw it. Everyone did. And, then, Reid ... surely, he makes it all worth it."

Kimberley lets go, grabs a tissue, and dabs it at her face.

"I'm sorry. I shouldn't have invited Jake. Or, at least, I should have asked you, first."

"Yes. You should have. Whatever."

I give her a rueful glance. "We're going to have to see each other eventually; it's probably best to get it over with. But, I don't want to talk about Hamilton Equities or Jake Winston, his benevolence or otherwise, tonight," I say. "It's my baby's first Christmas and he's all I want to focus on."

"It's all about Reid." Kimberley laughs.

"My baby's first Christmas."

I turn side-to-side in the mirror and stare at the stranger looking back at me. Grief has ravaged my body as well as my spirit. I look like a waif or a fairy in this black silk dress. Make-up does a pretty good job of hiding the dark circles under my eyes, but days of sorrow have taken their toll on my physical form.

"I'll probably be sporting a grey hair or two next."

"No, you won't." Kimberley doesn't fully mask her own sadness. It crosses her features, for a moment, and then, it's gone. *We all miss Evan.* "You look fantastic, Jules. We're not going to be sad tonight, or tomorrow. We're not." Kimberley steps back to survey me, one more time.

"Okay." She looks surprised when I agree. "Hey Kimmy? Thanks." I hug her close. "I don't know what I would do without you."

"Same," the PR wonder girl says back to me.

⁓⁓⁓

Bernard and Francesca Powers arrive from New Haven around five. My parents have been dead for almost ten years and Kimberley's family has been a part of my life for eight. I hug them close and take delight in the way they fawn over Reid. My seven-month-old looks like a little angel in his white sweater with a snowman imprint, little red vest, and black sweater pants with the black and white spat shoes Kimberley bought for him. I take a few pictures of the group with the digital camera Evan bought me, a couple of months before, and smile at the sight of my son and this quasi family surrounding me.

Within a few hours, Kimberley's promise of this party just being the close inner circle increases to more than thirty people as neighbors stop by, including Robert and Helen Hamilton, Evan's parents. Helen even makes an attempt to be nice to me, though we all know she longs for her first choice in a daughter-in-law, that one being dead and buried next to Evan. Lianne rescues Reid from the cloying woman's arms and takes him upstairs to get him ready for bed, while I try to make idle conversation with my grieving in-laws.

I'm on edge. Of course, I am. The unexpected appearance of Evan's parents and the inevitable question of: 'What are you going to do, Julia?' A question that's been posed by just about everyone in this room adds to my inner turmoil. *What am I going to do?* Tonight, I'm going to get good and drunk; and tomorrow, I'm going to stay in bed all day. After that? Who knows? Of course, I can't share these plans with anyone, Robert and Helen, least of all.

I can only hope they don't stay too long. Kimberley rescues me, after another ten minutes, and pulls me across the room from them, pressing a margarita into my hand.

"Sorry," she says with a heartfelt groan. "I invited them because I didn't think they'd come. And, if we didn't invite them, they'd hear about it. Shit. I'm sorry."

She knows my pain about them, too.

"Maybe, they won't stay long," I say under my breath.

"They won't," Kimberley promises.

⁂

Half past eight, I glance at my watch. As if, a visitation from Evan's parents isn't enough to fill me with anxiety, now, I'm bracing for the appearance of one Mr. Jacob Winston. I take a deep breath and another swig of my margarita, but neither steady breaths nor tequila, can calm the edginess raging inside of me now.

"Jules? Are you even listening to me?" Kimberley's brother Brian asks.

"What? Sorry. No. What did you say?" I touch his hand.

Brian shakes his head and grins. "You okay?"

"I'm fine. Just tired. I think I'll step out on the deck and get some fresh air. Can we talk a little later?" I give Brian a reassuring hug and escape through one of the French doors, watching him saunter off in the direction of the food table.

The roaring surf of the Atlantic welcomes me. The sounds of the party inside fade away, as I near the edge of the deck, lean against the rail, and look out at the dark ocean. I breathe deep and experience simple serenity from the crisp salty air that December always brings. Standing here, for a few minutes, reflecting, I realize I've been anxious, since the Hamiltons' arrival. I cannot be what they want to me to be. I'm not Elizabeth. Now, it's true more than ever.

I lean back against the railing with my back to the ocean and watch the party underway inside. Kimberley is draped in an embrace with

Gregoire; she certainly isn't suffering with doubt about Mr. Chantal, tonight. I lost her attentiveness, about a half-hour ago, with his arrival. For a girl who normally doesn't care for the one-woman-only type guy, Gregoire has made quite an impression on her. I watch the connection emanate from both of them and chase away the sadness that shimmers within me, just below the surface. I'm alone, in the after, again.

"You always spy on your family this way, Mrs. Hamilton?"

Jake Winston's recognizable southern accent greets me. I turn in the direction of the stairs that lead from the beach and spy a dark figure.

"You always arrive at a party on foot, Mr. Winston? And, all dressed up, too?" The sheen of his dark suit, white dress shirt, and silver tie reflect in the moonlight. "How do you do it?"

"Just talented at staying out of the surf, I guess." Jake takes the stairs, two at a time, and comes to stand beside me.

"And, how are you going to get back when the tide is full?" I look up at him.

He cocks his head to one side. "Very carefully," he drawls.

"Merry Christmas, Mr. Winston." I hold out my hand and he grips it firmly in his.

"Merry Christmas, Mrs. Hamilton."

He still holds on to my hand and this strange sensation travels through me. He must feel something, too, because he gives me this odd look as he lets go. "Julia…" he says, hesitant.

"You're not going to apologize, again, are you? I think you've done enough of that for both of us." I incline my head as I say this. "It was a weird night full of strange and very sad circumstances. That's all." I take a deep breath. "I just want to say, thank you. Thank you for saving me that night. I don't know what I was thinking. I just didn't see a way to start over, and there you were."

"And, now?"

"I'm fine," I say. "I was very sad. And well, still sad, but handling it much better."

I wince, recalling the intimate scene between the two of us, ten days ago. Being this close to him again stirs up these strange sensations all over again. And, just how much better am I handling things? The ocean swim, from two days ago, and Kimberley's subsequent rescue comes to mind. He gives me an intense look, and I glance away, before he can guess at my innermost thoughts. I lean my arms against the railing and look out at the darkness. The roaring waves of the Atlantic still make their presence known from behind me. "Thank you for the flowers, the cards. Very thoughtful. I could open up a flower shop with all you've sent, from London, too, no doubt."

"Are you sure you're okay?"

"Sure. Sometimes, I'm okay for as much as an hour at a time. Kimmy's here. Don't tell her I said so, but she's pretty militant about my regimen. Julia must get up today. Julia must get dressed. She's pretty tough." I glance sideways at him, see him smile, and I laugh a little. "Let's not talk about me anymore. Okay? I'm tired of being the center of attention." I search for something else to say. "I'm sorry about your wedding, about you cancelling it and everything. Evan was looking so forward to being your best man."

"Oh. Well, it just doesn't seem like the right time to be getting married." His tone is bleak and I try to discern what he's thinking, but now, it's too dark to really see his face as the clouds shift over the moon, obscuring the light.

"Well, postponing isn't a bad thing."

"I called it off, Julia. She's not exactly speaking to me, right now."

"Oh. Well. In a couple of months, things will look different. And maybe—"

"No." He shakes his head side-to-side. "Things are already different. I tried to explain it to her." He takes a deep breath. "Well, you just don't do that. Cancel, I mean. Days before, not in Austin, anyway. She's pretty pissed. Half the town is pissed. Sorry. I shouldn't be swearing. It's not your problem."

"No. It's okay. I love hearing about someone else's problems. I've had so many of my own." I grin over at him. A breeze comes up and I shiver at the cold. He slips off his jacket and puts it around my shoulders. "I'm sorry." I touch his hand. "It's sad, when things don't turn out the way we want them to."

We share this companionable silence; both seemingly lulled by the waves of the Atlantic. Our hands grip the railing only an inch apart, and this weird sensation dances between us, like an electrical current traveling a wire.

"I should go in," I say, breaking the moment. "Kimberley will organize a search party, if I'm gone too long," I laugh at my intended joke and he looks over at me in surprise. "I need to go check on Reid."

"I'll come with you. I want to see him."

Jake follows behind me and I hand him his jacket, as we slip inside. We're both served another round of drinks. Christian claims Jake's attention, so I climb the stairs to Reid' room, alone.

Lianne signals to me with a finger to her lips that my baby is already sleeping. We whisper about his schedule, knowing he should sleep through the night. I feel this twinge of guilt for not being sure of Reid's schedule anymore. Lianne squeezes my hand and assures me I'm doing just fine, when I admit this aloud.

"He felt a little warm when I put him down," Lianne says.

I rush over and lightly touch his forehead. He's just beginning to drift off. We take his temperature with the instant ear thermometer and exchange worried looks, when it registers one hundred and one degrees. We use the last drops of Infant Motrin and search all the upstairs bathrooms for more, but there isn't any, so we're standing in the hallway, deciding what to do, when Jake comes up the stairs.

"He's running a fever. He's been fighting a cold the last few days," I say. "Now, we're out of Infant Motrin. I don't believe this." Déjà vu with Evan comes back full force.

"I'll go," Jake says.

I shake my head. "I can't let you do that." I lean against the wall and close my eyes, for a moment. "I'll go. There's a Rite-Aid in Bridge-hampton, a little over a mile away. Maybe, they'll still be open, even though it's Christmas Eve."

Jake looks confused by my reaction. "I'll go with you."

I just nod. I'm unable explain this devastating feeling to anyone else. Lianne helps me put on my coat. I hand Jake the keys to the SUV without a word.

"Well, at least, it doesn't start with the letter *A*," I say with a shaky voice, once we're in the car.

"The letter *A*? Amagansett?"

"No," I say in a low voice. "Advil."

I watch him nod in the dark. "He was going to get Advil, when he swerved to avoid the little boy on the bike and hit the truck."

"Yes. I had a headache, so he went to the store for Advil. *For me.*" I swipe at a sudden tear and stare out at nothing but darkness and intermittent house lights.

"So you must blame yourself … for being human," he says.

"Yes, pretty much." I try to laugh through my tears and it breaks up the overwhelming sadness. "You know I'm paying over $200 an hour for therapy. Would you like cash or a check?"

"No charge." Jake glances over at me again. "So Motrin starts with the letter *M*. I think we're going to be okay, Julia."

"It's still Ibuprophen, just not called Advil. It's crazy, I know."

"No. I can see where the letter *A* would start to give you anxiety: Advil, Afghanistan, the Army."

I wince, remembering I talked with him about Bobby that fateful night. "Athens," I whisper, before I can stop myself. One of his hands slips off the steering wheel, when I say this.

"Athens, Greece?"

"Yes. My parents. When I was sixteen."

"I'm sorry."

I nod, trying to regain some semblance of control. *Why am I telling him this?*

"I don't normally talk about it." I give him a pleading look and search the darkness for the Rite-Aid neon sign. "There. On the left." He doesn't seem to hear me and has this faraway look. I reach out and touch his arm. "Jake. Right there, on the left." He pulls the SUV into the parking lot. "I'll be right back," I say.

"I'm coming with you."

He meets up with me on the sidewalk and keeps his hand in the middle of my back as we navigate our way through the pharmacy. This awareness of him travels through me again at his touch. It's confusing. There are so many things he does that remind me of Evan. They both have this thoughtfulness as a part of their nature. Both tall. Both handsome.

He smiles at me with reassurance as we make our way to the counter. I catch my lower lip between my teeth to circumvent these wayward thoughts about his attractiveness, but they come anyway.

On a scale of one to ten, with ten being gorgeous, off the charts.

Jake is in a league all his own.

He is so good-looking; it's disconcerting. He has these amazing eyes that just draw you in like warm sea water. His smile is like the glimpse of moonlight on a dark night. His lips are almost feminine, and when he smiles, they curve in this perfect oval shape that you just want to reach out and trace with your finger. He's angular with perfect geometric proportions in his jaw line, in his straight nose, in his forehead. His hairline is like a field of straight wheat bowed by a caressing wind. When he runs his hand through it, you can't help, but follow the movement and wish you could just reach up and do this for him. He's tall, even taller than Evan, with this muscular build, but long and lean.

He's a Greek god, not entirely real, certainly privileged, and utterly fantastic. All I know is time spins on, and eternity doesn't apply to me, the mere mortal, standing next to him. I think of Evan's fine traits and Jake eclipses even my dead husband's.

And, I shouldn't be having any of these thoughts, but it's a reprieve, from the grief that's invaded me for so many days, so I'll take it, knowing I'll have to contend with the guilt and shame that will come along soon enough. They'll be by any second, now.

He gives me an intense look and leans down toward my face. My heart races.

"Before, I forget to say this," he whispers in my ear, as he hands the cashier the money. "You do look amazing. Tragic, sad, but incredibly beautiful, Julia."

I'm too taken aback by the personification of one of my favorite mannerism of Evan's to do more than mumble, 'thank you', as this awareness of him rages through all of me.

My long black wool coat is unbuttoned and I glance down at my risqué neckline of the black dress and pull it closer around me. "Thank you," I say again.

There's this intensity in his blue eyes I want to understand. His own sadness over Evan is obvious and I almost reach out to touch him in sympathy, but being this close to him has revived all these feelings of attraction for him.

I'm pretty sure it's mutual. He just paid me the highest of compliments and he's looking at me now with complete concentration. It's both electric and terrifying.

As to the reason why we're having this bizarre connection in the harsh fluorescent lights of Rite-Aid, it's impossible to comprehend.

Minutes later, we're back in the car. He hands me the bag with the three bottles of Infant Motrin.

"So we won't be caught without it again," he says.

We. We won't be caught without it again.

His assurance draws me in and I move toward him. The faint smell of his cologne dances around me and I breathe it in. Polo Blue? Lacoste? *Armani. My favorite.*

I move away from him to the farthest point of the passenger door and pull my coat even closer around me.

Then, I busy myself with looking out at the dark night with profound interest, and fight the overwhelming urge to kiss him, again, while guilt and grief steal in to attack me from both sides.

The minutes tick by and the silence stretches on between us. He hasn't started the car.

Finally, I look over at him. He stares straight ahead, as if the answers are all right there somewhere. His hands drape the steering wheel, but he's motionless, except for his steady breathing, in and out. *Definitely, most definitely alive, the most alive human being in this car.*

"Jake? Is something wrong?"

He doesn't answer at first, but just shakes his head. "You know how you're unsure of something. A decision? And, then, it comes to you and you just know … it's right? Time goes by and it becomes even clearer?"

"Sure. I know it happens to other people," I say. "I wish it would happen to me." I look at him, uncertain, and, even more afraid, he's going to tell me.

"Okay. Well, let's just say, I realize it's the right decision."

"Okay, let's say it is." I nod my head, but not understanding him at all.

He doesn't volunteer anything more. He studies my face for a few seconds, finally smiles, and then, starts the car.

I try to concentrate on Christmas lights, knowing this day has been far too long, too intense, and that, this ebb and flow awareness of him is all too confusing for my mind, body, and soul.

99

CHAPTER

TEN

Absolutely, absolutely fine

I DREAM OF THE STRING OF PEARLS my mother used to wear for my father every Christmas morning. She wore them with everything, even her favorite jogging outfit. As a child, Christmas morning consisted of the usual classical tunes, but mostly Elvis songs playing from our stereo. A magical morning filled with fresh croissants, coffee, rich cream, and hot chocolate for me. I wake up in the middle of the night warmed by the dream of my parents for about twenty seconds, and then, hear Reid's screaming.

"Evan," I call out. "Evan, I've got to check on Reid."

Only silence answers me. Swamped with instant grief, I wipe away sudden tears with the back of my hand as I race to Reid's room.

Lianne is already there, pacing back and forth, with an inconsolable Reid. We give him a dose of baby drops and search the medical book for symptoms. I reach an on-call doctor at the pediatrician's office and quickly determine it's probably an ear infection. His remedy is: antibiotics, Infant Motrin, and sit up with him, but try to get some rest, predicting the pharmacy won't be open, before eight, because it's Christmas, for the medicine he's prescribing.

After another hour, Reid is worn out from screaming and falls into a fitful sleep in my arms. I gently rock him, afraid to stop, in case, he starts crying again. I convince Lianne to go back to bed, while Reid and I spend the rest of this early Christmas morning, upright, in the rocking chair.

I'm half awake going over, in my mind, the highlights of the Christmas Eve gathering the night before, which broke up around midnight. There was laughter, dancing, and plenty of margaritas.

Jake took it upon himself to teach us all the Two Step. We danced to John Mayer's *Why Georgia* and I think I surprised him with my dancing abilities. "Toe shoes, baby," I said, at one point. He had this amazed look, twirled me around, and grabbed my waist. He even took Lianne around the dance floor a few times. My French nanny was in awe of him, but seemed to feel even more comfortable around Kimberley's younger brothers than all of us.

Music transported me beyond everything and the lyrics resonated with my soul. Kimberley, Steph, and I did a special rendition of the Dixie Chicks version of *Landslide* we'd perfected at UCLA, years ago, at every karaoke bar in L.A., at the time. I'd had enough margaritas and performed my solo part, without falling apart in front of everyone, and experienced only happy thoughts of Bobby and Evan. The entire night was a temporary respite I very much needed.

Jake left with Christian and Stephanie to return to his place, where they'd all decided to stay. Gregoire squired Kimberley along with her family to some bed and breakfast in South Hampton. She'd only left, after several reassurances from Lianne and me, that we could manage, on our own, with Reid. Kimberley needed a break from me and my life. I already knew Gregoire had one final present for Kimberley he wanted to give her when they were alone. I'd witnessed a deep conversation between Kimberley's dad and Gregoire, earlier. I'm surprised she hasn't already called to tell me of her future plans, which have obviously changed, since yesterday morning's intense conversation. I smile and kiss the top of my baby's head.

Inner peace envelops all of me. Maybe, it's because I'm completely exhausted in taking care of Reid. For hours, we've rocked together, back and forth, while his cherub face rests between my breasts. I can feel his heartbeat, it intertwines with mine. There's this resurgence of love for this baby I haven't really felt this strongly, since Evan's death. And, it comes to me, this thought registers: I'm not alone in this world; I have Reid, he has me. This is all I need.

As the hours go by, Reid sleeps more deeply in my arms, although I remain fearful of waking him, so I vacillate between the idea of putting him down in his crib or continuing to rock him. But my arms begin to ache from holding him in the same position for so long, and at half past seven in the morning, I gently slide him into his crib, hold my breath, while he snuggles into his mattress, and finally, tuck him in with his favorite blanket.

Then, sheer exhaustion comes over me. I lean against the crib railing for support and close my eyes. I turn at the sound of Lianne in the doorway. She's already dressed and insists on going to pick up the prescription for Reid and be there as soon as the pharmacy opens. I'm too tired to argue with her. I follow her out to my car, press money and my keys into her hands.

"Coffee. A latte would be great, if you can find anything open."

I wave at her from the driveway, turn, and get a glimpse of myself in the underdressed attire of pajama pants, the red camisole, a castoff cardigan, and wild hair. I almost laugh at the spectacle reflecting back at me from the living room window as I trek back towards the house. I have this sexy clown combination look going on, a cross between a yoga instructor and a Victoria's secret model.

"Where's Lianne off to this early in the morning?" Jake Winston's now familiar southern drawl comes out of nowhere.

And, there he is, walking up the side of my house from the beach side, carrying two grande-size coffee cups, one in each hand.

"Reid has an ear infection. We were up…" I smother a yawn. "We were up half the night with him. She's off to get his antibiotic. He's sleeping, now."

"You should have called me."

"I don't know your number." I give him a rueful smile. "Merry Christmas."

"I should have called. I *do* have the number." Jake looks contrite. "Merry Christmas. I brought you a latte. I got a new espresso machine and had to try it out."

He hands me a paper coffee cup with a lid. I sip at it, trying to appear casual about my attire and wild hair.

"Santa brought you an espresso machine? You must have been a very good boy."

"Self-gifted I'm afraid."

I laugh at his admission and invite him inside.

"Self-gifting is the best kind of gift," I tease. "Well, before I met Evan I thought that. He was the best at giving gifts I'd ever witnessed." I set down the latte and pull my hair back into a ponytail, feeling self-conscious in front of this man I barely know.

"I should have called," he says, again.

"It's fine. It's no problem. I'm thinking Reid will sleep another couple of hours. Lianne will be back soon enough." I fail at hiding another yawn.

"Why don't I listen for Reid, while you try and get some sleep, since you were up half the night? My timetable is screwed up with London. I'm wide awake. I'll listen for him."

"Maybe, just a half hour, until Lianne gets back?" I can barely keep my eyes open, as extreme fatigue overtakes me, again. "Thanks."

I climb the stairs and fall across the bed. I really should get dressed. I think about putting on jeans and a sweater, but that's as far it gets. *Nobody should be that good-looking* goes this errant thought in my head, as I allow myself to think only pleasant thoughts about Jake Winston and his Christmas morning latte gift.

Sleep. Sleep proves to be another Christmas gift. I awaken, hours later, glance at the clock, and linger with the thought I've slept a full five hours, something I haven't been able to do in weeks.

"Well, I see you got your way about staying in bed all day on Christmas, anyway." Kimberley stands in the doorway with a benevolent smile, holding Reid. She sweeps into the room and sits down next to me on the bed.

I take my baby from her and kiss him on each cheek. "Merry Christmas, baby. Has Aunt Kimberley been taking care of you?" I glance at her over Reid's head of golden-blonde curls.

"He's better. The antibiotics are already working their magic. He's had a nap, three bottles, eaten three times, so there have been three outfits and four diaper changes." She grimaces at this last part, and I laugh.

"You've been taking care of him?" I ask in surprise. "Where's Lianne?"

"Well, Jake insisted she take the day off." She looks at me with purpose. "Apparently, she has a cousin in Manhattan, so he arranged a car service, and off she went. I just got here, an hour ago, so most of the stuff I mentioned, Jake actually did."

"What?" My mind races. "I've been sleeping and Jake Winston has been taking care of my sick baby because he thoughtfully remembered it was Christmas and gave my nanny the day off? I am so ... out of it. Selfish. Self-absorbed. Shit."

"Don't worry about it." Kimberley grabs my hand. "Everything's fine. He's making dinner. They're watching football. Stephanie ran out to get more wine and a dessert."

"Who's all here?" I hold my breath, afraid of her answer.

"Just the inner circle. Christian, Steph, Gregoire, Jake, Reid, you and me."

"That's the inner circle, these days?"

"Yep. Why don't you take a shower? Then, put on some jeans to go with this." She hands me a gift, wrapped in silver paper with a bright red bow. She gives me a sly look and escapes my bedroom.

"We said one gift, Kimmy."

"It's hardly a gift," she says from the hallway. "Wait 'til you see what Gregoire got me." I hear her lyrical laugh and actually smile to myself. *Oh my God. Kimberley's getting married.*

✦

Thirty minutes later, I descend the stairs with a modicum of trepidation and this butterfly feeling in the pit of my stomach and this strange pervasive joy. *What is wrong with me?* The timbre of Jake Winston's southern accent as he talks excitedly about some football play assails me, even before I race past the great room, and glimpse the three of them—Jake, Christian and Gregoire—engrossed with the flat screen television.

I slip into the kitchen, hoping to stay unseen, giving myself a few more minutes to gain composure. I'm still a little freaked out I slept for so long, forgot to appropriately reward my nanny with the day off, basically allowed a virtual stranger to take care of my son, who could serve as a heart defibrillator should I require one, and continue to wrestle with these cascading emotions of joy and sadness with the intuitive belief my best friend is getting married. Mommy guilt, widow

105

guilt, this bizarre awareness of Jake Winston, and my self-absorption in combating the mixed feelings of happiness for Kimberley and sadness for me, all follow me into the kitchen.

Kimberley hands me a glass of champagne and fingers my silky silver blouse. "You look awesome."

"Well, that's a start. Thank you, Kimmy. Now, show me the rock."

She whips out her left hand and there is the most exquisite sapphire I've ever seen. But, a sapphire isn't really our girl, Kimmy; I steal a covert look at her and note the tinge of panic, lurking beneath her excitement. She looks almost terrified, even as she says, "He did the whole on-bended-knee thing, I can't live without you, will you marry me, and I got this to match your amazing eyes speech, spoken first in French, and then, in English, so I could confirm what he was really asking me."

"Nothing wrong with a guy who loves white chocolate," I say.

"No, there's not," Kimberley says with a wan smile.

"Did we talk dates?" Stephanie asks.

"Please. I just got engaged, a first for me, a big first. Let's not rush things."

"Can you believe it? Our Kimberley's getting married. Gregoire's already talking about this summer. Believe me, you've got to get going, if you're getting married, here," Stephanie says.

The most experienced bridal planner among us goes on about securing the right location in Manhattan and setting the date and making arrangements, preferably by Monday, if possible.

I look over at Kimberley and confirm she's fading fast from the thrill of showing off her engagement ring and seems less certain about belaying back down this treacherous mountain of wedding bliss after the exhilaration of the climb.

The uncertainty and doubt she was expressing, just a mere twenty-hours ago, seems to reverberate from her, again, now. She's not her usual self, a precious hope diamond on display that everyone wants to see. I sense her uncertainty and half-expect her to race across the room, search her purse for those business cards she collected just yesterday, and place a frantic call to my psychiatrist or the toll booth guy for instant validation that she's available and always willing. Kimberley, the free spirit, doesn't like to be pinned down by anyone, unless it's sexual foreplay of some kind. I half-smile at this image and discover Kimberley glaring back at me.

"You okay?" I ask.

"I'm fine, absolutely fine," Kimberley says.

Steph and I exchange uneasy looks at her use of the code word, absolutely.

Jake comes in, interrupting a moment that needs disruption, and I watch my two best friends immediately respond to his captivating charm. The guy is obviously used to getting everything he wants. He's busy asking them for pots and pans and whisks and spatulas and making himself right at home, in my kitchen, while my two best friends are tripping over themselves to help him out. This is amusing, in and of itself, since neither one of them spends any time near a stove. Apparently, he's putting together some kind of pasta dish and grilling prime rib. I'm just watching this little scenario unfold with my family, as they fawn over him.

Christian and Gregoire drift in; and the champagne and congratulations start to flow. The more celebratory the scene gets, the more outside of myself, I feel. No longer exhausted, I just feel this vast emptiness ebb from me.

The baby monitor crackles with Reid's familiar first stirrings from sleep. I grab a baby bottle and slip away from this surreal scene, seeking solace again with my baby. After changing him, I sink into the rocking chair. His little hands reach up toward my face and I playfully touch his fingers, while he takes the bottle. The rhythm of rocking back and forth brings serenity. The clamor of hushed laughter and banter from downstairs fades away. I let my mind flow, grateful for the oblivion of nothingness. There's no sadness, no tears, just my baby and me.

The ringing of someone's cell phone pulls me away from my dreamlike state. Jake's voice drifts to me from down the hallway.

"Savannah? How are you?" His voice sounds stilted and it doesn't take long to discern what must being said on the other end. "I know. It's just … the timing's bad. How's your family? Okay, I'm sorry. No. I'll pay for it. I don't want to put your parents out." There's a long pause. "I'm not in London. I decided … to come back to Amagansett. Check on the boat. Christian and Stephanie have been staying at the house. I'm at Evan's. It seemed like the place I needed to be. Christian and

Stephanie are here and his brother Gregoire, her friend Kimberley. She's coping better than she was before … at the funeral, I mean. It's not like that. She was Evan's wife. He was my best friend. Look, I'm sorry. I don't want to fight with you. I didn't mean to hurt you. It's just … I didn't say that. Well, if I did, I'm sorry. Of course, I do. I do love you, Savannah. I just can't … marry you, right now. Jesus, we can't have this conversation on the phone. I know. Would you rather I'd just not shown up at the church and leave you standing there? I did what I had to do. I'm sorry." There's another long pause. "I'm leaving for London in the next few days. I'll call you. I'll call you. I said I would, and I will. Soon."

The hallway grows quiet. I feel this swirling sensation of inner turmoil at hearing this one-sided conversation, something I wasn't supposed to hear. A strange emotion I cannot name courses through me. I'm paralyzed with indecision. Should I stay here for a while longer with Reid or go? My baby sighs in his sleep. I get up and put him down in his crib and spend the next few minutes gazing at Reid.

With newfound resolve, I manage to chase away most of the conflicting emotions racing through my mind over what I just heard and block out almost every little snippet I've inadvertently been privy to, except two. Jake told her he loved her. And, he's going to call her. That much, I do recall.

I put my index finger to my lips and lay it across my sleeping baby's forehead. Then turn, intent on leaving Reid's room and heading downstairs, and there's Jake, watching me from the doorway. I have no idea how long he's been standing there. It's been a long ten minutes, since his call ended.

"Everything okay?" I say as I slip past him through the open doorway, hearing his footsteps right behind me.

"No," he says in this low voice. "I'm sure you heard me."

I stop and turn back to him.

"Little hard not to. The house is big…" I extend my arms around like Vanna White. "But, not that big."

I return his intense gaze, determined to wait him out, whatever it is he wants to say.

"I think it was better when she wasn't speaking to me. Now, she's just plain mad. Pissed. Pissed, I'm not in London. Pissed, I forgot to call her on Christmas, which I did. She's definitely pissed I called off the wedding." He grimaces. "You know, just beyond mad," he says in this forlorn southern drawl.

A very sad cowboy, indeed.

"Not used to being in trouble, I take it?"

His head whips up. He looks astonished that I've called him out on this, and then, he slowly smiles. "Right," he says. "I guess that's it." He inclines his head and gets this hangdog look that must just drive every female within thirty feet of him wild.

I'm amused, enjoying the power that teasing him gives me. "Have always gotten your way and things have always gone your way, I bet." I shake my head side-to-side. "No wonder you and Evan were best friends. Other than Elizabeth … I mean … up until his very last moment, he was the luckiest guy I knew." My eyes fill with tears and I try to laugh, shake off this moment that's turned gloomy within seconds.

"Julia." Jake leans closer to me. His finger catches a trailing tear running down my face. I practically shudder at his touch. The emotions and fatigue of the past twenty hours overwhelm me. His Armani scent comes at me and this heady sensation has me drifting toward him ever closer.

"What?" I say. I look up at him and he's so close and I lift my face even higher to meet his. The space embraces us both. We're inches apart, his breath blows at my hair, and mine reaches his.

This hallway, once just a rectangular representation of beige-colored walls with the proper adornment of Monet replicas, even though Evan wanted to get the real thing and I'd told him, "No, we don't need to spend money that way," metamorphoses into a sanctuary, protecting us both. We suspend disbelief and time, right here, and, even though there's a sleeping baby ten feet away from us, and the inner circle mills about downstairs a mere hundred feet from us and any one of them could possibly walk up those stairs at any minute and discover us, we move closer.

There's all these reasons why this shouldn't be happening that begin with: I was Evan's wife, and he was Evan's best friend and about to marry someone else. All these reasons.

But, no, there's only the two of us. The only reason that counts.

"I don't want you mad at me, too," he says.

Moment broken.

Mad at you? What? In the last few moments, my head's been swimming with all these tangled-up emotions, dealing with all these wants and needs and the powers of attraction from Dr. Bradley Stephenson's Hallmark lessons that I've been trying to undo, like a Gordian knot. *What? You don't want me to be mad? At you?*

"Why don't you take your chances?" I ask. His breathing is as erratic as mine. I gaze at him, and then, step back, glimpsing the edges of panic and terror in his eyes. "Oh that's right. You love someone else. You just told her that. And, you're going to call her."

Moment smashed, unsurvivable, and irretrievably broken, but good, now.

Jake looks astonished at what I've just said and the quick-tempered fury with which I've said it. Who says Kimberley Powers is the only brave one around here to tell it like it is? I've made an incredible comeback at lightning speed.

"It's not like that," he says. The defensiveness in his voice infuriates me further.

"Oh really? Because it certainly sounds like it. I love you, Savannah. I'll call," I say in my best imitation of a southern drawl. I've made a fantastic recovery from the edge of this almost passionate encounter and I'm not stoned or drunk, just running on constant idle with Dr. Stevenson's magic pills. Jake leans against the wall, catching his breath, and won't even look at me, while I attempt to laugh just as Kimberley would.

"Come on. Let's go see what's going on downstairs because *I know* neither Kimberley or Stephanie can cook." He follows behind me at a slower pace.

"So, who did all the cooking when you lived in Tribeca?"

I turn back, surprised, and left to wonder how he knew the three of us used to live there. "I did."

<hr />

A few hours later, we've eaten and watched enough football to satisfy the most avid fan among us, which seems to be a tie between Jake and me.

"When did you get so interested in football?" Jake asks.

He's been trying to make amends for the hallway incident, for the past two hours, with this solicitous we're-just-fast-friends schtick for our little crowd.

But, guess what? I'm still irritated with him, even though nothing really happened between us, it could have. We were both right there. And, now I'm burdened with even more guilt, as if I didn't have enough of it already.

"Julia dated the captain of the football team at UCLA," Kimberley says airily with a wave of her hand.

Drinking wine has made her careless about our unwritten rule: we don't talk about Bobby, or now, Evan. My waspish look in her general direction clearly communicates she's crossed the line. We don't talk about Bobby. It's a double-down secret. *She knows this.*

Stephanie steps in. "Kimmy. Double-down."

"Why? Why do we never get to talk about the past, Julia? Why do we keep all these secrets for you?"

"Why are you doing this to me?" I ask.

"Why don't we ever get to talk about Bobby? And now, Evan? You're not the only one who lost them, maybe, we all need to talk this through."

"Make an appointment with Dr. Bradley Stevenson. I'm sure he'd be willing to help you out, Kimmy. You've got his card. Why don't you call him?"

The three men exchange these puzzled looks, while I make a point of leaving to go check on Reid, because you can't trust baby monitors any more than you can trust people. So, it seems.

───※───

Earlier, Kimberley made a big production about exchanging more gifts, so I steal away in this latest awkward moment and grab a gift I'd wrapped weeks before for Evan, deciding to give it to Jake. There's no logical explanation for me doing this, except to admit I have no right to be mad at him.

As a simple gesture of kindness, I give him Evan's gift because there's no longer any point in keeping something for the sailboat he shared with Jake.

I can't find a point about anything, right now. The melancholy settles in all around me. I just want to go to bed and stay there forever.

"What is this?" Jake tears off the red foil paper, unlatches the Mahogany box, folds back the blue velvet cover, and holds up the sextant. I avoid his direct gaze. "Wow."

Christian takes it from him "Nice piece. It's an extraordinary find."

Jake gives me a surreptitious look as Christian hands the sextant back to him. "Are you *sure*, Julia?"

"He would have wanted you to have it."

"It's an amazing gift. I've always wanted one of these."

"Well, it's yours, then. He loved that sailboat, loved sailing with you. He'd want you to have it."

"We're still partners in the sailboat, if you want to keep it."

"We can keep it. I don't know how to sail, though."

"I could teach you."

We're looking at each other in this weird way, our gazes spellbound by the inexplicable connection neither one of us understands, while everyone else in the room is just watching the two of us interact.

"Anyway, Merry Christmas." My kind words have reached their limit. I take a breath and manage a smile.

I extend my hand, he takes it, and then, pulls me in for a hug. Our scents—his cologne and my perfume—co-mingle. For a few seconds, we both seem to succumb to the same heady sensation that almost led to trouble upstairs, a few hours ago. Then, I'm saved by the onrush of guilt and grief, one on either side, pulling me away from him. *Thank God for these rescuers, tonight.*

Jake hands me a gift wrapped in silvery paper. He gets this hopeful look. It's heavy. *A book.* I tear at the paper, guessing right, and breathe a sigh of relief, it's not something more personal, like my favorite perfume. Then, I see the title: *Complete Works of Shakespeare.* Bobby gave me an edition, years ago. I swallow hard and struggle to meet his gaze. "How did … you know, I love Shakespeare?"

"Surely, someone named Julia has played Juliet."

I played *Juliet* in the school play when I was sixteen. It was the last performance my parents ever saw me in, the last performance I ever performed. It was just before we left for Greece, and Jake's looking at me, like he already knows this.

112

"Julia, are you all right?" Kimberley comes up and puts her arm around me.

"I'm fine. It's an amazing gift." I give Kimberley a beseeching look.

"Oh," she says taking the book from my trembling hands, recognizing it, at once. "It's lovely, Jake. You okay?" she whispers to me. I nod and slip away from her.

"Thank you, Jake. It's very thoughtful of you."

I try to smile, to find some sort of balance again, but I sound hollow and faraway. For a moment, I'm even tempted to reach out to him, to touch his hand, and be rescued by the sensational connection that just touching him brings, but grief carries me away. The painful loss of all my loved ones resurfaces, surrounding me now, pulling me under. I'm already at the doorway.

"I'm going to check on Reid," I say, invoking my mantra for this day.

"Julia, are you sure you're all right?" Jake asks.

Heartbreak takes over. I've lost everyone I ever loved. I'm in the after, again. This day just needs to end.

"Absolutely," I say.

Both Kimberley and Steph look over at me at this declaration at the same time and channel an are-you-really-okay? look in my direction.

"I'm absolutely fine."

CHAPTER

ELEVEN

Seeking normal

THE DAY AFTER CHRISTMAS ARRIVES WITH the typical after-holiday malaise, more potent than ever. I successfully hide my disquiet from Kimberley, who finally acquiesces to Gregoire's insistence, that she return to the city with him, to get going on some of their wedding plans. He wants her to, at least, consider a wedding in Paris. Kimberley's determined to show him the romantic parts of Manhattan. I need to be alone, to just allow grief to have me, because keeping up the appearance of having it all together, all the time, is weighing me down.

Kimberley finally agrees to leave me, after I make a myriad of promises to her that I'm okay, and I'll be good. Ultimately, she's reassured by Lianne's unexpected return to take care of Reid and me, so Kimberley and Gregoire leave in the early afternoon. Soon, the house becomes unbearably quiet. With Reid down for his afternoon nap, Lianne is busy taking inventory of what we need to take to Paris and insists she doesn't need my help. At loose ends, the oppressive silence catches up to me, so I head out for a run, along the beach.

Running provides me with the much-needed rush of adrenalin I've missing for days. My heart pounds in my eardrums and I push myself faster and farther than usual. After three miles, I sprint toward an unfamiliar line of beach and somersault deep into the biggest sand dune. I attempt to catch my breath, knowing I'll pay for resting, at mid-juncture like this, with a few cramped leg muscles on the way back. Suddenly exhausted, I lie back against the sand and use the respite to take in the amazing scenery. A steady wind from the northeast accompanies the relentless saltwater, splashing at the shore. The Atlantic's waves strangely soothe me, lulled by its rhythmic sound, I close my eyes, and find solace in the natural confines of the sand.

❧

"You're a long way from home," drawls a too-familiar voice.

I stir awake, look up into the bright sunlight overhead, and discover Jake Winston. *Jake. The runner. We meet again.* He settles in beside me, breathing heavy from his own run, while the confusing memories of last night come rushing back to me, tinged with profound sadness.

"Uh-huh. Just had to get out of the house."

"The day after Christmas is always hard. I thought I could outrun it, too." He points towards the north shoreline.

"Uh-huh. Kimmy went back to the Manhattan with Gregoire. It got awfully quiet. I thought I wanted that, but then … running helps." *Why am I explaining this to him?*

Jake looks over at me. "I was going to call you. There are some things we should talk about. As the executor of Evan's estate, we should talk. I've got the paperwork at my house."

"We should do that sooner rather than later. I'm leaving for Paris at the end of the week."

"*Paris?* Why? I thought you were staying here." He sweeps his arm in the general direction of my beach house further down the southern shore.

"Kimberley needs to return to Paris. She's invited me to come with her. Christian and Stephanie left this morning to be with his family in Nice, and then, they'll be at their chateau for a month or so…" I stop talking because he looks so disenchanted, and I'm wondering why I feel the need to explain this to him, at all. "Can't we talk about this later?"

I push off with my elbows and come to a stand and start stretching out my legs. My body is already protesting the upcoming run. Jake stands up, too, towering over me.

"I'm leaving for London, tomorrow. There are a few things we should go over if you have the time."

116

The tone of his voice indicates this is a non-negotiable invitation. Part of me is angry with him for his sense of entitlement to my time, and part of me is intrigued to see the inside of his beach house, the place I've never been invited to, before.

"Fine," I say with a nonchalant shrug.

"Come on," he says in that charming southern drawl of his.

I trail behind him along the beach, for a few more minutes, and follow him up an old set of stairs leading from the beach to a house. I'm not disappointed by what I see. The exterior of Jake's home lies along the quaint spectrum of rustic with just the right amount of aging wood. He's left the exterior, alone, natural and unpainted, with the exception of the white-framed, oversized windows that run along the back of the house.

We traverse across the weathered planks of his deck, while I trail my fingers along the railing, enchanted that its normally rough surface is smooth and worn. I revel in the structure's permanence and its ability to withstand the elements of wind, water, and salt air. What a treasure. I sense this kindred spirit, this connection, to this place already. My smile is involuntary. This unexpected joy courses through me in just being here. Jake slides back the glass door, steps to one side, allowing me to enter first.

"Wow," I say to him as I pass.

It's the kind of beach house I always imagined having one day. It's not pretentious at all. It's welcoming, like a favorite blanket, so prized, it's the one you always seek out to wrap yourself up in. The interior is adorned with all the right comforts and just enough disorder to be charming. One whole wall is made up of long shelves made of Birch wood that overflow with books and framed photographs. There's a recent photograph of what must be Jake's family.

"My family, last Christmas," Jake says from right behind me.

"They're lovely," I say. "Your mother is beautiful." I stare at the older women's engaging smile and gold blonde hair. Jake has her blue eyes and his father's darker blonde hair. His sisters are replicas of his mother, blonde and beautiful. There's another photograph next to it with even more people. Spouses and offspring? There's a little blond boy and girl, dressed, alike, in charming Santa sweater outfits. They look to be about three. I smile over at him.

"My niece and nephew," he says after a long pause. "Lisa and Ted's three-year-old twins. Kelly's pregnant now; she and John are having their first in July." He points to the taller blonde in the photograph, standing with a good-looking guy in a blue sweater.

"Happy family." I blush, realizing I've just anointed his family with the name of a Chinese restaurant dish. I ruefully glance over at him, at my faux pas for this, and discover him, studying me intently, as if prompting me to say more or something different about the photographs.

"Mom's big on family," he finally says.

I nod and turn my attention back to his book shelf, running my fingers along the spines, noting Shakespeare, Hemingway, some of the latest best sellers, along with a sundry of law school books I easily recognize.

"I didn't finish," I say. "I was at Columbia. Then, Evan and I met." I shake my head side-to-side and grin over at him. "I got pregnant after missing only two pills. We got married." My smile fades, as I meet his gaze, for a moment. I turn away, undone by a strange potpourri of memories of Evan and our life together and the haunted look on Jake's face.

"I didn't know you went to Columbia. How much more do you have before you'd be finished and get a law degree."

"A semester," I say in an uneven voice. "But, I'm not going back. Bobby wanted to be a lawyer. Maybe, that's why I went. Now? Everything's different. I have Reid to think of. I want him to have a normal life. I want to be there for it. Reid's my focus."

"In Paris?" Jake sounds disappointed.

"Paris," I echo. "I'll probably do the PR gig with Kimberley for a while at *Liaison*, and then, I'll need to decide what to do for the long-term. Right now, I just want to be with my … family."

"Oh," he says with an understanding nod. "That makes sense."

I outline the black lacquer wood of another one of his framed photographs with my fingers, unseeing, as my eyes fill with unexpected tears. I wipe them away and turn to him, sad, all at once. Jake has this strange look on his face, as if he's expecting another kind of response from me, again. Disconcerted by his intensity, I move away from him.

"What about Evan's parents? They'll want to see Reid."

"Uh-huh. We'll work something out. I just need a little time."

I'm a little bit put off that Jake would be thinking of Evan's parents. Of course, he doesn't know the history of me and the Hamiltons, their unwillingness to accept me as Evan's wife. And now? Even less so. I'm disappointed, he would *side* with them and consider their feelings, not mine. "I'm not Elizabeth," I say without thinking, on edge, all at once.

"No one said you were."

"Uh-huh, well, that would be easier." He gives me a questioning look, but doesn't say more. And, God knows, I've said enough already.

I continue my tour of his place, needing some distance from him. I'm off balance. *I should go, but this place and its owner just draw me in.* Jake's home is the kind of sanctuary that no matter what time of year it is, winter or summer, it's the only place I'd ever want to be. Ever since I walked in, the place seems to have wrapped itself around me, making me feel right at home.

The seventies-style sunken living room is an easy three steps down, dominated by a long overstuffed sofa in dark brown leather with large red pillows strewn about. The walls are painted a crème white and the floors are a bleached hardwood. Birch, maybe. For the first time, in a long while, I sense tranquility, something I haven't really felt, since the early days in L.A. with Bobby, Kimmy and Steph. Jake's place provides some kind of unknowable respite from the chaos that my life has become, and I secretly find pleasure in this.

I steal a look at my host. At first, he's affecting a casual stance, but then, he's going around, straightening things up, stacking magazines, books, CDs. He carries a pile of clothing he's gathered from his first pass through the place, and looks momentarily flustered. I smile, taken aback by his display of self-consciousness. The man is a god from the heavens or another galaxy. I didn't think he did anything domestic.

"Sorry. I wasn't expecting company," he says with a slight grimace.

"You don't have to pick up. It's charming, just the way it is. It's a fantastic place, Jake."

"Thanks. It felt like home, the minute I walked into it. I had to buy it, used every last penny I had to my name," he drawls.

"But it's so worth it," I say.

"Yes."

Our gazes lock.

I know this man, but I don't know him. I should go.

I turn away from him and attempt to get my roller coaster emotions back under control. A covert side glance confirms Jake is just watching me explore his space. He gets this bemused look on his face, and then, starts stoking the fire in the fireplace. He moves on to his stereo. It's some technologically advanced electronics ensemble, destined to intimidate all but its owner. Some pop song fills the air. I smile over at him, appreciative of the way he's wired the room for sound.

I move on with my tour, beyond his line of sight. "Great kitchen," I call out.

It is ideal. The kitchen's not overly pretentious, just admirably filled with some decadent Viking appliances, I would be sure to put to good use. I run my fingers, along the white marble countertop and admire the marbleized gold thread running through it. The design is tasteful, something I would have picked out. Light, bright. A true beach house theme. I look out the kitchen window and glimpse the sandy shoreline to the north. Jake comes in.

"This is an amazing place. It's perfect. Just the right size, inviting, comfortable, really charming." I'm remembering bits and pieces of our conversation about his starting over and still looking for some of those answers. I lean back against the counter and smile at him. "What's so important, in London, that you would give up this life?"

He looks uncomfortable with my question. "I'm glad you like it," he finally says, then shrugs. "I was starting over."

"So you've said. And now?"

"Savannah … wants me to sell this place. She wants … wanted to settle in Austin, not London, or Manhattan."

My smile fades. "You can't sell this place."

"I don't know what I'm going to do." He runs his hand through his hair.

"It's Saturday," I say quietly.

"Yes."

"You were supposed to get married, today."

"Yes."

We share a long silence. A parade of emotions crosses his features: sadness, guilt, relief. I'm surprised to see the last one, but it's there; relief just emanates from him. I consciously step back from him.

"At least, I don't have to sell the place for *her*," he says with a slight laugh.

"Yes."

"We should talk about London. The overhead for the office, there, is too high. We're wasting money."

"I thought you liked London. I thought you wanted to be there."

"Everything's different, now." Jake gets this troubled look.

"Everything's different," I echo back to him.

We look at each other with renewed intensity and the inexplicable connection between us comes roaring back to life. There's a part of me that feels strangely at ease around him, as if I already know him, and another part that's deeply aligned to the increasing anxiety that being around him, this virtual stranger, always brings. It's like being near an electric fence: the logical part knows you shouldn't touch it, but the illogical part just wants to reach out and confirm this.

"Coffee, or something else?" Jake asks.

"Something else. Although you might have to take me home, I think I'm done with running for today."

"I'll take you home."

The way he says this makes it seem like a life-long promise. It must be that accent that has me so mesmerized by every word he utters. I shake my head, trying to clear it of these wayward, unfinished thoughts.

"I should call Lianne," I say slowly.

Because, apparently, I need permission from my nanny to be here, from *someone*.

"I forgot my cell phone."

"Call Lianne," he says, handing me his phone.

His gentle tone causes me to tremble as I take it from him. Now, I can't even concentrate and struggle to remember my home phone number. He finds this amusing and laughs a little, as he easily recites my home phone number back to me. Completely undone by him, now, I finally dial. As usual, my nanny is a godsend. Lianne has no problem with me meeting up with Jake for the afternoon to go over Evan's estate and the associated paperwork. Her reassurance steadies me a little bit; somehow, confirming for me that meeting up with Jake is a good idea, perfectly reasonable. *Permission granted.*

Jake pours chilled white wine into two glasses and hands me one. He arches an eyebrow at me and I can't decide if he's questioning my satisfaction with the wine or this whole encounter, all together. It would appear, we're both a little on edge.

I take a sip of the wine and furtively glance at him over the edge of the glass. He's even more attractive, today, in his navy running gear than he was in the casual allure of jeans and a polo shirt from yesterday or his fine suit of two nights ago. My mind tabulates his attributes at an astonishing rate.

The song *Chances* by Five for Fighting filters its way to me. I break away from Jake's concentrated, all-seeing gaze and my wayward thoughts related to his wardrobe, and drift back into his living room to hear it more clearly. The song's lyrics reach at me. The clarity of such heartbreak eases me my own. I recite some of the words and retrace my steps, looking for answers.

Eventually, I find myself staring out the huge living room windows at the magnificent ocean and attempt to get my bearings again. Soon, Jake comes up to stand next to me.

"I think you're closer to the beach than I am," I say with a little laugh.

"An old house has its advantages. Different setbacks, different era." He shakes his head. "Your house is four times bigger with an ocean beach view from every room."

"Nothing beats the allure of this place. It's fabulous. *Really.*" I sip the wine and remain at my post staring out at his view, but fully aware of him, standing right next to me. The song ends and I turn to him. "Don't sell it, Jake."

I lay a hand on his arm. He startles at my unexpected touch and splashes some of his wine onto the floor. He retreats to the kitchen, returns with paper towels, and begins dabbing at the floor. I get the distinct impression that this is something he normally wouldn't worry about so much. It appears he's on edge as much as I am.

I smile at him and say, "No matter what Savannah wants, you can't sell a home like this."

He looks up at me. "Sometimes, we have to do things we don't want to do." He sounds so resigned. I look at him more closely, trying to decide what he means by that.

"Some things we just can't *do*. Trust me. I know what I'm talking about. I've spent my adult life trying to find home. And, I walk into this place and ..."

I'm assailed by these confusing connections to him and this place. Disquiet returns full force. *What am I doing here? With him?* I walk away from him and stand at the center of his living room and contemplate my next move, suddenly feeling trapped, as if I've just discovered I'm in a maze and cannot find my way out.

"What do I know?" I finally say.

"I think you know a lot," he drawls.

His charming southern accent practically dissolves all the emotional walls I've put up. He comes to stand beside me and gets this thoughtful look.

I'm unable to look away. "Believe me, I don't know anything." We look at each other, again. I take a deep breath and let it out slowly. "I should go."

"Don't go," he says. "Stay."

We share another long-drawn-out silence, and hold each other's gaze, unable to look away. The words *go home* are now timed with my heart rate: *Go. Home.* Except, all I can do is stand here, looking at him, fascinated by the way he's looking at me.

It would seem we're both too captivated to do anything more. Then, finally, as if synchronized, we both take an unsteady breath at the same time, just enough to break the inexplicable spell between us.

"I should go home."

"I'll get the paperwork," he says, turning away from me.

His retreating footsteps sound out along the wood floor, while I slide down onto his sofa, suddenly too weak to stand.

———

"It's a lot of money." I cannot keep the devastating sadness out of my voice.

"It is."

We've gone over the finite details of Evan's estate, for the past two hours, and his net worth of two hundred million. I'm reeling from this fact, alone. I knew Evan had money, but, like so many things he and I never talked about, I just didn't know how *much*. This astounding revelation presses down on me like a vice, serving as an uninvited new kind of torture that reminds me that I am still here and Evan is not.

No amount of money is going to change any of that.

There is no consolation for me in any of this. I am all that is left. I am the charred broken remains; the one left behind again, after death's inferno effectively destroyed my life with Evan and took him from me. The reality of the after crushes me, once again. He's gone, incinerated for all time. I am the ashes left behind, soaked with too many tears, and burdened with an infinite future I cannot see. Our life together is finished. His money, so excessive, seems to be a personal affront that should have been incinerated alongside his body. Evan Hamilton was supposed to live forever. That was the plan. I begin to shake, engulfed in the suffocating loss of a life I will never have with him again. *It's over. Finished.*

Jake's voice breaks through to me. "There are properties in Malibu, Manhattan, of course, the house here. He and I were just finishing an acquisition in Telluride, Colorado. We should talk about that one." I hear him sigh, and then, he taps my arm. "Julia, are you *listening*?"

"No."

I feel hollow inside. Grief returns. My life is over, uncertain. I'm drifting. I'm alone, bereaved, empty. The enormity of it all: first, Evan's death; now, dealing with his company, the properties, the money—his assets. It's unbearable.

"I just wanted a normal life," I say. "A baby. A little house on the beach. Love. Happiness. Forever. I didn't want all of this other stuff. I just wanted … a normal life. *With him.*"

"I know."

Jake stares at me. Once again, I'm held here by his exquisite blue gaze, so different from Evan's.

Loneliness returns. This vast emptiness threatens to drown me. The need to be held becomes pervasive, an all consuming need. I'm undone, scattered, and broken into fragments. Part of me is distressed by this obscene amount of money. Part of me is undone for some un-knowable reason by the man in front of me. Part of me is inebriated by the chardonnay we've drunk over the past two hours. We finished the first bottle, and we're halfway through the second.

"I just want someone to tell me it's going to be okay. Tell me the lies. Just tell me *something*." I've spoken aloud. This is all, but con-firmed, by Jake's distressed look.

"It's going to be okay," he says after a long pause. "Julia, I … I can't. I'm your lawyer. You're my client. You're the chairman of Hamilton Equities, for Christ's sake. I basically work for *you*." He holds up part of the paperwork, as if it's a sword with special powers, wielding it in front of me.

I'm alone, bereaved, empty, *drunk*. I confirm this, as I stand.

Jake gets up, too. We're a foot away from each other.

"I just wanted a normal life."

"I know."

A tear makes its way down my face. Jake seems to watch its prog-ress, as if he's memorizing the tear's path, but gives me this I-can't-help-you-out kind of look.

I break away from his intense gaze, grab the half-empty bottle, and refill my empty glass. There's a part of me that knows I should care about this almost empty bottle. So like me, it seems. This almost empty bottle. There's a part of me saying, *go home Julia*. Yet, another part of me basks in this heightened inebriated state, revels in this astounding awareness of him, and desires to give in to this astonishing need to feel something with someone.

Dr. Hallmark Card's soliloquy about attraction, love, and his ongo-ing sermons about not being able to control these things, plays havoc with this widow's mind. My body wants Jake, and my mind says, *What the hell, Julia. Enjoy yourself because, frankly, your life can't get any more fucked up.* And, I haven't even taken a single pain killer to feel this way. I blame my devil-may-care attitude directly on being best friends with the promiscuous Kimberley Powers. *Kimberley* would give in these overpowering feelings of attraction and the need to be held; she would consummate this thing, this need of him. The saintly Dr. Stevenson would seem to be echo and encourage the same of me, in these cosmic circumstances. I close my eyes and try to remember exactly what the good doctor had to say.

"Julia, are you okay?"

"Uh-huh." I open my eyes and slightly sway.

The man before me, a mere six inches away from my face, right now, looks uneasy. The afternoon has definitely faded away. We're standing in the dim light of his living room. I turn away from him, steadying myself as I move along his furniture, gripping it as I go. "What time is it?" I turn back to look at him.

"A little after six," he says, glancing at his watch. "I should take you home."

"I'm not sure either one of us should be driving, even if it's just a few miles down the road." I sweep my hand across the room and stare directly at him. "Where's your restroom?"

He points toward the hallway. I watch him take a deep breath, realizing he's been holding it. I shake my head side-to-side and suddenly laugh at his helplessness. The man is afraid of me, right now. Somewhere inside, I enjoy this power over him.

His bathroom serves as a much needed respite.

Bless me, Father, for I have sinned. I'm about to. I surprise myself in recalling my Catholic upbringing. The memory of confession returns to me, all at once. I haven't thought of this childhood ritual, since my parents' death. For some reason, it makes me laugh, again. I feel the guilt for the inappropriateness and my attraction for Jake at the same time.

I spend the glorious minutes away from Jake and try to find my center. I dab at my face with wet wash cloth in an attempt to cool down these hot embers of desire coming to life inside. Despite my recollection of Catholicism and confession, nothing is putting out the passionate flames for him that radiate away inside. I stare at myself in the mirror for a long time.

Who are you? Who is this person that would be with someone else? Sleep with someone else? Who are you?

"I just wanted a normal life," I say to the girl in the mirror. She nods.

I take my hair out of the elastic band that's been holding it back, lean over, and brush it out with my hands. *Steady.* I grip the counter, as the effects of the wine courses through me. I finger-fix my hair and leave it down. I run a line of Jake's toothpaste along my index finger and hastily brush my teeth with it. This old college trick reminds me of times with Bobby. I examine the face in the mirror, again, and recognize the remnants of Bobby's Julia, the Julia, who was desirable and overflowed with happiness and love.

"A normal life, that's all I ever really wanted," I say to the girl in the mirror, again. I rummage through the drawers and find a discarded lipstick. *Thank you, Savannah?* I wipe off the end of it with my finger and apply a line of some sultry plum color to my lips. I put the lipstick away, tidy up his bathroom, and head out to his hallway.

The problem is: I haven't resolved anything. The desire for him runs through me like an out-of-control fever; and, I no longer care. That's the problem. Bless me, Father, for I *will* sin.

"I'll make you dinner," Jake says from the sofa. He looks compassionate, sitting there casually sipping his wine, apparently oblivious to his own sex appeal, although his eyes rake over me with renewed interest at my improved appearance. Apparently, fresh lipstick and finger-fixed hair is a sufficient enough turn-on. He holds his wine glass in mid-air, all at once, alert.

"I'm not hungry … for food." I tower above him, lean down, take his wine glass from him, guzzle the rest of it, and then, set it down.

"I should take you home," he says, suddenly uneasy.

"Take me … *home.*"

Within seconds, I climb onto his lap and start kissing the side of his neck. His pulse races beneath my exploring lips. He makes this inaudible, helpless sound. His arms come around me, pulling me closer. He whispers my name. I close my eyes and give into the amazing sensation of kissing him as his lips find mine. The magnetism between us is unleashed, once more, and neither one of us seems to be able to control it this time, as we move into each other. The connection between us begins to heat up, and I strip off my running jacket, and then, my t-shirt. He's kissing the tops of my breasts and unhooking my bra. The freedom and the warmth of his mouth set me on fire.

"We shouldn't do this," he says against my lips.

"We shouldn't," I echo back.

I move in closer, wanting to feel more of him. He comes to life, beneath my thighs. Need takes over, accelerates, and outruns all logical thought. I'm kissing him all over, and he's responding. I grab at his clothing, stripping off his white t-shirt. He's muscular and hot to the touch underneath. I trail my tongue along his chest and savor the saltiness of his flesh and hear his breath quicken.

"Oh God. Julia, we can't do this," he whispers.

Minutes go by and the intensity of our bodily explorations accelerates, though some part of me registers his growing despondency,as his movements become more labored, less responsive. Eventually, his arms slacken and he lets go of me. I stop for a moment, trying to ascertain why he sounds and feels this way, *different*, but necessity urges me on.

I need to feel alive, again. With him. Desperate, I press into his body, wanting him, needing this connection with him. I shove thoughts of Evan way down inside, knowing the shame of what we're doing will seek and punish me later for this indiscretion. With enough white wine working in combination with the inner peace of this place and this magnificent specimen of a man beneath me, I overcome the thoughts of my future and the inevitable meeting up with grief and shame that lies ahead, just waiting for me.

I'm here, in the here and now, and I want Jake Winston. All of him.

"We can't do this," he says again, more resolute this time. "Damn it, Julia." He abruptly pulls away from me. "You were his *wife*. I can't do this."

He stands over me now, still aroused, partially undressed *by me*. He finds his shirt, pulls it back on, and tucks it into his pants.

"If we do this, it'll be for all the wrong reasons."

"What?" I ask. I gulp at the air, knowing he's right, but angry with him, anyway, and even more furious with myself.

I pull on my t-shirt, my Capri pants, and then, my running jacket. I jam my bra into the outer pocket and grab my running shoes from the floor.

Before, he can stop me, I'm at the patio door sliding it open and racing through it. From behind me, Jake calls me back, but I run along the shoreline just out of reach of the waves at double-time. His voice fades away. I steal a look back and can barely make out his dark shadow, just standing there, watching me go. He's more than a half mile away from me, but so much farther than that.

In less than ten minutes, I'm back at my house, wet, weary, mortified, and definitely pissed off at myself, but also with him.

The phone is ringing, when I slip through the unlocked deck door. Lianne looks at me in confusion, as she goes to pick up the landline.

I attempt to smile, but shudder with too many competing emotions blazing away inside, all but incinerating me, now.

I'm sure I look like a crazed woman and confirm this, when I glimpse my reflection in the window glass. My windblown hair is going every which way. I reach up to smooth it back into place, but finally give up. Mascara streaks down my face. It's a combination of my eyes tearing up from the windy conditions outside, and something else I refuse to recognize. I wipe at a tear with the back of my hand and try to rub off the remaining streaks with my jacket sleeve.

"Yes, she just got here. Just a second." My nanny gets this thoughtful look. I bite my lower lip to keep it from trembling as I struggle to keep it together. "Mr. Winston wants to talk to you," Lianne says gently. She hands me the phone and heads for the stairs.

I'm grateful to her for the silent offer of privacy and experience a modicum of dignity, as I pick up the phone. I just hold the receiver to my ear because some distant part of me needs to hear his voice, while all the other parts berate me for this outward sign of weakness for him.

"I'm sorry. I shouldn't … have done that," Jake says. His remorse makes me feel worse. Tears trail down my face. "I shouldn't have said what I said. I *want* you. I do. I just … I want it to be right. I want it to *mean* something."

"It doesn't *mean anything*. And, I don't want to see you, anymore, Jake."

I hear him suck in his breath, shocked by my coldness, I suppose.

"I'm sorry," he says.

"Are you *done?*"

"I'm sorry, Julia. I don't want it to be this way. I'm sorry."

I don't bother to answer. Instead, I hang up the receiver and unplug the phone cord from the wall. Exhausted, on so many incomprehensible levels, I climb the stairs. Minutes later, I strip off my clothes, stand under the shower spray, and attempt to wash away the grief and shame that have already found me again.

CHAPTER

TWELVE

Navigating a Paris way of life

IT'S BEEN THIRTY-THREE DAYS. REID AND I are whisked away to Paris, France to a life without Evan, in a country we don't really belong. Grief has rallied to claim me and guilt over what almost transpired with Jake *again* makes a new frontal assault.

I've moved into the you-can't-possibly-understand-what-I'm-feeling-until-this-happens-to-you stage of grief, and, since I can't possibly be angry with Evan, I've projected this rage on to my two best friends and the persona of one Jake Winston, who remains in London. *Thank God.*

Kimberley is adamant about being there for me, at every point in time. She's conciliatory about Evan, protective, sulky, bitchy, loving, and watchful, sometimes all at the same time. Stephanie exhibits some of these traits, too. I'm at a loss as to how to handle either one of them, as we all try to navigate an unfamiliar way of life in Paris.

I don't have any patience left for Kimberley and Stephanie or their continued vigilance. *Come on.* If they could be inside my head for a single day and see how it feels: how every time I close my eyes all I see is Evan's last moments, or when I'm awake, I can't even conjure up his face, then, they'd know. If they only knew how I never really what day it is anymore, or can never gaze openly at Reid, since he looks more like Evan every day, then, they'd know how I feel. Frankly, I just want to stop thinking. If I could just stop thinking, maybe, all this grief over

Evan, and this guilt over Jake, and this overriding emptiness inside of me, would go away.

I harbor the secret of my latest encounter with Jake, and don't tell either one of them about it, while my despair intensifies. I am worse than ever, even Kimberley can see it.

"Five days," she says. She stares at me for the umpteenth time, this day, with an anxious look.

"Five days?"

"That's all you get. In bed. Five days. I'll let you have them, but that's it."

"Fine. Five days." I give her a quizzical look, wondering why she has caved, on this point, about letting me stay in bed. My lethargy has messed with my sense of time. I can no longer recall what day it is. One day just slips into the next. My nights are spent trying to find solace and elusive sleep, but nothing's working, most of all, me. The little magic pills from Dr. Stevenson and pure exhaustion make me practically incoherent, while grief and guilt take the rest.

"Lianne can take care of Reid, and I'll take care of you."

I nod. "Thanks, Kimmy."

It's only later that I figure out I literally slept through the first anniversary of our wedding on the tenth of January. Kimberley actually gives me six days in bed. Then, on the morning of day seven, she unceremoniously pushes me into the shower. I'm reminded of Jacob Winston, all over again.

Time, sleep, neither completely erases his image or the shame, that arrives with it, from my mind. The peaceful feeling we shared between us, for those precious first few hours at his place the day after Christmas, is long gone. In its place is this unknowable sorrow I try to ignore, while I forcefully embrace seething fury for him and the latest round of guilt that accompanies it.

Existing in a semi-fog with the assistance of the little white pills, I dully count the days, as they drift by. There have been sixty-three of those.

Christian handles the day-to-day operations for Evan's company. But, as time goes on, it begins to filter through to me, that there is much to be decided with the hedge-fund firm, and he can't possibly deal with it all and run his own company, too. The market is going crazy with the continual financial angst the New Year brings, as it reverberates on a global level, and Evan's private equity clients get more and more anxious, since the leader with the golden touch is, most definitely, deceased. I've relinquished all the responsibilities over to Christian to solve, but the guilt, of burdening him with my problems, starts to seep in to me. The pressure for decisions on what to do, both tactically and strategically, increases tenfold. "Talk to Christian" has become my mantra whenever someone reaches out to me, directly, to discuss Hamilton Equities. I'm overwhelmed with grief and the idea of serving as chairman of Evan's company, in any real, working capacity, terrifies me. Christian takes on the brunt of the responsibilities, as acting chief executive officer, and provides me updates on his and Jake's progress, while I dully listen and try to comprehend what he's telling me.

I've made one decision. I've hired *Liaison*, Kimberley, to do all the public relations coordination for Hamilton Equities. Evan and I had talked about doing this, just before he died. The one thing I know is, I need my little entourage—Kimberley, Stephanie, Christian, and even Jake—more than ever now, not just for my own consolation, but for the survival of Evan's company.

Paris in late February. I sit out on a garden bench wrapped in a thick wool blanket on the patio at Gregoire's chateau, where he so graciously invited all of us to stay, while we're here. I stare out at the winter landscape of France and try not to think about the things and places that start with the letter *A* that continue to haunt me. The earlier sessions with Dr. Stevenson, and now, Dr. Lila Grayson, here in Paris, still brings all this pain of the past decade to the surface for me. Pain, I thought I dealt with long ago, emerges and stays with me, now.

Gregoire's chateau vibrates with activity and people. Kimberley still insists on staying with me as much as possible, while things continue to pile up at the Paris office of *Liaison*.

My hand swipes at a stray tear. The opening and closing of the French door that leads out to the garden patio and Kimberley's lyrical voice breaks into my asylum.

"Yes. She's getting better. Probably, a few more weeks. Yes. I'll tell her. She's been edgy. Don't feel bad; she's not taking anyone's calls, but mine and Steph's." Kimberley looks over in my vicinity with an intense, we-will-be-talking-about-this-later stare. I return her gaze with my own determined defiant look.

"Thanks. No problem," Kimberley says with a laugh. "So two weeks, huh? Manhattan sounds good about now. Amagansett would be even better. I totally agree. Okay. It's not a problem. I have a team that helps me with everything. Well, we try to. Okay. Yes, I'll tell her." She presses the end-call button on her cell phone, then, walks around the garden, intent on examining last summer's long-dead flora, as if she can, somehow, resuscitate it, by staring at the vegetation long enough. I appreciate the silence, knowing it won't last and that Kimberley's going to be lecturing me about something, soon enough.

"Who was that?" I finally ask.

"Jake Winston."

"Jake? Is calling *you*?"

"He wanted to talk about the upcoming press release, announcing the closure of the London office and find out how you were doing."

"I'm fine." I glare at her, still undone by the man, even now. "Why is he doing *that*? Checking up on me?"

"He's the executor of Evan's estate. He's handling the things that keep cropping up at Hamilton Equities. He's helping Christian with *everything*, so whether you like it or not, or much less appreciate his efforts, Jake's doing everything he can to help you. We all are." The stress of taking care of me for the past few months catches up to us both. "Do you have to be so fucking *difficult* on top of everything else?"

Only Kimberley would dare say this to me, although, I'm pretty sure, there are a few others, thinking it, about now. Remorse sets in.

"I'm sorry. You can tell him to stop sending the flowers, the cards." I wave a dismissive hand through the air.

Flower bouquets and note cards continue to arrive from Jake on a weekly basis. I spend an inordinate amount of my time, cutting the heads off these very flowers, and tossing them away with an unspeakable perverse sense of pleasure. I leave the note cards unopened, keep them tied up with a blue satin ribbon, and hide them in the farthest corner of my suitcase, like some buried treasure, I intend to read someday. A secret part of me enjoys collecting these repentant acts of kindness from him. It's as if I'm extracting a piece of his soul with each one.

Somewhere, deep down inside, my ego acknowledges the unbelievable pain—this mortal wound of some kind—in knowing the man *actually* turned me down. These profound thoughts of him, in that regard, distress me at inopportune moments. These are the astonishing secrets that I do not share with anyone else.

He turned me down. It's unbelievable. Unforgivable, surely.

"If he would just stop sending the flowers," I say. I glance over at the pile of beheaded roses, acknowledging the cruelty I've doled out on these innocent flowers that should be directed at *him*.

"Tell him yourself." Kimberley stops pacing and comes to stand in front of me with her hands on her hips, essentially blocking my view of the garden and forcing me to look at her.

"I'm not going to tell him," I practically shudder as I say this. "How will that sound? Ungrateful. Bitchy."

"Oh we wouldn't want that," Kimberley says. "But *not* taking his calls, or responding to his emails, or much less *thanking* him for the flowers and cards all looks *so much better*."

I take a deep breath and let it out slowly. "If he would just stop sending them, the flowers, I mean … I wouldn't have to *think* about calling to ask him to stop sending them."

"Is your dosage too high?"

I know she's teasing, but it sets me off.

"You're such a bitch, sometimes."

"So true. I have this best friend; she's a great teacher. And, I *don't mean* Steph."

I half-smile. Stephanie was the most beloved kindergarten teacher in Manhattan before she married Christian. Now, they're so busy jetting between New York and Paris to take care of Evan's company and me; Steph has taken a year's leave of absence from her school.

"Very funny. They make me loopy. You *know* that. I'm going to stop taking them. *I am.*"

"I know. I think, you're getting better. Absolutely."

"Absolutely." I sink further into the lounge chair and pull the blanket closer and scowl out at the chateau's rolling green landscape that just exudes false promises about happily-ever-after's and fairy tales.

"It's curious … the flowers, the cards. What aren't you telling me?" Kimberley asks.

I practically shudder, knowing my ability to withhold information from her is seriously waning. She settles into the lounge chair adjacent to mine, grabs part of the blanket for her own, studies my face, and just waits.

"Did something happen in Amagansett while I was in the city?"

I carry the shame and will myself to keep silent, but her clairvoyant nature outruns my ability to hide this latest indiscretion from her. She gets up from the lounge chair, walks over to the pile of beheaded roses, and picks up a few. Then, she turns back to me.

"Are these his flowers?"

"Yes."

"Did something happen with Jake?" She saunters over to the chair again and refolds part of the blanket in around her. "Tell me," she commands.

"We met up on the beach, running, the day after Christmas." I wave my hand across the landscape, like this will, somehow, fix everything. "He invited me to his place to go over Evan's estate, the paperwork, which we *did*."

I can feel Kimberley sizing me up. She scans my face, like a laser beam. I look away from her, trying to find additional courage in the decaying landscape. I glance at the growing pile of beheaded flowers; the dead flora hurls silent accusations my way. *Look what you did to us, Julia.*

"What happened?" Kimberley asks into the long silence.

"We had some wine. His place, it's amazing. Simple. I don't know. It was so peaceful, just being there. Welcoming." I steal a look over at Kimberley. "I don't know. It felt like L.A. with Bobby." This look of understanding comes over her face, and she nods. "And, well, if he wasn't so damn attractive, if I hadn't been feeling so amazingly empty inside, I wouldn't have kissed him and it wouldn't have led to almost seducing him, *again*. God, Kimmy what is wrong with me? Who acts like this? I was celibate, after Bobby's death for something like three years, and now, I can't keep my mouth off of Jake Winston's."

The heat rises in my face.

"It's *disturbing*, on so many levels." I shake my head side-to-side

136

and feel the bitterness overtake me. "Don't worry; he turned me down."
My eyes fill with tears as the visceral pain surfaces over Jake's rejection
of me.

Kimberley stares at me. "Holy shit," she finally says. "For what it's
worth, and I'm only going to say this, *once*, because *I know you,* probably better than you know yourself: you're not ready for this, for *him.*
Jake is too much, way too soon."

She looks so concerned I feel a little bit anxious for myself. "That's
what he said, something like that. He said he wanted it to *mean* something and I … God, I was so angry with him. I left, he called to apologize, and, I told him I never wanted to see him again, and hung up on
him. I've been furious with him." I hang my head in shame, not daring
to look over at Kimberley. Then, I hear her laugh.

"Julia, honey, I love you, but you take sex entirely too seriously, and
thank God, we know this about you. Try to let it go" she says gently.
"There might be something there with him, but right now, it's not
something you're ready for." She sighs. "Maybe, I should talk to him."

"No!"

"Fine." She gives me a withering look.

"Nobody's *talking* to him."

Then, she leans back in her lounge, and closes her eyes. "Fine," she
says again, but then, she gets this bemused look. "Although I *was* just
talking to him."

"You know what I mean."

She keeps her eyes closed and I'm left to contemplate my forever friend. Kimberley exemplifies her characteristic seductress self—
her perfect ivory skin glows, her enigmatic blue eyes mesmerize even
closed, and her long mahogany tresses she hasn't really cut, since I've
known her, just shimmer. Her finest features coalesce in an outward
beauty she shows to the world. So many get lost in her amazing good
looks; they miss the best part of her—this zest for life that is solely
hers. This unique brand of magic that is Kimberley is what I love the
most. I'm left to wonder where it comes from. God knows, I need it.

"Kimmy," I say with amazement. "Thanks."

"For what?"

She opens her eyes, looks at me, her lips part, and she smiles. *There
it is.*

"For everything. For being so fucking magical."

"Fucking magical is my specialty."

We both laugh at the double entendre. I feel this sense of relief, I haven't experienced in so long, come over me.

I start to consider, maybe, it is time to get my life back on track. This admission, alone, has me contemplating working with Kimberley, again, at the job, she's been talking to me about, with *Liaison*. A few years ago, before I met Evan and we had Reid, I worked with Kimberley at *Liaison,* on a part-time basis.

The truth is, I can't keep spending all my time with grief and guilt. I did this with Bobby, and discovered the best thing, in battling heartbreak, is to keep myself busy and attempt to carry on, by embracing all things normal, although a life in Paris makes this somewhat of a stretch. Lianne can take care of Reid, since I tend to overanalyze my mothering instincts at present. The truth is, I can't do it all, perhaps, really, none of it, well, right now. My mind needs to be occupied with something else, besides thinking of Evan all the time, second-guessing my parenting abilities with Reid, and experiencing all these wayward thoughts of Jake Winston. I toss away the white pills, without informing my doctors or Kimberley, survey my closet for something to wear, and tap my way into the kitchen on the fourth Monday morning in February, where I find my best friend sipping a café au lait. She gives me an uncertain look.

"Going somewhere?"

"Going with you. To the office."

"Are you sure?"

I give her a beseeching look. "I'm not sure about anything Kimmy, but I've got to get on with it."

Kimberley doesn't say anything. She just retrieves another coffee cup, prepares another café au lait, and hands it to me. So, I start working at *Liaison,* again.

Liaison was founded five years ago by David Merchant in Manhattan. The public relations firm fulfills a particular niche and maintains exclusive focus on executive positioning and overall image branding and consists of an elite clientele. As David and Kimberley are fond of saying, leave the branding of products and the marketing of a company to others. *Liaison* specializes in speech writing, philanthropy work, and the images of its key clients. Image is everything in a client's public and personal life. *Liaison* makes it their business to know about all of it. *Liaison's* exclusive and loyal clients both openly admire and vehemently defend them, above all others (clients' lawyers, executive staff, and their own corporate PR firms).

David offered Kimberley a job a few days after we arrived in New York from L.A., just three weeks after Bobby was killed in Afghanistan. Her public relations background with the Hollywood scene made her a perfect asset for *Liaison*. He'd enticed her with a mid-six-figure salary, a senior vice president title, and told her she would be worth every penny. While Kimberley, Stephanie, and I lived in Tribeca, I'd inadvertently been involved with *Liaison* working part-time on the speeches or some of the key message profiles for Kimberley and attended Columbia Law School, essentially trying to get over Bobby's death. I didn't mind being in the background for Kimberley. She'd paid me, generously, as an ad hoc employee. I didn't consider writing press releases and speeches and doing research, writing per se. It wasn't something my parents would have understood. There was nothing literary about it, but since, I was able to attend Columbia, it had all worked out.

With admiration, I watched Kimberley assume the lead publicist role to CEOs, actors, movie stars, entrepreneurs, financiers. Anyone who was anyone, in need of image remediation or makeover, or a change in direction, or perception, wanted to work with *Liaison* and become a superstar.

I'd never seen Kimberley more dedicated to a boss than David Merchant. Now, working together for the past three years, David, the deal-maker, and Kimberley, the ultimate relationship manager, the two of them have become a formidable duo of public persona for the elite. The combination, of David's impeccable image and reputation along with the acumen of one Kimberley Powers, a dynamic woman, whose mind works like a think tank of a dozen men where she possesses an absolute deadly charm that could lure anyone, anywhere, anytime, is powerful, indeed.

With Kimberley's hiring, *Liaison* went from annual billings of ten million to thirty million within the first two years. *Liaison* exceeded fifty-five million with the opening of the Paris location, when Kimberley made partner.

I'd been enjoying her success and vicariously living through it, while trying to get over the loss of Bobby. Kimberley was the wind in my sail that kept me going. Then, in a magical whirlwind, I'd met and married Evan. We had Reid. We'd spent the last year building our life together, finding our way, while Kimberley got promoted and set up the Paris office. Then, my life descended into one of endless chaos in a single instant, just when I'd begun to let myself almost believe in the magic, again.

<hr />

"You look fantastic," Kimberley says to me, during my second week back.

I look down at my outfit and glance up at her. "Oh," I say in surprise. "I didn't really pay any attention to what I put on. It was the first thing in the closet. I'm just lucky my shoes match."

Kimberley smiles at me and I try to return it.

"We're having lunch with Christian. You up for it?"

Christian's company, Chavarria Equities, is *Liaison's* biggest client in Paris, and the main reason for opening the office, here. Christian runs a formidable hedge fund, just like Evan's. He and Steph hired *Liaison* to enhance the company's branding image and streamline the charity work they are both involved in.

"Sure. What's the agenda?"

"He wants to talk about the media plan. Give you an update on Hamilton Equities." I look over at her; doubtful. "Don't panic. It's just an update. He's not pressing you for any decisions." She gives me a speculative look. "Alexandre might be there."

I hold my breath for a moment in order to regain my equilibrium. It was bound to happen, running into Alexandre Chantal was only a matter of time. I have a brief history with Christian's older brother, Alexandre, from a few years ago. We went out for a brief time. It'd been three years, since Bobby was killed, and the oldest Chantal brother proved to be a nice distraction, that is, until I learned he was still in the process of getting divorced, but still married.

"I've met with the team. I can handle talking about the media plan," I say. "You'll have to handle everyone else." I give her a meaningful look.

"Deal." She sighs. "It's not like you weren't going to see him, someday. He'll be in the wedding." Kimberley practically shudders, when she says this last word.

I look at her more closely. She looks a little stressed out today, not her normal effervescent, fully-put-together self. "You okay?"

"I'm fine," Kimberley says with a dismissive wave of her hand. "Absolutely." She gives me the we-are-so-not-going-to-talk-about-this look. "Come on. Let's go over the plan."

A plan. Do we have one for my life, too?

Chapter

Thirteen

Handwritten notes

I'M REACHING FOR MY LIFE, ATTEMPTING to find my way back to it. Jake Winston and I begin this strange correspondence. I send him a handwritten thank you note for every flower arrangement that arrives each week. After my revelation to Kimberley, my anger dissipated, and I'd finally written to him in early March, stating: *I'll stop sending notes, when you stop sending flowers, Mr. Winston.* This seemed to only encourage him further, and all I can do is shake my head and laugh, when another exotic flower arrangement arrives, more beautiful than the last, which I no longer behead, along with a thoughtful note, which I've begun to read. He must be consulting his own book on Shakespeare.

I start running on a regular basis. It's always calms me down and it's working now. Grief loosens its grip. I experience more good days than bad. *Liaison* keeps my mind occupied, while Reid has the rest of me. His adoration for me repairs my broken heart, mirroring Evan's grey-blue gaze, Reid tracks me from across a room wherever I go, displaying his toothy nine-month-old grin my way all the time. Serving as his special planet, I bask in his continuous glow, my own personal sun lights my way.

On a Friday afternoon in the middle of March, Reid and I make our way to Stephanie and Christian's. Kimberley left early yesterday with Gregoire for Nice, to spend a long weekend with the Chantal family, and firm up their August wedding plans. With Kimberley out of town, Stephanie insisted that Reid and I come and stay with them.

I nose the car onto the long drive, leading up to Christian and Stephanie's old worldly chateau. Tall firs line each side, a welcoming ribbon that seems to indicate: this way, this way, Julia. I pull the car into the Chantal's circular drive, next to the enchanting lion statue spewing water down below into a beautifully carved stone fountain. It's like stepping into a fairytale. And, I just might be Alice, in Wonderland, lost and unsure of where I'm supposed to be.

This fantastic chateau was once a working vineyard that produced vintage champagne. Stephanie and Christian have been concentrating all their efforts into its transformation, to bring it to its former grandeur, after years of neglect by the previous owners. They've updated the interior and have been planting, trimming and reestablishing the gardens and outside grounds. It's Stephanie's personal wonderland. My hostess waves from the garden with sprigs of fresh-cut flowers and flora in her hands. I smile, when I see this. She's in her element with her wide brimmed straw hat that's tied around her fine blonde head. She raises her soiled garden gloves in my direction, evidence she's been digging in the dirt and tending to and cutting flowers.

She has it all figured out. Envy surges inside.

"Just go on in. I'll be right there," Steph calls out.

I carry Reid in his car seat into the spacious living room, set him down, and traipse back to the car to unload our stuff.

"Moving In?" Steph grins over at me, while lifting another suitcase from the trunk.

"Looks like it. I think we accumulate more stuff every day. Just so you know, three-fourths of this stuff belongs to Reid."

Christian should be home in an hour. He's bringing a surprise."

"A surprise," I say. "Like what kind of surprise?"

"I don't know. He wouldn't say."

I follow her inside, and we set up the portable crib for Reid in the guest suite, near the window, where just outside, Stephanie's planted an early spring garden of purple, yellow, and white crocus already in bloom. I mill about the room, appreciating its charm: the old-fashioned French Country chic with an elegant queen bed covered with the blue and white quilt to match, the headboard of polished burl wood, and a blue flowered porcelain wash bowl that Stephanie's placed on the dark wood dresser. The intricate white lace curtains at the window filter sunlight and cast lacy shadows on the pale blue walls, just adding to the magical feeling the room must impart to every guest that stays here.

The tranquility of this place is taking me in, filling my empty soul with a peace I haven't felt in a long while. The Chantals' transformation of this chateau is admirable. They've kept its distinctive old world charm and only added to its refinement with chic understated comfort.

This isn't a showcase home; it's a lived-in one, filled with love and charm and all the good things about life. Stephanie's warm touches are everywhere, from the freshly cut flowers and hand-blown glass vases in every room, to the latest photographs of all of us, displayed in antique silver photo frames throughout. *A home.*

Stephanie pulls me along on a grand tour to show me what they've done, since I was here, last, weeks before. All the while, I'm missing Evan and thinking too much about what could have been. *Evan, where are you?*

"I love what you two have done to this place. It's so charming. I'm envious."

"Thanks. It's home." She comes over to me and hugs me. "I'm trying to convince Christian to make this our permanent one, live here full-time, and give up the apartment in Manhattan, start our family. But, well, it's complicated. There's so much going on since…"

A shadow crosses her face. *Evan.* His loss affects us all.

I nod. "Love you, Steph."

A half hour later, we've baby-proofed the living room, and set Reid free to explore. Then, we make our way to the kitchen to work on dinner: toss a salad, whisk vinaigrette dressing, frost a chocolate cake, check on the roasted chicken, and finish plating the appetizers.

Well, I do these things, while Steph looks on, in that, sometimes, helpless way of hers, in awe and appreciation at my culinary skills.

"I miss this," Stephanie says with a wistful look.

"You and Kimmy, both," I say with a grin. "Do you starve? Now, that you don't live with me?"

"Almost. I warned Christian about it right away, but he doesn't seem to mind." She blushes. "He's ecstatic, you're going to be here, all weekend. It's been weeks, since he's had a meal of sustenance." She rolls her eyes and laughs.

"He's tired of soup, bread, and tea?" These are the three things Stephanie can heat up, toast, or steep. "I don't think so," I say shaking my head. "I think you could serve him a spoonful of uncooked rice, and he'd eat it, because you were the one feeding it to him. The man adores you. Cooking isn't everything." Happy memories of our time together in L.A. and New York flood my mind, then the loss of both Bobby and Evan takes over; I struggle to hide my heartbreak. "Hey, with Reid, it's harder to get anything done."

"You okay?"

"I miss my life, Steph. I wish I knew where it was." She gets this worried look. "I'm better though," I say. "Don't worry so much."

"I just want you to be happy."

"Let's not get ahead of ourselves." I swipe the frosting from a bowl with my finger and lick it off. "I have Reid, you and Christian, Kimmy and Gregoire. What more do I need?"

Stephanie clinks her wine glass to mine and follows me to the living room. We discover Reid has rolled his way over to the French doors that lead out to the patio, but now, he's stuck, and working himself up into a big cry. Stephanie picks him up and holds him close, kissing the top of his head, where his gold hair swirls like the curl of an ice cream cone. She sniffs his hair, getting a fix from his sweet baby powder scent, just like I do. "God, how do you stand it? He's so wonderful and amazing. I don't think I could ever put him down."

"Oh you would, when he's screaming in the middle of night and you can't figure out what's wrong, or he's teething and inconsolable, or spits up formula on your favorite silk blouse, or pulls your gold chain from your neck and breaks it with one chubby-handed swipe." I laugh. "Those are the times when you want to put him down, but you always want to pick him back up, too. He's the best thing that ever happened to me. The best thing Evan and I ever did together."

Steph hands him over with one last kiss. "He's amazing, just like you, Jules." She hesitates. "He looks, just like him."

"I know." I try to hide the pain and joy that comes in seeing that in Reid every day. "I'm going to feed him and see if I can get him down. Just watch the timer. I'll be back in fifteen. We're all set."

Stephanie gets this vexed look.

"You'll be fine. I'll be right back." I falter, lost in a moment, in saying Evan's last words to me.

I change Reid into pajamas and feed him his nighttime bottle. Together, we rock in the old-fashioned wooden rocker, near the bedroom window, where I stare out at Steph's garden, and absently hum a little tune, while Reid plays with my fingers. He gives me a milky grin, when he finishes, but is still wide awake. I kiss each side of his face and he grabs fistfuls of my hair.

Muted sounds invade, as I hear an approaching car come to a stop, and then, two car doors opening and closing, one after the other, signaling a fourth guest for dinner. I catch my lower lip between my teeth, feeling sudden disquiet with the idea of someone else invading this safe haven.

A few minutes later, I saunter into the living room with Reid in my arms and grin over at Christian, who is busy pouring brandy into four snifters.

"Well, he's wide awake, so I guess he needs to see his Uncle Christian, first," I say.

"Bonjour, Julia," Christian says easily. He sets down his glass, comes over, and takes Reid from my arms. In the next minute, he holds my baby up in mi-air. Reid giggles. "Bonjour, la petite enfant, Reid. Comme ca va?"

"*English,* Christian. How's he going to learn English, if you only speak French to him?"

"It's only right that his first word should be a French one," Christian says with a laugh. He looks past me. "Jake, what do you think?"

I turn and find myself face-to-face with Jake Winston, who stands in the kitchen doorway right behind me. My pulse soars like a rocket taking off.

"I think he should learn English, Christian."

His lips twitch with a hint of a smile. He exudes this amazing sex appeal, all over again, with his rolled-up white dress shirt sleeves, revealing his tanned forearms of golden brown hair, as if he's spent time in the sun. The persona of James Bond is back. Only this time, I'm not stoned out of my mind, overindulging in painkillers, martinis, margaritas, or wine, or singing *Landslide* or Christmas carols, or taking little white pills to battle grief, or even inappropriately draped in his arms at his place in Amagansett.

"Hello, Jake." A formal greeting. I sound like I've just stepped out of a Jane Austen novel.

He looks confident, as he extends his hand, and I shake it with a practiced firm handshake. We act, as if, we're doing a job interview with one another.

"Julia, you look…" The man seems intent on getting the word just right. "Fantastic." His blue-eyed gaze takes in my skinny black jeans, the low-cut blue blouse, and my black stilettos.

I boldly return his gaze. *Steady now.*

"How are you?" Jake asks.

"I'm doing fine. Absolutely fine," I say.

"So, this is the surprise," Stephanie says with a nervous laugh. She gives me the are-you-okay? look, as Jake walks over to the bar and picks up one of the brandies Christian's poured.

Christian looks over, he's been playing with Reid on the Persian rug, completely oblivious to the rising tension in the room, between his best friend and me.

"Jake flew in from London. He's going to stay the weekend, so we can start working on the quarterly report for Hamilton Equities."

And I should know this. I'm only the God-damn chairman of the company.

"Great. Absolutely great," I say with a practiced smile.

Steph pulls me into the kitchen with her as I use the code word, with the excuse of checking on dinner one last time, which is probably a good idea, since I'm chef for the evening. "I didn't know he was coming," she says with a groan. "Christian should've warned us."

"Not sure that would have helped. I'm fine. Really. Absolutely." Steph looks uneasy. "Sorry. That word just tumbles out at the sight of him."

"Absolutely," Steph says with a laugh. "God, it's hard to concentrate without just outright staring at him the whole night."

"Watch it, Mrs. Chantal. You're married."

"Absolutely." We both start to laugh.

During dinner, the three of them ensue in back and forth banter about the nuances of Paris, London, and New York City, while I remain caught up in an inescapable flood of anxiety. I'm out of sorts, undone by the man, because seeing him again brings back all these intoxicating sensations I shouldn't be feeling. Vivid memories come alive, the ones I harbor, in kissing him, almost kissing him, not kissing him, and just shaking his hand. I fight this raw hunger, this craving, in desiring to be unhinged and unchained from grief's shackles, for a while, to languish in the freedom of just feeling alive, for a few minutes, just one more time.

It seems we're at opposite ends of the emotional spectrum, this evening. While I'm all but drowning in this inner raging current of want and need, he's the stillness, that is water, and appears unbelievably tranquil. My covert observation of him asserts, he seems different, in a good way. Perhaps, he's more at ease because he's not fighting with Savannah Bennett on a cell phone about the cancellation of their wedding, or being seduced by the likes of me at his beach house. This last thought causes a new round of pandemonium to roil away inside of me.

Stop thinking about him. Stop staring at him. Just stop, Julia.

His southern drawl charms me, once again. I still the compulsion to put my hands over my ears, to keep from hearing it, so I can quell this reverberating sensation inside of me that responds in just hearing his voice again. *What is wrong with me?* His accent becomes even more pronounced, as he describes the things he likes about London.

Later, I attempt to converse with Stephanie about *Liaison* and give her the rundown on some of the clients I've been working with since my return, while Christian and Jake have a side conversation about the best places to ski in Europe. And, I'm trying to hang on to his every word like a school girl with her first crush.

"Kimberley wants me to think about running the team for Christian's account," I say to Stephanie. "Take a promotion and everything. VP Client Relations."

"That sounds great," Stephanie says. "But, is that what you want to do?"

"That's just it. I don't know what I want. Do I put roots down here, in Paris, or not?"

The two men have grown quiet. My conversation with Steph has been overheard.

"Is Paris the best life for Reid?" I ask in the ensuing silence.

"Is that what you want? A life in Paris? For the long-term?" Jake asks.

I look over at him, disconcerted by his dubious tone. Somehow, my son has made his way around the table to Jake. He holds Reid in one arm, while he tries to eat with the other.

"I don't know what I want." I sound defensive, even to myself.

Stephanie makes a point of clearing the dishes, attempting to compensate for my untimely outburst.

"I'm going to try and get him to go down. Excuse me," I say, leaning over to retrieve Reid from Jake's arms. I experience that damn electrical current, a jolt to my system, when I accidentally brush up against his hands, as I take my baby from him.

<hr />

Me. Overexcited by Jake, again, without reason.

Stop this Julia. You shouldn't be feeling this way, thinking about him.

Remorse, guilt, and shame march in; grief makes room for all three. I've assumed a heavy burden, while just making my way from the kitchen to the guest bedroom with Reid and his nighttime bottle.

A half hour later, I'm watching Reid as he drifts to sleep. I take my time, attempting to compose myself and overcome these feelings of vulnerability and confusion about Jake Winston. I'm self-conscious in his presence and all that's transpired between us. I try to reconcile the past with my present and can only wonder why this virtual stranger wreaks havoc on me, every time, I see him. I reach out and touch my sleeping baby's outstretched hand, so still, so tranquil. I close my eyes. *Evan, where are you?*

Footsteps come down the hall.

"Is he asleep?" Jake drawls, from right behind me.

"Yes." I open my eyes, kiss my index finger, and lay it across the bridge of Reid's nose. "Night, baby," I whisper. Without looking at Jake, I slip past him into the hallway.

"I like that kissing finger thing you do with him," he says from behind me.

I turn back to him, wary now, and look at him, quizzically. *Do you, now? Would you like me to do it to you, too?* I start to smile at this notion, and catch myself. "Uh-huh," I say.

"You really look great."

Don't be nice to me. I'm undone by you, stung by your rejection of me last time, and this whole tormenting thing that you do to me. "Thank you."

"I just. I just wanted to say—"

"Seriously? You're going to apologize again? Jake, *please.*" I touch his forearm and his warmth blazes beneath my hand. "I'm sorry. You're sorry. It was just strange circumstances, a very sad time, that played itself out in a very weird way. That's it."

"And, at Christmas? At my place?" Jake asks. "What was that?" He covers my hand with his, keeping me there.

"I don't know what that was," I say, not quite successful at keeping the dejection out of my voice.

His rejection from our last meeting cascades through me. My ego seems to hiss from deep inside: *don't forgive him.* I start to pull my hand away, but he holds on tighter.

"I'm sorry," he says. "Do you forgive me? Because I hear you've been cutting off all the heads of my flowers."

Christian.

"I've been nicer to your most recent bouquets. I've even read your most recent notes. It's not … it's unnecessary," I say with an airy wave of my free hand.

"So, no more flowers. Is that what you're saying?"

"I believe, I've said no more flowers, for some time now. Lovely though, loved the cards and notes, the flowers, but no more, okay?"

He studies my face. "Okay, but I've gotten so used to your recent thank you notes." His lips curve up slowly into this deadly charm smile he does so well, while his blue eyes just draw me.

Don't do this to me.

"You're so unbelievably polite and charming in the handwritten form," he says.

"Not so much in person," I say.

"No, you're incredible in person, too, but there's just something about your handwritten notes, I really enjoy. I can keep them forever and read them, over and over." He smiles again, but looks less sure of himself, as if he's taken this line of conversation, too far, revealing a completely different persona from the self-assured one he displayed at dinner.

"I'll get you a lock box to keep them in, with a key and everything."

Now, he looks as uncertain, as I suddenly feel. He swallows, while I just try to hold my ground, watching him, and sensing this strange power I hold over him, for once. "You look really great," he says, after long pause. "You're in a better place."

"A better place. The chateau's very nice." He's thrown off balance by my banter and gets this pained look. "Yes. I'm in a better place. Thank you." I'm getting more undone in being this close to him, again, in another place that is quickly becoming as intimate as his place was, in Amagansett, months before. "I … you didn't see me on my best day, any of those days, I guess. I'm sorry about that."

"I see you, clearly, every day."

"Every day? You've only seen me three times, before, Mr. Winston."

He looks uneasy. I start to laugh at his discomfort and my own, attempting to undo the tension. He slowly smiles.

"I'm changing my mind about the notes versus seeing you in person," he says.

We're right back to the day after Christmas. We both take unsteady breaths and stir each other's hair with this close proximity.

"Okay. Quit, while you're ahead," I say, feeling the unease.

This encounter is getting away from us, as the tipping point of vulnerability emerges. This has to stop, whatever, this is. I go with a reliable defense strategy that puts effective distance in so many relationships.

"Friends?" I ask with a bright smile. I extend my right hand.

"Friends?"

Jake seems momentarily taken aback by my suggestion. But in the next, he lifts my hand to his mouth, and brushes it with his lips.

The breathtaking sensation of being undone surges through me, as if he's flipped on a switch. I'm left without words. My lips part, but nothing comes out. *Why is he doing this to me?*

"Friends," I finally say, pulling my hand back.

"Maybe, it would be better, if you were pissed at me."

My bravado comes out of nowhere. "Who says, I'm not?"

"I'd know," he says, taking my hand in his, again. His ego bolsters him, within seconds, as his beautiful mouth spreads into a supremely confident smile.

"Would you? Are you absolutely sure?" I wield my power over him, like a sword, and slice right through his self-assurance, and now, he looks uneasy. Apparently, it matters, if I'm pissed at him. "I'll have to work on that," I say, affecting a charming smile.

I pull my hand back, move away from him, mostly intact, and walk away.

CHAPTER

FOURTEEN

These complications

SUNDAY. THE DAWN IMPLIES THE PROMISE of spring, a per-fect-weather day. Stephanie is up early and volunteers to watch Reid, while I plan to take a quick run around the chateau grounds, by myself and out of the vicinity of one Mr. Jacob Winston. I stretch out on the back patio, for a few minutes, and then, bend down to rework my shoe laces before setting off.

"Running again?"

I whirl around. There's Jake, sauntering toward me in a black jog-ging outfit, similar to mine, looking his usual breathtaking self.

Don't do this to me. You're supposed to be showering, breakfasting, and working on that damn quarterly report with Christian.

"Running relaxes me." I gather my hair into a ponytail and secure it with a red band. And, all the while, he watches. My heart races and I try to slow it down by taking deep steady breaths.

"And, you need to relax," he says with a teasing laugh. "Mind, if I tag along?" He's already begun stretching his quads, then moves on to his hamstrings.

"No," I say with a faint smile after a minute.

Yes. Jake's presence has been causing me emotional turmoil, since his arrival Friday night. I'm completely exhausted, not having slept well, two nights in a row. Just knowing he sleeps in the guest room across from me, causes my body and my emotions endless turmoil that goes up and down, like a roller coaster, as I experience all the extreme highs of adrenalin's rush and the inevitable lows that always accompanies utter fear. It's true; I might be incapable of coherent thought, ever again, because of *him*.

I've already packed my bags and Reid's things in the car, anxious to make my escape by lunchtime, although Stephanie will probably insist I stay, until Kimberley returns later this evening. Since arriving in Paris, I've been passed around like a child, peddled from one caregiver to the next. And, now, here's Jake in the middle of it all, wreaking additional havoc on me down to my very soul.

"How far do you want to go?" I ask. "I usually do four miles."

"I can handle it." His confidence reigns supreme. I just shake my head and do a few more stretches. "Ready?" Jake asks, and then, he takes off running.

Fine. Let's see what you've got. I press hard to catch up, then pass him after a few minutes, and keep going. He pushes himself to keep up at this too fast pace I'm adhering to, but after a couple of miles, he's fallen back behind me. I hear him groan, eventually turn, and discover he's stopped running. With a sigh, I retrace my steps and run back to him.

"Are you going to be like this the whole time?" He's doubled-over, clutching his sides, trying to catch his breath.

"Like what?" I press my lips together to keep from laughing.

"You know, bitchy. Ignoring me half the time. Maybe, you're PMSing or something?"

"Do you talk to all women like this? It's very … fetching," I finally say.

Fetching? Who uses the word fetching, anymore? What is wrong with me? Jake laughs at my word choice. I drop my head in embarrassment, but eventually laugh, too, and try to catch my breath.

"You're as bad as Savannah."

My laughter stops abruptly. "Savannah, huh? Really?"

I glare at him in irritation, turn back, and start running in the direction of Christian and Stephanie's chateau at an even faster pace, not bothering to wait for him. Equal doses of fury, jealousy, and misery come out of nowhere, at his mention of Savannah. Acknowledging I shouldn't be feeling any of these things, guilt attacks me from the other side.

"Julia. What's wrong?" Jake calls out.

"Nothing. I'm fine." I'm pulled to a sudden stop by him as he catches up to me.

"What did I do?"

"Nothing." I start to walk away, but he grabs me by the shoulders and turns me around to face him. I avoid looking directly at him.

"Well, it's obviously something."

I step out of his grasp, and start to draw circles in the dirt path with the toe of my running shoe, and attempt to get a handle on my emotions. He doesn't say anything, he just waits. When I look up, he has this bewildered look on his face, only a guy can convey, the innocent what-could-I-have-possibly-done expression, which covers a multitude of sins. It pisses me off, even more.

"I don't want to have a conversation, where we're discussing the merits of how I handle PMS, in comparison, to your girlfriend, fiancée, or whatever the hell she is to you." I look over at him, uncertain, exposed. *There you go, deal with that, Mr. Charm.*

The minutes go by.

Understanding must filter through to him because he begins to look uneasy. And I wait, like a fool, for reassurance he's not involved with Savannah anymore.

I'm ready. Say it. Because suddenly I need to know.

"Things … are complicated, right now." He gets this despondent look, runs his hand through his hair, and looks away from me. "For all of us."

"Things are complicated for *you?* Don't include me in your fine little, *all of us* assessment. You don't even know what complicated means." I start off down the path again.

He catches up to me and retains a firm grip on my arm this time.

"I'm supposed to do the right thing," he says. "But, I don't want to."

His uneven breathing stirs my hair and I can't look away from his face, awestruck by his amazing good looks and the intensity I see in his eyes. A memory stirs.

"Don't you want to know *why?*" Jake asks.

"Don't do this to me. No! I don't want to know why." I pull out of his tightening grasp.

"Julia, I know it's too soon." He gets this anguished look.

"And, it's complicated, but I want to say—"

"Complicated? Too soon? To say what? There's nothing to say. You're just an employee of Evan's company, my lawyer, and I'm just your client. You said so yourself, months ago."

His rejection of me from our last encounter vehemently races to the surface. A mixture of pain and wrath take over.

"Nothing more." I draw my hand across the horizon, like a Blackjack player indicates *stand down*.

"I'm just an employee." His eyes glint with anger. I step further back from him, when I see it. "You're right. You're the chairman of Evan's company, and I work for *you*," he says with a harsh laugh.

"You know what I mean," I say, undone by his anger. "I shouldn't have put it quite like that, but we have our roles to play, responsibilities. That's it." I do the *stand down* thing again.

He starts pacing. "I don't see you acting like the chairman. So, exactly, what role are you going for? Seductive widow, maybe? And *save it*, I'm aware you've been seeing Alexandre Chantal."

"What?" I ask, incredulous. "Seeing him? What?"

Christian probably mentioned the lunch meeting a few weeks ago to Jake. But why does he care?

"We're friends," I say. "We had coffee together and met with Kimberley about doing PR for his family's firm."

"Right," Jake says, shaking his head side-to-side. "I handle all the dealings with Hamilton Equities and you'll handle Alexandre Chantal. That's how it works? And, you're too busy gallivanting around Paris and working on some PR cause to pay any attention to what's really important, like being the Chairman of Hamilton Equities or the settling of Evan's estate—your future and Reid's. Just send me the money, when you're done, Jake. I'm working day and night to make it all work out for you, and you could give a shit. Right, Julia? You just said it yourself. I'm just the hired help. I *work* for you."

"He's just a friend," I say, on edge, all at once.

"He's *married*."

"We're friends. Yes, he's been getting a divorce from Eveline for two years, but he never does." I start to laugh, and Jake looks even more enraged. "Okay, we knew each other, a few summers ago. After Bobby. That's when Steph met Christian, Kimberley met Gregoire and I—"

"How nice you three were all paired off with a Chantal brother."

"We saw each other for a while, a few years ago, but then, I found out about Eveline and ended it." I look at Jake with defiance and watch this jealous rage cross his features. "He doesn't *see* me. He never did."

"Why should he see you, when you don't see anyone else? God, you're amazing. Evan's been dead, less than four months, and you're lining up your next conquest."

"It's not like that. I've seen him twice, since I've been here. We're just friends."

"Friends? Like we're just friends? Because what was happening at my place in Amagansett was not about being *friends*."

I recoil from him, when he says this, experiencing uncontrollable guilt and rage at the same time. "You turned me down." My accusation cuts across both of us. "You said you wanted it to *mean* something, but I was Evan's wife and he was your best friend." The words drip like acid. They sting, sear, and inflict incredible pain, and lasting damage upon both of us.

"You weren't ready, neither was I," he says with a heavy sigh.

"What? Are you making up your mind for both of us, now?"

"No," he says with uncertainty.

His obvious distress and sadness reach for me. I seem to splinter inside, all at once, as the heartbreak radiates outward from me. "You turned me down. What? Do you care about me, now? Make up your mind, Jake." My taunting surprises him and myself.

He doesn't say anything for a few minutes. He just looks at me with this haunted expression, and then, a parade of emotions crosses his face: remorse, anguish, frustration.

"God, you drive me insane," he finally says.

"Likewise." I succumb to insidious fury. It burns its way through me. "I didn't ask you to work day and night on my behalf. I didn't ask for any of this. But here you are, judging me, my life, and the way I'm handling things, when you don't even *know* me. And, you turned me down, so don't criticize me, because I'm moving on with it!"

My eyes begin to sting. *Don't cry. There are no spectacular feelings left, in being around him, today.* I stomp away from him, but he grabs my arm and pulls me back.

"I turned you down for all the right reasons. And, I do know you,

Julia. I do. I know you better than you know yourself." Then, he looks at me with this pleading look. "But, when are you going to really see me?"

"What? What are you talking about? I see you, you're standing, right here."

"You don't even know who I am." His anger flashes like a blinding light. I hold up my hand to shield myself from its intensity. "I don't even know why I came here. I had a life. I moved on. And yet, here you are, standing here, telling me I'm just an employee, just your lawyer, you're just my client. Look at me, Julia. For once in your life, just look at me. If you could just see me, if you would trust me, this could all be different."

"*Trust* you? Trust you? I don't even trust myself. I can't even see myself. I'm broken, Jake. Why can't you see that? I don't want to ever feel heartbreak again. I don't want to be close to anyone. This thing, whatever the hell it is that keeps happening between us, needs to end. I'm too broken to start over. I can't do it."

I start down the path again, determined to outrun him and whatever this is between us. Soon enough, he catches up to me.

"Julia," he drawls in that tantalizing accent of his.

Resolute, I shake off his tight hold on me and back away from him. "What do you want from me, Jake? I've got nothing left to give or be for you, for anyone." I blink back tears in frustration and wipe at my face with the back of my hand.

"I'm sorry. I didn't mean to upset you." He gets this pained expression. "It's just … there's a lot going on. Everywhere I turn, it's fucking complicated, okay? And, you're going to have to step up. Christian can't run the company forever. The clients are getting more and more anxious over Evan's death. With the market downturn, we're just trying to keep it all running. *For you.* You can't hide out in Paris, forever, Mrs. Hamilton. You're the chairman."

I'm stung by his words. *This is all about the business to him.*

Disillusionment overtakes me. The anger just drains away. I lean against a tree along the path and sink to the ground, feeling defenseless and undone. I close my eyes, trying to find balance, equilibrium of some kind.

"I just wanted to be lost for a while, so I didn't have to run into anyone that knew my story, or knew Evan."

I open my eyes. Jake towers above me, breathing unsteady, just watching me. Eventually, he slides down the tree, sitting down next to me, our thighs practically touching.

"I just wanted to be lost," I say again. "That's all. Just lost. But, the inner circle always finds me. If it's not Kimberley, it's Steph. Both of them propping me up, telling me everything is going to be okay. But, it's not." I pause and try to catch my breath. "Evan's dead and no matter what anyone does or says … he's not ever coming back. It's just like Bobby, all over again." I look over at him, trying to make him understand. "Sure, things are complicated, but who cares? Why does it even matter?" I brush back a tear and try to control the pain making its way to the surface again. "I'm barely holding it together. I have nothing left, but … Reid. I'm alone, lonely."

I stop talking and look away from him, cajoling myself to keep it together, but the anger surges inside for all of it, and I aim it directly at him.

"I'm sorry running a damn hedge fund wasn't on my list of things I wanted to accomplish in life, neither was working at a PR firm, or being a widow at twenty seven and raising a child by myself, but apparently life isn't about getting what we want or even what we need." I shake my head side-to-side overcome with desolation.

"Running a hedge fund wasn't on my list of life wants, either," he says. "I just wanted to be an attorney in a small town, get married, have a family, and a reasonable life. But, I guess I don't get to do that, either."

This conversation just got very dangerous. I can see it ignite in him as much as myself.

I get up and step back away from him. I give in to this prevailing need to hurt him, in some way, as if his feeling my pain will, somehow, take it away from me.

"Let's stay away from the Hallmark stuff, shall we? I get enough of it with my counseling sessions. Go back to London or New York or wherever it is you're going to be, Jake. Just let me know, so I can be someplace else."

I race down the path in search of the safety of the chateau, where Stephanie and Christian and Reid await me. I can hear him running up from behind me. Soon, his arms come around my waist and pull me to a hard stop.

"Julia," he says in anguish.

I can barely breathe because of the tight hold he has on me and the way he's just said my name. With willful determination, I free myself from his arms, but then, he bestows me with that unique expression of his, the one that can mend broken souls, maybe, even mine, and would melt ice cream if it were within twenty-five feet of him, right now. *Oh God.*

"I'm sorry," he says. "There are just some things you're going to have to be involved in." He grabs hold of my hand. "I had to make the decision to close London, decisions you should be making."

"I thought you wanted to be in London," I say in confusion. *Why are we talking about London?* "That's why I held off on that decision." I lift my head, defiant now. "See? I do pay attention, sometimes."

"The reason for going to London doesn't exist anymore. I'm going home to New York." He looks like he has more to say, but he hesitates and studies me. "What are you going to do?"

I sense this expectation in him, as if his destiny depended upon how I answer, but I'm angry with him, again, because of what happened in Amagansett between us, because his problems seem so much simpler than mine, and because he's never said where his relationship with Savannah Bennett really stands, and yet, he's kissing my hand in hallways and generally wielding chaos throughout all of me, whenever we're together. I pull my hand from his.

"I don't know if you've noticed, but my life has all but fallen apart. I'm just trying to keep it together on a day-by-day basis."

He stares at me with this renewed intensity. For a moment, I lose myself in his blue-eyed gaze, turquoise today. I'm momentarily caught up in the spectacular moments of kissing him in Amagansett and when I look at him, I know he's remembering the same thing. He reaches for me and begins stroking my jaw line with his exquisite fingers. I've missed what he's said. "What?"

"Come home. Come back to New York, to Amagansett," he drawls.

I pull out of his embrace, recalling his rejection of me last time, and wield all the pain that I still carry at him now.

"No. There's nothing for me there."

His anger reaches me from all sides. "Right," he says with a bitter laugh. "You do what you want. You're the boss. I'm just the hired help.

Thanks for reminding me, Mrs. Hamilton."

Jake takes off running and I just watch him go, assailed by this powerful sense of loss at his leaving.

CHAPTER

FIFTEEN

Living in a room without oxygen

I PULL THE SEDAN INTO THE PARKING garage of *Liaison's* Paris office and make a conscious choice to sit in the car, for a few minutes, and revel in the absolute stillness. The utter absence of human contact soothes me. Reid is with Lianne for the day, so my mommy duties are taken care of. Kimberley is already here at the office, so she's off-duty from her mommy duties in taking care of me. And, I'm alone.

On a subconscious level, I acknowledge this is the start of my fifth week back at *Liaison*. And, on a more conscious and very grateful level, I breathe a deep sigh of relief because Jacob Winston is now safely ensconced back in London and will be on an airplane to New York, within hours. Like a general from World War II plotting points on a map using tiny colored stick pins, I'm making it a priority to know exactly where he is, at all times now, so I can ensure I am somewhere else.

For the first time in four days, I can actually breathe. I gulp at the air. His physical presence, where he dropped back into my life, has ended. I luxuriate in the relief this brings and disregard the tidal wave of remorse, swirling its way toward me because of the fireworks displayed by both of us, just yesterday. Last evening, Jake left for the airport with Christian for his flight to London without saying good-bye, without saying another word to me; and, I let him go.

I lean back against the headrest, close my eyes, and allow myself to wallow in the one continual persistent thought that pervades my system: How does everything go from being almost perfect in my life to *this*? Now, there's just this vast emptiness, this nothingness, not even Reid can fill for me, this day. *Evan, where are you?*

After another ten minutes, where I indulge in the absolution of incredible silence and reflect upon Evan uninterrupted, I start the mental rundown of all the things I have to do today. There's the team meeting to go over the week's assignments and client updates. I need to talk to Kimberley. I have to check email. I should call Jake and apologize. Check email. I can't put it off any longer. I have to check email. Talk to Kimberley. I should call Jake and apologize.

If I say these things often enough, will I actually do any of them? Besides, talk to Kimberley? Probably not, but this last wayward thought is enough to compel me to get out of the car, propel me into the garage elevator up to the lobby and onto the floor elevator that whisks me up to the top floor of *Liaison's* Paris office.

I'm a living miracle and I'm almost smiling. I greet all the staff with "Bonjour" and make my way to one of the corner offices. Vice President Client Relations is handwritten on a post-it note in Kimberley's familiar script. The note, this sticky reminder on the glass door to my office, welcomes me. I guess Kimberley has made that decision for me, and I breathe a sigh of relief for having one less decision to make.

It's Monday, the day after Sunday, the day after the latest fireworks with Jake. I struggle to put one foot in front of the other and contrive a look of happiness for the team. Monday.

There is a new list of complications that arrive with this day. Jake is the very first one. He invades my mind every five minutes. I stare at my computer and contemplate the inbox logo of unopened email and watch the number tick higher. My hand hovers over the mouse, it wants to click and open correspondence, but my mind doesn't. I just gaze out the window at Paris, without really seeing it. Just when I think I've begun to conquer the grief and achieve some semblance of equilibrium and find balance, things change again, like a kaleidoscope. I wonder, once again, how does everything go from being almost perfect to *this? Evan. Where are you?*

My mother loved to do origami. From the time I was four-years-old, we would sit together with these amazing colorful squares of paper between us and form intricate figurines: cranes, swans, dragons, and flowers of all kinds. The last origami crane I made with her was during the fateful trip to Athens and it's in a box at the beach house in Amagansett, along with all the other mementos of a magical time so long gone. Today, I think about the origami crane and my mother. The ancient Japanese legend goes that if one makes a thousand origami cranes, a person's wish will be granted. In Japan's culture, cranes are considered to be mystical or holy creatures representing good luck and the birds are believed to live for a thousand years. I'm guessing Mr. Jacob Winston has never even seen an origami crane. I decide this might be the best way for me to apologize.

After meeting with my team, where I pretend to lead, and more or less agree with everything, and make no real decisions, I slip out to the gift store a couple of blocks down from our office, in search of unique paper for this secret project. I also buy a small silver box with a key, some place he can store all those notes of mine he's said he's saved. My fervor for starting this is unexplainable. My mother used to say origami freed her mind, allowed her to think through a story line that wasn't working and come up with the answers, all with just the simple act of creating something beautiful and giving herself permission to think things through.

I'm not sure what is driving me to do this for Jake, but my mind could certainly use some answers. It takes the better part of a half hour to fold the crane into the intricate folds because I'm so out of practice, but I finally succeed. I think my mother would be proud of my efforts and my reasons for doing it. And, just as she once promised, the answers come to me as I work with the intricacies of folding this beautiful paper, allowing my mind to let go.

I regret saying so many things I shouldn't have said to Jake and I have to make this right with him. Making one crane leads to the next one. I end up making nine cranes out of this black and white lacy wrapping paper and the last one out of bright red velum. Then, I suspend them, using fine clear thread, with the red one hanging from the center.

Then, I handwrite a note on white vellum paper:

Dear Jake,
Sometimes, we see our world in black and white
and, sometimes, we just see red. All the while,
we miss the beauty suspended, right before our
very eyes. I'm sorry. Friends?
Julia

I'm holding the mobile up to the light by the window, admiring my creation, when Kimberley comes through my office door. She has this haunted look, as she sidles by me, toward the largest window that frames a perfect view of the Eiffel Tower. She seems off-kilter, just by what she's wearing, alone, as she's dressed in a conservative navy blue outfit that is so not her. The only standout in what she wears is a bright yellow scarf tied loosely around her neck. None of this ensemble portrays Kimberley's normally edgy signature style.

"Do I even want to know what you're doing?" Kimberley asks. She looks weary. *Weary?* Kimberley is never weary, tired, or undone, and she exhibits all three of these attributes, this Monday. She plops down in my desk chair and begins turning it in circles.

"Don't ask, if you don't want to know," I say.

"Why not? It'll be entertaining in an otherwise pretty fucked-up day," she says with a heavy sigh.

"Okay, you have my attention. Go ahead. What's happened?"

"No, you start," she says.

I study her face for a moment, but then she spins away in my chair toward the window. I shrug and hand her the handwritten note for Jake as she comes around again. She reads it, and then, looks at the mobile of cranes I'm holding.

"Wow, that's so amazingly beautiful." She gets up and examines it closer. "It's exquisite." She gets this sad look and moves over to the window away from me. I watch her gaze at the fine view that is Paris. "So, what happened?"

"What didn't?" I say. "Jake Winston was at Christian and Stephanie's this weekend and I spent the better part of it avoiding him because…"

"Because?" Kimberley asks, turning from the window.

"Well, as you know, he has this way of making me feel completely undone. I can't explain it. I'm devastated about Evan, but Jake stirs up all these emotions. I'm roiling inside with this unbelievable…" I make an effort to wrap the mobile in white tissue and place it inside the silver box with the key and seal it in a larger cardboard box for mailing. I stall in answering her question, but she knows it.

"What? *Say it*, Julia," she says, exasperated. "Just say it."

"I can't. It's too soon. I can't say it."

"I'll say it, then," she says, nodding. "He makes you crazy. He makes you feel outside of yourself. There's an invisible line between the two of you, this tethering, an electrical connection." She looks elated. "Yes, kinetic energy. That's what it is. And it makes you feel alive and bound to him from the very first moment."

"Is this my story, or yours?" I ask in surprise.

Kimberley gets this funny look. "Did I just use the word *bound* in a sentence describing my connection to a *guy*?"

"Yes, you did," I say. "And, thank you for that analogy because that's it, exactly. I feel, electrically connected, bound all at the same time. I mean, what the hell is that, Kimmy?"

"I don't know." She looks miserable and happy, all at once, as if she's discovered how to make lightning, but isn't quite sure of its purpose.

"He makes me feel like I'm going to implode, burst, or something even worse," I say. "What would it be though?" I begin to pace. "God. We're in the hallway at Steph's and he says the most amazing things and he takes my hand and kisses it. *My hand.* He brushes it with his lips. That's it, just my hand. I feel like I would walk across fire for him. What is that all about? I can't get him out of my mind, how he makes me feel. He's haunts me, in a good way, and a bad way. I *loved* Evan, and I feel guilty, having all these feelings for someone else."

"Guilt is the worst," Kimberley says. She has this grim expression. I stop and look at her more closely. "Go on," she says with a wave of her hand.

"But it's what he *doesn't* say about Savannah Bennett, that really puts me over the edge. All he said was: 'things are complicated, right now', and then, he doesn't explain any of it." I tape and label the box with the address for the New York offices of Hamilton Equities.

"Things are complicated. What things?"

"That's just *it*. He doesn't tell me what those things are. And, I'm just furious with him half the time. What's *wrong* with me?" I start pacing, again, and carry the package in my hands as I go. "We had this huge fight, *colossal*, and said some things we shouldn't have said." I hold up the box. "This should be there by the end of the week, and then, maybe, he'll be ready to forgive me, by then."

"What did he say, exactly?"

I shake my head, trying to remember everything Jake said. "He wants me to pay more attention to Evan's company. Be the chairman. Make decisions. Move back to New York."

"You should go," she says in this quiet voice.

"What? No. I told him there's nothing for me there."

"You said that to him?"

"Yes." I catch my lower lip between my teeth, remembering his anger after I said it.

"God, Julia if you said that to him. How do you think that makes him feel? If he's in New York now; and you're saying there's nothing there for you?"

"It's not like that." I make the Blackjack *stand down* sign, but she doesn't see it because she's back to looking out the window, again, apparently, for answers of her own. "We're friends. That's it."

"Friends," Kimberley says with derision. She turns toward me. She has this bleak expression, very un-Kimmy-like. "I don't think men and women can be friends with each other."

"You don't really believe that, do you? I *have* to be friends with Jake. He's my attorney, he's taking care of Hamilton Equities, and the settling of Evan's estate; he, basically, works for me. That set him off too, when I brought it up." I slide down onto the sofa. "We have to be friends."

Silence.

"Kimmy, are you even listening to me?"

"I'm listening," she says in a faraway voice. She has her back to me, again, but I see her reach up and wipe at the side of her face.

"Are you *crying*?"

"No." She shakes her head emphatically. "But Jules," she says in this choked-up voice. "I need you to tell me everything is going to be okay."

Oh shit.

"Well, I hate to lie on a Monday," I say.

She tries to laugh, but it comes out as this strangled cry. Her face is streaked with black mascara.

"What's going on?" I ask, suddenly uneasy.

"Want to get out of here?" Kimberley asks.

Kimberley settles into the passenger seat of my car and looks over at me. "You want to go get a cup of coffee?"

Kimberley doesn't *do coffee*. She swills it on her way to someplace else, on her way to work, or a meeting, or an event. She doesn't sit down in a café, and have coffee, and *talk*, not even with me. *Ever.*

But fifteen minutes later, that's what we're doing. Sitting and drinking café au lait in some charming café, about ten blocks from *Liaison's* office in Paris.

"It's cute, isn't it? Charming. I discovered it, a week ago," she says.

This is news. Kimberley doesn't discover anything. It is *found* for her, researched by others, and approved of by her. I must have this incredulous look on my face because she finally smiles, something she hasn't done, in the last hour. This serves as another clue as to how bad things really must be.

"Don't look so surprised, Julia. We're just having a chat."

Kimberley doesn't chat, either.

"Why don't you just cut to the chase and tell me what the fuck is going on." I haven't invoked this particular tone with her, since Evan died. It's actually exhilarating to realize I've still got it in me to do it.

"Nothing is going on," she says in this angelic something-is-so-going-on voice.

I recognize this tone. She's used it, only once, in her life with her one and only heartbreak, when Peter Sayers broke up with her, while we were at UCLA, and now. When things are at their absolute worst for Kimberley, she goes into her most protective mode. The worse things are, the more angelic she sounds. It's completely out of character, and we both know it.

I glance down at her left hand, the sapphire is still there. She sees me do this. A shadow crosses her features.

"Please don't make me guess," I say.

"I don't know where to start."

She raises her arms in this helpless gesture, somehow, imitating what Stephanie does when she's trying to cook something and it doesn't turn out. I stare at her even more intently because Kimberley has never been helpless a day in her life.

"Start with this weekend and work backwards because, somewhere in there, I know this café has something to do with what you're going to tell me."

She beams at me. That's the only way to describe this look she gives me. Somehow, I've set her free and she's sitting in this coffee shop, drinking café au lait, and *talking*. This Kimberley has a whole new magic show going on.

"I feel like I've been living in a room where there's no oxygen, and I'm just finding this out," she says with a nervous laugh. "Can you imagine the incredible torment, in discovering you're going to die slowly, because the air you're breathing in doesn't contain oxygen? I've been feeling this way, for a while, and the closer the date gets, the worse it becomes." She nods and gets this anxious look. "Julia, I'm being fitted for a wedding dress that belonged to his mother. It's *off-white*. I don't *do* off-white, as you well know. Yet, here I am, trying on this exquisite antique of a dress, and I look in the mirror and think, this isn't me, is it? And, I, literally, cannot breathe. I had to take off the dress and shut myself in the bathroom, for a while. And, all these Chantal family members and friends are looking for me, wondering where I've gone to, and I'm hiding out in the bathroom, freaking out." She gets this pained look and takes a deep breath.

"And, Gregoire is oblivious. He doesn't even see it, or *me*. You always used to say that, after Bobby died, how you wanted someone to see you, the way he did. I never understood that, until now. Because when you finally meet someone who gets you, well, it's an amazing thing to be seen."

She smiles, this incredible smile. It lights up her whole face. Kimberley's been touched by the magic she has always wielded for others.

"We're not talking about Gregoire Chantal, are we?"

"No," she says in a low voice. Her eyes fill with tears.

"Gregoire is the nicest guy and I love him, but it's not enough, you know?" She shakes her head side-to-side in disbelief. "We're still in Nice, and, I tried on the wedding gown, again, after my bathroom calamity, and his mother comes up to me, and says, "It's just going to be wonderful, when you two live in Nice, full-time." I just nod and wonder what she's talking about, and so, I ask Gregoire, when we're alone, that night, and he tells me, yes, most of the business dealings with his father's company are done in Nice and he's been told he really needs to get back to it. *Told*, Julia, not asked. And, he wants to get back to it, leave Paris, and return to Nice."

"What did you say?"

"I was floored. I mean, I have this amazing job, here, in Paris, where everyone dreams of living." She shakes her head. "But, I always thought I'd return to Manhattan, eventually." She frowns. "And, it dawns on me that living in France for the rest of my life is not a part of my plan. You know, how you don't know where you want to be, right now? Well, I feel that way, too. But, the one thing I do know is, I don't want to be married and live *here* for the rest of my life. Steph's got it all figured out and it works for her. She has the fairytale chateau life going on here. And, Christian is amazing, but he *sees* her. He would go wherever she wanted him to go and she would do the same for him. There's the difference, right there."

"Sometimes, I think it's not the place so much, but the feeling," I say. "Wanting to share it with someone, who sees you, is everything, and, if you live in a great place, that's just a bonus. I would have followed Bobby anywhere he wanted to go. Place didn't matter. Heart did. God, I sound like Dr. Stevenson, Mr. Hallmark Card, himself."

I start to laugh and Kimberley gets this bemused look for a moment. "What?" I ask.

"Well, Gregoire isn't our dear Christian, who, by the way, runs his own company, and doesn't work for the family business. When I told Gregoire, we needed to discuss the option of living in Nice, he said, 'Kimberley, you can't work forever; Nice will be our home.'"

She takes a deep breath.

"And, that's when, I really felt like I couldn't breathe. He'd already made the decision for me, the same way he orders for me, when we dine out." She gets this introspective look.

"He wouldn't be able to save me, if I was suffocating, because he doesn't see me at all."

"So what are you going to do?"

"I'm going to have to tell him I can't marry him." Kimberley makes a face. "I feel relieved just saying it. I can breathe, again. And, I've got to talk to David about this office and putting Frederic in charge." She looks at me intently. "Because you and I need to go home."

And, there it is, the sudden release of oxygen into the room for both of us. I can breathe again, too. She's right. We need to go home.

"Are you going to tell me who can see you?" I ask.

But Kimberley isn't paying any attention to me; she's captivated by the person coming through the entryway of this charming café. Of course, it has to be someone who knows most, if not all, of my double-down secrets already, just like she does.

CHAPTER

SIXTEEN

Wait and see

ASTONISHMENT IS DEFINED AS A STATE of surprise. Synonyms include: astoundment, awe, bewilderment, confusion, consternation, dumbfoundment, shock, wonderment. There are others, but these are the ones that parade through me, like marching bands on Main Street. I'm merely a spectator watching Dr. Bradley Stevenson and my best friend Kimberley Powers drink café au lait drinks and *chat*, while I just sit here in, well, astonishment at this turn of events.

An hour later, we're making plans for Le Bristol because Dr. Bradley Stevenson is starving, and he made reservations, weeks before, when he knew he'd be in Paris.

Now, we're dressing in Brad's master bathroom at his hotel suite and changing into dresses from Kimberley's suitcase she stashed in my car, earlier. I begin to suspect her preparation for tonight's event has everything to do with the handsome doctor rather than any trips she's taken to Nice. I'm relieved just to see her put on one of her more chic black dresses and step out of the somber one she wore to work all day.

I grab my cell phone and check in with Lianne about Reid. My nanny assures me that he's just fine. "Go to dinner. When is the last time you've been out, Julia? And, you're in *Paris*," Lianne says with a laugh. "Have fun."

Fun?

What is that?

I'm still reeling with shock that my former psychiatrist, Dr. Hallmark Card handsome man, is probably involved with my best friend.

I look over at Kimberley. Pure joy emanates from her. She seems to float, instead of walk, over to me. It's magical. I reach out and touch her hand, so I can feel it, too.

Le Bristol is one of the most exclusive restaurants in Paris. I haven't been here before, well, I haven't been anywhere in Paris. I've been drifting in a daze, for these past few months, in the City of Light. So, Le Bristol is a pleasant surprise in combination with the unbridled amazement that continues to reverberate through me that Dr. Bradley Stevenson and Kimberley may be seeing one another. Him, seeing her, and her, seeing him, literally.

Stunned by what's taking place between them and watching it unfold, it's as if I'm witnessing one of Shakespeare's famous plays come to life. I'm still struggling with using my handsome former doctor's first name. He seems to be in some kind of spell of his own making, as he appears to hang on to every word our dear Kimberley utters.

When the waiter hands us the dinner menus, Kimberley looks at hers, then looks at me, and then looks at Brad.

"Brad, what are you going to have?"

Kimberley looks unsure as to what's she's supposed to be doing with the menu. She fidgets with it, opens it, and closes it. I'm not surprised, since she's been letting Gregoire Chantal handle these decisions for her, for the past year. But, it's what Brad does next that assures my loyalty to him, forever.

"Kimmy, just cruise the menu and order what sounds good. Just because we're here, and, it takes forever to get in, doesn't mean it needs to turn into an event." He bestows an amazing smile her way and she responds in kind.

I'm reeling from the fact he called her *Kimmy*. I'm the only one that calls her that. The only one she *allows* to call her Kimmy. But, here's Brad, using my favorite endearment for my most magical friend. *He sees her.*

"What are you having?" Kimberley asks him.

"I was thinking of a hamburger, shake, and fries."

"It's a four star restaurant in Paris. I doubt they even have that here." Kimberley laughs.

"They'll figure it out," Brad says. "Have what you want. That's the point of eating out."

The waiter comes over for our order. Brad shreds the French language and ends up asking in English for an American-style hamburger, shake, and fries. Somehow, he and the waiter get his order all worked out.

I'm just enjoying the show.

Kimberley is still considering the menu, so I order a gourmet burger, just like Brad, and a salad. And then, we wait for Kimberley, who seems to be negotiating world peace with the menu, at this point.

"Just have what you want, Babe," Brad says to her.

"Well, I don't know what I want."

"I think you do. I think you just want me to make the decision for you, but I'm not going to. She gets like this every time we go somewhere to eat," he says to me.

I just nod. The dynamics, going on at this table, is fascinating. And, how many places have they been to eat together?

"Fine," Kimberley says. She playfully tosses her hair and peruses the menu for a fourth time. "I'll have the gourmet burger with blue cheese, a side Caesar salad, and an iced tea."

Brad inclines his head. "See? That wasn't so hard, and now, you get what you want."

Kimberley just radiates under his tutelage. I've never seen her like this. Then, he looks over at me and winks. I'm reminded of our needs and wants discussion, from months before. Oh my God, he completely understands her magic. And, why not? He is the wizard of magic, himself. I'm soaring high in the privilege of just watching this connection between them ignite.

"Do you want to keep a dessert menu?" The waiter asks in his best English.

I laugh, knowing we have provided enough fodder for the kitchen staff to laugh about for weeks: the Americans ordering hamburgers at one of the finest restaurant in Paris.

"No. I have dessert all figured out," Kimberley says with a suggestive look. Her eyes never leave Brad's face, and his fine lips curve into an unbelievable smile, just for her.

"Should I leave or something?" I ask.

"No, we want you here. We're just having dinner," Kimberley says.

"Looks like a lot more than dinner to me." I grin over at both of them. "So, what brings you to Paris, Doctor … *Brad?*

"I told him he should come," Kimberley says. "Take a break from Manhattan and see Paris."

I look from one to other, confused. "You told him that, huh? When did you tell him that, exactly?"

"I ran into him the last time I was in Manhattan." She gets this enchanted look. "Last month?" Kimberley asks this, like she's forgotten what month it is.

"February?" I ask.

"Yes, it was February." Kimberley nods. "I don't remember the date though."

"It was late February," Brad says. "February 26th, at four in the afternoon, to be exact. At a Starbucks in Tribeca."

"Near the apartment?" I ask in surprise. Kimberley looks so captivated she looks like she might float away. I'm trying to put this all together. "How long have you been here, Brad?"

"I just got in last night," Brad says. "I'm attending a conference. I leave Sunday. My flight's at seven Sunday night."

Kimberley looks miserable, when he says this. *Holy shit.* "So, you just ran into each other at the coffee shop, here in Paris, too? That's a lot of coffee talk for a girl, who doesn't normally sit still long enough to drink coffee, or chat, for hours."

Kimberley looks over at me. "Julia, we want you to be okay with it. Because if you're not, we'll have to work something else out."

Her blue eyes sparkle with tears. I'm taken aback.

Not a crier, our dear Kimberley.

"Kimmy and I want to ensure you're okay with it," Brad says. "Because if you're not, I'm stepping aside."

Our handsome doctor takes a needed breath. I think he's been holding it.

"So, Julia, are you okay with it?"

It has become a very big word, indeed.

I study Brad. Dr. Hallmark Card seems a little disheartened, now. Where's all that grand philosophical schtick about love, attraction, wants, and needs?

"Well, you pretty much know all my double-down secrets, so there's really no problem, there," I say slowly. "The only thing I would say is Kimmy personifies all that is miraculous about this world, but since you're a wizard, yourself, you should be able to handle and appreciate her brand of magic." Then, I smile, this benevolent smile. "As long as you understand, we're kind of a package deal, I'm cool with it."

The way they gaze at each other says it all. I've given them a gift and I didn't bring anything.

Later, I look over at Kimberley as we finish our American meal of hamburgers and fries, Paris style, while Brad excuses himself for a few minutes.

"Kinetic energy," I say.

"Yes," Kimberley says.

"We talked about this."

"Uh-huh." Kimberley glances up at Brad, as he crosses the dining room toward us, she practically shimmers with light, and then, looks over at me.

"I'm seeing it. It's so beautiful."

"Yes."

"The bound part … seeing that, too. How does it feel?"

"Amazing," Kimberley says.

"That's what I thought."

It's two in the morning, Paris time. Our newest addition to the inner circle, Dr. Bradley Stevenson, accompanies Kimberley and me to the bar at his hotel and we talk for hours about everything: Gregoire and how Kimberley was going to tell him, *Liaison* and how Kimberley and I are thinking of handling that with the Paris staff and David, Reid, Christian and Stephanie, Evan, Bobby, holidays, birthdays, Kimberley's family, my parents, Brad's parents, Kimberley, Brad, and me.

My best friend looks at me in amazement half the night. I don't think she was aware of how *open* the Pandora's Box of my life has been with Brad. I've never disclosed this much with her, before, or shared how I felt about any of it. There were never deep discussions about my feelings or *me*. And now, here we are, having whole conversations about all aspects of my life, her life, and Brad's. I know she's pieced together what's happened to me over the years, but I think the freedom in being able to talk about it, liberates her, as much as it does me.

"What about Jake?" Kimberley asks. I give her a surreptitious look. "Her funeral liaison. Jake Winston," she says to Brad, who nods and looks a little uncomfortable.

How far does patient-doctor privilege go for former patients?

"He's been helping her through all the estate stuff and he's working with Evan's hedge fund clients. He was Evan's best friend. He's a *great* guy," Kimberley says.

"So what about him?" I ask. I'm defensive, tired, and undone, all at once. "I can't even think about Jake. Let's not ruin a perfectly wonderful evening, talking about *Jake*."

"There it is. Did you see that, Brad? That thing she does with her lips. She kind of purses them, and involuntary half-smiles, when she says his name."

"I do not."

"You kind of do, Julia," Brad says.

I look over at him, a little disenchanted. "I don't want you two ganging up on me about Jake. I don't know what's going to happen with him."

"Well, I do," Kimberley says. She waves her hands in the air, dispensing her brand of magic on me, right there.

<hr>

Kimberley and I take a taxi back to Gregoire's chateau. Gregoire is still in Nice and due to fly in to Paris tomorrow morning. We look at each other and share this sense of unease, knowing what will transpire for her, when she talks to him, tomorrow.

"I'm surprised you came back with me," I say. Kimberley had just hugged Brad and kissed the side of his face, and then, left with me.

"We've decided to wait." Kimberley gets this impish look.

Now, this is news.

"What?"

"My idea. He's game, but I want it be special and so we're going to wait a while. Wait and see how things go. Let it simmer for a while, and then, we'll see. I have to deal with Gregoire. I want to be fair, be free." She frowns. "And, I just want to wait and see."

"Wait and see," I say. "A novel idea for you, Kimmy. Why do I think this is tied back to the bound thing?"

She doesn't answer me, just floats away, in this bliss she's discovered with Dr. Bradley Stevenson, and calls out an airy good night on her way to bed.

Now, I'm wide awake going through the revelations of this past evening and the early morning hours about Kimberley and Brad. There's this sense of loss in knowing Brad and I won't be having frank conversations under the guise of the doctor-patient relationship, anymore. But, I like him, and I don't need counseling sessions anymore.

Intuitively, I already know he'll always be with Kimberley and has a better understanding of my friendship with her than anyone else has ever had. Kimberley entering into a relationship with Brad will take all of her attention and focus away from me. There's a part of me that's set free by this turn of events. I'm ready to be on my own, revitalized in witnessing the magic that is uniquely theirs. Maybe, it will lead to my own.

My mind drifts towards later this morning. Kimmy's already arranged to meet up with Gregoire. I feel sad about their ending, which leads me to inevitable thoughts about Evan. I take steady breaths and try to focus on all the wonderful memories of him and not let the sadness prevail. *Evan.* When I walked down the aisle at our wedding, the way he gazed at me, there was no one else that day, not even Bobby. When Reid was born, the intimacy in welcoming our son forged our relationship together, however imperfect we'd been with each other in the past, we were both committed to our future, committed to a normal life: a marriage, a baby, each other. *Evan. I miss you.*

Before turning off the light, I check my cell phone, and discover a text message from my assistant, telling me she got the package to Jake mailed off to the Hamilton Equities office in New York. I text back a thank you and feel relief, for a moment, but then, worry I've sent him a gift and the note in the first place.

The good feelings about doing a silly origami project for him disappear. I'm meandering toward these anxious thoughts about sending him the note and the mobile, since he probably won't understand its significance, when my cell phone actually rings.

It's Jake.

"I thought, I'd try something new."

My heart is pounding so loud, I can barely hear him. "Something new," I say, uncertain.

"Calling you in the middle of the night there, and knowing right where you are, this very second." He starts to laugh.

I take an unsteady breath, realizing I've been holding it, since I took his call.

"I'm sorry," I say quickly. "I'm sorry for saying the things I said. Don't ask me to name them, right now, because I'm incredibly tired. I haven't slept well for three nights. I shouldn't be mad at you. I've got to stop doing that." I take a breath. "So, I'm sorry Jake, just know that. I sent you something. It should be there in the next week or so."

"A note?" Jake asks.

I hear this longing in his voice. I close my eyes. This amazing sensation travels through all of me in just remembering his face from … yesterday? It's only Monday or early morning Tuesday. *Oh God.*

"There's a note, but there's something else too. You'll just have to wait and see."

"Julia, I just want to say, I'm sorry. I know this is a rough time for you, even though things are beyond complicated, with other people, I shouldn't take it out on you."

"We're leaving Paris," I say in a rush.

Silence. Not the response I was expecting.

"Julia," he says my name, as if it's the last note of a song, but not a high one, a low one, out of tune. "I should have said this in person. I should have told you this, while I was there."

"Things are complicated," I say.

"Yes. You're going to have to trust me. I think I know what's going on, but it involves a lot of people and—"

"Things are complicated for me too, Jake. And I have Reid to think of and I have to figure things out, too. I just want you to know—"

"You're not going to tell me we can just be friends, are you?"

"Okay, what do you want to call it, then?"

He laughs his attractive southern cowboy laugh. It takes my breath away. "Wait and see," he says. "Let's just wait and see."

I smile because he's used the exact same words Kimberley did, just an hour ago. I take it as a sign of some kind.

"I can live with that," I say. "For a while."

I can feel his happiness through the phone line at the last part of what I've just said. "Wait and see, Jake. Let's just wait and see."

"I like these phone calls. Let's do this again, soon."

"Okay. Call me, when you get my note."

CHAPTER

SEVENTEEN

You are here

EVAN—THE ISLAND IN THE MIDDLE OF my life's ocean that I've been forced to leave behind. The days pass and take me farther away from him. This unsolicited reality of an ocean's waves roll over me, again and again, intent on drowning me with the only truth it holds: my island is far from me, now. I'm tossed along in life's boat held up by the inevitability of gravity that's taken various forms: the dispensations and endless explorations of my mind, an overly solicitous inner circle whose sole intention is to keep me afloat, and a baby that needs me.

Death is … so permanent. It alters everything. This relentless wrecking ball comes at me from every angle in a different way, then the day before.

My island gets farther away. This glimpse of him, only I can see, gets smaller with each passing day. The more I go looking for him, the more I discover him missing. I can't tell anyone. Permanent fear settles in. How do I explain the profoundness of his love? And, it's long absence from me, now? I can't hold on to him, anymore. At one time, his love occupied every cell of my being. Now, it gets deeper inside of me, yet, somehow, just out of reach. The prolonged longing for his touch causes me to search for him, but I find him nowhere. How do I explain this to anyone?

Guilt arrives; an unwelcome visitor coupled with time's passing as my island all but disappears. I struggle to remember what he looked like and can only resurrect his image with photographs. My memory of his whole persona becomes distilled snippets: his kindest word, his best smile, and our closest moment. All fleeting, less real, more imagined.

His birthday, even the day we first met, all slip by me. Memories languish, while time swallows me whole. This automaton existence propels me forward, while I stop counting by the hour, by the day, even by the week, but still search for the glimpse of him in the face of every stranger. Five months slip past me.

And, I am here. And, he is there. On that island. More than an ocean away from me, now.

On some level, my body and mind both know time isn't going to bring him back, but acceptance comes in degrees, with the inevitable rolling of each ocean wave to this shore, this life. My island's all but gone now, a passing glimmer in my mind and so far away from me now.

I am here. And, he is there and lost to me, forever.

<hr />

You are here.

The building map diagrams the fortieth floor of Hamilton Equities. I lean closer to get a better look.

You Are Here. The words are written in big bold letters. In case of fire, go here. There's a thick red line that zigzags across the map, outlining the way to the stairs. To here.

I look around and locate the red exit sign and the sign depicting stairs. *Where do I go to get back to my island?* I gaze at the building's map again and wonder where he is. Where's my island, now? Because not a day has gone by that I haven't wanted to go there and be where he is. But, I am here. I look at the sign, again, for an answer, for anything, that might signal where he is.

You are here.
Am I?

<hr />

"Mrs. Hamilton." I'm engulfed in a warm fleshy embrace and the faintest hint of Joy perfume. Evan's assistant.

"Mrs. —" I panic, trying to remember the woman's name. Evan talked about her all the time. *Think, Julia. Think.*

"Call me Maggie, dear. Mrs. Talbon makes me sound so stuffy." Her laugh resembles the giggle of a girl more than a woman with silver hair. She crushes me in her sweet embrace. "Everyone calls me, Maggie. Evan did, too."

She touches my cheek with hers and starts to pull away. I miss her touch already and fail in letting her go. She fingers my hair and touches my face. Then, she moves in for a tighter embrace, before she finally steps back from me.

"Call me Julia," I say.

"You look wonderful, Julia." Her voice is wistful, and, I know, she wishes it were true. She squeezes my hand and smiles, while her brown eyes bestow sympathy and simple promise.

"Not really," I say.

Her embrace has unchained me from my outwardly-composed-I'm-fine self. My eyes sting with unshed tears. Maggie sighs, reaches out, and pulls me to her, again.

"You look a little tired, but still lovely, Julia. I'm so glad you've come." She glances at her watch. "They're not here, right now. Some big meeting uptown." She looks unsure, for a moment, and inclines her head. "But, never mind that. Let's just get you settled."

"I don't plan to stay. I mean, I don't know why I'm here. Kimberley told me to meet her here. I had some time, so it seemed like a good idea to come by … and, here I am."

I point to the You Are Here sign, as a way of explanation, and run out of words. *Why am I here?*

Maggie Talbon folds her arms across her chest, tilts her head to the other side, and studies my face, once more. Then, she takes my hand and leads me down the hall.

Mahogany lines all the walls and we tap our way across the slate floors. The entire hallway portrays this restrained prosperity. I'm over-whelmed with the memory of the first time Evan brought me here. I'd teased him about the opulence of this place. He'd laughed, and said, "We have to look like we make money to play, Baby."

I smile, remembering how often he called me that.

Maggie swings open the corner office door to Evan's glass wall view and steps back. I glance at the humongous desk and the white leather sofa located, nearby. My smile deepens. We made love right there on that very sofa, late one night, on one of our first official first dates. There weren't too many of those, since he proposed a month after we'd officially met, but I definitely remember that one.

"I'll get you some tea," Maggie says from behind me.

"That would be … wonderful." I'm buoyed up by her kindness, and comforted by being in this room, again.

You are here.

I swirl in the executive leather chair and catch glimpses of the spectacular views— the greenness of Battery Park, the long-gone promise of Ellis Island, the shimmery blue of the Hudson, and the symbols of wealth that gleam in the austerity of glass and stone. I carousel by it all, only stopping long enough to sip the tea, Maggie Talbon brought me. Her last words continue to console me, somehow. "I'll just leave you to it."

Leave me to what, I'm not sure. I don't know why I'm here.

I close my eyes and feel my island's proximity stir closer with the faintest hint of his cologne that still permeates from the leather of his chair. Armani was my first gift to him. "It reminded me of you," I'd said as he opened it. I still remember his genuine look of surprise at my unexpected present. We'd only seen each other a couple of times, and both of us had already admitted, we weren't even sure, where this thing between us was going, but he wore it every day, after that. And, two weeks later, four weeks after we officially met, we both knew where things were going.

You are here.

I stir awake at the sound of voices, just outside Evan's office door. Christian's distinct French accent and Jake's southern one echo in the hallway and ricochet back to me. I haven't seen Jake for two months.

"She's going to have to be told. It's not something we can hide from her forever," Jake says. "I know you all want to give her more time, but we've run out of it, Christian; and Wells, just basically told us that."

"I know. It's just ... she's had a lot to deal with in Paris, just returning here, and Reid's first birthday is this weekend. It's going to be hard
for her, without Evan," Christian says. "Maybe after that, we'll tell her."

I fling open the Evan's office door. Both their faces register shock
at seeing me. "Tell me what?"

Jake recovers first. He tries to smile and sticks out his hand. "Julia,
it's nice to see you again."

I'm assailed by the memory of Bobby's first greeting and can feel
the heat rise in my face at seeing Jake Winston, again, after the fireworks of our last encounter. My anger starts to build; I haven't heard
from him, since our *wait and see* call, two months ago. Not one word
about my note or the origami crane mobile that accompanied it. *Complications, really?*

"Jake." I incline my head towards him and ignore his extended
hand. He looks uncertain. I lift my head in defiance. *No, I'm not going
to make it easy for you.*

I glance over at Christian who gives me an even more anxious look
than Jake is now. Christian shares the same peace-making trait as his
wife and strives to protect me as much as Steph and Kimmy do. "Tell
me what," I say in a firm voice.

"Not here," Christian says. He shoots Jake a pleading look, and
then, looks back at me with a forced smile. His normal reassurance is
absent and apprehension moves in on me.

"Oh good, you've found Mrs. Hamilton," Maggie says from behind them. "I just stepped away, for a moment. Can I bring anyone
coffee or something to eat?"

Both men say, "No," at the same time.

"Well, well, this is quite the reunion," Kimberley says from down
the hall. She does double-time to catch up to us, her heels click along
the floor in quick succession.

"What exactly do we need to be telling Julia?" She pushes her way
past Maggie with a warm smile for the older woman, and then, glares
at Christian and Jake. Next, she throws her arm around my neck and
pulls me to her. "I thought we all agreed we were going to wait?"

"Tell me what?" I ask. I am here.

⁓⛧⛧⁓

My inner circle, including Brad and apparently Jake, gather around the dining room table at Kimberley's apartment in Tribeca. There was a brief two minutes of consternation at Brad's arrival, but I think the interaction between them has tempered our close-knit group enough, so they understand that Brad and Kimberley are the real deal. Everyone seems in awe of their magic as much as I was the first time I saw them together in Paris. Except for Jake, who arrived after Brad and doesn't seem to understand the dynamics of what's going on at all. I'm restless and get up to peruse the loft; it holds so many memories for me. I feel Jake's eyes upon me as I cruise around.

"Thomas Wells is like the canary in the coal mine, the first warning sign of trouble," Jake says. "He's the first sign of things to come. He thinks the market is overcharged and he's pulling out, while he can. There will be others. A hedge fund works like a bank account. We use other people's large sums of money to play with in the market—and when they want their money, after a contractual amount of time, we give it back to them. But when, everyone wants their money at the same time after the required term…"

"We can fold," I say into the ensuing silence.

"Right," Jake says. "Look, I'm sorry we didn't tell you sooner, preparing you, instead of springing it on you like this. I wanted to, but everyone else wanted to wait. And there's validity to that strategy. Why worry you about something none of us can control? But now, we have to try and figure out a plan, of some kind, before all the investors want their money, all at once. If that happens, Hamilton Equities could be wiped out, depending upon market conditions and timing."

"There's no confidence in my being chairman. Is there?" I stare at Jake, willing him to answer.

"No," he says after a long silence.

"The financial sector is still largely a man's world," Kimberley says. She comes to stand beside me and takes my hand.

"We thought we could stave this off, a little longer, but the market isn't cooperating, and the media is picking up on any negativity they can find, and Evan's death happens to be one of them." She lets go of my hand and retrieves a newspaper article from her folder and hands it to me.

I scan the headline: *Widow Assumes Chairman position at Hamilton*

Equities. What's next? The picture with the article is less than flattering. I look lost and out of place. The photo captures me walking in front of the Hamilton Equities building from months before with the caption: *Chairman makes rare appearance at the office.* The article starts, "As new chairman of Hamilton Equities, we hope Mrs. Evan Hamilton is finding the financial answers she seeks, but we have our doubts. Few have seen her grace the offices of Hamilton Equities, since the unexpected death of her young husband, Evan Hamilton. She's spent most of her time away in Paris." I stop reading and glance around the table at all of them. Stephanie pushes back her chair and comes over and puts her arm around me.

"It's all a bit much to take in, isn't it, Julia?" Stephanie asks. "First Evan. Now, his company. I say we table this discussion, until after Reid's birthday celebration, tomorrow. Then, let's just spend the weekend at your beach house and figure this whole thing out. Jake, are you going to be able to make it?"

Jake hesitates. "I won't be able to be there, until late Saturday afternoon, but I'll try to make it." He gets this distressed look. I look across at him, but he avoids looking at me directly, now.

Complications. Most certainly.

I wrestle with my anger for them in keeping this bad news from me, especially Jake. Stephanie and Brad are as stunned as I am at the news that Evan's company is in jeopardy, and they're the only ones I'm not mad at, right now. I've drifted away, both from the conversation taking place all around me and physically from all of them, as I peruse the pictures along the fireplace mantel.

Brad comes over to me. "You okay?"

"Absolutely." I force a smile.

"Uh, hey, Julia, I know about the code word, *absolutely*," Brad says.

I glare over at Kimberley, who, from a distance, is tracking her handsome doctor's every move. She gives me a questioning look, as if to say, 'what did I do?'

"So, are you all right? I'm asking as a *friend*."

"Let's see," I say with a bit of irony. "I've been in New York for only a few days. I'm still on Paris time. My nanny isn't feeling well. My son is turning one tomorrow and I haven't even frosted his cake or bought him a single gift. And, now I find out Evan's company is in trouble, has been in trouble, for a while, from what I gather." I shrug. "I'd say I've had just about enough for one day."

"But, you're handling it."

"Yes, Bradley, my good *friend*, I'm handling it."

He puts an arm around me and squeezes my shoulders. "See? It's so much better being friends. I could never do this in the office," he whispers.

I laugh. From the surprised looks at the table behind us, I believe the inner circle is astounded at my response. "You're not going to freak out, when Kimberley and I do tequila shots a little later, are you?"

"No, I picked up the tequila on my way here." Brad grins.

"You are so awesome," I say.

"Do you two want to join the business discussion or have I missed out on why we're all here?" Jake asks from behind us. "Good friend of yours, Julia?"

Brad and I turn with his arm still around me and we're confronted with Jake's seething anger, as he stands there, clenching his jaw and staring at us. And, my own anger ignites.

"Brad is seeing Kimberley, Jake. He's a psychiatrist and he worked with me in December. So, yes, I'd say he is a great friend. He calls. He writes. He doesn't lie, cheat, or steal. He's fun, but he doesn't play games. And, he certainly doesn't keep things from me. He's an *awesome* friend."

"You really want to do this, now?" Jake asks.

"No. There's nothing more to say." I glare at him for a moment. "Okay. Let's discuss business, that's why *you're* here."

He flushes and staggers back from me, and I wince, knowing I've just delivered a pretty low blow. He's done so much for Evan's company, and me, but I'm tired of the complications he's referred to so many times, the game he's been playing.

"Clients are beginning to bow out," Jake says, retaking his seat at the table, again. "I can't make any traction with any new investors. They're all waiting on the sidelines to see what we're going to do long term about hiring a CEO. The best thing we can do is plan our strategy around that objective."

"I agree. We need to set a precedent by choosing a CEO," Christian says. "That's our next big move, signaling to our clients and the market we're in this for the long term."

"But are we in this for the long term?" I ask. "I mean, what are we doing this all for? He's gone. He isn't coming back and unless one of you takes this role on, I don't know what we're trying to save it for."

"Let's not make any hasty decisions about the company, right now," Kimberley says. "Let's take the weekend to think about it. We'll all be at the beach house. We can decide what to do this weekend. Okay?"

"I agree. Tomorrow, Reid turns one and we're all going to be there. I'm sure Julia needs to pack, so I think we should table this conversation, for now," Stephanie says.

The peacemaker tries to still the troubled waters, but the undercurrent is too powerful.

"No." I surprise myself by speaking. "I don't want to have a big discussion about this all weekend. We decide now." I look over at Brad, and he subtly nods, which strengthens my resolve to keep going. "We need a CEO. The finance world doesn't accept women at the helm, so that leaves out Kimberley, Stephanie, and me. Fine. Whatever." I do my little *stand down* Blackjack move. "Christian can't do it because his own company is suffering, and I know this, firsthand, because I've been leading the Paris office team on straightening out the strategies and messaging. You know, I love you, Christian, but you've been completely absent with a lot of it, and I know it's my fault for not taking care of this sooner, but I'm ready to now." I see him nod.

"Julia, I don't think we should…" Kimberley struggles for words and looks more worried and uncomfortable by the minute.

I look over at her. *What do you know that I don't?*

"What? The choice is obvious," I say. "Brad isn't qualified to lead a hedge fund, and I know, he's saying, *thank God.*" I smile over at Brad. Then, turn and stare at Jake. "So that leaves you, Mr. Winston. Do you want the job or not?"

Everyone is looking at me with these very peculiar expressions, like I've missed the punch line of a joke. Jake looks miserable, like he wishes he were any place else, but here, or didn't have to say what he's about to say. "I can't take the job as CEO. I'm moving to Austin."

Austin. Another letter *A* word. I look at Brad for understanding. *Are you getting this? Do you see why I hate this letter so much?* Because I already know Austin and probably Savannah are the complications he's spoken of. Jake won't even look at me, now. And, I'm shaking, trembling head to toe, as if I'm drowning. My island's gone and I am nowhere near the shore. I look at Kimberley, and then, Brad. *Help me.*

"Julia," Jake says my name, as if it's a cry for help and he's drowning, too.

Breathe.

"Okay," I say into the uncomfortable silence. "So, that leaves us with a search firm to find a replacement CEO for Evan, unless, there's someone in-house, some superstar, no one's mentioned." I look around. "No? Okay, Kimmy, you lead the charge on that one. Let's do a press release around it. You and I can write it up this weekend. Let's do another press release on me, returning from Paris ,tying in the whole *Liaison* connection. God knows, I've earned it over the last few months."

I smile at her and she's looking at me, like I'm insane. *Maybe.*

"We should really build strategies around that because some of *Liaison's* clients could certainly benefit from Hamilton Equities, right? Or, vice versa," I say. Then, I look directly at Jake. "So, this should help you out with the new client acquisition problem, until you leave for *Austin.*" I practically spit the word out at him.

"Savannah handles the human resources stuff at Hamilton Equities," Jake says, though he sounds like he's having trouble breathing. "I can ask her to do the CEO replacement search,"

I give Kimberley a questioning look. *She works for me?* Kimberley subtly nods. *Oh, this is surreal.*

"Perfect," I say to Jake in the growing silence. "Bring her, tomorrow. We'll fill her in on our requirements for a CEO. Everyone think about that criteria and we'll put together the list. That's it." Everyone is staring at me with their mouths half-open, except for Jake and Brad.

"I'll get the tequila," Kimberley says.

"Yes, absolutely, bring the tequila, and we'll chat on the way to Amagansett."

Keep it together. I take a deep breath and move over toward Brad and Kimberley, while searching my purse for my cell phone. I'm intent on getting a taxi and heading back to Evan's penthouse to pack as soon as humanly possible, before I completely fall apart as the news of my financial woes begins to sink in, and Jake's announcement that he's moving to Austin overtakes me. His complications are pulling me under, most of all.

I could lose everything, but hasn't that already happened?

"I have my car," Jake says. "I'll take you home."

I look past Jake at Brad and Kimberley. She holds up tequila and limes. Brad just has this inquisitive stare that, too often, gets me to share my secrets.

"No. You know what?" I gaze at Jake with open hostility, ignoring the despair that etches his features. "I don't need anything from you. You've done enough." I walk away from him towards Kimberley and Brad. "Kimmy, can I just borrow some of your clothes? Let's just go. I've got a cake to frost and things to do for Reid's party."

You are here.

Am I?

CHAPTER

EIGHTEEN

Battle lines

THE FIRST SATURDAY IN MAY DAWNS with perfect ocean weather and nothing but blue sky and a calm sea, signaling there will be no sadness on this day. Tranquility stays with me. I refuse to let the grief about Evan and everything else I'm unwilling to name to attend this birthday party.

Jubilation swirls through all of us, as we watch my one-year-old son dig in to his first birthday cake in the shape of a circus bear. Once Reid discovered no one cared if he puts his thumb directly in the center of his cake, he stuffed fistfuls of cake and frosting into his little mouth as fast as he could. The look of glee in being able to do this all by himself was precious.

Evan's parents stopped by, during this hilarious moment, and it was a rare scene to see them enjoy their only grandson's delight so much. His squeals are infectious as he proceeds to get cake and frosting everywhere, including his clothes, face, and hair. Reid wears his circus birthday hat, claps his little hands, and plays with the red and yellow balloons tied to his high chair. This is enough amusement for my child and his laughter enchants all of us. He is the magic this day.

"This is the inauguration for a lifetime of loving chocolate, you know," Kimberley says.

She takes a picture of the larger circus cake that I've decorated depicting a circus elephant and monkey peeking out of a red circus tent shaped cake.

"Did you stay up late to get all of this done? Do you have to be Martha Stewart with the cakes? Now, Brad is going to want one of these."

We all laugh.

Kimberley and I keep up with digital camera duties together because we don't want to miss anything he does today. After cake, ice cream, and presents, things slow down and Reid sits in the center of the great room playing with his new toys until naptime.

Where Jake is becomes the running conversation topic by mid-afternoon. We continue to wait for him, but then, finally convene at the dining room table to put together a list of leadership qualities for the new CEO search for Hamilton Equities.

We've just finished, when Jake and Savannah arrive. Instant tension permeates all of us, as soon as Savannah Bennett enters our atmosphere. Even Dr. Bradley Stevenson, Mr. Hallmark Card, himself, seems to be at a loss, as to how to handle this unexpected force.

This much, I know, Scarlett O'Hara lives. She's alive and well and breathing in the perfect dark-haired goddess form of one Miss Savannah Bennett, who uncannily resembles the classic movie star Vivien Leigh, who played the part of Scarlett, only with a self-possessed personality and none of the famous actress's *good* traits. Savannah doesn't grace a room, she cloaks it. A cloying perfume, whose scent lingers on, long after the physical embodiment departs. A poison star or a wayward sun, one cannot stare at her, too long, for fear of blindness, or perhaps, incineration. A burning star at the center of her own universe, we serves as bit players, smaller planets or moons set to orbit around her, or distant stars she's flung to the farthest point of the galaxy, after colliding with her all powerful gravitational force. My utter destruction would be just fine with her, evident within the first minute of her meeting me. After Jake's introductions, I silently communicate, *is she for real?* to Kimberley. She can only nod.

I just don't know how real, quite yet.

Jake is stuck within her orbit as an extraordinary planet seemingly unaware of her thermonuclear powers. He accompanies Savannah everywhere she goes, ensuring she has what she needs or wants. If he strays away from her trajectory path by showing any interest in anyone else, even something as simple as offering to get one of us a glass of wine, which most of us practically guzzle, while in her presence, Savannah demands his attention be centered back on her within the predetermined time limit of twenty seconds.

Competition with me began for Savannah, from the moment she walked in. This perfect stranger has waged a secret battle with me, I didn't expect to be drawn into, as she makes pointed remarks about my beverage offerings, food choices, and cake-decorating abilities. "You're quite amazing, Julia," she says, at every turn. But it's the way she says this that leaves little doubt to her true feelings about me.

My consolation is, everyone appears to be on edge with her arrival. It's not just me. The celebration seems to have hit a mystifying lull, like a ride at an amusement park that suddenly slides backwards, the first indication something's not quite right, before disaster follows. This sense of dread, its inevitability, settles all around me. A storm's coming, the planets are preparing to realign.

Jake and I have this implied truce going. I focus on ensuring my son's first birthday is memorable, and feel relief about the strategy we're taking with Hamilton Equities. I'm averse to further exploring the feelings I have with Jake's *complications* that he alluded to a few months ago in Paris. I can center myself by focusing on Reid, this day.

As the party moves towards late afternoon, I begin the preparations for grilling steaks outside on the back deck. Jake volunteers to do these and heads out the French doors with a plate of filets, while Savannah airily announces she's a vegetarian.

"Really? And, you're from Texas?" Kimberley asks.

For her teasing remark, Kimberley is rewarded with a contemptuous icy stare from Savannah. This would be funny at any other party, but not this one. We scramble to find her some suitable alternative entrée, but like Goldilocks with porridge, nothing is quite right for Ms. Bennett.

"I've been nauseous for days with this pregnancy. I'm hoping, I feel better at the end of June, when we get married."

Momentarily stunned by what's she's just said, I watch her sip at her glass of water, quietly reeling at her news, as if I've just been punched in the stomach. I stand, frozen for a few seconds, and then, move toward the refrigerator, and pretend to look for something, while I quake inside at this news, although I should have figured out this *complication,* already. She's evasive, when Kimberley asks her, how far along she is. I flit around the kitchen, pretending to be busy, while dully listening to every word she utters.

"Well," she drawls, "When Jake returned from London in March, we had quite a reunion." Her radiant smile is almost too bright, and I force myself to look away.

A few minutes later, I escape upstairs to check on Reid, since Lianne left us for her cousin's place in the city, a few hours before, still not feeling well. From the upstairs bedroom window, I watch Jake as he talks with Christian out on the deck. A child would mean everything to Jake, this much I do know about him: he would choose a life with her because of a child. It all makes perfect sense, his hesitation in Paris, the complications he spoke of, and, here they are. I shouldn't be feeling this way. This connection between us, whatever this is, can't happen.

I look out at the Atlantic. The endless light blue horizon and the vast royal blue swells meet in perfect symmetry, a linear alliance with nothing between them. There is no land in sight. My island is nowhere to be found. He's nowhere to be seen. "Evan, where are you?"

This underlying sense of chaos greets me, when I return downstairs. With Jake and Christian out on the deck grilling steaks for everyone, Savannah's needs have gone unmet and she's unhappy. I discover Brad methodically searching through our soda supply for an acceptable one for Savannah that doesn't contain aspartame. Kimberley and I are maneuvered into putting together an appetizer that doesn't have any beef, chicken, soy or dairy in it, because she's starving, and just cannot wait to eat, any longer.

She displays this disquieting, satisfied smile as we serve her. Peace has been restored among the planets, temporarily. Savannah is happy, for now.

The filets are grilled to perfection. It's the one communiqué I make a point of telling Jake, as we sit down to eat at the dining room table, while Savannah goes on and on about the hazards of carnivorous living. That's what Savannah calls it, 'carnivorous living.'

After Savannah's long-winded dissertation on the hazards of eating steak, Jake appears so disheartened, I thank him, again, for playing chef. "Perfectly cooked filets, Jake. Thank you."

He gives me a grateful smile, and I return it. Turning to Savannah, I glimpse pure hatred, as she trains her gaze on me, but, in the next moment, she contrives this wide smile, which is all Jake sees, when he looks over at her.

Kimberley pours more red wine for all of us. "Cheers," she says.

I give her a pleading look to behave herself and not cause any unnecessary trouble with Savannah Bennett, who seems intent on waging a personal battle with me and appears to be waiting for the just the right moment to strike. She converses mostly with Jake and with the rest of the inner circle, as little as possible, but with this perfected banter, and completely ignores me. The feeling that I need to protect myself becomes almost insistent, as the party goes on.

I follow Kimberley out to the kitchen for coffee to mitigate the buzz from too much wine, and to take a respite from Savannah, herself.

"Watch yourself," Kimberley says. "She doesn't like you."

"Uh-huh. Got that. What do you think her problem is?"

"You, most definitely. Insecurity about *him*." She inclines her head towards Jake, as he enters the kitchen, asking what he can do to help. Minutes later, Jake follows me out onto the deck, where I attempt to put things back in order, collecting plates and utensils left outside. Through the glass doors, I see Kimberley is engaged in a conversation with Savannah and I take a deep breath.

"Julia, look, I need to explain this." He runs his hands through his hair, his signature stress sign.

This whole situation between us has become unbearable. The jubilation of this day ebbs away from me and fury begins to take its place.

"She's pregnant, you two are getting married at the end of June. She *told* us." I shrug, striving for nonchalance, while rage works its way through me.

How could I have been so stupid? So weak? How can I do this to Evan's memory?

"Congratulations. I knew there were complications and I figured you were still engaged to her for some reason. Stupidly, I thought you'd have it all worked out, in a few months, while I was still in Paris running things for Kimberley. Yes, you've got it worked out, all right."

The roar of waves, hitting the beach, seems timed to my words.

There's this massive pounding at the shore.

"I want to do the right thing."

"Then, you should, Jake. A child changes everything. Be happy. You'll have a wife, a family, live in a reasonably-sized town; I assume Austin is small enough for you." I try to laugh, but it comes out this agonized cry.

"You never called me," Jake says. "No explanation for why you stayed behind in Paris."

"What? No. I waited for you to call me, to let me know, you'd gotten the crane mobile. My apology note? When you didn't call, I assumed you didn't accept my apology, after all."

"The what?" He looks confused.

"The crane mobile," I say. "You know a thousand cranes bring you good luck? I sent it to you from Paris. It has nine black and white little birds, cranes, with a red one in the center."

"Yes, we have one of those. Savannah bought it for me, two months ago."

"No, Jake." I shake my head side-to-side. "I *made* it for you. I sent it to you. You can't buy them, you *make* them. I made it for you. I sent you a note too, apologizing for the things I said to you in Paris, for everything."

I shake out the grill cover and he helps me put it back on. We're just looking at each other with so much to say, but neither one of us saying anything.

"Why would Savannah lie about it?" Jake finally asks. "I never got your note."

"Why are we even talking about this?" I can't control the anger any longer and just unleash it on him. "You're getting married, in what, seven weeks to *her*? I thought we had an understanding, this wait and see thing. But you're engaged to her, marrying her, and she's having your child. That's a lot more than a *complication*."

He's just standing there, not saying anything, looking distraught. Then, I see this flash of anger come over him.

"I had a life. I started over. I moved on and Savannah and I ... it's complicated. Then, she tells me she's pregnant and the answer seems so clear. And then, I see you again, and this thing between us just reaches at me. You drive me insane, Julia. I had a life. I started over. But, here you are … if you could just see me."

"What are you *talking* about? I don't know what you want from me."

I race down the stairs that lead to the beach and start running toward the shoreline away from him, but he follows.

"I have to do the right thing," he says above the roar of the waves.

"Then do it, do the right thing. Go to her. Go now."

"If you could just—"

"Don't you dare put this on me! I may have fucked up many things in my life, but I didn't do this, you did. Wait and see? Well, I *see* it all now."

Jake grabs my arm. "Please, Julia. If you could just wait and see."

"No! Let go of me. I've heard enough."

We both look up at the same time and see Brad at the top of the deck stairs with Kimberley and Savannah following right behind him. I slip from Jake's grasp.

"Julia, are you all right?" Brad asks, when he reaches us.

"Absolutely." I give him a pleading look and avoid looking at Jake. Brad nods with understanding.

"Let's go for a walk, Jake," Brad says.

I try to get a hold of myself and these racing emotions. Out of the corner of my eye, I see Kimberley and Savannah retreat from the steps toward the house, and then, watch the two men walk further down the shoreline just out of reach of the crashing waves. The sky begins to darken, signaling a storm is coming.

When I reach the top of stairs, Stephanie calls to me from the open doorway. "Julia, we're off to the store for more milk for Reid. Do you have a list going?"

"Yes, I'll get it." I walk past Savannah. "Can I get you anything?" I ask.

"I have everything I need." She studies my face briefly, then saunters back over to the railing, and watches Jake, as he walks down the beach with Brad.

"We need more mixers, too, Steph," Kimberley says.

"Just come with us. Brad's out at the beach. We never get you to ourselves, anymore."

Stephanie throws her arm around Kimberley and drags her out

the door. I watch the three of them get into Christian's car and drive away.

A chilling breeze blows in from the open kitchen window and catches my attention, for a moment. It serves as my only warning.

The storm is here.

Chapter

Nineteen

It's the little things

Disquiet swirls inside as I turn from the window. "Alone at last," Savannah says with a little laugh, from right behind me. "I haven't seen you sit down, once, today, Julia. Can I call you that? Mrs. Hamilton seems so formal. Let's have a drink and just chat." She pours wine into a glass for me and soda water for herself into another.

"Sure." I sit across from her in an opposing chair and toy with my wine glass, while she settles in on the sofa. She seems almost thoughtful, perhaps preoccupied. Then, she smiles.

And, it comes out of nowhere, without intended provocation on my part, and hits me at full speed, like a meteor, hitting the Earth causing instant destruction, it eliminates the life, I thought I knew. Instantaneous. This poison star.

"We were together for a while," Savannah says. "Over a year ago, now. Yes, the spring before. March. He took me to the place in Malibu. Have you ever been there? It's amazing." Her violet-blue eyes sparkle, like she has a high fever. "Yes, an unforgettable time for both of us."

She nods, moving her head ever so slightly, effecting perfect decorum. Then, she pauses with keen interest to ensure I've heard everything she's just said.

Disbelief begins to run its course through my body, while my mind sifts and comprehends her words.

Evan. She's talking about Evan.

Then she laughs, one of those wicked laughs, not intended to be funny, while my mind races through calculations of time. Over a year ago. March. We were still in New York, living at the penthouse. I'd just discovered the shrine to Elizabeth. We'd had a huge fight about … what else? Elizabeth. He'd left so angry, and told me, later, he'd flown to California to figure some things out. Late March. I couldn't fly because I was eight months pregnant.

Fear begins its slow drum beat inside. "What are you talking about?"

The fierce rolling waves of the stormy ocean reach at me. Drowning is so certain.

She laughs, again. It's this tinkling, coquettish practiced laugh. I amuse her.

"Oh, I think you know, don't you? The wife always pretends to be the last one to know, but you're really the first. Right? Marriage…" She shakes her head. "It's such a permanent web, but we all want it."

She gets up from the sofa, grabs a bottle of white wine off the counter, fills her glass, and finishes it in one long swallow, then, pours herself another. *Not pregnant.*

She slides back to the sofa and leans towards me. "When Jake asked me to marry him, at first, it was terrifying to say yes, but I did, because everybody wants that—to be happy, married, secure. I mean look at him, he's gorgeous. And, he has those special traits we all need: loyalty, trust." She sighs and shakes her head. "Evan could never quite adhere to those, at least, not for long, or rather, with anyone still living." She shrugs with nonchalance and leans back. Her arms are draped across my sofa, while she swirls the wine glass with one hand.

"I trust Jake, but you…" She moves her head side-to-side. "You could never be sure of Evan, could you Julia?"

I never could.

She looks at her red-nailed manicure, as if she controls time and has plenty of it. I wonder if she even has a heartbeat, this poison star. I'm staring at her, unable to look away from her intense gaze, even as I feel the burning.

"He actually took me to that wretched cemetery in New Haven. Can you believe it? But, who could compete and win against a dead woman, like Elizabeth Hamilton? I saw it in him, right away, his endless quest in still loving her so much, searching for her persona in every woman he's with, or marries. I might look like her, but I could never be her. Who wants to be second, anyway?"

She frowns, and then, shakes her head, as if to clear it of an unpleasant thought.

"He didn't want you to find out. With a baby on the way, he wanted to try and make it work. With *you*." She looks surprised by her own remark, and then sighs. "We both agreed it was best to end it. I had Jake, he'd asked me to marry him on Valentine's Day. Evan had you. Our affair was just one of those things—an intoxicating heady experience, an amazing high. He wanted me; and his need was so great. I wanted him because he could satisfy me, in ways, no one else ever could." Savannah gets this bemused smile. "But, we knew we had to end it."

She looks sad, for a moment, and then, it's gone. Her features harden, like she's made of porcelain. She has perfect doll features: impenetrable, unaffected, and lifeless.

Then, she waves her hand in front of my face, as if to say, pay attention, this is important. "He took care of me, of everything. He was so generous. He gave me a promotion, money, stocks. We had this secret between us, and we agreed to keep it. We were both secure in knowing we could always start it up, again, if we needed to. I was right there at the office with him, working closely with him, every day, while Jake was away in London. Just the idea of it kept us going. But, I had Jake. And, he had you and the baby. Life went on. And Jake and I were getting married at Christmas time, and that was my focus." She nods. Then, her eyes narrow and hate just shoots from her, as if she's been suddenly lit afire and found her purpose. "And then, it all falls apart. Evan dies." She says this with such vehemence, as if it was just inexcusable of him to do this to her. "Jake cancels *everything*. I couldn't believe it. Your damn friend Kimberley couldn't move fast enough to send out those cancellation notices. You two are quite a pair."

"And *you*." She stabs a red fingernail into my hand as I hold my wine glass. "You ... you just couldn't handle *anything* on your own. Could you? And, Jake, like the good guy he is ... he's helping you out, at every turn. *Your* life's ruined, and, somehow, you're interfering with *mine*."

Her chest heaves, as she tries to catch her breath.

"Well, it's not going to work that way. Jake's mine. He's marrying *me*. We're going to be together, in Austin, where we both belong. And someday, when the time is just right, I'll let him know about our tidy little hedge fund account. Then, we can live the lifestyle we really want. You've really inspired me, today. It's been quite informative. He loves your kid; imagine how much he'll love one of his own. I intend to make that happen. Someday."

She laughs, as she pours herself another generous glass of wine, and swallows it down, reminding me of a black widow drinking its liquefied prey. "Evan insisted we keep our little affair quiet, but I believe the arrangement we had, died with him. And, you always knew. Didn't you, Julia?"

I make a guttural sound and search for words. I clutch my midsection wanting the venomous words she's spewing to just stop, to somehow not reach me, but they already have.

"There's no point in telling Jake. It would just make you look vindictive, and I'm sure you wouldn't want that. Perfect Julia being vengeful? Not possible." She laughs. "It'll be our little secret." She stands, runs her hand down the front of her black skirted thigh. I stand and face her, but shock ripples through me, and I can't form any words.

"I think we're finished here. I just wanted to be clear. Amazing what we have in common after all, you do look ... just like her. From her portrait in Malibu? Hey, if you ever get out there, can you look around for my black bikini? I left it there and it's my favorite. Evan was supposed to bring it back, but, you know, how men are about the little things."

I nod. *The little things, yes, it's the little things.*

"I should have kept it going a little longer with him, but he really wanted to make it work with you. Devote himself to you and ... Reid? Is it? So, maybe, in the end, he really did love you, Julia." She bestows me with a benevolent smile. "Yes, I think he did."

She retrieves her white sweater from the back of the chair, slips it on, and lifts her long dark hair away from the inside of the collar with one hand. And I just watch, from a place so far away, I can barely see her anymore, as these roiling waves of despair crash within and all but drown me. "Tell me this, did you have Evan buried or cremated?"

"Does it matter?" I ask, dully.

She's landed every crushing blow squarely upon my soul.

"No, I guess not. It really doesn't matter." Her smile disappears. "He's dead, either way."

She turns toward the French doors, just as Jake and Brad come across the deck. My throat constricts and I gasp for air.

By the time I look to where she was standing, just moments before, Savannah is opening the doors and calling to him. "Jake? We should get going. It's been a big day for everyone and I'm sure Julia wants to turn in early. She's told me she's tired." Savannah turns back to me, takes my hand, and squeezes it, then, lets it go.

Jake comes up to us. His kind nature consoles me, although I feel so far away already. I glance over at Brad and try to smile, but then, Savannah claims my attention, again, by reaching for me.

"You do look a little tired," Savannah says. She looks at Jake then, and dazzles him with her radiance, but he hesitates and half-smiles at me. "Jake?"

He looks back over at her and she nods, satisfied she has his attention, and then, she shifts her trajectory gaze back on to me.

"It's been so nice to finally meet you, Mrs. Evan Hamilton. *Julia.* It was a lovely party. Just so *sweet.* You have a beautiful child, there. I'm so sorry about your loss, about Evan."

Instinct for my survival, in some form, kicks in. This might be my only chance to save him from her, as well, so I take it.

"I'm so sorry about your own loss," I say in an even voice. "Thanks for thinking enough of me to share your story about losing the baby. Jake, I'm so sorry for you, for you both."

I glance over at Jake. *Help me.* But, he's reeling with his own devastation, reaching for her.

"Savannah, you lost the baby?"

She's stunned at my words, my comeback. She just stands there, for a moment, in disbelief that someone has dared to take her on. She hesitates. Her lips part, like she has something more to say. Then, she seems to recover, looks at Jake with this knowing lover's smile, as if to say, I've got this.

It's incongruent: her smile, his devastation.

I can't stop, now. I just keep going, fighting back, and landing blows she's not expecting. I grab her hand.

"Did you want to take the wine you opened with you? I'm not a white wine connoisseur."

Her frozen smile looks out of place. I retrieve the open bottle, cork it, and hand it to her in less than sixty seconds.

Last salvo.

"He was cremated," I say. "You asked and I never answered."

There's this vacuum of stunned silence, from beside me, as Dr. Bradley Stevenson comes closer to me, inadvertently, providing me with his strength, as well.

"You asked her about his burial?" Brad asks. His incredulity bolsters me further.

I remain standing, insulated from her poison star attack for a few more moments. I'm all powerful, gazing at her, holding my serve.

"Savannah?" Jake asks. "Why would you ask Julia a question like that?"

She recovers, affecting this pouty look. "I was … upset about losing the baby. I'm not myself. I didn't know how to tell you. I know how much you wanted it. And, Jake, you know, I just want us to be together and happy. I wanted to be able to give you what you want." A tear rolls down her cheek.

I watch her performance with sickening fascination and wonder where the tears come from. She feigns a heartbroken half-smile for all three of us and makes her way to Jake's car. She opens the door, looks back, and wipes at her face.

"Jake? Can we *please* go?"

With naiveté, I look over at Jake for acceptance, absolution, unity, all three, but he's despondent. His world's just fallen apart.

"She lost the baby," he says more to himself.

I'm careful with my answer. "She indicated she wasn't pregnant. She drank two glasses of white wine. I don't know. She told me a lot of things…" My voice trails off, I realize he can't even hear me, he's too devastated.

My newest heartbreak is pulling at me, and I begin to struggle with all these revelations and his response to her.

"I have some things to take care of," Jake says. "She needs me."

Perhaps, he's not a lost planet, anymore, but he's still within her orbit, not free of her, cruising along a collision path towards her. I've given him a lifeline, but he has to see it, to reach for it. He glances out at his car, where she waits, and then, looks back at me. His allegiance to her, even now, cuts across my soul.

"Then, go." All the pain she inflicted upon me in the last half hour begins to surface in this instantaneous fury. "Go to her. Choose her. She's all you see."

"Julia, you don't understand. She needs me."

I see his torment, but I can't believe he doesn't feel mine.

"Then, go."

Drowning seems most certain as I watch him leave.

My mother personified two great women: Jacqueline Kennedy Onassis and Princess Grace Kelly. Diana Hawthorne dressed impeccably, exemplified manners in all matters, civil or otherwise, and personified a way of life that embraced the arts and the art of fine living. She spoke and wrote eloquently about ordinary things and found the good in everything and every person. It's what I loved best about my mother, and, on this day, in this hour of evening, at this suspended moment, at twenty-seven years of age, I realize I have two choices: I can cry out and behave just as badly as the woman, who just left with Jake Winston, or I can emulate my mother or Jackie Kennedy or Grace Kelly.

The answer comes to me in a single defining moment, in knowing that any one of these three beautiful women would have taken the high road upon hearing the story Savannah Bennett has just told. At their very worst moments, these women were at their very best. Ethereal, calm, poised. So, this is me, too.

"Julia, are you all right?" Brad asks.

I turn toward him. *Smile.* "I think so."

"That was quite the revelation about her losing the baby. It's strange, she hadn't told Jake." Brad's looking at me and I struggle to stay poised and in control.

"She sat there and guzzled half a bottle of wine, while you two were walking the beach," I say. "There's no baby. I don't think there ever was. A girl like her." I grimace. "She's not interested in being a mother any time soon and that's what she told me."

My breath becomes unsteady. Shock renders my body, almost useless. I move slower, now, clutch at the kitchen doorway for balance, and then, make my way over to the counter and lean against it for support. I reach for normalcy and attempt to stave off the heartbreak, over Evan's infidelity and Jake's apparent allegiance to Savannah and her continual vicious lies, from overtaking me. The pain just keeps mounting. I'm not sure I can outrun this despair.

All the while, Brad's just watching me. "I'm asking, *as a friend*, if you're okay." He studies my face intently. His sincerity for my well-being almost causes me to break down.

"I'm telling you, as a *friend*, I'm fine." *A little smile.*

"Why don't I believe you?" Brad asks.

His scrutiny of me is interrupted by the arrival of the rest of my inner circle, especially Kimberley.

"Where's Jake and Savannah?"

Kimberley bounds into the room like a welcoming breeze on a hot day, reaches for Brad, and kisses him, like she's been gone for a week. I start to laugh, when I see this, but then, have trouble stopping.

I busy myself with drinking a glass of water. *Swallow, slow swallows.* I take advantage of Kimberley's open seduction of Brad in my kitchen, and try to regain my composure, though it's getting more difficult, as desolation begins its inevitable journey through all of me. Christian and Stephanie come through the door, carrying all the groceries. They give Kimberley a bad time for not helping bring things in from the car.

"Where's Jake and Savannah?" Stephanie asks.

God. Will you people stop asking me all these questions?

"They had to go." *Smile over at Brad.* "How was the beach walk on this perfect day?" *Be buoyant, gracious, poised.*

"It was great. Jake is … he's a great guy. I like him." Brad bestows me with one of his I-know-your-story-Julia-don't-try-to-hide-it-from-me looks. "I just want to know, *as a friend*, if you're okay."

Kimberley's looking from Brad to me. "What's going on?"

"I am. Fine. *And smile.* "But, I've been thinking, you guys should take off. You don't need to babysit me all weekend. I'm fine."

"Brad has a house in East Hampton," Kimberley says with a hopeful smile. "He was going to show it to me. Do you mind?"

I watch as he grabs her hand and kisses it.

"Go. I have to get Reid into the bath, ready for bed. So, no, I don't mind. Go."

Stephanie and Christian decide to go head and leave for Jake's place, where they're staying for the weekend. We all exchange hugs and kisses.

"I'll call you tomorrow."

"Only, if you're sure," Kimberley says.

"I'm positively sure." I hug Kimberley and then, Bradley. "Thanks for coming. How did you know the Teddy Ruxspin Bear would be the big hit, Dr. Stevenson?" *Gracious, smile.*

"Kid toys are my specialty. Are you sure you don't mind us leaving?" Brad asks.

"I don't mind. I'm fine." I turn away from his inquisitive look. "Kimmy, can you help me? Between the two of us we can manage to get these gifts upstairs." *I'm logical, calm, poised.*

"Sure. Jules, are you sure you're okay?" Kimberley gives me the once-over what's-wrong-with-you stare.

So not okay, but look at me smile and nod and convince my little magical friend how really okay I can be.

"I'm fine." I smile again, as I follow her up the stairs. "Really, I'm fine. Absolutely."

Kimberley whirls around at this and scrutinizes me.

Help me, Kimmy.

I falter.

There's a bleak moment, just a moment, and then, I'm poised, in control, and smiling.

"I'm fine."

I'm my mother this night. So call me Diana, or call me Jackie, or call me Grace.

I'm poised and ethereal as I wave goodbye to the last of my inner circle.

My island is gone. There's no shore in sight. These insurmountable waves of desolation overcome me.

Drowning is most certain.

CHAPTER

TWENTY

It's important to have a plan

PUBLIC RELATIONS, ALSO KNOWN AS *PR*, is all about maintaining a public image. Whether it is an organization for profit or non-profit, a business or celebrity, the goal is the same: look good in the eye of the public. And, every good public relations firm has a plan in place, *several*, in fact, because plans are the essence of the trade. In PR, being prepared for anything means starting with a plan.

There's the strategic plan, where strategies are determined by how a company or individual defines itself. How they want to be viewed or seen. For example, *Liaison* devises a strategy based around ABC Company's point of view about the environment. The company's message is: we respect the environment, but we also respect people's right to drink bottled water, if they so choose. And, guess what? ABC Company happens to sell bottled water and they don't consider their stance on the environment to be in conflict because the company does not believe their water bottles impact the environment, if recycling is utilized. The public perceives ABC Company as a supporter of the environment because they support recycling efforts, yet, the company sells bottled water which impacts the environment, but their reputation is perceived as environmentally conscious because they've said they are, and this is the message the public perceives.

A strategic plan, it's a beautiful thing in the PR business.

Get it?

Now, every good PR firm also has a crisis management plan. For example, let's say ABC Company's CEO has an extramarital affair and it makes all the papers because he's dating an environmentalist, who leads a protest against his company about bottling their water in plastic. Oh, this is a good one. The PR firm will determine the client's messaging in response to this unsavory story hitting the papers.

A spokesperson for ABC Company might say: "We support our employees and ensure they get help with their personal problems, when necessary. We consider this salacious story to be without merit and possibly untrue and we do our best to support all our employees in coping with these types of unfortunate challenges that may arise in their personal lives. ABC Company feels this is a personal matter between Executive X and his wife, a personal and private matter, and has nothing to do with ABC Company. We believe in our employees, here at ABC Company, and encourage them to follow process and fully support them, ensuring they get appropriate help, when needed, so they are productive employees. Just like we believe in recycling and believe bottled water is not a detriment to the environment. We want our customers to feel empowered and safe in drinking ABC Company's pristine water. That's our goal: satisfied customers and great employees."

Crisis averted.

So, all I need is a plan. Two plans. One for Hamilton Equities with both, short and long-term strategies, and another plan to mitigate the crisis taking place inside of me. A plan. I start with the easy one first and draft an email to send off to Kimberley's personal email account, when I'm ready.

DRAFT - Private Confidential Message
To: Ms. Kimberley Powers
From: Julia Hamilton

Dearest Most Magical One – Kimmy,
As you read this note, I want you to keep in mind how much I love you, and, I know, I'm putting a ton of shit on your shoulders to

do in my absence. Please help out Steph, too, because Reid is with her and Christian at my house in Amagansett, and I'm not sure how long I'm going to be gone, and I wasn't exactly forthcoming about it with Steph. I just don't know how long this is going to take. A week? Maybe more. Tell Dr. Hallmark Card not to worry. And don't you, either. I'm going to be fine.

So, for this crisis management plan, my number one goal is to ensure Reid's future. For the short term, because I just need to take this break, I want to move forward with the tactics we talked about yesterday. Do a press release announcing Jake Winston as acting CEO. Pull his file; (I guess we've never done that) just to ensure there are no surprises and beg him to do this for us. It's not going to be long term, just for six weeks. It would really help us out. If everything checks out, do the release, and get it out there ASAP to settle down the clients and the media. As you always say, "Keep those doors shut and locked, but do have an open sign on the door."

Also, go ahead and send out a release that clearly states I've returned to Manhattan to Hamilton Equities (fine, use the title chairman of the board, COB) to mitigate the media coverage about my previous absence and play up what we've done with Liaison in Paris. Also, tie in Christian's role in working with Hamilton Equities, over the past six months. Now, I know you're getting pissed off, at this point, reading this, because I'm straying into to your strategic area of expertise, but I learned a few things while I've been in Paris, so give me a break.

Please talk to David about a Liaison sponsorship of Hamilton Equities executive search program. But, let's talk about this one if Jake is willing to be acting CEO for a couple of months that may be all we need. We'll talk soon.

Kimberley Your Eyes only - Crisis management: pull all HR files and take them to Amagansett. Pull all the client lists. Freeze accounts on particular investors. Look for ties and / or connections to company employees. Pull files on everyone, including me, and you. Just do it. You'll understand why soon enough. We'll have a verbal conversation, in the next couple of days, and I'll explain why I'm doing this. We can tell Christian and Jake more at the appropriate time. But, Kimmy, you and I, will determine the time frame. (You can include Brad because he knows my double-down secrets as much as you do.)

Please start the Liaison team on research into the following objectives. (If you need to hire people, do it.) I want to establish foundations or donate to the following entities: Reid Hamilton trust fund (Jake should be able to do this or his partner); families of soldiers killed or wounded in Afghanistan; childhood counseling after family tragedy. (Can you talk to Brad about this one?) I want to establish an annual literary scholarship for Yale University in the names of Robert and Diana Hawthorne for aspiring writers. (Steph can probably look at this one for us.) Money isn't an object; we just need to make it all happen.

I need a complete list of all assets tied to Evan's estate. Can you please work with Jake on it, so, when I get back, we can discuss this, first? It's important to determine funding dollars for planning everything else.

You can trust Maggie Talbon to help us with anything that looks suspicious. She can pull files and get stuff to you. I hope you know what I'm talking about here.

It's down to you, Steph, Christian, and Brad for this inner circle. And, soon, you'll understand why I'm saying this. For now, let's keep her close by. Know thy enemy and all that shit.

Okay, I'm tired, and I'm swearing, and soon you'll understand why. I love all of you so much. You ARE the BEST family, a girl could ever have. It's your brand of magic that keeps me going, especially now.

Love,
Julia

<hr />

Then, I start developing my own personal plan, a crisis management plan. I have a lot to do and many handwritten notes to write. I just keep telling myself, I just need some time, some time, alone, to think things through and that's the main message in most of my notes to everyone I care about: Kimberley and Brad; Steph and Christian. That's my inner circle now, the only ones left I can trust and believe.

Julia's personal plan. Day one: sleep in Malibu. Day two: sleep in

Malibu. Day three: call Kimberley and discuss ramifications of memo sent earlier. Day four: call Steph and check in on Reid. Day Five: return to NYC to get things rolling.

Optional Second week – Have Reid join me in L.A.? Continue to decompress. Just think things through, and then, return home at end of second week.

A plan with options is always good. A plan with contingencies is also important. The important thing is to have a plan and try to stick to the plan and be open to modifications, as warranted.

⁓⁓⁕⁓⁓

After a few hours of sleep, I awaken and watch Reid as he sleeps. With the lightest touch I feel his fingers. I play with his hair, fingering the swirl at the crown of his head. I kiss my index finger and trace his forehead down to the bridge of his nose. He stirs awake, for a moment, and looks at me with adoration. The tears come, and I let them fall, as he closes his eyes, sighs, and drifts off to sleep. "I love you, baby. Mommy loves you, wherever I am."

Reid is so incredible, the best part of me, and I really hope whatever's going to happen to me that I'll be able to come back and be his mother again. That's my first wish: for Reid to be all right without me and never even know I've been gone. I've been absent, for the past five months, living this automaton life without — *don't think his name.* What's a few days, or a week, or a little more? *Why didn't you love me?*

⁓⁓⁕⁓⁓

At eight in the morning, Kimberley calls.

"It's Sunday," I say. "What are you doing up so early?" I've been up for three hours already.

"Calling you. You let me go without telling me the big news; Savannah isn't pregnant." She's indignant.

"Oh, did I?" I'm nonchalant and so very tired.

"What's wrong? Brad's worried about you, and now, so am I." She sighs. *Oh Kimmy.* "Look, I know things were beyond surreal with Jake and Savannah yesterday. I just want to make sure you're okay."

"I'm really fine. I'm tired. Savannah's … quite the piece of work."

"That is the understatement of the year."

219

Kimberley laughs and I get myself to laugh, too.

"I'm putting together some action items for the strategies about the CEO search," I say.

"Great, I can drop by and we can talk more. I'm only ten minutes away."

"No. You spend the day with Brad. Take the day off, Kimmy. I have to get some things done and I'm going to ask Stephanie to come here and watch Reid. So, have a great day with Brad doing whatever it is you do, when you're not doing what you really want to do."

"As if my celibacy status isn't hard enough to keep, you have to bring it up" she says.

"Pull your email later. Your personal account, not the company one," I say.

"Okay. Now, you're acting very mysterious, but you're okay, right?"

"I'm fine. Will you stop?" *Laugh.*

"Stopping."

Call ended flashes on my phone.

Oh Kimmy.

<hr />

Stephanie arrives around ten after my casual phone call asking her to swing by, while I've been racing around town and packing my suitcase, including Evan's laptop, the plans, and my passport, everything I could think of. I've placed the notes for everyone in manila folders and marked them all and put them in the office. I've been to the store and fed Reid his breakfast. I'm exhausted by mid-morning, but try not to show it, while Stephanie is casually drinking her coffee and looking at me with keen interest, most likely having by tipped off by Kimberley. I imagine her saying to Steph: Check on Julia; why don't you? I take a deep breath. *Smile.*

"I need a huge favor." *Calm, poised, in control.* "It's big. If you don't want to do it, I'll understand, but I don't … trust anyone else with him."

"Julia, what's wrong? Is this about watching Reid? Because I'll do it. I'd love to," Steph says. "Lianne's still in Manhattan, right?"

I nod.

"It's about watching Reid." I hold my breath, so thankful, she didn't ask me for how long. "I've got some things to do in the City, for a few days. You and Christian can stay here or at Jake's, either way, it would be great and watch him ... for me." *Breathe.* "And, after that—"

"You'll be back," Stephanie says. "Great. We'll take good care of him, I promise. I think we'll probably stay here, Savannah is stressing out even my easygoing Frenchman."

We both laugh. *I smile.*

And, walk away and don't cry.

"I'll be back as soon as I can."

"No hurry. Take your time."

I hand her his schedule and we go over it together. She seems fine. I give her a big hug and kiss Reid one last time, and try not to think about the significance of this goodbye with my son, or with Steph.

On the flight to L.A., I call Kimberley.

"I need you to go to my place in Amagansett. There's a list of everything I need you to do. I've sent an email to your personal account, and there are envelopes there for everyone: you, Christian, Stephanie, and even Brad."

"Where the hell are you? Steph just called and said you left Reid with her this morning and you were going to Manhattan, for a couple of days, to do some things. What *things*?"

"Kimmy, I'm not coming back for a while."

"Damn it, Jules, you're scaring me. Where are you? Tell me. I'll be right there."

"No. This is something I have to do on my own. I don't want to drag anybody else down into it."

"Drag anybody else *down*? What are you talking about? Julia, are you okay?" Panic begins to reverberate in her voice. The more agitated she becomes, the calmer I get.

"I'm not sure, but I'm going to find out soon enough. Just know, I love you, Kimmy, more than anyone else, except for Reid." I try to laugh. I can hear Kimberley talking to Brad in the background.

"Julia, it's ... Brad."

I smile, because we haven't quite figured out our relationship, yet. He's not my doctor, and he's with my best friend, and he pretty much knows every double-down secret that Kimberley does, except for this last one, about Savannah and Evan. I'm not going to tell him or Kimberley about that one, until, I know, if it's true or not. ,

"Tell me, what's going on," he says gently.

Ignoring his request, I ask a question of my own. "You'll take care of her, right? Because she is the real deal, the magic."

"I know. I'll take care of her. So are you, Julia. You're the magic, too. Whatever's going on with you, I know, you can handle it, but, if you didn't want to handle it all by yourself, you could tell Kimmy, or me. You know that, right?"

"There's that Hallmark card stuff, you say, that I really like about you. I'll fill you in the next time I see you."

There's a rustling sound. Then, Kimberley's back.

"Julia, please, tell me where you are," Kimberley says. She has this singsong voice going, she portrays this crisis worker, talking the jumper off a ledge.

"I can't. I love you, Kimmy. I'll call you soon. Help out Steph with Reid for me. Pull the emails. I'll call. I love you, Kimmy Powers."

I hang up the phone because I think I'm finally going to break down and cry. And, people in first class are beginning to notice this about me.

CHAPTER

TWENTY-ONE

Malibu answers

Los Angeles. I take a taxi from LAX to the house in Malibu. The journey along the Pacific Coast Highway begins to relieve my broken soul.

The cleaning service has been coming in, on a regular basis, and I left word with them, late last night, I'd be flying in. Lemon-scented cleaning solutions greet me, when I walk into the Malibu house at seven at night, West Coast time.

In a daze, with too long of a day, I watch the last of the bright orange sun, as it slides down the horizon out of sight. A gift to behold, this sunset, on the West Coast, and it reaches me in some small way.

I make my headquarters in the guest room, the bedroom farthest away from the master. I'm not ready for the journey into that particular room. It may no longer be a sanctuary and I'm fearful of what I might discover there.

I sleep the entire night into the next evening, plagued with night-mares about Evan, Savannah, and Elizabeth. The only one that soothes me is Bobby. He's the one, who tells me, that everything is going to be okay. I so want to believe him.

Day three away from Reid. I deviate from the plan. I forget the plan, for a moment, and it leads to my first mistake. This can happen with a plan and the important thing is to get back on track, but I don't do that soon enough. When I crawl out of bed, I make my way down the hall to the master bedroom.

Once there, I'm assailed by the memories of Evan and me, the honeymoon we spent, here, in this house, in this room. I stand in the center of it for a long time and slowly turn, taking in the gigantic bed, the stunning view of the Pacific, an endless stretch of blue, and think of Evan and me.

There was so much promise and a future ahead of us. He seemed excited about having a baby with me, something unplanned that forced us to a crossroads, sooner then we might have been, but he seemed to want me, want a baby, and want our life.

Now, his permanent absence activates a new kind of heartbreak. Silent questions seem to scream from the walls.

Did you ever love me? Did you?

Is silence my answer?

In a long while, it occurs to me that I need to know if what Savannah Bennett said was true or not. A desperate search ensues with a frenzied inventory of the entire room. I pull out every drawer and go through all the contents of each one. Finally, in one of the last drawers, my actions produce the black bikini, corroborating Savannah's story.

Somehow, I stay grounded. There's still no reaction to her story. I am beyond numb, beyond even drowning. I wrap it up in tissue paper and put it into the gift box I brought, especially, for this task.

I go back through drawers, until I find the swimsuit I left here on our honeymoon the January before last. My laugh echoes back to me in the bathroom, when I recall it was so cold that I never even wore it.

Not as cold, in L.A., in May. I rhyme again, and I try not to think about that other time, with bees and the state patrolman, but, I do.

Overcome with sudden sadness, I slide down the wall to the floor and close my eyes. And, just for a moment, I let in the sorrow.

He never loved me.

Later, I pull myself up off the floor and slip into the hot tub, and then later, the pool. Repetition occupies my mind and all I do is count laps, until I can't do anymore.

Exhausted from swimming and this heaviness in my heart, I watch the sun slide toward the horizon on day three in Malibu. I rhyme in time. A miracle, this sun, it illuminates the coming night sky with orange brilliance, until the very last second, I reach out and cover the last little orange slit with my hand and say goodbye.

Thoughts of Bobby keep me company. I keep hearing him say, "Everything's going to be okay, Babe." And, I so want to believe him.

"I know." My voice echoes poolside.

My plan begins to disintegrate in handling this news, in the persona of my mother. I can feel it leaving me, and I'm caught in this vast emptiness, and from far away, I start to worry about the plan, and even me.

A different day. Day Four? If so, the plan says: call Kimberley. I turn on my cell phone and wait a few minutes. It registers fifteen voicemails. I left her a note, didn't I?

Most are from Kimmy with variations of her saying, "Where are you?" She finally breaks down and says, "Where the fuck are you, Julia? Call me, now!"

Oh boy.

I deviate from the plan. I don't call Kimberley. I call Stephanie, needing to know Reid is okay. But, Christian answers. "Julia, how are you?"

"Christian … look, I'm sorry I had to leave you and Steph with … Reid. How is he?"

"He's good. He misses you, Julia. Where are you?"

"It's … hard to explain. I don't feel like I'm anywhere, right now. But, the sunsets are … orange and bright. Really amazing."

"Julia, Steph's right here. She wants to talk to you. Where are you, Julia?"

"Tell Steph, hello." I press end on my cell phone as I hear Reid babbling in the background. "Good baby. Mommy's okay."

***

I mark the days off on this white board now. There have been five. Six? Five or six. I realize I haven't done more than drink water, swim, and sleep. It occurs to me that, maybe, today is the day I should do something else. I find the keys to Evan's Porsche and head out. Have to love a man, who has a car at every house, and multiple houses at that.

I did love him, didn't I?

I think, I did.

I did.

I did, but not so much anymore.

There's this weight in my soul, and it gets so heavy, in just thinking of him, just thinking his name, or saying it aloud, within these echoing walls. Even then.

Shifting gears in this car proves too hard. I get confused. Which way do I go to get back to the house? I don't think I've strayed too far, but far enough.

"Lady, are you lost?" a guy asks, who looks just like Bobby.

"No."

"Do you want to be?"

I stare at his too-white smile. *I'm reminded of Jake. Jake? Don't think about him. Not good.*

"Do you want to be?" he asks.

"Do I want to be, what?"

"Lost."

"Absolutely."

There's a pool. We're high up in the hills of Malibu, away from the beach, now, at this gorgeous house. The Pacific is so vast. It's big from up here. I step into the pool. I just step in. The water is warm and I swim a while. Now, I shiver in my clothes, staring at the sunset and the vast Pacific. It's so vast. Endless. I look for the guy who has the too-white smile, but he's left me.

Of course. Of course, he's left me. Everyone does.

It occurs to me that I should eat something. I have this weird high going, from the drink he handed me, before, and now, he's left me. Of course, he's left me. Everyone does.

I can't find my car keys. Finally, Bobby figures it out.

Keys are on the car floor, Babe.

"Thanks, Bobby, I love you so much."

I wake up at the beach in the car. It's a beach that is vaguely familiar. The place is deserted, and I assume it's morning because the sun is behind me, when I'm looking out at the ocean.

You are here.

I laugh, when I see the sign and study the map. Somehow, I've made it to Marina del Rey.

"Bobby, did you bring me here? Because, you remembered. This is our beach, our place. We were supposed to get married, right here, on this very beach. I'd stay, but I have to get back. How far can it be to Evan's house in Malibu? Check that, *my* house in Malibu. Evan's dead. That much we do know; right, Bobby?"

He doesn't answer, and I can't wait around for him, because it is most certainly time for me to get back.

Five people give me directions to Malibu. Five people take turns, during this long day, to ask, "Lady, are you lost? Or, the variation of this one, which is: "Lady, are you okay?"

"Yes, I'm lost. Can you give me directions to Malibu?"

"Yes, I'm okay. I'm just tired, so very tired."

"Lady? Yes, I'm a lady. I guess. I'm twenty seven and I have a son who just turned one. And bees are mostly he's, except for the queen. And, Evan's dead, but he must have loved me because he came back. And, we had Reid, and Evan said, 'We're going to have this wonderful life.' And, I believed him. I thought, we did. I suppose, we did. But, it didn't last. It never lasts. And, why is that? These are hard questions that are going to take some time to answer. And, if I could find my house, and just sit down for a while, I would answer them."

"I have to get back to the plan. I had a plan, and now, I don't know where the house is, where I've left the plan, but I have to get back to it. I can't keep messing around with this stuff. My son needs me. I know he does and the longer it takes to process this, the less time I'll have with my son ... he'll be older; I'll be older and he might be old enough to realize that I've left him and I don't want ... Reid ... there it is. I forgot his name and I can't believe I did. I don't want Reid to know I ever left him. God, we should have just named him after you, Bobby. Because you, I will never forget."

I know, but Evan didn't want you to.

"The sun's starting to set. It's bright, blinding. I can't see. I'm pulling over, on the shoulder. The sign says, Pacific Coast Highway. I'm just trying to get to Malibu. You would think I would know. Wouldn't you?"

Are you okay?

"Well, yes, I think so. I'm just trying to sort things out. Figure it out. That's all. I have a plan. Every good ... like Kimmy ... has a plan."

"Do you think he ever saw me? Ever?"

He saw you, just like I see you, now.

"You've always seen me. That's hardly fair. Maybe, after Reid was born, maybe then. Maybe, he finally figured it out, then. It's just, who does that? Who would leave his pregnant wife and go off? Who does that? I wasn't going to think about this. I was going to deal with this later, and now, I can't find the house where the plan is."

What's your favorite color?

"You *know* this. Okay, I'll tell you, again, because you're just being funny. My favorite color is black because I love the night sky, black licorice, and I feel sorry for the color black because no one ever chooses it as their favorite. So I did, a long time ago, and it's still my favorite."

White chocolate or dark?

"White. You *know* this."

Favorite place in the world?

"Wherever you are."

And, if I'm not there?

"The place that brings me back to you. Okay, I'm tired we have to stop talking. I'm going to rest in the car and figure out where Malibu is. I know it's not hard to find, but I just can't seem to … find it. Good night. Thank you for being here with me."

<hr />

"Glove box. License. Registration. Here you go. I'm just trying to get home. I'm a little tired. I've been driving for some time."

"Do you need a lift, Mrs. Hamilton?"

"Yes, could you give me a ride? Oh, that would be so wonderful. I mean, if it's not too much trouble. What's your name?"

"Grant."

"Grant? Are you kidding? I met a policeman, whose last name was Grant, once before. He was there, at my husband's accident. Evan, my husband, died, over five months ago."

"I'm sorry to hear that."

"Well, yes, we've all been very sad. And, everyone is sorry. Sometimes, that's all we can be is sorry. Everyone is. Sorry. They're … just so … sorry. Yes, it would be better, if people didn't die. Because, if they didn't lie or die, then, they wouldn't have to be sorry, or lie, or die. That would be nice. Wouldn't it?"

"Mrs. Hamilton, are you okay?"

"Absolutely. I'm absolutely fine. Can you call me Julia? Mrs. Hamilton, the real one, the one he loved, is dead. And, it makes me sad, when people call me that. Call me … Julia. And, thank you for the ride. And, they'll just tow the car? That's magical. Isn't it? Thank you, Officer Grant."

"Is there anyone I can call?"

"No. There's no one left. We could try Bobby, but Afghanistan is a very long ways away, and he can only call, at certain times, and this isn't really an emergency. I'm just tired, that's all. Thank you, again, Officer Grant. You're very kind."

Ten marks on the board. I count them again. Is that right? I've got to get back to the plan. Where's the plan? I was supposed to call Kimmy, again, three days ago. I should probably call her, now. But I'm going to wait because I'm so tired, and I should really eat something.

Julia, you need to drink the water.

"Bobby, is that you? The room is so dark. Is it morning, yet? Where are the lights?"

It's nighttime.

"Bobby, I knew you'd come. The light switch is on. But, no one is here. Where are you?"

Drink something, Julia. You've got to eat. You're getting sick, and you have to be able to get to him. Get home.

"Home. Home is where? Yes, I want to get back to Reid. I want to. If I just wasn't so tired, if I just wasn't so sad."

The stairs. It takes forever to get down them. I hold tight to the rail and almost fall. My body won't move right. It's been too long, since I've eaten, too long, since I drank that party drink with that silly guy.

"Water. Still water, right from the tap. No one drinks tap water, anymore.

I'm wasting it. I'm watching the steam of water as it flows down the drain. Fascinating. This water."

Lean down and taste it.

"It's good and it's been too long, since I had water, so now, I have this new thing for water. Right here. Right now. Water. Bobby, can you turn the water off?"

⁂

Water helps. I don't feel so loopy, when I wake up. The water must have helped me.

"A little help is all I need. The ceiling is so high and so white above me. And there are the glassy walls that lead to beach."

I'm here. Get some rest. Tell me, where you are.

"Malibu. I told you. You're right here with me."

Where are you, Julia?

"On the living room floor. With Elizabeth's grey carpet. It has swirls and everything. That part I like. Evan said we can't change it. I wanted blue. But, it doesn't matter what I think, or want, or need. Should it be blue?"

It should be blue, if you want it to.

"You know that's what I love about you. You'd follow me anywhere, wouldn't you? Just like, now."

I'm coming. I'll be there soon.

"Soon. I knew you would."

⁂

Standing. Move toward the sliding glass doors. A perfect Malibu day. White sand, blue sky, and the surf. The Pacific, not the Atlantic. No letter *A* issues, here.

I pull the afghan off the sofa, wrap it around me, and go outside. To the beach. To the waves. The Pacific is calling me.

"Julia."

"Kimmy." I sink to the sand. "It's soft. I don't care, that it's in my hair. Hey, I rhyme."

⁂

"Her vitals are good. She's dehydrated. They want to keep her overnight for observation. The IV is just to get fluids into her faster. It looks like she hasn't eaten in days, so they'll run one for fluids and one for nutrition." *Dr. Hallmark Card ... is that you?*

"I don't like it." *Kimmy?*

230

"Baby, she's really going to be okay. They're not going to let you stay the night. They want her to get some rest. They're giving her a sedative, so she'll just sleep."

"I want to stay."

"Then we'll stay. I'll go make it happen."

"And, this is why I love you."

"Not the only reason, I hope."

"I just love it, when you're insecure, Bradley."

"I just love you, Kimberley."

Sunlight. Streams of it. Windows. Sunlight. Is there any other kind? It's bright, no matter what. Slats at the window. How long since those were dusted? People don't think about that. They should. Blue sky. A nice day. In L.A.? It doesn't feel as cold here. That's nice. See Bobby? Some things change.

Voices in the hallway. I can't open my eyes. I try but it's too much work. I'm so tired.

"I just don't think it's a good idea that she sees you, right now. You might upset her more." *Kimmy?*

"I have to see her. I need to talk to her." *Jake?*

"I have to agree with Kimberley on this, Jake. It's just not a good idea, until we know more of what set her off. Something happened that triggered this, and we have to figure out what it was." *Thank you, Dr. Hallmark Card. Perfect sense, you.*

"Is she going to be okay?" *I'm fine. Just tired.*

"I think she's going to be fine. It's just going to take some time. Kimberley and I are going to take her back to the Malibu house, when she's released, which is probably going to be later today, or tomorrow morning." *I'm fine, Bobby, tell 'em, I'm fine. Just tired.*

I open my eyes to L.A. sunlight. A typical hospital room greets me, although even the eccentricity that is Los Angeles sneaks its way into this room with a few wild colors splotches of red and yellow with black modern artwork gracing the walls. I haven't been in a hospital since ... oh, the night of Evan's funeral, which leads me to thinking of Jake and the most sensational and saddest night of my life. How can it be both? *Jake.* Thinking of Jake leads me to think of Savannah, which makes think of Evan and her together, which makes me so sad. Five days, then. How many will it be now? The sessions with Dr. Bradley Stevenson. *Brad,* now. *Geez.* It's hard to reconcile all that's transpired. But, Kimberley's happy, and it's all I want for her, Dr. Bradley Stevenson, her true one and only.

The door swings open, and there's Kimberley, looking rather festive and unnatural, again, in a pale pink jogging suit, I've never seen. She's donned her usual hospital drama attire, just for me. I smile at her.

"Well, I see your wardrobe hasn't changed for hospital duty," I say.

"Welcome back," she says. She sets down her coffee, runs over to me, and won't stop hugging me.

"Glad to be back."

And, I am.

⁂

How to lose fifteen pounds in twelve days without really trying. Suffer heartbreak. Break down, literally. Stop drinking water. Stop eating. Stop everything, and make yourself sick doing it. Twelve days. We can do it for you, too.

I'm released, after one day, from Cedars-Sinai Medical Center having been treated for dehydration and exhaustion—a typical Hollywood ailment that doesn't raise any unnecessary red flags with any of the medical staff, here. But, Dr. Bradley Stevenson is struggling with all of this.

Hippocratic mumbo jumbo, my previous history, and his propensity to be responsible, at all times, has him on edge, as we wander around the Malibu house and languish poolside, my first day back. After a satisfying lunch, where they both make sure I finish my meal, that Kimberley bought from some gourmet market in town, we sip lemonade and contemplate the background noise of sand and surf, and the things, so far, not being said.

Brad can't take it anymore.

"So, Julia, I'm in the capacity of *being your friend.* I can't treat you in the state of California, since I practice in the state of New York," Brad says. "And, since you've just been treated for dehydration and exhaustion and nothing more, and I'm not your doctor anymore, under the auspices of psychiatric care, because I'm going to marry Kimberley, do you want to talk about it, *as a friend?*"

This little bit of news that they're getting married is only a surprise to one of us, but Kimberley hardly smiles, when he says this. Worry lines etch her beautiful face, and I reach out and grab one of her hands. Then, I look over at Brad.

"You're one of those people that will pull the Band-Aid off in one swell swoop, aren't you?"

He looks disconcerted, for a moment. "Well, yes, I guess I am."

"And, this is what I love about you."

Kimberley beams, literally lights up, when I say this.

"So you want to talk about it?" she asks.

"I do, with both of you. Brad knows my double-down secrets as much as you do, Kimmy. Let's take a walk."

The Pacific, a constancy of rhythmic blue and white waves, plays an endless song as soothing to my soul as a lullaby to a child. We walk along the shoreline, among the palatial and eclectic collection of the wealthiest and most beautiful, where the rich and famous intermingle, and pretend to be ordinary. I have a sense of belonging among them, sharing in this same sentiment, in this same wish, for normalcy, among the extraordinary, in this twenty-seven mile stretch of sandy paradise that is Malibu. I link my arms with Brad and Kimberley's, as we journey along.

"You remember our huge fight about the beach house, about Elizabeth. He left me for a few weeks and I moved in with you. You were making the final plans for Paris. And, he came here. Then, he came back."

I look at Brad. "And we worked it out. I was eight months pregnant. He'd come back. He was different, different enough that I ignored the signs … of his infidelity."

"Oh, Julia." Anguish crosses Kimberley's features.

"I knew. I just didn't want to know. I wanted everything to be perfect. And, since it wasn't, I just ignored it. I was scared. Scared, to be on my own, but I knew. He was so remorseful. He went overboard on gifts and I should have known by that, alone. The thing is, I could never be Elizabeth, and we'd known that, but after he came back from being with someone else…"

I swallow and take a deep breath.

"He was different. I think he wanted to love me. He wanted things to work out. After we had Reid, there was no doubt. I'd finally done something Elizabeth had never been able to do, given him a child. And together, we were finally looking forward, instead of back. He wasn't Bobby, I wasn't Elizabeth, but we had Reid. Together, we were building a life and going forward. I'm not excusing what he did. I'm not even remembering it differently. He was broken over Elizabeth's death and he was coping in the only way he knew how. I was broken too, over Bobby, and I'm not perfect, either."

I look at Brad.

"I know that, now. Bobby wasn't perfect, either, but he was there for me. He loved me and I never had any doubt. With Evan, he was always on a quest in search of finding *her*, finding her replacement, whether he was married or not …always searching."

I look at Kimberley. "That's what she said. And, she's right."

"Did you know *her*? Did you know who he had an affair with?" Kimberley asks.

I stop walking, let go of them, and step toward the waves lapping the shore. Turning back, I look, first at Kimberley, and then, at Brad. They stand there, watching me, waiting.

We have walked about a mile down the beach now and I look back out at the far swells of blue surf, knowing that what I'm about to say will surprise, at least one of them.

"I didn't know her, but Jake does."

"*Savannah*? It was Savannah Bennett?" Kimberley gasps. "Evan had an affair with *her*? Does Jake know?"

I shake my head side-to-side.

"No. Savannah told me Evan gave her the job promotion at Hamilton Equities to have her close to him, in case, they decided to start things up again. In case, it didn't work out with me." I frown. "Jake doesn't know. And, we're not going to tell him, Kimmy. I don't want to be in the position of delivering that kind of news, the double betrayal of your fiancée with your best friend. No, thank you. I'm done. I want out. That's it." I run my hand along the horizon in my now familiar Blackjack *stand down* move. "Done."

"As a *friend*, I'm asking, what you mean by being *done*?" Brad asks.

"Well, Brad, as a *friend*, I'm telling you that I want to liquidate his company, sell all his assets, except for, perhaps, the fine house, here." I wave my arm wide in the general direction of the glass structure, a mile from us. "I'm moving on. I have a list of where I want the money to go. Reid is my priority."

"And, I am telling you as a *friend*, it's an awesome idea."

"Did he just say awesome, Kimmy? Wherever, did you find him?"

Kimberley laughs. "Well, I had this best friend, who needed a little help after her husband's wake, and he was there, to talk her through it."

Kimberley grabs Brad's hand and they smile at one another. I have to turn away, for a moment. Then, I glance back and almost smile.

"Well, I'm just glad I was able to help the two of you out."

"Jake's here," Kimberley says. "In L.A."

"No. I don't want to see him, Kimmy. I'm done with all of it. All connections to Evan."

"Are you sure? He says he has something he wants to say."

"Tell him, he can write me a note. I'm moving on. Here. To L.A. I'm going to live on the beach with Reid and love my life on the West Coast."

"Are you sure? Because, remember, Brad has a house in East Hampton, and we could finally be neighbors."

"That would be grand, wouldn't it?" I link my arms with both of them again, and we keep walking. "I'll think about it," I say, after a few minutes.

"You do that."

I squeeze her hand. "Don't worry, I'm fine. *Really*. I said I'd think about it." She still looks unhappy. "*Fine*. I'll split my time between, here and Amagansett. We can use this house for sunny family vacations." I look over at both of them with a sly smile. "You *will* be having children, so Reid has someone to play with, won't you?" Kimberley gets this frustrated look. "Please tell me you're not still holding out on him?"

"We are discussing our future and hastily making plans because waiting is proving to be extremely challenging," Kimberley says.

I look over at Brad and he's just smiling, his generous-six-ways-to-Sunday-handsome-self smile. Oh, to be Kimberley, and finally have someone who sees you.

CHAPTER

TWENTY-TWO

Connections between people, places and things

E'RE AT LAX, AND I'M ASSAILED by a memory, from nine years ago, when Bobby leaned up against the very wall I lean up against now. From a distance, I watch Kimberley, she hangs on to Brad and kisses him, a dozen times, goodbye, while they wait for the security lines to diminish. We're early, so we have a little time. Watching them, I feel this longing for that kind of connection again, for someone to see me that way, again.

I close my eyes. I wanted it to be that way with Evan, but now, I don't know if it ever was. The pain of his infidelity strikes a new blow at my heart and psyche. All I can trust and love is the inner circle and Reid.

The loudspeaker overhead disrupts my reverie. I open my eyes, stare across the gate area in search of Kimberley and Brad, and discover Jake Winston, fifty feet away.

He's leaning up against the wall, opposite from mine, and has the Calvin Klein Jean advertisement golden-boy persona going, today, with a white dress shirt open at the neck and the rolled-up sleeves and the designer blue jeans hugging his hips, just so. His looks and stance reflect Bobby's, from all those years ago. It's as if I could just walk right over there, and start my life over, again. The appeal for doing this thunders away at me inside. I could just go over there and start this whole thing all over again. It's there, but, I don't. His words, *she needs me,* plague me still. I just can't do it anymore. The plan is to cut all connections to Evan, all of them. We have to stay focused on the plan.

I slip away towards the crowd, looking for Kimberley's quirky L.A. chic, black beret that she's been sporting the last couple of days and Brad's blonde hair. Thirty seconds of scanning draws me to them, but I've forgotten my stealth moves and start walking towards them, out in the open.

He calls my name. His southern drawl, so familiar now, reaches me, even through the newest pain I carry. I slow down and attempt to concentrate, on reaching Brad and Kimberley, because just the sound of his voice begins to draw me in, again, to his amazing sphere of existence.

Will I ever be free of him? Do I want to be?

"Julia," he says, from right behind me. He reaches for my hand and some kind of gravitational force turns me around to face him. "Are you okay? I wasn't even sure it was you. You're so thin." I see him, taking in my black jeans, black t-shirt, and black bomber jacket. Shock registers on his face at my gaunt appearance.

I've combed my hair, there's that.

"It's me." I hang my head, embarrassed at my appearance, undone at the sight of him, and then, glance back up at him with a rueful smile. "How are you, Jake?"

"I'm headed to New York, again." He looks uncertain. "What happened to you, Julia?"

He scans my face for some kind of answer. I wish I had one for him. "A lot of things. I'm still working through them."

"I just wanted to see you, to talk to you, to know that you were okay, but Brad and Kimberley said you didn't want to see me." He gets this pained expression and hesitates. "I had a lot of expectations of you. Things you couldn't see and I don't want to do that to you anymore."

"It's nothing you did, but I can't be more than what I am, Jake. I've done enough of being what other people wanted me to be, especially with Evan. And, I won't do it, again. I am just me, after all."

"I wish you'd tell me what happened, so I could understand."

I sigh, and look over in Kimberley and Brad's direction. They're watching me closely.

When was I going to stop living with the secrets of my pain? When was I going to let go of them?

"Evan had … an affair. I came here to confirm it. That, it was true. And now, I'm working through it."

"Evan had an *affair*? When?" He's incredulous. It's beyond his comprehension. His reaction makes me feel slightly better. If his best friend didn't see it, why would I have seen it?

"Before Reid was born, in March, over a year ago. He brought her … here."

"Here?"

"To the place in Malibu."

I look past him at Kimberley. She's giving me the are-you-okay? look. I subtly nod. "Kimmy and I are staying in L.A., for a while longer. We have some things to work out with the company. I was wondering if you could help us out a little longer."

"I don't know. It's complicated." He looks uneasy, again. "I have to get to Austin. Figure some things out."

I nod. "Of course. Okay, well, if you change your mind, the job's still yours." *Smile.*

"Thank you for everything you've done for us, for Reid and me."

"Where is Reid?"

"Steph and Christian have him. I thought you knew that?"

"No." He looks at me closely, as his sweet breath caresses my face. "I just came out, when I got your call."

"I called you? When?" My heart begins to race. *I called him? When? Oh God.*

"Four days ago. You said you were lost in Marina del Rey and trying to find your way back to Malibu." He looks confused. "We talked for a long time, Julia. Several times. Don't you remember?"

"I wasn't myself." I look down and discover we're still holding hands. He grips my hand tighter and pulls me closer to him. "What did we talk about?"

"You talked a lot about sunsets and water. You called me Bobby, quite a bit. I guess you weren't yourself." He looks disappointed. "You were so *open* about everything."

"What did I say, exactly?"

"I'll send it to you in a note sometime." His eyes glint with anger.

"That's what Kimberley told me you said to do."

"I'm sorry that you came all this way for nothing. I have some things to work out." I look away. "I thought he loved me, and now, I don't know."

"I think he did."

I pull out of his grasp and wave my hand through the air in agitation. "He left me and took her to Malibu, for two weeks, when I was eight months pregnant. Who does that? Who knows how long it went on? He paid her stocks, money, promoted her." I stop. I shouldn't be saying any of this to him. I start again. "It's not easy when trust is broken like that. I thought the grief was bad." I wince, trying to control the pain that resurges. He grabs my hand, again. "I keep wondering what I did, what I didn't do. Was it me? Was it her?" I shake my head side-to-side, and then, look at him with defiance. "Now, I'm trying to look forward, instead of back. I don't want any ties to the past, to *him*."

"To me," he says. Now, Jake looks distraught. His lips part, as if he has more to say.

"I'm sorry. I hope you understand."

"No, I don't understand, but just know, you can always call me, and I'll come find you." He lifts my hand to his lips and kisses the inside of my wrist. "We're not even in a hallway. Look at the progress we've made, Julia."

He gets in the security line, and I watch him as he advances to the front. When he's through, he turns and waves at me, one last time. It takes all the strength of will I have left, to let him go.

⁓⁓⁑⁓⁓

Kimberley drives at a high rate of speed, while I languish, next to her, in the passenger seat of this silver Porsche 911, while my hand trails out the open window and the wind pushes against it, and I force it to stay there. Gravitational force, this wind, the only one I currently follow.

It's another great day in L.A., where it's sunny, without clouds, and with a just little breeze. *What's not to love about L.A.? This Hollywood scene?*

It's surreal, filled with beautiful people and perfect weather. *Why leave?*

240

"The new Julia is supposed to share with her best friend Kimberley what was going on back there, with the most stunning man, hands down, we've ever known, except for Bradley." She grins over at me. "The new Julia is supposed to be open with her feelings, and share them, with me, her old best friend Kimberley Powers. *Old*, in the sense we've known each other a long time, not in the sense that we're closer to thirty, instead of twenty, and that some, *not us*, would consider that old. *Sophisticated* is the word I'm going for here."

"There's nothing to say."

"Damn it. That's what you always say. Come on. We're on a new page of life. We've left the old one behind. Remember? Out with it, friend, how do you *feel?*"

"You know what your problem *is?*" I ask with growing irritation. I turn towards her as she speeds along in this fantastic sports car that I can only see as another token from Evan, an act of contrition that doesn't make up for what he did, doesn't excuse any of it, just another nice asset transferring away some of the pain from me, just by being *mine*. "You need to get laid, and you just put the only guy you want to do that with, on an airplane, so, please, don't make this about *me*."

"True," she says with a laugh. "But, you just did the same thing."

I'm about to argue this point, but I've dispensed with telling lies, and have committed to sharing more about how I feel about things, as part of my new plan, the new Julia's-moving-on plan. I think of Jake kissing my wrist, again, and the sensuous feeling that comes with it, and actually smile. "True," I finally say.

I go back to watching my hand fight the gravitational force of the wind. The only one I currently follow.

"Now that wasn't so bad, was it? Admitting, what you *want to do* and have *done to you* with Jake Winston, is the first step, in achieving that particular goal."

"He's not part of the plan."

"Well, he should be."

"You knew him." Kimberley stands above me, poolside, casting a long shadow, blocking my sun, and didn't hesitate to wake me. "Or rather, he *knew* you."

"Who knew who?" I ask, slightly irritated.

She sighs and holds up a legal size sheet of paper.

"I did dossiers on everyone, all of us, per your memo." She gives me one of her just-deal-with-it looks. "Miranda just sent everything over, about three hours ago, and I decided to play around with it, for fun, and you'd *asked*. So, I'm just flipping through everything, and it's starting to form a pattern, and so, I decided to work it up, and this is what it looks like," Kimberley says.

She lays out ten sheets of paper in a kind of timeline. There are photographs and one long line with dates, names, and small captions.

"I did it on everyone." She hesitates. "You, me, Brad, Christian, Stephanie, Jake, Savannah, even Bobby. You better take a look at this, Julia."

Kimberley is the best at her craft, *the best*. Her job is to ensure a public persona that matches the goals set out in the strategic PR plan, for whomever she's working with, which really means, knowing more than the client. So, she knows the secrets, sometimes, before they do. She has a wide ranging network and her mind really does work like a think tank of twelve men. She makes the connections between people, places, and things, all the time. By the time Kimberley has finished vetting her clients, there are no secrets left.

There are no secrets left, here, either, when I look at what she's put together. The feeling of exposure and, even, a resurgence of pain, returns, as I view the connections she's put together of my life.

"Start here," she says. "His parents went to Yale with yours. It makes sense because Jake's father is also a writer, Jonathon Winston. It looks like they kept in touch with your parents pretty regularly. There's correspondence Miranda found in that box you keep from New Haven. Don't look at me like that, Julia. You disappear, I don't know where you've gone and you didn't call when you were supposed to. It took some time to figure out you were in Malibu. So, we started going through the things at your house to try and determine where you might have gone."

She gets impatient and points to the timeline. "They visited you and your parents that summer. You went to Athens, two months later. After that, Julia Hawthorne disappears. There's not even a school registration with that name. You're off the radar for almost three years, in Chicago." I nod, trying to chase away the memories that come with those lost years. "Then, you met up with me in August of 2000 after you turned eighteen. We're in L.A. with Bobby."

She draws a vertical line from my life timeline, to the one below, she's marked as Jake's. She looks at me.

"Jake's *there*, Julia. He transferred from Texas University to UCLA in the fall of 2001. He played football with Bobby. Here's the team photo with his name listed. He must have known Bobby or you. Do you remember him?"

"No." I get up and start pacing along the edge of the pool. "I don't know. All I ever saw was Bobby. I've got to sit down."

I slide into one of the deck chairs and put my head on the table and feel the cool glass. *Jake is part of my past?*

"Look, I don't want to upset you. I just think it's more than a little interesting Jake's popped up into your life at various touch points. He was your first kiss, right?"

"What? I ... well, I guess he was." My mind is reeling and it must show on my face.

"You talked about it, once, when we first met up, on the way to L.A. on the plane. You said there had only been one guy, who moved you, and that was the guy you met, just before your parents died. You couldn't remember his name or his face, just that he had golden hair and a perfect smile and blue eyes."

How is it you remember this conversation, and I don't?"

"I don't know. I can't explain my clairvoyance. Just hear me out. You told me about him on the plane, *before* you met up with Bobby. Look, I loved Bobby, too. Don't get me wrong, but, Julia, the two of you connected right from the start. I'm thinking, maybe, just *maybe*, that connection had more to do with finding someone, who reminded you of your first kiss, Jake Winston, than Bobby Turner, himself."

"You know, this whole new Julia needs to share every fucking thing with you has really gotten to you. I think you're taking things a little too far."

"Don't get pissed at me. *Look*. I just see the pattern. The ties and connections are all there. He's been in your life, at several junctures. Your first kiss, at UCLA, he's Evan's best friend, and now, again, when Evan's ... gone."

She continues to draw vertical lines through my life time line as well as Jake's.

"What's your point?"

"God, just look at the pattern. Forget you, for a moment. Look at him. He's at UCLA for a year, and then, he transfers to Yale. He graduates with a B.A. in English Literature and goes to Yale Law School in New Haven, Connecticut. Okay, maybe his ties to school are with his parents, but you used to live there. He's friends with Evan and Christian, from the start, so that's 2003. You meet Evan in July of 2008 and marry him in January of 2009. Jake's been friends with Christian and Evan, since 2003. But, you never meet him, even the day of your wedding. And what happened that day? He was supposed to be the best man, but he's a no show."

"He said he came, but he wasn't there very long," I say.

"Why?"

"He didn't say. I didn't see him. Stephanie told me that he was up at the front of the chapel with Evan, but when I came down the aisle; he wasn't there. Evan said he just left without an explanation. They didn't speak for two months after that, and then, they worked it out," I say. "Jake had proposed to Savannah by then, and moved to London. I don't know. I was focused on Evan and having a baby. Then, Evan and I had our big fight over Elizabeth in March."

"Was he speaking to Jake, by then, again?"

"I don't know. Savannah was working at Hamilton Equities, by then. She and Jake must have started dating, sometime, the year before, he left for London. He said he wanted to start over."

"But, Evan is getting it on with Savannah in late March, *here*, betraying both you and Jake."

"I don't know what you're getting at."

"Evan is out of sorts because of your reaction to Elizabeth. He's angry, and he already knows a girl, who looks a lot like Elizabeth, and so, he does his normal pattern and hooks up with Savannah. I think it explains it a little bit. He wasn't speaking to Jake. Savannah was there, and willing."

"I really don't want to talk about this."

"I'm sorry. If it helps, you can imagine what my own dossier looks like, which I've already verbally shared with Brad." She hugs me.

"You aren't *married*."

"Evan was faithful to Elizabeth, but it pretty much ended there, although his pattern shifts, after Reid is born. No more women, just you."

"I don't feel any better. Who's this?" I point to the line with another long list of names."

"That's Savannah. She's very busy for a twenty-two-year-old, but I'm not judging." Kimberley laughs. "She's been with Jake, since mid-2008, but she's been with quite a few others, during that same time frame."

My head is spinning with all she has put together, and I already know how she does it. It's amazing what's goes on in coffee shop conversations, lunch meetings, business meetings, what's printed in newspaper articles and press releases, what's written in online blogs, said in phone calls, revealed in photographs, found on the Internet. *Connections. Ties.* It just takes someone looking, to connect it all together, to see the patterns.

Kimberley nods. "I'm going for some iced tea. Want some?" I watch her saunter off toward the sliding glass doors, but then, she turns back. "Oh, and she was never pregnant."

"How do you *know* this stuff?"

"Trust me. I'd know." And, Kimberley would.

I sit in the blazing sun and stare at the timeline, and the photos of people and captions that make up my life. Ties and connections, even Dr. Bradley Stevenson talked about these with me, but I never saw them that way, until now.

Kimberley returns, and hands me a glass of iced tea.

"So, what are Jake's complications?" I ask.

"Yeah, I'm wondering about that. Savannah Bennett and her family are big fish in Austin, Texas. Her upstanding family owns about half the town. The Winstons are the literary darlings of that particular universe. Jake's dad has done very well with his books. He's made all the best-seller lists. They live well. They have a place just outside of town—a ranch. It's curious Jake didn't settle there. But, I guess he was out looking for you."

"Will you *stop*? We don't know that, Kimmy."

"Right. It just looks like it."

"You're giving me way too much credit. I'm just the girl, at fifteen, who kissed him. Nobody remembers their first kiss."

"You did."

"I'm broken, my life turned tragic." I shake my head and look over at her. "I had to hold on to something, a vague memory of a guy, who made me feel complete, was just a fantasy of one of the last days of magic I had, before I got pushed into harsh reality and learned what the real world was like."

"You're not cynical. That's what is so amazing about you. You should be, but you're not. You'll start over, you already are."

Kimberley gets up and heads inside, to call Brad, I'm sure. It's been, at least four hours, since she last spoke to him. I lie back on the lounge chair and attempt to recapture the lazy feeling I was enjoying, before Kimmy abruptly mapped out my life for me.

An hour later, Kimberley calls my name. "Julia, you have a visitor."

I sit up, and spy her walking towards me, chatting up the guy walking behind her, who seems, somewhat, familiar. I recognize his voice. Officer Grant. He's carrying a bouquet of flowers. Kimberley walks ahead of him and gives me the be-nice-he's-here-for-you look. I stand up, feeling awkward in only my red bikini and sun hat, and force myself to smile.

"I just wanted to make sure you were doing okay. These are for you." He hands me the flowers, and I take them, and he's just looking at me, and I'm at a loss. I remember his voice, but that's about it. "Brian Grant. My name's Brian."

I shake his hand. "Julia Hamilton, well, soon to be Hawthorne." I look at a speechless Kimberley, who I haven't informed of this news. "I'm going back to my maiden name. How are you? Thanks for coming by."

"Sure."

Brian smiles. He has a nice smile, his grey eyes crinkle at the corners, and he has dimples. He's about six foot one and his hair is dark brown. I'm appraising him and doing this quick tabulation of all his characteristics, and comparing each one to Jake Winston. He's good-looking, but not GQ good-looking, like Jake, which is a relief.

Brian Grant is different in every way. *This is good. This is normal. I want normal.*

"So, Julia, would you like to go out to a movie or something tonight? It's my night off. I thought … maybe, if you weren't too busy you might like to go out … with me."

I so don't want to do this, but he has this charming, hopeful look, and I cannot turn him down. "Sure, that would be great. Let me change. Kimberley, do you want to come with us?" He looks disappointed, when I extend this invitation.

Kimberley says, "Oh, no, I've got a hair appointment. I'm late as it is."

"You do?"

"Yep, late. Go ahead, Julia, have fun."

I'm up changing into jeans, silently swearing, now that Kimberley and Officer Grant have interrupted my afternoon siesta, when she sneaks into my room. A few minutes before this, I heard her downstairs plying our guest with an iced tea and cheese and crackers, which is about all we have in the way of food around here. The new Julia has not been focusing upon her culinary efforts, at all.

"Okay, I think you should do it," Kimberley says.

"Do what?" I ask.

I brush lip gloss across my lips, and then, finger-fix my hair. I can't remember the last time I looked in the mirror or put on makeup, so I'm surprised to see this green-eyed woman with dark hair and subtle gold highlights and a hint of tan. I look good in my skinny black jeans and sleeveless white blouse. There's the promise of the Julia from the UCLA days. My lips even curve upward in the hint of a smile. I'm moving on. This is what moving on looks like. I'm going on a date with a normal guy. *A date. Me. The new Julia.*

"You know, if the timing is right, the moon is full, and it feels right, I think you should take it to the next level. I think you *need* to do this. He's a nice guy. He's a cop, for Christ's sake. I did a quick background check on him. He's clean as a whistle."

I give her a withering look, and she laughs.

"I had the software program up. He's been on the LAPD for four years, went to UCLA and everything. He kind of reminds me of Bobby, just with dark hair. Just think about it. Call it revenge sex

247

against Evan. You *need* it. You are too wound up and, since you sent Jake Winston away…"

"You're killin' me. I'm going out with him, just to get away from you."

"Sure." She grins. "Just remember who loves you best."

"Uh-huh, well, if my people would quit dying on me, you wouldn't be at the top of that list." I smile, as I say this, and Kimberley just laughs as she bounds out of my room.

There's something going on with me in L.A. I feel life slowly coming back into me.

⁕

Brian and I go see the movie, *The Ghosts of Girlfriends Past*, starring Matthew McConaughey and Jennifer Garner. He finds our seats and the theater is fairly deserted. He politely excuses himself, and then, returns with buttered popcorn, diet sodas, and plenty of napkins. The movie is sweet; it's about a guy and girl, who grew up together, grew apart, and find each other at the end.

Brian's holding my hand and I'm thinking of Jake. I'm supposed to be cutting all ties to the past, and here I am, thinking of a guy I kissed for the first time, almost twelve years ago.

⁕

Back at Brian's apartment, I'm thinking I probably shouldn't have gone out with him. I've just learned too much about the ties and connections in my life, to be sitting here, listening to Phil Collins, as he sings one of my favorite songs, *Against All Odds*, and of course, I'm thinking of Jake, again, even as Brian kisses me.

I'm on autopilot, when he's stroking my back and as my body responds and his hand explores what's underneath my silky blouse. And, this feeling is so good. I want normal. I want to be with a nice police officer, who says he hasn't stopped thinking about me, since ten days before, when he found me on the side of the highway, lost and out of sorts, as he put it. And I still like him when we're falling back onto his sofa.

And, I'm ready to do this.

Aren't I?

But then, I'm calling him, Jake, instead of Brian, and promptly burst into tears, and the nice police officer tries to comfort me, while I just cry, and that seems to be where we, pretty much, started, ten days before; and, when the date ends.

I tell him, at least five times, as he drives me back to my place, that I'm sorry, and I think, he's really beginning to believe me, or thinks I'm crazy, which I probably am. He's a nice guy and tells me, he's just glad, I'm okay. I kiss him on the cheek, goodbye. And, that's the end of Julia's revenge-sex-against-Evan date, which really seems to be revenge sex against myself, involving no sex, whatsoever. A normal date that managed to hurt Brian's feelings, upset me, and remind me of Jake.

Where's the plan? I'm supposed to be moving on from the connections to my past, which appears to be, namely, Jake, at this point, since everyone else is dead.

The new Julia is feeling a little bit undone, a little bit put out, and it doesn't bode well for Kimberley, when I walk through the door at one in the morning, and she's still up.

"I know what the complication is," Kimberley says. I see her astonished look at my tear-streaked face as she starts to form a question.

I say as softly as I've ever said anything, "Fucking *save it*. I don't want to talk about it."

"His parents are about to lose the ranch. His dad got into some REIT fund, about three years ago, invested all of his royalties from his books, and lost it all in late 2008 like so many with those kinds of investments. It looks like Jake tried to help him out, but all Jake's money is tied up with a property in Telluride, Colorado that he paid twelve million for and is underwater because of the housing downturn. It looks like he's trying to short sale it. It appears he bought the house in Telluride on Evan's behalf. Do you know *anything* about this?"

"No."

"So, his parents are about to lose their house, but there's this saving grace because the Bennetts own about half the town and Savannah's father is the president of the bank that owns the Winstons' ranch."

"Geez! This is like a damn western cowboy movie out of the seventies. Who *lives* this way? How much do they owe?"

"Ten million."

"These are all very *solvable* problems, Kimmy."

"Not to people who don't have money to throw around or give away." She makes a face.

"All right. Let's just take care of it all. It's not hard. It's a couple of phone calls and money transfers. But I want it to be *anonymous*. I'll take care of it, but I don't want Jake to know."

"What is your *problem*? How did things go with the nice Officer Grant?"

"I pretty much ruined his night, when I called out someone else's name, when we were progressing to something beyond kissing."

"Whose name?"

"I shouldn't have even said anything."

I stomp up the stairs and she races up them behind me, while I strip off my clothes as I go. I turn on the shower, and step in, and slide down the wall, and let the continual stream of water fall over me, and don't say or feel anything more.

CHAPTER

TWENTY-THREE

Kite without a tail

TWENTY-NINE DAYS IN L.A. WE'VE MADE our obligatory calls to Christian about all things Hamilton Equities, to Stephanie about Reid, to Brad about everything else, to my private banker about everything to do with Austin and Telluride and anonymity. And, we've spa-ed it, drunk it, sunned it, pooled it, and talked it through. And we've gone over the plan a hundred times.

"I'm going to have to hire temporary staff to get this all done," Kimberley says.

"Do it." I look over at her with my Jackie O black sunglasses and my wide brim sun hat that shades my face and just smile. "Money is no object."

"It will be, when you spend it all. Oh, excuse me, *give* it all away."

"You know, it's not about the money."

"Yes." She sips her margarita through a straw, loudly, on purpose, to annoy me. Kimberley isn't one hundred percent in favor of the plan to give all the money away.

"Have you ever thought about opening your own PR firm, Kimmy?"

She sighs, leans back in the lounge chair next to mine, adjusts her sunglasses, and then, her sun hat, the one identical to mine that we bought together on Hollywood Boulevard, a few days ago.

"Yes I have. It would be a huge undertaking and to do it right would cost a lot of money."

"Well, I just happen to have a lot."

"Oh God, I don't know, Jules, that's a whole other thing—big commitment, gigantic deal."

"I know, but it would be fun. You and me."

"Only if we run it on both coasts. Mix it up a little bit, but keep it small because I think the boutique approach works best. And pick our clients: no bankers, except for Christian, no lawyers, except for Jake, and no doctors, except for Brad. It'd be fun to focus on high tech. Those guys don't seem to be so uptight. Well, manageable, if uptight, anyway. I'd like to expand it, too, in terms of specialties, and look beyond the executive positioning stuff, get into product and company strategies, and more crisis management. Because, let's face it, a crisis is when we're superstars." She shakes her head. "We're actually great at them, but we leave that money on the table, all the time, and leave it to others to handle."

"Well, only if you put some thought into it," I say with a laugh. "When should we start?"

Kimberley grins over at me, and says, "I thought, we just did."

Later that afternoon, I watch a father and son at the beach fly a kite. I settle down into the sand and sip from a bottle of water and just watch. They attempt numerous times with their kite. The father holds it up in the air, the little boy takes off running and it falls to ground, again, but they keep trying.

My dad and I used to fly kites.

"The key is the tail, Julia. That's what controls the kite's direction and allows it to fly. The tail makes all the difference." I remember asking him what the string was for. "It anchors it down, so it doesn't fly away. See? But, it's the tail that keeps it flying, instead of crashing into the ground." I remember looking at my dad and asking him, if he was the kite or the tail? And, what was Mom? He told me, my mom was, most definitely, the kite, and he was the tail. I always wanted to be the tail, be like him, but I realize that I'm much more like my mother, with the colors, even the dramatic flair, and the desire to fly. No wonder, I was spinning out of control, I haven't had a tail, since Bobby.

I walk over to the father and son, and help them fashion a new tail for their kite. Within a few minutes, the kite soars high overhead.

And, we watch its perfect flight.

A kite with a tail is added to the plan. And, I tell Kimmy, it's time to go home.

So on the thirtieth day, Mommy came home.

Kimberley barely stops the car as she drops me off, so intent is she, on meeting up with Brad at his place in East Hampton. "I'm ten minutes away, at the most," she says.

"Nice. Tell Brad hi. Don't do anything I wouldn't do, which considering my love status is very very sad for you." I laugh, while she gets an all-knowing smile that conveys that celibacy may no longer be a part of her plan. "And, thanks."

"For what? Having a fabulous time in L.A., and getting a tan?" Kimberley's still wearing her sun hat all the way from L.A. to show Brad, personally and up close. "Get some rest. I'll see you, soon."

I walk through the front entry calling Reid's name and he runs at me, saying, "Momma, Momma."

Not forgotten at all.

"I told you he missed you," Stephanie says from the great room. "See Reid? Mommy's home." I go over to Steph and hug her for a long time.

"I can't ever repay you for taking care of him, both you and Christian," I say.

"Julia, taking care of him was a privilege. He's so wonderful, just like you." Steph starts crying first, then, I do, for a long time, because the new Julia doesn't hold in her feelings anymore.

When Christian arrives, I tell them everything that transpired with Savannah Bennett and Evan. I've had thirty days to deal with it, so I give them some time to process it.

"Jake doesn't know about Savannah. I told him I had some things to work out because I discovered Evan had an affair, but I didn't tell him who it was," I say.

"Don't you think you should?" Stephanie asks.

"As I told Kimberley, I don't want to be the one to deliver the news of a double betrayal of his fiancée and his best friend. He's going to have to figure out what he wants in his life, for himself. I don't want any ties to Evan, beyond the two of you, Kimberley and Brad, and for Reid's sake, Evan's parents, periodically. That's it. I'm moving on." I run my hand along the horizon in my permanently adopted Blackjack *stand down* move. "Done."

"I'm just so sorry," Christian says. "I knew Evan was … I knew, he was despondent over Elizabeth. I just didn't realize what he'd done to you. I don't know what to say."

"I'm not sure I know what to say, either. I mean, I know this stuff happens, I just didn't think it would happen to me. I wanted a marriage, a family. I thought he did, too." I look away and stare out the large window at the swells of the Atlantic. Gentle, today. "Anyway, I've made some decisions. Reid is my priority. As for Hamilton equities, it's time to let it go. I have a list of where I want the money to go."

"Julia, are you sure?" Christian asks.

I look over at him. "That is one thing I am definitely sure of. Kimberley and I have put together a plan." I provide a basic outline of how I want to sell assets, dissolve Hamilton Equities, and give away most of the money to important causes. Then, I share with them, a little, about what Kimberley and I did in L.A., in terms of beach, fun, and sun. "It's not as cold anymore in L.A., Steph. It was nice, freeing. I bought a kite." They both look at me in surprise.

"What?" I ask, and then, smile at them. I share the father and son kite story with them and they're still looking at me with this kind of wonder.

For a while, we share in necessary silence. I look over at Christian and know he's still upset about everything I've just told him and Steph, tonight.

"I just can't believe it. It's just so sad," Christian finally says.

"I know, you're so amazing and we didn't realize Evan had hurt you so," Stephanie says.

"All right, you two, don't worry about me, okay? We tried to make it work. We were just two broken people. who loved the ones who had died the most, and we were just trying to cope. I'm not excusing his behavior." I look over at them. "But, he's not the only one, who's in love with Savannah Bennett."

"What about that? What about Jake?" Stephanie asks.

"It's complicated." I wince at using Jake's favorite phrase. "Jake told me there were complications, and I know, now, they all have to do with Savannah. I don't know. We have a connection, but I'm not..." I sigh and start again. "My sphere of trust is pretty clear to me, right now. It includes: both of you, and Kimberley and Brad. With Jake's ties to Savannah..." I shake my head and look directly at Christian. "I can't include him in the circle, right now. I can't. He's a wonderful guy, but his fiancée came into my home and did her best to destroy me, so forgive me, if I don't want anything to do with her."

"I'll talk to him, just outline the general plan, that's all," Christian says with reassurance. "Someday, everything is going to be all right for you, again. You're an amazing person, Julia. Steph and I believe there's love for you in this world and it's just going to take some time to find it. This, we know."

"Reid's my priority, right now. I just want a normal life. Something happened in L.A., out of all the bad I went through, something good, and I'm just trying to figure out what it all means for me. For me and Reid."

Later, I spend a few minutes out at the beach and just listen to the roar of the ocean waves. It's my new favorite thing to do.

The restorative powers console me, even here, on the East Coast, so different from L.A. and Malibu. The salt air and light breeze swirl around me, serving as a protective cloak. I feel alive, more alive, than I have in months.

And, here's what I know: I'm not drowning anymore. I can't see my island. He's gone from me, forever now, but I'm standing on life's shore again.

I am here.

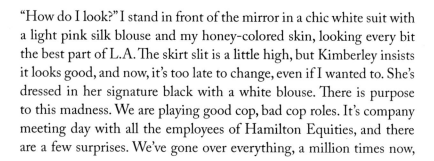

"How do I look?" I stand in front of the mirror in a chic white suit with a light pink silk blouse and my honey-colored skin, looking every bit the best part of L.A. The skirt slit is a little high, but Kimberley insists it looks good, and now, it's too late to change, even if I wanted to. She's dressed in her signature black with a white blouse. There is purpose to this madness. We are playing good cop, bad cop roles. It's company meeting day with all the employees of Hamilton Equities, and there are a few surprises. We've gone over everything, a million times now, but I'm still nervous. I smooth down my skirt, fidget with my blouse and hair for the tenth time, in an hour.

"You look great, perfect. Quit worrying."

"Who's all going to be there, again?"

"Everybody. We've briefed Christian. This is really a non-event. I've had the packages prepped for those getting them. Everything's done."

"Do you think she'll be there?"

"Oh, yes."

"And, Jake?"

"Not sure. Christian was working on it. Jake's been busy packing his apartment, still intent on moving to Austin."

"We should have told him." I shoot her an anxious look.

"Julia, we've been over this. People see what they want to see. If he hasn't figured out Savannah Bennett, by now, on his own, then, he never will."

Fifteen minutes later, I'm standing at the end of the long conference room as the employees of Hamilton Equities file in. I seek out the familiar face of Maggie Talbon, Evan's assistant; she gives me a reassuring smile. Maggie's been briefed on the gist of what is taking place today. She's been helpful with all of the confidential stuff and she's expressed interest in following Kimberley and me into our new endeavor of a PR firm of our own with select clients. I look over at Kimberley, and she points to the papers in my hand with the detailed agenda. Christian gives me a reassuring pat on my shoulder, as he takes the seat to my left. Then, I glance up in time to see Jake slide into the chair, next to Christian. We haven't seen each other, since my return from L.A., a week ago. My breath quickens at just the sight of him. *Stick to the plan, Julia.*

I look around the room, again, and remind myself there is really only one enemy in this camp, and she takes the third chair, down the row, next to Jake, and gives him one of her more seductive smiles. I look away, and Kimberley catches my eye and nods and gives me the get-on-with-it-look.

Fine.

"I want to thank all of you for these past six months of support, since Evan's death. He loved you all so much, loved working with you. It's a privilege to stand up here and see all of you, here, and acknowledge what you've accomplished. Your perseverance and dedication are so touching. I know it hasn't been easy, and I just want to thank you, one more time."

I pause. *Breathe, Julia.* Don't stare at Jake in his fantastic navy blue power suit. Turn to the right and look at Maggie. *Smile.*

"I've just returned from L.A., where on one of my last days there, I was watching this little boy and his dad at the beach as they were trying to fly this kite. It wasn't working. Dad kept flipping it up in the air and the boy would take off running and it just kept crashing to the ground. I could see what's wrong with it, so I went over and helped them make the tail longer. And, we watched it fly."

Jake's looking at me with a new concentration I haven't seen before and I smile a little, and nod, and, he does, too. I look around the room. "With a kite, it's the tail that keeps it going, allows it to swirl and dive, and fly the way it should. Sure, you need the string to keep it from flying away, but it's the tail that makes it soar. Without the tail, it doesn't fly. You have to have the perfect tail, to keep a kite flying. You need someone dedicated to the markets that can sense the winds of change, make the proper adjustments, and keep the kite in the air. That was Evan. And, now, no matter what we do, our kite won't fly."

I look around the room and pick up my notes with a shaking hand and take another deep breath.

"So, we're closing Hamilton Equities. We're going to inform our clients of this decision and assure them of our goal in making this as smooth a transition as possible. We'll transfer their assets to another firm, such as Christian's, or one of their choosing, or cash them out. As you all know, Christian and Jake have been tireless in their efforts to keep Evan's company going, but they both have their own pursuits, and we can't ask them to delay their own priorities, any longer."

I seek out Christian for reassurance. *Breathe.*

"I have my own priority, and his name is Reid Hamilton. A one-year-old doesn't need very much, just a mother, who can give him all the love in the world." I smile over at Maggie Talbon, as she clasps her hands together, in the middle of her chest, and beams at me.

"The reality is, I have a background in public relations, not finance, and my focus is on Reid and his future. There's no doubt we could continue to fly this kite with your amazing efforts and dedication, but it will never be the same without Evan."

I pause, while Kimberley and her team hand out the compensation packages to everyone. From a human resources perspective, we've left Savannah out of this whole process, but she doesn't even seem to notice. She's busy flipping through the handouts, when I glance in her direction. *Breathe, Julia.*

"I've tried to ensure, you are well taken care of, for the next two years, until you find other employment. We can provide letters of recommendation should you need them. Change can be difficult, I know. The past six months ... have been hard for all of us. Please let us know what you need." I look right at Jake. "Sometimes, as I've recently learned, some things change and you really just need to find a tail that can make your kite fly to see where it takes you."

He's looking at me in complete surprise with his mouth half-open. *Look away.*

I pace the floor a bit to regain my momentum, because I've completely lost it, with the look I've just exchanged with Jake. Everyone is smiling at me. And, maybe, they're thinking, that poor crazy girl, she's off her rocker, and it's absolutely true, because she's giving away most of her money.

"Okay, moving on, because I'm still jet-lagged from L.A., apparently." I laugh, and glance at Kimberley, who has this wide smile, and she's pointing to the papers in my hand. "Oh yes, I have several charities I'm interested in supporting, and we're dividing Evan's assets among them. We'll continue to support the Elizabeth Hamilton Cancer Research Foundation and are in the process of establishing foundations for the families of soldiers killed or wounded in Afghanistan as well as children who experience family tragedy. Dr. Bradley Stevenson is helping us with that one. We've also established an annual literary scholarship at Yale University in the names of Robert and Diana Hawthorne for aspiring writers. I'm open to other causes any of you would like us to consider for support, so please let me know, if you have any." I take a breath. "That's it. Are there any questions before I hand it over to Kimberley?"

"You're giving away all his money to charity?" Savannah asks. "Why would you do that?" She looks incredulous.

"I'm giving away quite a bit of it. We're starting a PR firm and we'll need some seed money for it, but yes, these are the things I care about, and as long as Reid's future is taken care of, this is what I've chosen to do."

"This just doesn't make any sense. It's ludicrous! He worked hard for all that money, and he spent it, and enjoyed spending it. And, you! You're just giving it away to cancer patients and soldiers and their families and screwed-up kids and writers?"

"Savannah, what are you saying? Jake asks. "These are Julia's wishes. She doesn't even have to tell any of us about this. It's her decision, what to do with her money." Jake looks at me, and I smile back at him, savoring this brief moment, as he defends my actions.

"I've been incredibly lucky from a financial perspective and I think it's important to give back, if you're able to," I say. "My son is my priority and a comfortable life, not an extravagant one, is fine."

"I just don't think Evan would have wanted you to do this," Savannah says. "And, I just think it's … you're just…" She gives me a withering look and shrugs. "Fine."

Intuitively, I know she's not going to say anything more. She's said enough to try to rattle me, but no one else. I seek out Jake, again, for support, but now, he's quietly talking to Christian.

"Kimberley, can you and your team go through the strategy for informing our clients?"

I breathe a subtle sigh of relief that my part is finished and slide into the chair Kimberley's just vacated directly across from Christian, Jake and Savannah. Jake is studying the papers Kimmy's team has handed around and doesn't even look up at me. I feel this stab of jealousy, in watching Savannah place her hand on his left shoulder, and talk to him in a low tone, and he's nodding, but not really saying anything to her.

Why can't he see who she really is? Even now?

"Thank you, Julia. We've compiled a list of the clients that need to be informed of our decision to dissolve the company," Kimberley says. "This is the complete list with all the contact information for those we have. Please review it and, tomorrow, we'll divide up into teams and make the calls. Among the papers, you'll find the acceptable script for calling our clients, and, of course, this is all confidential and needs to follow protocol. It's our hope with Julia's generosity with your severance that we can count on you to uphold the terms of your employment with us. Let's quickly review the client list and identify the teams, so we can get this going tomorrow morning."

While everyone is reviewing the handouts, I'm just trying to breathe and keep it together, Jackie O style, and thirsting for a margarita. Right now. I wish I was on a beach, somewhere, helping a father and his son fly a kite. I can't even look at Jake anymore, I'm done in by seeing him with Savannah. Now, I'm feeling guilty about some of the things we haven't told him, leaving him out of the inner circle discussions and plans because of his ties to her. It's not his fault. Minutes later, I'm losing my poise, and I just want to go to the beach, and not be here, anymore.

Maggie Talbon comes over with a cup of tea. *For me?*

"I'll just leave you to it. I'm right outside the door," she says. I give her a grateful smile.

Tea. Not a margarita. Tea. Okay. All right. Breathe. Smile. Poised. In control.

Dr. Hallmark Card would be so proud and I so wish Brad was here. I look over at Jake. He's reviewing the client list and glances up, and smiles at me, that reassuring one. I like that one. His eyes are this glacier-blue, today, this amazing glint, they just sparkle my way, and he looks like he should model Calvin Klein underwear and women would buy it right off of him, because he is beyond description and on a scale of ... *Oh God. Look away. Drink the tea.*

I catch Kimberley's eye. *Can I go now?* She subtly shakes her head. *Tea.*

"That's it. We'll meet tomorrow to discuss strategy."

Employees are beginning to file out, intent on reading their compensation packages, to determine if they have any questions before we meet again.

Timing.

"Oh, one last thing," Kimberley says, just like we practiced. "There are a few accounts that are unidentifiable. Perhaps, Evan had money set aside for specific purposes, for investment strategies for him, or key clients. If we can't identify whose assets they might belong to, beyond Julia, we're going to transfer those to the escrow account, and, eventually, liquidate the funds to the ones identified for charitable contributions."

Kimberley glances over and shoots me the get-ready look. We practiced that, too.

Savannah is just sitting there and staring at a piece of paper she clutches in her hand. Then, she looks up and over at me. The poison star gaze, direct, searing, I can feel it from here, six feet away from me across the table.

"What happens to the funds you can't identify, again?" Her voice is faint, as if she's having trouble getting air.

"If it can't be identified, it'll go into the escrow account and we'll liquidate it for the charitable causes," I say, on cue, just like we practiced.

Then, Kimberley jumps in. *Thank God.* "For example, the SB Investments? That one? All indications are Evan coordinated all activity with that account. The trades' history confirms his account code for making all the transactions associated with it. Since we're not able to identify who he was making them for, we'll transfer the money back to the escrow account." She looks down at the client list. "Yes, the entire sum of $12,600,012 and change will go into the escrow account, since there's no identifiable person, except Evan, associated with it. No worries."

Kimberley rewards Savannah with her most angelic smile, the one she saves for the resignation of a bad client, which she's done, just turned them down, turned them out for bad behavior.

"There weren't too many of those, just a few," she adds.

Kimberley shrugs her shoulders with nonchalance and looks around the room as most of the employees file out. Two of the last stock brokers that are about to leave, promise to take a look at the list and see if they can find out more information from the account files.

"Great, thanks," Kimberley says sweetly.

Timing.

Now, it's only Kimberley, Jake, Christian, Savannah, and me.

"SB Investments?" Jake asks. He turns to Savannah. "Can I talk to you?"

"Just a minute, Jake." Savannah is looking directly at me. "Julia, what do you want? I'm sure we could work something out about the SB Investments account." She actually smiles.

The girl is a wonder. She's enjoying this and thinks she can hurt me even further.

I look over at Kimberley, in awe, because this is all playing out, just as she and Christian had predicted it would. Brad, too. Stephanie and I were the only holdouts, thinking no one would be that motivated by money, alone.

"We should take this offline," I say, just the way we practiced. Savannah has this smoldering look, again, and it becomes clear, even to my naive way of thinking, it was always about the money for her, and never about Jake, or Evan.

"No," she says. "There's no need for that. What do you want?"

"What are you offering?" My response is not part of the plan. Christian and Kimberley both shift in their seats, when I say this.

Savannah looks confused, as if no one has ever dared ask her to give up anything before. I can see the tipping point coming in her. She's looks more unbalanced, more desperate, as her breathing becomes erratic, and the panic sets in. Her violet-blue eyes become more opaque because as she, now, knows, I hold all the cards. And, she wants her money, one way, or the other, at the expense of everyone else, even Jake.

I steal a look at him, but he's focused on the client list, and then, asking Christian a question. I'm getting confused by how calm everyone is. I glance at Kimberley who subtly nods—it's our signal—to go ahead, and again, suggest we take this offline, just as we practiced.

This whole thing is so surreal, a play happening in slow motion, Shakespeare, no doubt.

"It's mine. What … do you want?" Savannah asks, again.

"Well," I say, standing up and moving to the head of the table again.

Not in the plan.

The plan was to get her to confirm knowledge of the account, which she's just done. Stop there. Let it go. Play her out, with everyone predicting she'll come to me, in the next day or so, in private, and we'll tell her what we already know: she has no rights to the money, whatsoever. But, she seems to have that figured out already, and now, she's playing me.

So, I deviate from the plan.

"Truthfully, I'd like you to share with the group the story, you told me, that has caused me so much heartbreak, for the past five weeks," I say. I sense, Jake looking up and over at me, but I concentrate on Savannah and hold my serve, look directly at her, and withstand her fiery gaze. "But no, I think there's been enough suffering, among all of us, in relation to *you*. So, I'll ask you, again; what are you offering?"

I start for the door, just as Kimberley has prepared me to do. I steal a look at Jake, and see the clenching of his jaw and know he's just beginning to figure out what I've said, and watch this latest revelation come down on him.

"Him," Savannah says.

Her single utterance hits me, like an unexpected storm gust off the ocean. This sudden rage for what's she done to us, and what she's doing to him, for money, takes over. I whirl around and face her, my hands clenched, knowing what I'm about to do is so not a part of the plan. I glance over at Kimberley, and she looks a little scared because I'm sure I have this crazed look, like I've just woken up and realized where I am. And, maybe, I have. Because I just got back from L.A., where I bought a kite, and the new Julia can handle this.

"Here's my offer." I look at my watch, glance at Kimmy, then Christian. "I cut you a check for the amount Kimberley just read off and you are out of this office, out of this building, out of this city, and out of my life, and his, and his family's, too. That's the deal. It's non-negotiable. You have five minutes to decide what you want to do. Five minutes to clear out, and five hours, in which, to make it happen, verified by an escort of this firm, or the check becomes invalid. I'll cancel the whole God-damn thing, and you won't see a dime. *Ever*."

She doesn't even hesitate. She doesn't even get that vexed look, as if to say I'm thinking this through. She just stands up in her perfect poison star form with her chic designer suit, smooths down her skirt with her flawless manicure, and rewards us with one of her most radiant smiles, Scarlet O'Hara style, that clearly conveys she's just having a set-back. It's just been *one of those days*, at Tara. She doesn't even glance in Jake's direction, when she says, "Done."

263

I take a shallow breath and hold it, for a moment, while she just watches me. We stare each other down. I allow myself a little smile and she smiles back.

The rest of the room is dead silent.

"Well then, cut the lady a check, Christian," I finally say.

From the credenza, I grab the silver gift box with her black bikini swimsuit inside, and slide it—*jam it*—across the conference table her way. I can't even look at Jake.

"You left this in Malibu," I say.

And, I walk out.

Chapter

Twenty-Four

Find a tail that makes your kite fly

AGGIE MEETS ME IN THE HALLWAY, takes hold of my arm, and leads me to the executive elevator down by Evan's office. She loads me up with my laptop on one shoulder, and my purse on the other, and drapes my white suit jacket across my outstretched arm. Kimberley's arranged a reception for the employees at The Peninsula hotel. I'm supposed to be going there. There's a car and driver, downstairs, waiting for me. I'm trembling, but I try to hide it from Maggie.

"Oh, I found this." She picks up the long florist box off the foyer table. "It had Mr. Winston's name on the gift card envelope. I assume you want to give it to him, tonight, before he leaves for Austin?"

"Right." The shaking mysteriously stops. This numbing sensation takes over. I attempt to smile at her, as she hands me hands me the long silver gift box. It contains one of the kites I bought in L.A. I was going to give it to Jake, but now, I don't know, if I'll ever see him, again, after what just transpired in the conference room.

"I found these, too." She hands me a set of keys. "They go to Evan's car. His black Mercedes is parked in the garage. I don't know … maybe, you want to be on your own."

"Yes, maybe, I do." Voices begin to filter to us. I anxiously scan the hallway. "I just want to go home to Reid." I blink back tears and try to smile.

"Then *go*. They can handle things here, now. You don't have to."

Maggie gently pushes my loaded-up self onto the private executive elevator and presses the down button. "We'll talk next week."

"Thank you."

The elevator whisks me down to the parking garage, where I walk around in a daze, loaded down with all of this stuff, and look for Evan's car. Minutes later, I discover a black Mercedes, covered in a fine film of dust, located in a parking space marked *Reserved for:* Evan Hamilton.

There it is, just one more token item, that compensates me, in some innocuous way, for what Evan did to me. I wipe away sudden tears with my only free hand, hit the unlock button on the key fob, and toss everything into the trunk.

As soon as I shut the car door, the enclosed space swallows me up. Silence, absolute silence greets me. I sit back, close my eyes, and replay what just took place.

Two dominant emotions rain down on me: euphoria for standing up to Savannah and this profound disenchantment with Jake's passive reaction to her greedy vile behavior.

Don't think about him. It's over. It's done.

I glide the car out of the garage and onto the crowded streets of Manhattan. I'm a long way from Amagansett, but I'm definitely going home. I console myself with this thought, as I navigate the traffic.

It's another fifteen minutes before Kimberley calls. "Nice adjustment to the plan!"

"I can't really talk … right now."

"Hold up. Take a breath. Everything's fine. I'll be with you soon at the hotel."

I grimace, knowing she'll figure out soon enough I'm not going to the hotel. *Stick to the plan. The plan, Julia.*

"Take another breath," Kimberley says in a consoling tone. "My God, your mother would be so proud. *Jackie O* would be proud. I just can't believe how you handled everything. You are a superstar, and so ready to fly, soaring already. My God, it was fantastic, such a rush."

"You're killin' me." I do my best to concentrate on the road. "Is she gone?" I grip the steering wheel tighter.

"Oh yes. She's gone, cleared out. Christian and Jake had her sign some paperwork; I'm not sure what that was all about, but it's done. Christian escorted her out of the building and on to the airport," she

SEEING JULIA

says with a hint of wonder in her voice. "Unbelievable, huh? I knew she'd take the cash. Hold on a second, I have another call."

The cell call goes silent. I nose the car onto the ramp for the Brooklyn Bridge.

Kimberley breaks in. "Where *are* you? That was the driver, asking when you're coming down. He's been waiting for the last twenty minutes. I waited to call you because there's no cell service in the garage. Damn it, Julia! Where are you?"

"Don't panic. I'm going home. I just want to see Reid, walk the beach, clear my head."

"Oh, Julia." Kimberley sounds so disappointed. I start to feel guilty about leaving her to handle everything.

"I just need some time to figure things out, now that everything's finished." The vestiges of heartbreak begin to weigh me down. "I'm still dealing with Evan's betrayal, and now, Jake must hate me for provoking her."

"Don't be so sure," she says in a low voice.

"I just want a normal life, Kimmy," I say with a deep sigh. "That's all I ever wanted."

"A normal life sounds good. I *get* it. I know. I just want you to be happy."

"I want that, too. For me, for Reid."

"Why do I have the distinct impression you're leaving me again?"

"Not for long and not until tomorrow or the next day. L.A. sounds good, for a while."

"But, for how long?" Kimberley asks.

"Not long, a week or two. I want to check out the house. The painting should be done; the new carpet—"

"Maybe, you should just slow down. Wait a little while. I'll go with you. I've got some contacts lined up for the business. We need to come up with a name."

She's babbling, kind of panicked sounding, and I'm wondering why. "What's going on? We can talk about all of this, later."

"Nothing," she says with a nervous laugh. "It's just, well … Brad and I were going to come out tomorrow, to barbecue, to play on the beach … with you. You know, that *normal* stuff you want to do."

I've never seen Kimberley frolic on a beach in my life. Kimberley languishes in lounge chairs near pools. She generally gazes at sandy beaches and ocean waves, from a distance, like they are part of a backdrop required to serve as props at an upcoming event she's planning. She doesn't *play* on the beach.

"*Really?*" I ask. "You'd do that with me?"

"Yes," she says, a little defensive at my skeptical tone. "We'll fly kites and everything."

I smile, trying to imagine Kimberley Powers flying a kite on the beach.

"A margarita in one hand, and kite string in the other?" I tease. I envision Kimberley, enlisting Brad to fly the kite, while she just watches. I laugh. "I don't see you flying kites."

"Brad thinks we should all be leading more normal lives. He wants to spend more time at his house, there, too, with me, you, Reid, everybody."

"What aren't you telling me? Is this some kind of convoluted plan to keep me here?"

"Of course! How are we going to see each other, all the time, if you're in L.A.?"

"Let's just start with tomorrow. I'll leave for L.A., after the weekend. Come out in the morning."

I hear her sigh. "All right, then, we'll be out in the morning. To fly kites."

"You don't have to fly kites with me. Just come out. And, I'm sorry to leave you in a bind with the reception thing, but I just wanted to be *done,* for a while. Maggie said she'd take care of it. You're not mad, are you?"

"No," Kimberley says. "But, I plan on putting the suite we reserved for you, to good use."

"Really? Done with the celibacy idea, huh?"

"No! It's fascinating what you can find to do with someone, besides have sex. We'll have room service. Maybe, take a bubble bath. Sometimes, he reads to me: Shakespeare, poetry. It's illuminating, this celibacy thing," she says.

"Who are *you?* And, what have you done with my promiscuous best friend Kimmy Powers?"

She laughs. Then, there's a long pause. "Maggie, huh?"

"She gave me the keys to Evan's Mercedes. It was parked in the garage, just sitting there, begging to be driven. Use the suite. Put it to good use," I say with a laugh. "Tell Brad, hello, and you may share with him my stellar performance, if you leave out the part at the end."

"Leave out the ending? That was the best part. Julia, you did so awesome today. I almost cried at your kite story. And, I, quote, "Some things change and you really just need to find a tail that can make your kite fly to see where it takes you." End quote. My God, Julia, it was amazing the way you said it, and who you were looking at, when you did."

My throat tightens. "How is he?"

"Surprisingly upbeat. I believe, in following your kite analogy, she was his anchor, the string keeping him in place, and he was trying to fly without a tail."

"You're mixing it all up. I'm the kite, he's supposed to be the tail."

"Did you just say you love Jake Winston?"

"We were talking about kites, in the sense of *kites*."

I'm losing my composure and can't track what Kimberley is saying quite as well. I must be having a delayed reaction to confronting Savannah. I really just need to lie down and process this whole thing, but I'm driving *home*, to Amagansett.

Beholden to this new plan.

"I'm pretty sure we weren't talking about kites," Kimberley says. "Just a sec."

The phone goes silent, again. A few minutes pass.

Then, she's back. "Look, I have to go take care of this reception thing. Call me, when you get home. And, at least, *promise me*, you'll be at the house, when Brad and I get there tomorrow morning."

"Your general distrust of human nature is running incredibly high."

"I have this best friend who taught me *everything*, I know," she says.

"I'll still be in Amagansett tomorrow morning. I promise."

"Okay. See you, then. And, Julia?"

"What?"

"You're amazing. Everyone sees that."

"Don't get all sentimental. I'll see you, tomorrow. Let's pick up, where we left off in L.A. Tell Steph and Christian to come out, too.

We'll have a big party, some of us will fly kites, and all of us will drink margaritas, and welcome summer. The normal stuff."

We're both laughing as the call ends.

A half hour later, my cell phone rings again. It's Dr. Hallmark Card, himself.

"Brad, I wish you would have been there," I say with a wan smile. The thrill of besting Savannah Bennett resurges, for a few extraordinary minutes. "You would have been so proud of me."

"That's what Kimberley said. How do you feel?" Brad asks.

"I feel … liberated, airy in a weird way, like I've taken in too much oxygen. Everything's clearer. Freer. Yes, that's it. I had to take on Savannah Bennett, and, I did." I frown as the scene with her charges through my mind, playing like an endless film loop. "All she wanted was the money and she took it."

I take an unsteady breath, unable to say his name.

"Now he's free. He might not see it that way, for a while. I still can't believe she betrayed him like that, took the money over him. He might not accept it, or believe it, even now, but he's better off without her."

"And you? Are you okay?" Brad asks.

"I'm okay. Here's the thing I've come away with in all of this: all we can be is who we are, and that includes me. I want a normal life, for Reid, for myself. Maybe, someday, that will include someone else. For now, it's just Reid and me, but, as you say, no one controls the power of love." I try to sound upbeat as I recite his best Hallmark line. "I'm not as sad, anymore. I'm not even that angry at Evan, anymore. I'm letting go, I guess."

"How does that make you feel?"

"More vital? A little more self-actualized, I guess."

"Give yourself some time to process it all," Brad says in his all-knowing way.

"Exactly! That's why I'm going home to Reid." I hesitate. "You were the catalyst, you know. You asked the questions and opened the Pandora's Box to my past, and helped me acknowledge and work through all the pain I was holding on to, saving me, because you can see me, just like Kimmy."

"You saved yourself. You're moving on." He pauses. "You finally see yourself and know who you are. Just know, there are others that can see you, too, Julia, more than you think."

"What? Don't start with all the Hallmark card philosophy, Brad."

I try to laugh, but I'm caught in the crossfire of competing emotions about standing up to Savannah Bennett, yet losing Jake in the process.

I sigh. "Just focus on Kimberley. She has a very exciting evening planned for the two of you." I smile at the thought of him reading Shakespeare to her. "All I can say is: I hope you've rested up."

I end the call and toss the cell phone into the passenger seat, intent on concentrating on the drive and rejoicing in the fact that I'm going home to Reid, in pursuit of a normal life, starting now.

With more traffic than usual, it takes more than two and a half hours to get to Amagansett. I pull the Mercedes into the driveway, grab my cell phone, and note three missed calls from Jake. *Not calling.* I take phone off silent and make my way into the house, only to learn from Lianne that Reid is already asleep. Slightly let down, at this news, I spend a few minutes gazing at my sleeping child.

The exhilarating high of besting Savannah Bennett trickles away. My spirits reach an all-time low. Exhausted and determined to outrun the malaise, I put on a pair of jeans and wrap myself into a nice long black cardigan sweater as the June night cools off. I make my way to the beach, just as twilight descends, and the moon begins to rise. Lianne was planning to spend a quiet night, here at the house, but now, that I'm home, she's called her latest boyfriend, and is getting ready to go out.

I walk the shoreline and head north at a fairly fast pace, knowing I need to return soon, so Lianne can leave for her date. I run toward the farthest post, skirt around it, and head back down the shore just out of reach of the crashing waves. That's when it comes to me: this realization that somewhere along way, between my time in L.A. and now, I've made peace with the letter *A* as it relates to Athens, Afghanistan and the Army, even Advil. I haven't actually thought about any of these things in weeks. I slow down and begin to walk the beach just out of reach of the frothy waves.

I'm free.

I'm not haunted anymore by the memories associated with my past and all of the loss. As I told Brad, the anger for Evan is all but gone. He wasn't perfect and neither am I. Maybe, I clung too tightly to the memory of Bobby, even when I was with Evan. Maybe, he sensed that.

I stop, realizing this might be true. I stare out at the darkening skyline and the waves.

"Less than perfect, but I loved you, Evan." The water meets up with the white moonlight in synchronized harmony and shimmers back at me. The almost full moon casts a long shadow of me across the sand. *I can see myself.* This is who I am. Just Julia. I'm no longer the fiancée or the widow left behind. I'm Reid's mother, Kimmy's best friend, Steph's, too.

Julia, less than perfect, and that's enough.

I hold out my arms to the pitching swell of the Atlantic and watch the waves churn toward the shore and me. I say goodbye to my island, to all of them.

I am alive and well on the shore. I am here.

The ocean answers this profound insightfulness with a huge rogue wave that comes out of nowhere. It swirls around me, for a minute, soaking my running shoes and jeans almost to my thighs, before retreating. I laugh and feel lucky I didn't fall in and get pulled into the surf. I move farther up the beach, away from the unpredictable surf and eventually climb the stairs to home.

At the top step, I slide off my wet running shoes, shimmy out of my soaked jeans, and start towards the French doors.

"Lianne, I'm back. I just have to change," I call out. "I got soaked by a ... wave." I look up and find myself face-to-face with Jake. He's just standing there in the moonlight. "Jake! You scared me. What are you doing here?"

He saunters over, reaches for my hand, pulls me to him, and brushes his fingers up against my neck. "Yep, definitely have a fast heart rate, maybe, you are scared, just a little." His thumb moves back and forth across my neck, while my pulse just pounds away beneath his touch. "You are very much alive though, and that's very good," he drawls.

"Please don't do this to me." My body betrays me and moves closer to him.

"What am I doing to you, exactly? I'm checking your pulse, like a good boy scout." He moves even closer. "Lianne left for her date. I've been watching Reid and waiting for you." He gives me a mysterious look. I escape his hold and step away from him.

"What are you doing here, Jake?"

"I tried to call you, but I guess you weren't answering your cell phone." He gives me a derisive look; his eyes narrow. "At least, you weren't taking *my* calls, just everyone else's."

I ignore his accusation. "I just wanted to get home to Reid."

"We had everything planned out," he says, shaking his head. "This awesome suite at The Peninsula. Champagne. Music. Candles. All planned, and, as usual, no Julia. And Maggie Talbon helps you out, by giving you the keys to Evan's car, which has been parked in the same spot for more than six months, except, for today, when I go looking for you, and discover, it's gone. It takes another ten minutes to get back up to the office to find Maggie and learn her part in all of this: your escape. I have to hope that I can get to where I think you're going, before you head to someplace else. Because, let's face it; you are never where you are supposed to be. But, here you are and here I am. On this deck, with the ocean playing its special brand of music and you're stripping down to your skivvies, just for me. It's another step in this arduous, and, I do mean, arduous journey, but I'm fine with how it's turning out." He slowly smiles. I react to him by stepping back even further, until I feel the railing behind me. "It's okay, Julia."

He has this expectant look, as if he's waiting for something. I take in his navy blue pinstripe suit and the impeccable white dress shirt and red tie ensemble and I can feel myself being drawn in to the magnetism of him already.

Did I ever tell you, that's my favorite, Jake? Did I tell you? The new Julia should be saying all these things. *Say it.*

"Love the tie," I say.

Better. Keep going.

He smiles and moves closer to me. "You like my *tie?*"

His Armani cologne starts doing a seductive number on my senses.

"I like the suit and the whiteness of the shirt contrasting with the red ... of the tie. It makes you look ... fetching."

We smile at each other, remembering this particular word exchange while in Paris. Then, his words, from earlier, get through to me. "We had everything planned? *What plan?*"

"You weren't the only one with a plan today. Your inner circle, which is also *mine...*" He grins at this declaration, but then, it morphs into distress. "Christian filled me in on what Savannah did to you. I had my own suspicions about her and Evan, from some things she'd said, things he'd said. I'd begun asking about the SB Investments account, over three months ago, and then, today, she confirms it. We had to plan it out because it was complicated, as you now know." He sighs. "I just want to say I'm sorry for—"

"I'm sorry Jake. I can't believe she did what she did to you today, but I know, in time, you'll realize it's the best thing. She's not a nice person. She would end up hurting you, even more than she already has. I just couldn't stand by, and let that happen."

I walk through the open French doors, and he follows me inside.

"So you pay her twelve point six million dollars and change, just for me?"

I whirl around. *The new Julia responds.* "It was a good deal. I would have paid more."

We are in an electric situation, here. I really need to go and find a pair of jeans, instead of standing here, in just a cardigan and my underwear. I escape to the laundry room and toss the wet jeans onto the dryer and search through the stack of clothing for something to wear. *Nothing.* It's all Reid's baby clothes.

"How much more?" Jake asks, from right behind me. "Because my mom called, on the way out here, and told me someone paid off their loan. And, my bank's calling me, and asking how they can help me invest the sizable amount of money recently deposited in my account of some fourteen million and change. You've had quite a day, Miss Benevolent One. And, I was just wondering, how much more you were going to *dole* out?"

There's a discernible edge to his tone and I'm stunned to hear it. "Don't be *mad*. I had the money—it was Evan's money."

"You're pissed off enough at him to sell all his things ... and give away his money to all your important *causes*."

He shakes his head and looks at me, uncertain.

"And, my parents? How'd that come about?"

"Where's the anonymity that I was guaranteed?" I say with irritation.

"Well, Kimberley—"

"God! I should have known. Well, since your parents knew *mine,* it seemed only right." He looks stunned. "Yeah, I know who you are," I say.

CHAPTER

TWENTY-FIVE

The normal stuff

I MOVE PAST HIM, RACE UP THE stairs, and afford myself a quick glance in Reid's room, before sprinting to the bedroom and grabbing a few clothes. I close and lock the bathroom door, strip off the rest of my things, and step into the shower in less than two minutes. I'm intent on rinsing off the saltwater and pulling it together, though there's this overriding thought pushing at me that causes a new round of anxiety: *Jake's here.*

The shower doesn't really help in calming me down. Ten minutes later, my mind and pulse still race.

I get dressed in a pair of black jeans and a simple white blouse. Soon, I'm fumbling in the mirror with mascara and make-up with shaking hands. I comb my hair and start to fix it. I'm trembling so bad, I give up and pull it back with a headband. After a few more minutes, I give up on the makeover, too, dismayed at the panicky feeling overtaking me.

What am I doing?

He's probably left, by now.

I ruefully glance at the girl in the mirror and shake my head side-to-side. "Get it together," I say to her.

With trepidation, I unlock the bathroom door. Jake's standing in the bedroom doorway.

"I was going to fix dinner. Do you want to eat or something?"

He pushes away from the jam of the doorway, coming towards me.

"Sure, I'm starving, since I had to race out here to ensure you weren't off to somewhere else."

"I'm not going anywhere for a while. Well, L.A., in a few days…" My voice trails off at his irritated look.

Then, he takes my hand, holds it tight, and he pulls me along the hallway. It's semi-lit with the gold sconces that light our way, every couple feet or so on each side. I'm looking around at the swirls in the carpet, the paisley pattern of the gold wallpaper, and trying to breathe, somehow, and sensing his aggravation with me.

I know we're at a crossroads, or on a collision course, of some kind. I'm caught up in trying to remember the plan. I know this much, what's happening, right now, is so not a part of it. I can't really recall the plan, at this very moment, but I know this much: Jake isn't in it.

He suddenly stops, and I walk right into him.

"Sorry," I say. My breath is getting erratic. The airy feeling, from earlier, catches up to me. I feel like I'm going to pass out. "I've got to check on Reid."

"I thought you already *did*."

I can feel him, staring at me from the doorway, while I'm in Reid's room. *Breathe Julia. Just breathe. Take your time. Slow down and think this through.* I tuck in Reid's blanket and sweep his hair away from his forehead. I kiss my finger and trace along his temple down to the tip of his nose.

"Let's eat," I say, slipping under Jake's arm draped across the open pathway of the doorway.

"Uh-huh. If I wasn't starving, I would argue this point," he says, from right behind me.

We traverse the stairs in silence. "I thought you had a plane to catch to Austin?"

"Change of plans." I steal a glance at him. He gives me this defiant look. "So, when did you figure out it was me? The guy you kissed at fifteen," Jake says.

"Kimberley figured it out, while we were in L.A."

"Kimberley."

I look at him in surprise. He sounds so disappointed. "I really don't remember you. I'm sorry. I blocked out a lot of stuff after my parents died. Years worth of stuff…"

"What *do* you remember? About me?"

"You liked Nirvana. You had a great smile. You were a fantastic kisser." I look away from him, then back again. "I was fifteen. That's all I've got." I feel a little guilty about my indifference. "It's been a long day."

"Right."

I sense his disappointment, as he studies me, for a while, and I practically wilt under his scrutiny. He seems to be taking his time, trying to put it all together.

"I told you, in L.A., that I put a lot of expectations on you, before." He looks at me intently. "And, I don't want to start doing that now. I wish you remembered more, but I remember enough for both of us."

I'm stunned by his words. I think it's the most sincere thing that anyone's ever said to me. The new Julia would like to tell him this, but the old Julia takes over.

"You can stay for dinner, if you want," I say.

My benevolence is underwhelming to both of us. He doesn't hide his disappointment with me, now.

"I want," he says simply.

I stand at the refrigerator and silently bless my nanny for restocking our supply of groceries in the past few days. The last ten minutes have been unbelievably tense. Jake seems to be reeling from my sustained indifference and I'm combating every other emotion that exists between the two of us: relief, sadness, despair, guilt.

I seem to mirroring Jake's demeanor by degrees. He feels it first, and then I do. The chasm between us grows wider. He's on one side. I'm on the other.

The alarm for the refrigerator goes off, signaling the door's been open too long, and brings me back from my troubled reverie. I try to keep my focus on the task, at hand, retrieving steaks, lettuce, tomatoes, a cucumber, an onion, and green beans. My arms are loaded up. I turn, closing the door with my hip. Jake's standing, right behind me. He takes each item from me, one by one, and sets them on the counter.

"You carry a lot of stuff, Julia. You carry such a heavy load, burdened down with so much, never asking for help from anyone, except Kimberley or Steph, or, sometimes, Christian, or Brad, but you never ask me for anything. I was just wondering, if you could ask me to do something for you. Anything."

Silence.

The new Julia wants to say something, while the old Julia doesn't. New Julia wins out. "Tell me what you want from me."

Now, he's coming towards me again. I take a step back, but then, I'm up against the stainless steel of the refrigerator. His smile gets even wider. "Where are you going to go?" He kisses his index finger and brushes the bridge of my nose with it, the same way I did to Reid, earlier.

Oh God.

"How are you?" Jake asks.

"I'm fine. Yes. Absolutely." He starts to laugh. "What?"

I don't hide my annoyance because I'm freaking out, on too many emotional levels, right now, to care. The crazy electrical connection between us is back again, in just being in the same room with him.

"I've been hanging out with Brad, quite a bit. And, I'm aware of the inner circle code, in particular, with the word, *absolutely*. That's when you say, *absolutely*, it really means things are not okay and you need some help. And, I was wondering, if you could tell me what you need help with. Just lay it out there, as you did on the phone in Malibu, when you thought I was Bobby, but you were actually talking to *me*. You know. Tell me, how you really feel." His tone is gentle, caressing.

I feel this stirring of life all the way to my soul, when I look up at him. He's just waiting for me, holding his breath, waiting for me.

"Can we just focus on the *food?*"

He looks disappointed, but then sympathetic. He nods.

I make a salad, while he just watches me. I chop at the lettuce, slice the tomato, cucumber, concentrating all my efforts, so I don't wield the knife the wrong way. I make a vinaigrette dressing and start to steam the green beans. Turn the indoor grill on. He disappears, after a few minutes, and I take the moment to take a deep breath and tell myself not to completely freak out.

We're having dinner. That's it.

Kimberley calls. "You forgot to call me back, to let me know you got there."

"Sorry," I say.

"So, you're home?"

"Yes. How's the party?"

"It's fine. Everyone's having a good time. Maggie's great. She's going to be awesome for the PR gig. So, how are things there?"

"Good. Fine. We're having dinner."

"So, he made it. Good. Feeding 'em first is always a good idea." She laughs in that wicked way of hers.

"You could have *told* me he was coming," I say.

"No way. Would have ruined the surprise. Sometimes, not being prepared is best."

"There's a plan. We go with the plan," I say in irritation.

"Of course there's a plan. There are *several* plans, Julia. You have yours. We have ours." Kimberley laughs again. "Okay, I'm going. I'll see you tomorrow. And, Julia? Don't overthink it. Okay? Let yourself go. You're where you're supposed to be."

"Fine," I say. "Stop telling me what to do."

Jake returns to the kitchen. He's changed into jeans and a black t-shirt and looks even sexier, which sends me, in a completely different way. A part of me wonders where he got the change of clothes, but since I'm trying to focus on getting dinner ready, and control my reaction to his every movement around the kitchen, I don't even ask. He gets busy putting the steaks on the indoor grill and adding salt and pepper just the way I would. Then, he's opening a bottle of red wine he's brought and pouring it into two glasses. I'm trying not to openly stare, as I inadvertently watch his every move. When he goes to set the table, I start breathing freely again.

Twenty minutes later, we're sitting down and eating dinner. Normal stuff, something we've never done before, alone with each other like this, eating dinner. We talk about Kimberley and Brad getting married, about Reid. The normal stuff. My mind drifts to the nice officer Brian Grant. *He deserved better from me.* I feel awful for how badly things turned out with Brian that night. Jake must see this because he stops eating, and looks at me.

"What?" he finally asks.

"I had this date with Brian Grant, the nice police officer, who stopped me in Malibu. We did the normal stuff: we went to a movie, shared popcorn, laughed a lot. You know just normal stuff. Then, we're back at his apartment and things are progressing." I sigh.

"Well, it didn't end so well, and I feel terrible about that."

"Didn't end so well for whom? Back at his apartment? What happened, after the normal stuff?" Jake gets this incredulous look. "Progressing to what? Did you *kiss* him?"

"I'm sorry, I brought it up." I glare at him, feeling even worse for Officer Grant, although the look of jealousy on Jake's face is somewhat comical. "It was just nice. Normal stuff. That's what I want. The normal stuff."

"We can do normal." Jake gets this distressed look.

"It was a date. We didn't do anything more than kiss."

"You *kissed* him?"

I give him a withering look, and begin clearing the dishes. "You've been with Savannah Bennett. At one point, you believe, she's pregnant *with your child*, and you're asking me, if I kissed a police officer in Malibu. Seriously, Jake?"

"We can do normal. I promise. We *will*." He's looking at me with this intensity, like he's intent on finding a way into my soul.

I practically toss the stoneware into the sink when a new wave of uncertainty overtakes me as he comes into the kitchen. He looks at me in surprise.

Normal is finished. We've had dinner, and he still hasn't said anything that tells me anything.

"We can do normal," he says, again.

"I don't know, Jake. I'm not sure we can. Somehow, I'll always wonder, if you're here, out of some obligation to your parents, or even the Savannah thing, which I still don't completely understand."

He starts pacing, back and forth, across the kitchen floor, and runs his hand through his hair, every so often. "Okay, I had reservations about coming here," he finally says. "I *do* feel a little bit bought and paid for. I don't know what to think. You didn't talk to me about it. You just came up with your own God-damn plan, with Kimberley and Christian, and cut me out of it. And now, you're talking about this Grant guy. I don't know what to think."

"You're not bought and paid for," I say. "You're free to go anytime you want. I just wanted her gone."

"Why?"

"Because of what she *was* to Evan. Because of what she *did* to me."

He's holding his breath. His face is a parade of emotions: anger, frustration, disappointment. He seems to be going over the exact words I've used, trying to find the counterbalance. He's looking at me with such intense concentration; it emanates from him across the room, to where I stand, willing me to say more.

The new Julia is confused, out of sorts, unwilling.

"I don't know how to trust you," I say without thinking. My words cut across him. He literally flinches, when I say this. I sigh and try to think of what to say to him. "How do I know you're not just here out of some obligation to your parents? I don't know what you want from me. I don't. I'm not perfect. I married someone who expected that from me, and when he discovered I wasn't Elizabeth, he went searching for someone else and found your fiancée."

I finish the rest of my wine, avoid his direct gaze, and attempt to get my composure back.

Finally, I look over at him and say, "I couldn't tell you about their betrayal. I couldn't do that to you. Maybe, that makes me a horrible person. Perhaps, you do feel bought and paid for, but, you're not. I don't want anything from you."

He stands there for a few more minutes, just waiting for me to say more, but the old Julia wills silence and wins. After he leaves the kitchen, I angrily wipe away at a tear and start putting dishes in the dishwasher. He soon returns with more dishes from the table. His continual silence is far worse. I can see him processing this whole thing, everything I've said, and everything I haven't.

"Fine," he finally says. "Let's just get some things straightened out, right now." He dials his cell phone and flashes me a defiant look. "Mom? Look, I need you to talk to Julia," he says. "Yeah, she's the one." There's a long pause. "She's right here. I know. Well, she thinks I'm here out of some kind of obligation for what she's done, and I need you to set her straight."

He hands me the phone and stalks from the room.

"This is Julia." I wince, dismayed at my nervousness.

"Oh my God, Julia, it's Laylie Winston. I can't even put into words what you've done for us. Of course, we were close to your parents, but it doesn't seem right that you would take up our cause. Jake said he had it all worked out and we were trying not to worry too much, but now, we're just so touched and overwhelmed by your gesture. He's loved you, since he was seventeen. He went all over Europe, trying to find you, after learning what happened in Athens to your parents, but you were already gone. All this time, he's been searching for you, and we'd told him, he needed to move on, but he was always so determined to find you. We're so thrilled the two of you have finally found each other and that you're both finally sitting down and talking it through."

"We had dinner."

"Oh that's good. Feeding 'em is always good." She laughs and I start to as well, as she echoes Kimberley's exact words. "Julia, will you come see us, soon? Jake talks about you and Reid, all the time. He's sent us pictures, but it's not the same. Come to the ranch and stay with us, a while. I know it's not the beach, but there's nothing like the sound of the wind, rustling the grass in the middle of nowhere, when it's really *somewhere*. It fills your soul and we all need that." She laughs again, this tinkling sound, like wind chimes. I'm just drawn in to her, so much like her son. "What you've done for us can never be put in to words, and Jon is pretty good with those." I hear her crying, though she's been laughing, and this is reaching at me, too. "Come see us, soon."

"Okay, we will. I promise." I wipe away another tear with the back of my hand.

Jake comes in. He looks uneasy, when he sees my face, before taking the phone from me.

"Mom? Yeah, we had steak, salad, green beans. She's an awesome cook." He looks over at me with this contrite look. "I don't know. She's never made me a pie." He starts to smile. I back away from him because just seeing his smile plays havoc with my emotional defenses. "Sure, you could show her your famous pie crust recipe. I'm sure she'd like that." He pauses again. "She said she'd come? Really?" He looks over at me, again, in surprise.

Now, his family is drawing me in. I turn away from him and walk into the great room. This is getting way out of control.

Damn it. This is so not a part of the plan.

I hear him say, "Okay, Mom, I have to go. I will. I'll call you, in a few days. I love you, too."

Jake follows me into the great room, stands across from me, and leans against the fireplace mantel with his arms folded across his chest, and watches me, as I continue to pace the floor, trying to recall the plan. *I've got to get back on track. Back to the plan.*

"What's wrong? Are you...? Tell me, what you're thinking, what you're feeling," he says.

He's been well coached. Kimberley? Brad? Christian? Who has been telling him how to handle me?

I look over at him, as the rage begins to surge. "I haven't seen you, since LAX, when I sent you away, and told you to send me a note with what you wanted to say. Now I've just blown up my life: sold all his assets, dismantled his company, and paid off your girlfriend or whatever the hell she is to you, because I don't know what she is to you. I've taken care of things in Austin, Telluride, whatever." I jab my hand through the air. "And then, you put your *mother* on the phone with me. And, you know, it just pulls me in, Jake. You *know*, I want those things."

"What things?"

His contrived innocence infuriates me further. "A normal life with a family, a mother who strokes your hair for no reason at all, who teaches you to make perfect pie crust, for Christ's sake. She *invited* me to the ranch. She said we should just stand out on the prairie and listen to the wind rustle the grass. She knows it's not the ocean, but she said it fills your soul."

"Okay." He nods with some kind of enlightened understanding. "Mom's always had a way with words and what she's describing really happens. I would go there, when I could, and just think of you, somewhere, out in the world."

"See? That's what I'm talking about. You say things like that and then you..." I shake my head. "I think I've made so much progress, like today, with Savannah." I start pacing again, trying to recall the damn plan.

"What Julia? Tell me."

I stop and look over at him. *Say it. Just tell him.*

"I'm scared. Of you. And, of what this is." I swallow hard, but the tears come anyway. I brush at them in irritation. "I can't lose anyone else, Jake. And, I don't know how you feel about anything, including *me*, not really. I don't know where we stand. And, I told you, and myself, I was giving up all connections to Evan. And yet, here we are, and I feel more connected to you than I ever did to Evan. Why is that, Jake? Tell me, why that is."

The new Julia is talking way too much. I employ the hangdog expression he's done to me, so many times, already. He hesitates, as if he's struggling to get the words just right.

"What?" I say in irritation.

He slowly smiles. "That's what she said you'd do. Kimberley said, eventually, she warned me it would take some time, a long while, but if I would just wait, if I could just slow down, and not put too much pressure on you." He looks hopeful, like he's concentrating on catching a small butterfly with his hands. "You would tell me how you really feel. And, now you have." He looks amazed, as if he's just discovered the secret path into Wonderland. Maybe, he has. "So you want to know what I want from you. You want to know where you stand. You want to know how I feel about you."

"Yes, let's start there." I can barely breathe. He walks towards me and trails his fingers down my neck, feeling my pulse.

"I've loved this girl for a long time and she was lost to me. Then, I found her again at UCLA, but she was in love with someone else, and she didn't even see me. I went on with my life, still searching for this persona of this girl I'd always loved. Then, Evan's getting married to someone he's just met and down the aisle comes the girl from UCLA. So, I had to get away. I took the job in London, since she was lost to me, so I wouldn't see her every day. I was starting over. They had a baby and I thought she was lost to me forever. Then, Evan dies." He shakes his head. "I'm set to marry a girl, who looked a lot like the one I'd lost, but was different in every other way and she tried to destroy the one I really love, just when I'd found you again, Julia. In talking to Brad, I'd say it doesn't get more complicated than that."

He strokes my face with his hands, then, gently kisses the tip of my nose. "I love you, Julia. I've loved you for a very long time. I'd follow you anywhere because this incredible thing between us makes us connected forever, so don't be scared. I'm not going anywhere."

He puts his arms around me and pulls me closer. I encircle my arms around him and pull him closer. He starts kissing my neck and my racing pulse beneath his lips gives me away. He lifts his head and smiles at me. His eyes are this incredible turquoise-blue with just this hint of gold fleck on the outer circle, amazing eyes. I'm so close to him. I haven't been this close to him, in such a long while. I'm reminded of the golden boy he was from long ago with that same smile and the same enchanting curvature of his lips. The same heady sensation—this magical connection—returns that I haven't allowed myself to remember or feel, until now.

"So, do you think you can learn to trust me? Trust this?"

"I want to."

He traces my eyelids, plays with my lashes, wipes away at the tears drying on my face. "That day at my place..." he says.

"The day you turned me down."

"Trust me. It was hard to turn you down. I almost didn't. Even when I did, it was one of the hardest things I've had to do. But, it was the best thing, for the moment. You weren't ready."

"And, you were? Because, somewhere in there, Savannah came back into your life." I don't attempt to hide my insecurities about her from him.

"I'd started over, Julia. I don't deny that." He gives me this pleading look. "And, even after Evan died, there were so many complications keeping us apart." He hesitates for a moment. "I know, I hurt you, turning you down when you needed me the most, but I had to do it, to ensure we had a future together, free of all the complications."

He looks distressed. "What's wrong?" I ask.

"There's something else. I need to tell you."

I hold my breath and, somehow, know this will have something to do with Savannah.

"What?" I ask, moving out of his arms and away from him.

"We didn't give Savannah the money. Christian called, while you were in the shower. He managed to convey to her that blackmail and fraud are pretty serious crimes. She had no right to your money. She knew that, so we didn't give it to her, and we had her sign an agreement to that effect, so she won't be bothering you, or me, ever again."

There's this protracted silence between us again.

I'm reeling from what he's just said and struggle with the competing emotions of having just declared ourselves and reconciling all of that with what he's just told me.

"I've been feeling bad about confronting her and feeling sorry for you," I say slowly. "The whole bought and paid for speech had me going."

I was upset with the *concept*." Jake half-grins at me in that charming way of his. "I'm already yours, for free," he drawls. "Let's not lose sight of the end goal, here."

"Which is?"

I stand with my hands on my hips, trying to ascertain how pissed I should be with him, but then, he affects that damn hangdog expression and I cannot even conjure up a single thread of anger. I've got nothing.

And, he's coming over to me, and he swings me up off the ground and lowers me back down to his lips. His kiss is long and demanding, effectively extinguishing any semblance of anger I might have found.

"So, you've think we've waited long enough, is that it?" I ask, breathless when he lowers me down.

"I think we've waited long enough, yes. Please tell me you think so, too."

I look at him for a long time, like I have a choice in this matter, this thing with him. I'm caught in a fast moving current of profound emotions for him. They grow stronger, by the minute, even when I should be mad at him. My body and soul have already determined how this is going to go, and my mind quickly catches up. "I think we've waited long enough." I give him a provocative look. "But, I want to go home."

"What do you mean? This is home, isn't it?" He gets this hopeful look.

"No. I want to go to the place that feels like home, as soon as I walk through the door."

His lips curve slowly into a wide smile. "I know that place," he says.

CHAPTER

TWENTY-SIX

Exchanging gifts from L.A.

I LEAVE A NOTE FOR LIANNE, BUNDLE up a sleeping Reid, and load him into the backseat of Jake's SUV. Then, I secretly stow away the florist box, containing Jake's kite, before he sees it. Jake throws his overnight bag, my hastily packed suitcase, the diaper bag, the portable crib, and as much food and wine, as he can carry into the back of the SUV. It's epic, our enthusiasm to get to his place, as if we're planning for a storm and destined to be housebound, for days, in taking all of these provisions with us. It takes twenty minutes to load it all and another fifteen to get to Jake's and unload it.

We set up the crib in Jake's spare room. I gently lay Reid down and he snuggles right in, asleep within minutes, oblivious to the tumult involved in transporting him here. For a while, we just stand together, gazing at him. We spend another twenty minutes putting everything away, but move around the house completely aware of each other. Apprehension settles in, between us, within a half hour of our arrival. Now, we're hesitant, shy, and unsure.

The peaceful feeling I experienced the last time I was here is nowhere inside of me; disquiet takes over. *We're going to do it. Have sex.* It's these thoughts that paralyze me, follow me around, no matter where I go.

This reflective certainty leads to others, the incomplete ones. Did I shave today? Should I shower again? Should I tell him about the birth control patch? Will he *ask*? What if he doesn't ask? Well, he'll eventually *see* it. Should I tell him, first? Does it matter? What if all this buildup of us being together is all for nothing? What if he's disappointed by my body? The way I look? The way I have an orgasm? What if *that* doesn't happen? Well, it probably will because he practically has me doing this every time I look over at him now.

Maybe, I'm not the Julia he's fantasized about and supposedly loved all these years. I'm probably not. Let's be realistic, I'm *not* that Julia. I don't know who I am, most of the time.

Maybe, I should call Kimberley.

I catch my lower lip between my teeth, as uncertainty takes all control. He flashes me one of his amazing smiles and I return it with a simple nod. I'm twenty feet away from him and the man is pulling at me in this weird, celestial way. I can feel the tether circling my heart. It tugs at me, guiding me to him, like a science fiction tractor beam. The bond with him is real enough. It's all the other bits and pieces, these insecurities, surfacing within me, that I'm unprepared for.

He turns on the stereo, but keeps it at a reasonable volume. Some love song fills the room. I can't even begin to follow the lyrics, I'm too fragmented. He's busy opening champagne and generally setting the mood for seduction. I'm impressed at his orderly way of stoking the fire, lighting the candles, selecting the music, and pouring the champagne. Apparently, the man has a plan, but I find little solace in this.

Jake hands me a glass of champagne. I swig it down too fast, and start to cough as the carbonation hits my throat. He gets this curious look.

My hand trembles. Champagne splashes onto the floor. I race to the kitchen, return with paper towels, and begin swiping at the wood floor. He gets down on the floor with me, sets down the flutes of champagne next to us, and takes the paper towels from me, and starts cleaning up.

"Julia? Are you okay?" Jake tosses the towels to one side, and stands up, pulling me along with him.

"Yes. Absolutely." I sound like a terrified school girl doing it for the first time. I give him a rueful smile.

"Why don't we take it slow? We'll just watch a movie or something."

He turns off the stereo and turns on a few more lights. His television comes to life. Five minutes later, we're sitting on his leather sofa together and watching the Matthew McConaughey movie I saw with Brian in L.A. Twisted fate comes to life, right there, on the screen. *How epic. How apropos.* I shrink further into the leather sofa, feeling worse, and absently sip at the champagne. I keep cajoling myself to at least try and focus on the movie, but all I'm fully aware of is *Jake*.

My mind wanders. Will I ever be able to sit next to him and achieve a normal heart rate or take a steady breath? Or, am I destined to experience this out of control pulsation and erratic breathing, all the time? Will I ever be able to concentrate on anything else, besides him? Will I spend years, not knowing the plots of movies or the lyrics to songs because all I can feel and see is him? And, where does this certainty come from? That I'll have *years* with him?

The fear creeps back in, the persistent stalker. What is this? Where is it going? Where are we going? Can I survive this much happiness? Here's the other side of despair for me, this incalculable bliss. Both overpower me in the same exact way. One seems to stay forever; the other is so fleeting, I can never fully trust it will last or let myself believe in it. I grimace, recognizing this astonishing truth about me. Can I let myself be this happy? Forever?

I stare at his fine profile. I've only allowed myself these glimpses of him all this time. I could reach out and touch him this very moment. He's so close. He's right here.

But will he always be? This is what I'm most afraid of, allowing myself to love him and losing him. *Too.*

I look away from him and back to the television screen. It's gone dark.

"What happened to the movie?" I say in a low voice.

"I turned it off five minutes ago," he says, turning toward me. "I thought you were hyperventilating or something. I thought I might have to save you with mouth-to-mouth resuscitation."

"Oh."

I'm embarrassed, undone by him. My breath gets even more jagged. I hold it for a moment, trying to maintain some sort of self-control in front of him, but he sees me doing this.

"I'm not going to pressure you, Julia. I want it to feel right."

He sighs, takes my hand and rubs the inside of my wrist back and forth with his thumb. "You know how you finally get what you want? You know what the gift is, you've finally gotten what you always wanted, but there's this moment, when all you want to do is, stop and just savor it, before you ... unwrap it." He shakes his head in that charming way of his. This enchanted look crosses his features. "That's where we are."

"Am I the *gift* in this scenario?"

He nods, runs his free hand through his hair and gets this rueful look. "I think we both are. To each other. A gift. Something like that." His smile disappears. Now, he's shy and affects his infamous expression. The ice cream must be melting in the freezer at this, just like I am. I can't look away from him now. He has such an incredible hold on me.

He leans over and kisses me, then. It's this tentative, exploring kind of kiss. His lips barely touch my face. His kiss feels like the finest paint brush gently caressing canvas with these light incredible memorable strokes. I close my eyes, taking pleasure in this exquisite contact with him. When I open them, he's pulling back away from me. I override the uncertainty and outrun the fear; I grab his shoulders and bring him to me. I kiss him the same way he's just kissed me. He responds to my loving touch. I discover his heart rate runs as fast as mine does and smile against his lips at this. Maybe, he's scared, too. I kiss him more urgently now, pressing more of my body into his. The inevitability of all of this arrives, like an ocean wave, beholden only to time and the inevitable shoreline. This is the two of us. After a few minutes, we pull apart. We both appear undone by this heady passion that hints at how all consuming it will be for us.

"I got you something in L.A." I slip out of his arms and walk unsteadily back out to his foyer and return with his gift.

He reads the card first.

Jake,

Some things change; and you realize you really just need to find a tail that can make your kite fly to see where it takes you.

Love,

Julia

"Really?" He looks even more excited as he opens the box. "You got me a kite? I've always wanted to get one. Fly it on the beach here. It's one of those things you never take the time to go shopping for and never do often enough."

"Uh-huh. My dad was a kite man, quite the kite-flyer. He was the tail that gave my mom her direction and ability to fly. Yes."

He gets this captivated look. "You just told me about your parents. And, how you feel about kites and, somewhere in there, was an analogy about your mom and your dad."

He stares at me with this look of wonder, rereads the note for a third time, and then holds up the kite.

"Oh." I wave my hand through the air. "It's part of the new Julia. I have to share more of myself and not shut people out so much. It's part of the plan." I give him a weak smile. My mind races because there are so many things I should say. "I helped your parents because I could. I helped you with this mysterious place in Telluride because you've helped me through everything and I owed you that; Evan owed you that, most of all. But I didn't really want to take anybody out, not even *her*. I wanted you to be free of her," I pause and try to smile. "For me. For you, but mostly me. The truth is, you deserve so much more." I stop, while my mind spins with all these profound thoughts. "I just want to be a great mom, spend some time on a beach, fly a kite, maybe, visit a Texas prairie to hear that wind, and have a life. With you." I gasp. "Did I just say that out loud?"

"Yes. You did." Jake looks dazed for a moment by what I've said. Then, he takes my hand. "Just know. I'm here with you because I want to be. I know you helped my parents for all the right reasons that had nothing to do with me. Kimberley said I just need to let you talk, and so you have, and I just want to say: I *brought* you something from L.A., too. You told me to write down what I had to say in a note. So I did, *weeks* ago."

He lets go of me and reaches into the pocket of his jeans and pulls out a folded paper. A nice vellum paper that looks miraculously familiar. It's the note card, I sent him from Paris along with the origami crane mobile.

He's taking his time with this folded vellum note. I feel like I'm going to pass out. I feel like I'm going to, at the very least, hyperventilate, so I rest the side of my face against the coolness of his leather sofa and close my eyes because it's all become a little bit too much.

"I don't know where this is going," I say.

"Just a second, I'll show you."

He takes my hand again. I open my eyes. He opens the palm of my hand and places the folded note card on it.

"My note," he says. "You told me to write down what I had to say. So I did, forty-four days ago, in L.A." I'm looking down at the folded note in my hand, while Jake unfolds it. "This is all I need."

He's written the word *you* on the note and taped a diamond ring to it.

I stare at the word *you* and the engagement ring. Slowly, I level my gaze upon him. What he's written on the note and taped to it reaches for me at a soul level. It causes me to express my innermost thought aloud. "I trust you."

"You already gave me a gift," he says in wonder. He slowly smiles, pointing to the kite he's placed near the back door ready to fly tomorrow.

Love for him just courses through me. It's like an exquisite narcotic, eliminating all the pain, all the loss, and all the heartbreak, all at once. Joy surges in. I'm not completely sure I can handle this exchange of recognizable pain for absolute bliss. I lean back against his sofa and trail an arm over my face, while shock reverberates through me.

I hear him tearing the tape from the note. I peek out from the shield of my arm and confirm this. "I've had this ring for a long time," he says. "Since, I was seventeen." I lower my arm, unable to look away from him now. "I was going to wait. Kimberly thought it would be best to wait." Jake gazes at me closely. "But, I don't think so. I think twelve years is long enough."

"Jake," I manage to say in this raspy voice.

One second he's sitting right next to me, and in the next, he's kneeling at my feet, taking my hand, and slipping the ring on my finger. I'm still too stunned to get any more words out beyond his name.

"I've already checked on marriage licenses in East Hampton. We have to wait twenty-four hours after we fill out the paperwork, but I don't want to wait any longer than that. Maybe, until Monday, that's it. Do you? I want to fly a kite and hang out on the beach with you and Reid. I want us to be a family. I want to start now." He hesitates, probably related in some way to my weighty silence, which effectively unsettles us both. "Of course, my family, especially Laylie Winston, is going to want a big thing in Austin. We'll have to do both. Okay?"

The last part, the mentioning of his mother, has me reeling again. All these insecurities return. Maybe, Jon and Laylie Winston wanted Savannah Bennett for a daughter-in-law. The Hamiltons' disdain for me still stings, a constant reminder.

"I'm not Savannah. I'm not Elizabeth," I say, before I can stop myself.

"I don't want you to be," he says. "Julia, Baby, what are you *talking* about? My parents *love* you, have always loved you, just like I do."

Jake traces my jaw line again, the bridge of my nose. He settles in next to me and takes me into his arms, while remorse courses through me because I've ruined the big moment. He's asked me to marry him and I still haven't said anything. Yet, instead of being angry with me, he's reassuring me.

"We'll figure it out. We'll take it slow. Okay? I shouldn't have asked you, yet. It's too soon. Kimberley's right. You're not ready for all of this." He waves an arm around the room and I shiver missing the warmth of him already. "I've never loved anyone else, like you."

I turn in his arms and study his fine face. The new Julia answers. "I've never loved anyone else like you, either. So *yes*, let's get married," I say, allowing the incredible bliss to rush in at just saying the words.

CHAPTER

TWENTY-SEVEN

All I see

REFLECTING BACK TO SIX MONTHS AGO when I thought my life was over, and then, I kissed him; it's been a long wait. If he's going back to when he'd thought he found me again, seven years ago, only to discover I was with Bobby Turner at UCLA and the only one I ever saw; it's been a long wait. If we're going back to a year and half ago, when I walked down the aisle and married Evan, with Jake realizing I was, in some way, the girl from UCLA; it's been a long wait. And, if we're going back to twelve years ago, when we first kissed and made all these promises about staying in touch, but then, that magical world fell apart for both of us; it's been a long wait. There have been enough complications between us, enough unhappy endings and betrayals by other people, that have kept us apart for far too long. It's been a long wait.

It's too dark to fly kites, too windy to sail. We're not hungry. We're not thirsty. Although Jake's opening another bottle of champagne because it's the one he's been saving to drink with me. He's the sexiest one in the room, so why wait?

I'm getting impatient, as I stand gazing out at the night sky. I'm starting to experience the earlier fears in contemplating the fantasy of us. We're finally going to be together, to consummate this thing between us, but I've begun to wonder if it will lead to anything other than disappointment for one of us.

For him?

When Jake hands me a glass of champagne, I drain it in one long swallow, like I'm trying to win a contest. He looks at me in surprise, but follows my lead and does the same.

"I know what I want to do," I say.

My desperate attempt for bravery gets interrupted by my ringing cell phone. This effectively destroys the moment and my last vestige of courage at the same time as I pounce for the cell phone, already knowing who it will be.

"Kimmy." The way I say her name sounds like a cry for help. Jake looks uneasy, when he hears it.

"Why should you two get to enjoy each other's company, while the rest of us are entertaining employees? I realize you two have a lot to *talk* about, but I'm just checking in.

I force myself to laugh. "Fine. We're *fine*."

Jake's looking at me intently, making it difficult to concentrate on anything else other than what we were about to do to each other, causing a new round of panic inside of me. *Am I ready for this? For him?* I watch him carry our champagne flutes outside on the deck and breathe a subtle sigh of relief.

"I've barely had time to declare my feelings, kiss the man, accept his proposal, and then, you're calling me, interrupting absolutely everything."

"You said *absolutely*." How Kimberley is able to laser right in on my insecurities is an amazing talent only she possesses. "Are you *okay?* And what do you mean by his *proposal?* Are you getting *married?* I thought he was going to wait."

"We're not waiting. We're getting married soon, maybe, even this weekend."

"You said *absolutely*. Maybe, you need to slow it down, Julia."

"I'm through with slowing down." My voice trembles, doubt comes for me. My clairvoyant friend can hear it all the way in Manhattan.

"Oh Julia. You haven't even slept with him yet, have you?"

The disquiet reverberates from deep inside of me. *What am I doing?* "We're working on it. We're going to test those waters."

I don't even get a chance to really dwell on the fallibility of her argument that she's been holding out on Brad. I think the idea of me marrying Jake so soon has caught her completely off guard. Kimberley is the self-indulgent one among us. I'm the very definition of self-control, except when it comes to Jake, apparently. My bravado wanes further at this silent admission. What *am* I doing?

"You know what your problem is? You haven't done this in a long while," she says gently. "I know you. You're busy putting up every obstacle you can think of to ensure it doesn't happen and generally freaking out."

"The new Julia doesn't freak out," I say airily. "And, are we talking about me or you? Because I'm *fine*, on this end." But, my voice trembles and I know she hears it.

"Maybe, both of us," she finally says. "Look, you took my call. You didn't have to." She sighs. "Is it going to be too much to ask for you to *wait* until Brad and I get there before you marry him? And, maybe, wait for Steph and Christian, too?"

"I can wait for all of you. We have to wait twenty-four hours after the marriage license application is accepted in East Hampton. It might be as late as Monday."

"East Hampton? I just can't believe you're rushing into this," she says in a daze. "At least, sleep with him first to ensure you're sexually compatible."

The absurdity of what she's just said finally reaches me. I start to laugh and the overwhelming doubts about all of it— me, Jake, sex— disappear. "Are we talking about me or you?"

"I'm not sure," she says. "Brad and I will be out in the morning. We'll do breakfast first, and then, talk about your future."

"My future is certain. So is yours," I say. "And, we're at Jake's place. Do you know how to find it?"

"I'll find it. Are you sure you're okay?"

"I'm fine. I'm great. Fabulous." I laugh because the surety of Jake has finally hit me.

"It's all happening so fast," she says.

"I know, but it feels right, most of the time, when my best friend isn't freaking me out, unnecessarily. Sexually compatible," I say with a silly laugh "My God, Kimmy, look at him. What's not going to be compatible?"

"Jake loves you, you know. He told me that," she says.

"He *told* you? When?"

"This afternoon before he left. He was beside himself that you'd left and so intent on catching up to you. He said he's always loved you. And Julia? I believe him. Just *wait* for me, okay? I want to be there when you say "I do" and start this new normal life of yours."

"I want you to be there. Hey, Kimmy?" I say, taking a deep cleansing breath. "Thanks."

"Okay…" she says with a little hesitation. "I'm off to the suite with Brad, so *don't call.*"

"What happened to the celibacy idea?" I ask.

"I think you just changed my mind about all of that," she says with a nervous laugh. "Maybe, L.A. *did* change all of us," she says. "Probably *you*, most of all, but maybe, all of us in some way. Go, Julia. Go greet your life with him. I'll see you in the morning."

"Not too early."

"Not too early," Kimmy says with a little laugh. "It will probably be more like the early afternoon."

Jake is out on the deck, leaning against the railing, staring out at the dark ocean. The roaring of the Atlantic greets me as I walk toward him. Now, I'm secure in the knowledge that I will love him for the rest of my life and have come to accept that there are no guarantees in how long that might be, but time with him is all I want and need.

If there's a look of love, I see it on Jake's face, when he turns at my approach. It's there in the way his lips part, when his eyes connect with mine, and track my every movement. There's this sense of expectation, significance, even permanence that we share between us when our eyes meet. He's seems to grow more uncertain as I draw closer. I grab his hand. It's warm with a hint of heat and sweat. I'm a little surprised to discover he's nervous. The man can stop traffic and have any girl in any room he's in.

Everything is so clear to me; the stars are aligned right where they should be when I look up at the night sky. I smile and glance back at Jake, he gives me an evocative look, but looks uneasy just as I was, minutes ago. I reach for his hand and pull him along inside with me. I have enough bravado for both of us now.

"What's wrong?" I ask.

"Nothing, I'm fine," he says. "Sure."

"I've noticed you say *sure*, when you're really not sure. I was wondering, since you normally take care of everything and never ask me for anything, if there's something I can do for you. *Anything*. Ask me to do anything."

"Okay. I want you to do that thing you do to Reid, where you kiss your finger, and then, trace the ridge of his nose. I've wanted you to do that to me, since the first time I saw you do that to him. Christmas night. The night I knew that no matter who I hurt or who hurt me or whatever happened as long as I was breathing I had to be with you. Sure, it was Christmas Eve, the night before, when we were in your car, getting Motrin for Reid, when I confirmed who you were to me and knew I loved you, had loved you for a long time already, and would love you for all time, but it was when I saw you do that for Reid on Christmas, that made me want you, forever."

I swallow hard, too moved, by what he's just said to speak right away. "Do you say these things to all women or just me?"

"Just you. You're all I see."

I kiss my index finger, trace his forehead, and trail down the tip of his nose. "You're all I see, too, Jake. That's why I love you so much." This is the first time I've really said this aloud and I think that's what he's been waiting for me to say. This incredible smile transforms his face. "I love you, Jake. I always have."

Together, we enter his darkened living room. He fumbles for one of the light switches and swears in the dark as he bumps into something. In the next moment, light floods the room and I involuntarily cry out.

"Sorry," he says from across the room. "Damn it. I had this whole seduction scene planned out so everything would be perfect and nothing's going right." He dims the lights, stokes the fire, refills our champagne glasses, and hands me a flute, but he still looks on edge.

I'm strangely composed, just taking it all in. "Jake, it's okay. We've got time."

"We've already lost three hours with dinner, phone calls, and heated discussions." He drains his glass and tops it off again.

"I'm not going anywhere."

"How do I know that? It's been quite a ride trying to keep up with you, Julia. You could change your mind tomorrow. You can have anybody you want. Officer Grant called me a couple of times, wondering how you were doing. I guess he checked your cell phone for who you dialed last, when he stopped you that night in Malibu. And now, I know *why*, since he knows what it's like to kiss you. So, who knows?"

"I *know*. I'm not going anywhere without you." I kiss my finger and trail it along his jaw line. "Have I ever told you how your southern drawl turns me on? The sound of your voice sends these shock waves through all of me. Say something."

"No." He shakes his head side-to-side and half-smiles at my teasing.

"I love the way you say *no*. Say it, again."

"No," he says in his oh-so-famous-southern-drawl.

I step back away from him, watching him. He's just standing there, smiling at me, now. Trust seeps into him as it has for me. His white smile is like a lighthouse beacon in the darkness. His shirt is lit up from the reflective orange glow of the fire and the moonlight streaming in the window. A shadowy pattern plays across his face.

"You look like one of the black and white origami cranes," I say with a little laugh.

He turns away and disappears through the doorway to the next room. I feel this let down that he would just leave like this. All this sensual buildup, and then, he's just gone. But then, he's back again, holding the mobile. He hooks it onto his dining room chandelier. It starts spinning. I'm watching it and smiling. Then, I look over and find him just staring at me.

We meet in the center of his living room, ready to move forward together. I kiss him and he kisses me back. A fantastical radiance seems to burst between us, when we touch each other. I pull him closer and put my arms around his neck. His kiss consumes me and seems to set me ablaze. I feel alive in a way I've never felt before. We close in on the space between us and our bodies seem to connect at every juncture. This kinetic energy envelops both of us.

My mind seems to splinter with uncontainable elation. He slowly undresses me, unbuttoning my blouse, pulling off my jeans, casting my bra and panties aside, with a knowing smile. I stand before him naked, but decidedly brave and committed to him already.

With fervent enthusiasm, I undress him in a matter of minutes, undoing his belt, the buttons to his jeans. I slide them off with unadulterated intention. I strip off his t-shirt and pause to caress his amazing body. There are no more restrictions, no more barriers, and no more social mores ruling us. The will of others no longer separates us. The liberation in being free to love each other transcends us both to a new place of our own making. His breathing is as erratic as mine. This discovery makes me smile and I know we are where we are supposed to be.

There's a part of me that wants to slow all of this down and capture these first moments, but there's this other part beholden to this urgent need to connect with him. It overtakes the sentimental wishes as I reach for him and pull him to me, needing to hold on to him as we meet up with this inexplicable connection that's always been there between us. With enthusiasm, we fall back against the sofa and he finds his way to me, covering my body with his own and kisses me all over. His vulnerability is evinced in this physical desire for me, though my insides flow with a similar response, but he has no way of knowing this. Then, his fingers intimately explore me there, too, and I smile up at him.

No one else is here, but the two of us. We immerse ourselves in this amazing union and when he moves inside of me, there's this incredible sense of fulfillment. He is the most precious part of me that's been missing for so long. He is the missing link; I'm whole again. His sexual prowess and mastery as a lover, effectively vacates my past, except for him. All I can see is Jake. I'm mesmerized by his powerful presence, while my body involuntarily responds to every sensational touch with him. In sharing this miraculous connection he lights me up from the inside and he tells me I do the same for him.

We recognize our first time together and surrender to this irresistible frenzy, this urgent need, that requires destiny be realized. It's clear to both of us we're inseparable, complete, and able to withstand the changing tides, and what this life together might bring for us.

We lie in front of the fire wrapped up in the same blanket; our bodies intertwined. Within his embrace, my body naturally curves down the length of him. It's, as if, we spent a lifetime together already. He settles his chin in the arch of my neck and every so often, he kisses the side of my face, each kiss is like an imprint, an inextricable tie to him. We're exhausted and satiated at the same time, both fully aware that our life together stretches out before us because we're together at last. We joyfully accept this reality and playfully start planning our future.

Jake reaches over and pours the last of the champagne into our glasses and hands me one. He trails his finger along my breast, traces further down, spending a few tantalizing moments at my abdomen, and then moves onto my inner thigh with true intention. I moan at his touch, while he laughs in this provocative way at my powerless reaction. I drink a little champagne, then set it aside, and turn toward him again. Coming to life inside, I guide him into me and become mesmerized by the suggestive way he says my name in the heat of our lovemaking. But then, he stops in the midst of our magnificent ride, just as we've found our unique rhythm. His hand traces over my left hip bone.

"What is this? Birth control?"

I look down to where he's touching me, then, sheepishly look up at him. "Uh-huh."

I lean up back on my elbows and see his eyes rake across my naked chest. He fondles my breasts, while I try to stay focused on answering him.

"I tried the Pill, but I only missed a few of them, and then, surprise … Reid. I guess I'm one of those women who can get pregnant pretty easy," I say with a little laugh at my joke. "So to keep my cycle more on track and since the Pill doesn't work so well. Evan didn't want any more kids," I say without thinking.

"Well, I'm *not* Evan and *I do.* I want at least four, well, *three* more."

He gets this mischievous smile, works at the edges of the patch at my hip, and tears it off in the next minute. He starts moving into me again.

"Let's get started on that baby, right now," he drawls.

But I'm reeling from what he's just said. "Four?" I ask, incredulous. "Shouldn't we at least *talk* about this?"

I slide away from him, just out of his reach.

He looks down at me in surprise, moves closer to me again, and kisses my face. "Julia, you're a fantastic mother. I missed seeing you pregnant with Reid." His fingers trail along my stomach. He gets this wistful look. "I don't want to miss anything else with you. I want to experience it all—a family, a normal life—with you."

"I want that, too. I do. I just ... *four* kids? I was thinking more like two." My mind is having difficulty wrapping itself around this idea of a family of six, even if it is with Jake, who I've secretly anointed in the past few hours as the love of my life.

I've lost my concentration in what we were doing and he's torn off the patch, effectively ending my quest with birth control. I'm busy trying to remember what the instructions said about how long the medication lasts, while he's looking at me with this renewed intensity, and perhaps, realizing this about me. He gets this disenchanted look, stands up, and strides away from me across the living room, perfectly comfortable with his naked, munificent, beautiful, god-like body.

A few minutes go by, before I realize he's not coming right back. Soon, I hear the shower running. "Not so perfect," I say to the empty room. "Julia, less than perfect. Jake, less than perfect, too." I attempt to smile at the reminder of this recent life lesson.

He's standing under the running water with his eyes closed, shampooing his hair; his desire fading away, but still evident. Naked, I step inside, surprising him in the next second with a daring touch that demands his full attention. His arms come around me. He lifts me up off the shower floor. I make a face at him and he starts to laugh. "Let's never be so mad at each other that we take a shower without the other person. Okay?" I say.

"I'm not mad," he says with a sheepish grin.

Then, he shows me that he isn't mad. Anymore, at least.

I kiss him, and then, demonstrate my willingness to consider at least one more child, as I abandon all thoughts of birth control and encircle his waist with my legs. I'm determined to finish where we left off in the living room, just minutes before.

***

The water runs cold, eventually, stirring us both from this latest mesmerizing encounter. He turns off the shower, wraps me in a towel, and then says, "That night, when I put you in the shower in your black silk dress, I was desperate to save you and already knew I couldn't live without you. I was so scared I was going to lose you, just when I'd found you again. And, you were so sad and I just wanted to make everything all right for you again."

"And, you have." I reward him with my most benevolent smile. After a while, I say, "I'll do *three*. That's it." I employ my infamous *stand down* move. He takes my hand and brings it to his lips.

"I can live with that," he says. "For *now*."

Hours later, we lie awake in bed, holding each other and sharing in this inexplicable wonder that we're finally together. I settle further into his arms and listen to his heart beat, enchanted by its steady rhythm. Contentment travels through me, vacating a need I've always coveted, but have never fully realized, until now. I lift my head and look up at him. He looks happy, too. I put my arms around his neck and kiss him.

"Have I told you lately that I love you?"

"Not lately, not in the last twenty minutes or so." Jake plays with my hair. His hand travels back and forth in a soothing rhythm. Then, he stops. "Do you think it will always be like this?"

"I think..." I say, gazing up at him with a secret smile. "It's always been this way between us."

"*See?*" Jake says. "You *do* remember me."

Sometime, during the night, I awaken and discover Jake still holds my hand. I slip away from him, stare out his bedroom window for a few minutes, and glimpse the stirrings of dawn as it meets up with the Atlantic. It's an extraordinary moment watching this union. A sign.

Behind me, I hear the distinct rustle of bed sheets. I smile.

"Julia? Come back to bed, Babe. We have a big day ahead of us. Kite-flying, sex, Reid, a marriage license, more sex when Reid's napping, a barbecue, the inner circle. A *big* day." Jake laughs.

"I'm just greeting my new life."

"Well, come greet it over here," he drawls.

I turn to him and smile.

And, he's all I see.

ACKNOWLEDGEMENTS

With Gratitude

THIS IS A SPECIAL THANK YOU to a group of women who served as my Beta readers for *Seeing Julia* during the fourth of July weekend of 2010. I was on a short deadline to complete the novel and Melissa Schaub, Darla Heitman, Colleen Coady, and Cheryl Oliver took the time out of their busy holiday plans to help me out, by reading the final draft of this novel and providing valuable feedback. Additionally, these four have read several versions of *Seeing Julia* and have encouraged me throughout the process with this particular story. This final version may not please them all because I had to cut out some awesome scenes, but their support has been invaluable to my success with this novel.

I'd also like to thank all my teachers and classmates at The Writer's Studio for their invaluable feedback on my writing which also shaped this work. Additionally, I would like to say a special thank you to Lori Zue whose editorial review helped shape this original story. inally, I would like to express my gratitude to all those who have inquired or encouraged me along the way. It helps so much with the writing process. Thank you, all of you, for your encouragement, support, and love.

And, to all my readers: thank you so much for reading my work.

Katherine Owen

Afterword

Thank you so much for reading Seeing Julia! I hope you loved reading it as much as I loved writing it.

If you enjoyed Seeing Julia, I would love to ask you for a favor. Please go back to wherever you purchased this book (Amazon.com, etc ...) and leave an honest review of the novel.

Authors live and die by their reviews. The few extra minutes it takes you to leave a review really helps out!

If you use Twitter, Facebook, or Goodreads, it would also really help me out if you let everyone know why you enjoyed Not To Us as well!

And, thank you so much for reading my work!

About the Author

Anointed a female fictionista by an overzealous Georgia Bulldog fan, I immediately took it for my job description.

I write. I write a lot. And, when I'm not writing, I think about writing a lot. You may think we're having a conversation, but invariably I'm stealing your name, asking how to spell it, or describing the look on your face in five words or less. I write dark, moody stuff with the sometimes funny. I write lyrical, fantastical, amazing stuff. My readers complain they can't put the book down because just when they think they've figured the story out, it changes and becomes something else.

I spend hours on photo sites looking for the right look for my book coverart. I know the models and photographers by name. It's part of my over-controlling tendencies. I like controlling everything to do with my books.

I am married and have two children and they all like having me home, but complain that I write too much. Add to that the twittering and the face-booking and the wordpressing and google plus-ing and checking Amazon and now, Pinterest; it's a full-time gig. And, I take classes with The Writers Studio, so I'm "literary" besides.

When I'm not writing, I like to drink good wine or champagne and look at my awesome view which I rarely see from my writing refuge.

Don't ask.

So. That's a little about me.

Here's the standard stuff. I am a graduate of the University of Washington with a Bachelor of Arts degree in Communications with a major in Editorial Journalism and a minor in English Literature. My debut novel, Seeing Julia, won the Zola Award and First Place with the Pacific Northwest Writers Association in 2010. So far, I've written and released three novels: Seeing Julia, Not To Us and When I See You. I'm busy writing my next novel, *Finding Amy*. Look for its release mid-summer 2012.

Katherine Owen

Author, Author! Q & A

WHAT INSPIRED YOU TO WRITE *SEEING JULIA*?

This novel was a long, arduous journey. An early version was 190,000 plus words long and took place in Paris the entire time. It's in a box hidden away. This final version is the result of various critiques that I received over the past few years. *Seeing Julia* from Chapter Four on is all new to most readers, including the ones that read it early on. As for the story, I think of it as a tribute to my dad. Losing someone you are close to alters your life's course. I wanted to explore that theme in my writing. The idea of developing a character who loses her parents at the age of sixteen was compelling. The story went from there. Then, the questions began: What if she lost someone else she cares about? How would such tragic events define her?

CAN YOU TALK ABOUT EVAN?

In the early versions, Evan was perfect, almost saintly, however, this made it difficult to get Jake and Julia together in the time frame that I wanted to from a social mores point of view. So, I started thinking: What if Evan wasn't so perfect? What then? How would it affect Julia if she learned of betrayal after his death?

CAN YOU TALK ABOUT SAVANNAH BENNETT?

Savannah was a late-comer to the novel. I had her as a background character in all the earlier drafts. She was still a complication for Jake, but not so out front and center, when she arrives on scene in this final story. Savannah kept coming back to me. I wrote Chapter Nineteen after I thought the novel was completely done. My sister read the update and said, "No one could be that mean." I disagreed. I think someone who is threatened can act out this way. So, I left the chapter alone, refined it, and weaved it into the plot line. It changes the entire complexion of the story and has the desired effect. It created the necessary tension for all of these characters. She was fun to write. Her goals are clear: to get what she wants, at any cost.

WHAT IS YOUR WRITING PROCESS? HOW DO YOU GET THE IDEAS FOR STORIES?

Well, I don't do outlines. I've tried them in the past, but, for me, an outline just slows down my writing process. I don't know where the story is going to go when I first start writing it. The characters, *literally*, take me there, on a journey. They visit me at night or when I'm doing the dishes or driving my car. I see scenes in my head and try to write them down when the inspiration comes to me. Sometimes, I talk to my husband and tell him what I'm thinking of. Often, he tells me to put in something with a mystery to it (kidnapping, murder, anything with a spy theme to it) and every time I say *no way*. Regardless, he has helped me tremendously with the plotting of all my novels. He keeps me grounded, especially when my ego starts to soar too high with the praise from others for my work. Another thing to know about my process is: I've taken writing classes with *The Writer's Studio*. I cannot say enough about what I have gained in my writing with these classes through this amazing program. The prologue of *Seeing Julia* as well as Chapter Four were a direct result of my coursework. As I've noted before, I steal ideas all the time: names, occupations, mannerisms, word choices, scenes, people, places, and things. Watch out! I'm always on the lookout for the unusual circumstance or name for the plot line of my next book.

WHAT'S YOUR FAVORITE SCENE FROM SEEING JULIA?

Just one? Chapter Four was a challenge to write in trying to convey the heartbreak and outline the horror that Julia experienced, when she came upon the accident and had to relive it, in describing it to Dr. Bradley Stevenson. Another favorite for me is Chapter Nineteen with Savannah because it was just such a turning point in the story and so unexpected. Also, I enjoyed writing Chapter Twenty-One because I had to write in a way that conveyed her emotional breakdown, yet stay with Julia's point of view. Finally, there's Chapter Twenty-Two—the scene between Jake and Julia at LAX. It's probably my favorite because they are so far apart in terms of mindset, yet so close in their connection in so many other ways.

WHAT'S NEXT? I'm writing, writing, writing.

WHAT'S THE BEST WAY TO REACH YOU OR PROVIDE COMMENTS ABOUT YOUR NOVELS? Please visit my website: http://www.katherineowen.net. I would love to hear from you.

BOOK CLUB DISCUSSION
OF

SEEING JULIA

Book Club Discussion of Seeing Julia

1. From the Prologue last lines: "My new reality would take away the magic, turn my dreams to nightmares, make my memories imagined, when before ended and the after came."

What is Julia referring to in terms of the after? How do her parents' deaths, then Bobby's, and now Evan's, shape her view of the world? Considering all Julia's losses over the past decade, do you think she's fairly normal? Or, do you think her past losses define her in some way?

2. From Chapter Two with Julia thinking: "I've been here before. I've done this before. At sixteen, I buried my parents, at twenty-three, my fiancé, Bobby. And now, almost four years later, my husband, Evan. I'm here, again, in the after. Here's what I know: death abducts the dying, but grief steals from those left behind. There is less of myself with every loss."

What do you think Julia means by this last statement? Do you think it's true that there's less of her with every loss? Do you think she's cynical about love? Or, do you think she outwardly projects this, while inward she still longs for it? Do you think she is emotionally broken from all that has happened to her?

3. From Chapter Two when she tells Jake:

"I'm not starting over. Not this time." I'm emboldened, suddenly anxious to share my secret. "It's too much. Too hard. And for what? So I can lose it all again? I believed him. I believed him, when he said we could have a wonderful life together. I believed him. Look what happens when you believe them. He's gone. They're both gone. My life is over. I can't do it again."

Julia is referring to both Bobby and Evan in these lines. Do you believe her and think she is really set upon killing herself? Was that her intent? Or, did she really just make an error in judgment? What do you think Jake is thinking at this point? Is it possible that he is just as desperate as she is in trying to find his way? Why or why not?

⌒

4. In Chapter Three in the hospital, Stephanie asks Julia: "What about Reid? He needs you, Julia." And Julia thinking: "I have not really considered my seven-month-old son, not since the day Evan died. The grief just took me. I have not been able to really look at Reid for fear I would glimpse too much of Evan's face in his features and literally break down. My son serves as a constant reminder of all that I've lost. Grief has had its way with me, breaking me apart." When Julia says to Stephanie, "I'm not...good for him."

Do you think Julia really believes this? That she's not good for Reid? Do you think Julia judges herself too harshly? If she does, why do you think she does that?

⌒

5. From Chapter Four: "There were these seagulls. Just calling, cooing, whatever the hell it is they do. These seagulls flew overhead in frenzied formation, diving, seemingly spying at the unexpected activity. They flew away, all at once, disturbed by the building crescendo of unfamiliar sounds, I guess. I kept wondering: why do they do that? Are they frightened? God-damn birds."

What do you think Julia is really describing here? The voyeurs at the scene? Herself? How do you think Julia feels about death? What are her views? How does it affect her? Is she fearful? Accepting? Defeated?

⌒

6. Also from Chapter Four: "The thing was, I knew, even then, I was saying goodbye to happiness. I felt it seeping away from me. Gone forever. Just this feeling of suspended disbelief. Suspended disbelief. You know; the feeling you get, after you've cut yourself, a silly accident where the carving knife goes astray. You're cutting tomatoes and then, you've cut yourself. It's stupid, really. And, you stare down at your finger and before the pain starts, you watch the hint of blood ooze from sliced skin. Then, in the next instant, it's everywhere. The horror...spurting blood that can't be stopped... the horror takes hold. And then, the pain comes."

Do you think Julia really thinks that her happiness is gone forever? Why or why not?

⌒

7. From Chapter Seven with Dr. Bradley Stevenson: "So, how did it make you feel that you could never be Elizabeth?" And, Julia thinking: "I hesitate with my answer, knowing it could turn the tables on a lot of things we've discussed here. All the pretty, trussed-up stories I've put together for him so far could disappear."

"Our marriage wasn't perfect." There. I said it. Just saying it out loud causes some sort of release inside. I breathe easier. "I wasn't perfect and neither was he. We weren't perfect together."

Were you surprised to learn that their relationship (Evan and Julia's) was less than perfect? Do you think this is a breakthrough moment for Julia to admit this? Do you think she is beginning to view the truth of her world? Of herself? Why do you think people often hide the truth about their relationships from everyone around them?

⌒

8. From Chapter Seven when Dr. Bradley Stevenson asks: "What did she look like?" His question stops me in my tracks. His perceptive ways are so eerie. I'm taken aback and unable to answer for a few minutes. Finally, I say, "Long dark hair, blue-violet eyes, slender, tall, she had a Liz Taylor in Black Beauty thing going on." Reluctance sets in. Do I really want to put this together for him?

"Like you," he says. Pandora's Box opens. Chocolate anyone? An abundance of heartbreak. Rare happiness. Plenty of self-destruction. Take your pick. Julia's got everything in here.

This is a big revelation for the reader about Julia. Why do you think she is finally opening up about her life? Do you think she's angry, on some level, that it's never worked out for her? With Bobby? With Evan? How do you think she handles it?

⌒

9. From Chapter Seven right at the end: "I can't believe I kissed him," I say in a low voice. "I'd just lost Evan ten days before. Drank enough alcohol and took enough pain killers to escape the grief for awhile. And, he was there and he made me...feel something. Alive again, I guess. Kimmy knows.

She said it shows I'm living that I want to go on." I turn around to face him. "What do you think it shows?"

Why do you think Julia confesses the whole Jake scene to Dr. Bradley Stevenson? Would you tell someone about something so intimate and morally questionable? Do you think it helps Julia comes to terms with it? What do you think of the psychiatrist's response to her?

"No one controls the power of love," he says.

"I didn't say I was attracted to him. And, I certainly didn't say I love him. I don't even know him."

"Love has nothing to do with knowing someone. And, everything to do with need."

Do you think he's right? Does his view of the world help Julia see hers differently?

10. From Chapter Eleven with Julia thinking: "I revel in the structure's permanence and its ability to withstand the elements of wind, water, and salt air. What a treasure. I sense this kindred spirit, this connection, to this place already. My smile is involuntary. This unexpected joy courses through me in just being here."

What do you think Julia recognizes in Jake's beach house? About her life? About him? Why do you think she has such a strong reaction to his place? What does it represent for her?

11. From Chapter Sixteen with Brad saying: "Kimmy and I want to ensure you're okay with it," Brad says. "Because if you're not, I'm stepping aside." Our handsome doctor takes a needed breath. I think he's been holding it. "So, Julia, are you okay with it?"

It has become a very big word, indeed. I study Brad. Dr. Hallmark Card seems a little disheartened now. Where's all that grand philosophical schtick about love, attraction, wants, and needs?

"Well, you pretty much know all my double down secrets, so there's really no problem there," I say slowly. "The only thing I would say is Kimmy personifies all that is miraculous about this world, but since you're a wizard yourself you should be able to handle and appreciate her brand of magic." Then, I smile, this benevolent smile. "As long as you understand, we're kind of a package deal, I'm cool with it."

What do you think Kimberley's friendship means to Julia? Brad's? What do you think Kimberley represents for Julia? A mother? A sister? Is Kimberley's brand of magic really as simple as her ability to embrace the world with ease and acceptance? Is this what Julia admires? Or, is it more than that?

12. From Chapter Seventeen with Julia thinking: "Death is...so permanent. It alters everything. This relentless wrecking ball comes at me from every angle in a different way than the day before. My island gets farther away. This glimpse of him, only I can see, gets smaller with each passing day. The more I go looking for him, the more I discover him missing. I can't tell anyone. Permanent fear settles in. How do I explain the profoundness of his love? And it's long absence from me now?"

What do you think Julia is most afraid of? Forgetting Evan? Not forgetting him? Both? What else? What do you think she is referring to with: "The more I go looking for him, the more I discover him missing. I can't tell anyone?" Do you think most people hide their grief this way?

13. From Chapter Nineteen with Julia thinking: "And, it comes out of nowhere without intended provocation on my part and hits me at full speed, like a meteor hitting the Earth causing instant destruction. It eliminates the life I thought I knew. Instantaneous. This poison star.

"We were together for a while," Savannah says. "Over a year ago, now. Yes, the spring before. March. He took me to the place in Malibu. Have you ever been there? It's amazing."

Were you surprised by this chain of events? Why do you think Savannah is so cruel? Why does she take the risk in telling Julia? Do you think anyone can be this cruel if the circumstances present themselves?

14. From Chapter Twenty-one: "There's a pool. We're high up in the hills of Malibu away from the beach now at this gorgeous house. The Pacific is so vast. It's big from up here. I step into the pool. I just step in. The water is warm and I swim a while. Now, I shiver in my clothes staring at the sunset and the vast Pacific. It's so vast. Endless. I look for the guy who has the too white

smile, but he's left me. Of course. Of course, he's left me. Everyone does."

Do you think Julia really believes this? That everyone always leaves her? Do you think she has a right to feel this way, given her history and what's happened to her?

───

15. From Chapter Twenty-Two with Julia thinking: "His looks and stance reflect Bobby's from nine years ago. It's as if I could just walk right over there and start my life over again. The appeal for doing this thunders away at me inside. I could just go over there and start this whole thing over again. It's there. But, I don't. His words, she needs me, plague me still. I just can't do it anymore. The plan is to cut all connections to Evan, all of them. We have to stay focused on the plan."

Why do you think Julia rejects Jake at this juncture? Is she broken beyond repair at this point? Or, is it something else? Is she afraid to repeat similar patterns? If Jake resembles Bobby so much, for example?

───

16. More from Chapter Twenty-Two with Julia saying to Kimberley: "I'm broken; my life turned tragic." I shake my head and look over at her. "I had to hold on to something, a vague memory of a guy, who made me feel complete was just a fantasy of one of the last days of magic I had, before I got pushed into harsh reality and learned what the real world was like."

"You're not cynical. That's what is so amazing about you. You should be, but you're not. You'll start over; you already are."

Do you think Julia is cynical? Would you be?

───

17. From Chapter Twenty-Three with Julia thinking: "She just stands up in her perfect poison star form with her chic designer suit, smooths down her skirt with her flawless manicure, and rewards us with one of her most radiant smiles, Scarlet O'Hara style, as if she's just having a set-back. It's just been one of those days at Tara. She doesn't even glance in Jake's direction when she says, "Done.""

I take a shallow breath and hold it for a moment while she just watches me. "Well then, cut the lady a check, Christian," I finally say. From the credenza, I grab the silver gift box with her black bikini swimsuit inside and slide it—*jam it*—across the conference table her way. I can't even look at Jake. "You left this in Malibu," I say. And I walk out.

Why do you think Julia risks alienating Jake with this scene with Savannah? What do you think she came back from L.A. with? Closure? What does the kite-flying with her dad represent? Do you think she finally understands what her dad was telling her about his relationship with her mother? Do you think Julia understands herself better from this experience in L.A. and the recalling of her past?

18. From Chapter Twenty-Six with Julia thinking: "The fear creeps back in, the persistent stalker. What is this? Where is it going? Where are we going? Can I survive this much happiness? Here's the other side of despair for me: this incalculable bliss. Both overpower me in the same exact way. One seems to stay forever; the other is so fleeting I can never fully trust it will last and let myself believe in it. I grimace, recognizing this astonishing truth about me. Can I let myself be this happy? Forever? I stare at his fine profile. I've only allowed myself these glimpses of him all this time. I could reach out and touch him this very moment. He's so close. He's right here. But will he always be? This is what I'm most afraid of, allowing myself to love him and losing him. Too."

Do you think Julia has the right to be this fearful? Do you understand why she feels this way? How do you combat the fears of loss? The fear of death? How could someone who has experienced so much loss ever completely give herself over to another person? Do you think she succeeds in doing this with Jake?

19. From Chapter Twenty-Six with Julia thinking: "I smile, uncertain. My mind races because there are so many things I should say. "I helped your parents because I could. I helped you with this mysterious place in Telluride because you've helped me through everything and I owed you that; Evan owed you that, most of all. But I didn't really want to take anybody out, not even her. I wanted you to be free of her," I pause and try to smile. "For me. For you, but mostly me. The truth is you deserve so much more." I stop while my mind spins with all these profound thoughts. "I just want to be a great mom, spend some time on a beach, fly a kite, maybe visit a Texas prairie to hear that

wind, and have a life. With you."

This is Julia's profound truth. Why do you think she finally trusts him enough to say what she really wants and feels? Do you think she acted in the right way to do what she did with the money in giving most of it away? Would you have done that with the money?

20. From Chapter Twenty-Seven with Julia thinking the following: "He gets this disenchanted look, stands up, and strides away from me across the living room, perfectly comfortable with his naked, munificent, beautiful, god-like body. A few minutes go by, before I realize he's not coming right back. Soon, I hear the shower running. "Not so perfect," I say to the empty room. "Julia, less than perfect. Jake, less than perfect, too." I attempt to smile at the reminder of this recent life lesson."

Do you think Jake is being selfish by reacting this way to her telling him Evan didn't want more kids when Jake wants four? Do you think Julia handles Jake well in this situation? As a reader, is it a relief to know Jake is less than perfect and has some flaws of his own? Do you think they have some challenges ahead in their relationship? Or, do you think Julia has finally found the man and a family she can belong to? A normal life?

ALSO BY

KATHERINE OWEN

NOT TO US

WHEN I SEE YOU

Please visit her website: http:www.katherineowen.net, for the updates about her work and her latest novel releases.

CONTACT INFORMATION

Connect with Katherine Owen in the following ways on social media:

Website
http://www.katherineowen.net

Twitter
https://twitter.com/#!/KatherineOwen01

Her blog
http://www.katherineclareowen.com

Facebook
https://www.facebook.com/KatherineOwenauthor

Goodreads
http://www.goodreads.com/author/show/998458.Katherine Owen

Or, her latest obsession: *Pinterest*
http://pinterest.com/katherine_owen/

The *easiest way* to find out more about her novels and other interests would be at her website: ***http://www.katherineowen.net***. Come visit.